TIP OF A BONE

For Emily,
a great walking partner!

Christine Finlayson

Christine Finlayson

Adventure Publications, Inc.
Cambridge, Minnesota

DEDICATION

To my family, especially Steve.

DISCLAIMER

This is a work of fiction. The names, characters, businesses, places and events are either fictitious or used in a fictitious manner. Any resemblance to real persons, living or dead, or actual events is purely coincidental.

Cover design by Lora Westberg
Book design by Jonathan Norberg
Edited by Brett Ortler

10 9 8 7 6 5 4 3 2 1

Copyright 2013 by Christine Finlayson
Published by Adventure Publications, Inc.
820 Cleveland Street South
Cambridge, MN 55008
1-800-678-7006
www.adventurepublications.net
All rights reserved
Printed in the U.S.A.
ISBN: 978-1-59193-439-4

TIP OF A
Bone

ACKNOWLEDGEMENTS

Writing a mystery doesn't happen overnight, and I'd like to thank the many people who've supported me during this journey.

A huge thanks goes to my husband, Steve, and our kids, Evan and Siena, who have encouraged me throughout the writing process and given up family time so I could stare at the computer. I'm also grateful to my mom and dad, Pat and Bruce, for their ongoing support, and my sister Cady, who always reminds me to follow my dreams.

My writing group has provided honest critiques, beginning with early drafts. Ann Littlewood, Angela Sanders, Evan Lewis, Marilyn McFarland and Doug Levin, your input has been priceless. (Likewise to former group members, including Nancy LaPaglia, Joe and Michelle Lewis, Richard Cass and Joe Jablonski.) Ann, Angie, and Evan: you guys win the *Endurance Award* for multiple readings and still offering crazy-helpful advice.

Special thanks to other critique partners as well: Micki Browning, for her great law enforcement insights; Bonnar Spring, my favorite grammar guru; Kat Brauer, who inspired Maya to be more hip; Carol Cole, who gave a Newport perspective; Liz Voss, a thoughtful editor and early fan; and Becky Kjelstrom, who campaigned hard to eliminate my adverbs.

I'd also like to thank Elspeth Pope and Hypatia in the Woods for seeing my mystery's potential and for the residency at Holly House. To the Oregon Writers Colony, thank you for peaceful writing retreats and terrific workshops by Robert Dugoni, Marjorie Reynolds and Larry Brooks. The Willamette Writers provided a quiet space for making final edits. Bless you all for supporting Northwest writers!

I'm also grateful to those who answered technical questions, including Chuck Harman, Ben Jones, Lieutenant Malloy in Newport, and the guy at Ossies Surf Shop. Thanks also to Pat Dennis, Leona Grieve, David Henry Sterry and April Henry for your important help at critical junctures. To Andrea Somberg, who provided kind words at just the right time, and to Janet Reid, who really is the finest shark in the sea, THANK YOU.

This book wouldn't have come to fruition without the great folks at Adventure Publications, especially Brett Ortler (editor), Gerri Slabaugh (publisher) and Ryan Jacobson (marketing).

And—last but not least—a huge thank you to the people of Newport, Oregon. You're lucky to have such an amazing place to live.

AUTHOR'S NOTE

One of the joys of writing fiction is being able to transform real places into a creative world. The businesses, people and events in this book are products of my imagination, but I couldn't resist including a few real-life favorites. The Sylvia Beach Hotel and Rogue Ales Brewery are coast landmarks, and you really can drink Shakespeare Oatmeal Stout and other beers while gazing at the bay. You can also enjoy the local Killer Coffee, head north to the Pelican Pub, or watch Newport's Survival Suit Races and Blessing of the Fleet.

A note on geography: Oregon coast residents will recognize there is no road from Newport along the south side of Yaquina Bay, nor is there a boat repair or marina there. It's called artistic license—that's what makes fiction fun.

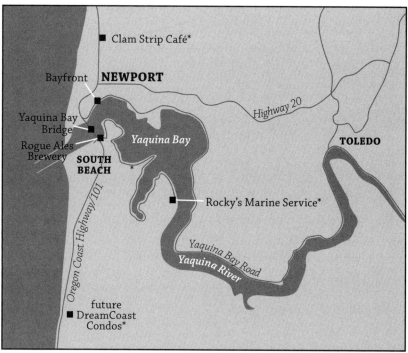

for illustration purposes only, not drawn to scale   * fictitious

FEBRUARY

Near Newport, Oregon

One

Stay away from trails. They'd told her that in training.

Sara Blessing pushed aside wet branches and clinging spiderwebs as she bushwhacked through the forest. She couldn't see a thing outside the glow of her headlamp. Even the moon hid behind a gray shroud.

So freaky dark.

Her hiking boots caught on a tree root and she stumbled, falling to her hands and knees. The backpack slammed into her spine and her shin collided with a rock. She stifled a cry. Birds screeched warnings and small creatures scurried.

"Sorry," Sara whispered. "Go back to sleep." She struggled to her feet and heaved the pack into place. Nobody could call her a quitter. Nobody.

Her instructor, a gray-haired hippie with skin so etched it looked like bark, had drilled the new recruits on their stealth techniques. He'd warned them to avoid roads. Avoid people. "Don't take established trails," he'd said. "You're warriors. You must watch your backs."

In retrospect, Sara thought, *it was crappy advice for a pitch-black night.* If she'd walked up the gravel road instead of clawing through this over-grown jungle, she'd probably be there by now. But no turning back—she'd left her mountain bike by the highway, a steep trek downhill.

In the woods behind her, something rustled.

Company?

Sara flicked off her headlamp, heart galloping. She'd told no one where she was going. Not a soul.

Rustle, rustle.

It's probably an animal. She forced herself to breathe deeply, inhaling the forest's cool, damp tang until her heartbeat slowed. Rain dripped onto mossy ground. Trees creaked. A stream splashed over rocks.

Another rustle.

Sara shivered as she slid a hand into her pocket and pulled out a Swiss Army knife. Leaving the blades closed, she clenched the knife in her fist and turned. No whisper of movement. Just black woods, black night.

She waited.

Finally, she clicked her headlamp back on. The glowing light dipped, washing across gnarled roots and low shrubs: sword ferns, evergreen huckleberry, salal. Thick moss covered the ground. Her gaze tilted up, searching the canopy of spruce and hemlock. Gusty winds rocked the treetops, making the branches quiver and sway.

There it was again.

Rustle, rustle.

Scrape.

Oh. Sara let out her breath in a relieved whoosh. *The wind.*

"Chill out, girl," she grumbled as she slipped the army knife back into her pocket. She'd gone face-to-face with cops in riot gear, dodged pepper spray, and resisted arrest with style—so why get spooked now? Her shoulders slumped. Ever since she'd found that strange bone here . . .

Sara checked her GPS watch. *Better get going. They'll be here at dawn.*

The straps of her pack dug into her shoulders as she continued hiking. Mud sucked at her boot soles. It was slow going, but she soldiered on, the headlamp beam bouncing in front of her. She followed the curves of a stream, picking out a vague trail. The water rushed and roared, swollen by winter rains.

At last, she reached the clearing. Underneath the so-called breathable fabric of her clothes, sweat cloyed against skin. But she was here.

Her throat tightened. The headlamp's glimmer barely hinted at the destruction. All around the old cabin, acres of trees had been butchered into stumps, the land scraped clean and crisscrossed by bulldozer tracks. Work crews had left behind piles of slash and construction debris. Everything wild was gone. Before long, concrete foundations would cover the ground like gravestones.

Not if I can find the rest of the bones. Sara pulled up her jacket hood, tucked her long hair inside, and powered the headlamp to high beam. She stepped into the clearing.

As she walked toward the abandoned cabin, rain slanted through the glow. Despite its moss-coated roof and peeling paint, the cabin's gingerbread trim made it look charming. She snorted. Hansel and Gretel charming.

She headed for the spot where she'd found the previous bone and paced off a grid, studying the ground intently. Nothing there. She moved another twenty feet and repeated the process. And then again. And again.

They had to be here. They had *to.*

Sara raised her head and scanned the site.

Her light caught on a patch of bare, lumpy ground, not far from the cabin. Had it been disturbed by scavengers? She hurried over. Dropping to her knees, she brushed off a few millimeters of soil. *There was a lump here.* Her fingers moved faster and faster and dirt crumbled away, exposing something hard. Something pale.

Just under the surface lay two bones, their tips cracked and yellowing.

Yes! Sara swung her backpack to the ground and pulled out her camera. The flash pulsed through the night, capturing the pale bones against dark, soggy earth. She re-framed the photo and zoomed in. After documenting her find, she grabbed a camp shovel from her pack and snapped the folding parts into place.

The shovel slid in easily, revealing two long shafts. Mud smeared her hands as she tugged the bones free. She wrapped them in cotton rags, slid the bundle into her pack, and picked up the shovel again. Dirt mounded beside her. Sweat ran down her back in sticky rivulets and her shoulder muscles ached, but nothing else appeared. *Two bones? That's it?*

She was about to give up when the shovel clinked—the sound of metal hitting glass. Breathless, she scraped around the imbedded object with her fingers. It was a tiny brown jar: cracked, its contents long ago spilled. She squinted at the faded label. DANGER.

Even better than bones: evidence. Ammunition. She photographed the jar, each camera click sending strobes of light into the blackness.

As the flash faded, she heard a faint rumbling. *It must be coming from the highway.* She returned to taking photos, so engrossed she barely noticed the rumbling noise getting louder. Closer.

Headlights washed across the clearing.

Sara snapped off her headlamp and hit the ground, flattening her body to the dirt. The engine's rumble stopped. She dared a peek: a medium-sized pickup truck. Two people climbed out and the doors slammed closed, loud as gunshots.

Do they know I'm here? Her stomach heaved. *There's no way.* Reaching for her pack, she waited for the right moment. Every instinct screamed to flee, to run for her life, but she'd never reach the forest. Could she hide in the abandoned cabin?

Slowly, oh-so-slowly, she commando crawled toward the rundown house, her belly sliding over dirt and rocks and twigs. She tried not to make a sound. The backpack pressed on her, weighing her down, but she kept crawling.

Behind her, two flashlights waved.

The cabin's front door eased open with a whine of protest. Heart strumming, Sara entered. She climbed to her feet and took a few cautious steps, blinded by darkness. Her hip bumped something soft, and her breath caught. She reached out to touch it. An old couch? Carefully, she inched past the obstacle.

Her hiking boots tapped across linoleum, taking her down a narrow hallway and into a back bedroom. A place to hide. The room smelled musty, hinting of mice and mildew, and it was bare except for a bed with cold metal posts and a bare mattress. She prowled along the dark walls until she found another door. A closet with shelving. No refuge there.

The bedroom's grimy windowpane offered a slivered view of the truck. Everything outside was still. No sign of the intruders. Why had they come? Why now?

Oh, shit. Sara froze. *The shovel.* She'd left it sitting by the hole . . . and the cops had her prints. They'd get her on trespassing. She paced the room, choking down stale air and fingering the locket that hung from a thin leather cord around her neck. *Stupid, stupid, stupid.*

She was about to leave—take her chances outside—when the cabin's front door creaked open. Loud male voices carried through the house.

With a quicksilver movement, Sara slid under the bed, shoving her backpack in front of her. Dust flurried. She huddled in the corner, holding back a sneeze, and wrestled the army knife from her pocket. Three puny blades.

"Maybe you were seeing things," one man said. "Ghosts and goblins?"

"I saw something," the other guy insisted. "And it wasn't a frickin' ghost. We need to check it out."

His voice nagged at her. Young. Somehow familiar.

Sweat beaded on her forehead as their heavy footsteps crossed the linoleum. Clump, clump, clump. They stopped just outside the bedroom door. *Please don't come in*, she prayed. *Please.* Her face was pressed into the floor, and something reeked—dead mouse?—but she couldn't move. Could barely breathe.

The door opened.

A flashlight beam crept across the room and brushed by the bed. Her heart thudded as one pair of footsteps drew near. All she could see were boots. Rugged boots.

The man clunked over to the closet. The door swung open. He shut it hard and moved toward the bed. Toward her. A beam of light brightened the floor in front of him.

"We shouldn't be in here," the other man said from the hallway. "Let's *go*."

"Not yet." The boots halted by the edge of the bed. At any moment, he'd peer underneath the metal frame and expose her hiding spot.

She held her breath.

"Must have imagined it," he muttered at last. When his flashlight beam swung into the hall, she gulped for air. Their footsteps thunked across the linoleum again, this time retreating. "You're right," he called to the other man. "Nobody's here."

So close. Sara remained under the bed until the truck's diesel engine rumbled to life. Only then did she crawl over to the bedroom window. Keeping her body to one side, she peered through the dirty pane. Taillights glowed red as the truck U-turned and drove away, heading down the gravel road to the highway. As she watched it leave, she rubbed the silver locket again. Her touchstone.

Adrenaline gave way to exhaustion, every muscle aching and stiff from the evening's labors. She retrieved her backpack, crept through the house to the living room, and pushed a flap of curtain to one side. She looked out—the truck was gone.

Sara turned on her headlamp and squealed in surprise. On the wall immediately above her was an old deer mount with twisted antlers. It had lost one eye, and the remaining glass iris glared at her.

She let out a shaky breath and moved the light. Apparently, the construction crew had adopted this cabin as their trailer. They'd filled the room with a beat-up couch that sprouted wads of stuffing, a card table with two folding chairs, and a small file cabinet. A Mr. Coffee sat on top, along with non-dairy creamer and a stack of cups.

She hesitated, wanting to search the files. *No.* She had the photos. The bones. Time to get out of here.

Sara opened the front door. Was that a sound in the clearing? She flicked off her light. The hairs on the back of her neck edged upright, but nothing moved outside. Nothing she could see, anyway.

Closing the cabin door behind her, she walked back toward the pit where she'd found the bones. She stopped dead. This was the right place. But there was no shovel. And no hole. While she'd been cowering inside, those two men must have filled it in and smoothed over the top—as if she'd never been here, never found the two bones. Or that small jar, leaking poison into the ground.

What the hell were they up to? She fell to her knees, scraping at the dirt with her bare hands. The bones were the cake, the photos icing, but the cracked jar would be the cherry on top—a precious bargaining chip.

A muffled footstep sounded behind her. Scrambling to her feet, she twisted to look. Oh my God. A man. Coming toward her.

Sara swooped down and grabbed her pack. *Run.* Her boots pounded against the uneven ground as she flew over rocks and construction debris. She kept running, the pack bouncing on her shoulders. *If I reach the woods, I can hide. If I reach the woods—*

She thudded to a stop. In front of her was a muddy stream bank. Below that, rushing water. She looked left, then right. *Totally screwed.*

He shouted at her. Sara raced alongside the creek, searching frantically for a place to cross. *There?* She stepped down, balancing on a slick, dark rock. Water roared. She jumped to another rounded stone, teetered for a moment, then regained her balance. The stream ran high, bulging at its banks. Current tugged at overhanging branches.

He shouted again as she jumped to the next rock. Startled, she lunged for the opposite bank. Her boots skidded across the rock's wet surface and she slid into the water, arms flailing.

Help me. In seconds, the flow knocked her flat and her mouth filled with numbing-cold creek. *I can't breathe.* She coughed up water and struggled to stand, straining to grab a rock, a branch . . . anything.

Hands tugged at her pack, yanking her from the creek. Sara tried to twist away from the man's rough grasp. He reached for the thin leather cord around her neck and whispered something, his breath hot against her skin.

Sara fought with animal panic. She knew that voice now.

MARCH

Two

Maya Rivers' hand wavered as she aimed the dart. The bulletin board on her bedroom wall was covered in pink Post-it notes. Handwritten messages to herself.

With a grunted "Aiyah!" worthy of any martial artist, Maya let the first dart fly. *C'mon, bull's-eye.* The shaft sailed through the air, ricocheted off the plaster, and clattered to the floor, taking a tiny chunk of wall with it. Whoops.

She picked up another dart and aimed more carefully. This time, it nailed pink paper. Maya peeled the skewered note from the board and read her Positive Thought for the Day aloud. "I love my job! I meet new people every day!" She tried to juice her voice with delight, but it was useless. Maya crumpled the paper into a ball, hurled it across the bedroom, and tried a third dart.

"Every challenge is a fresh opportunity!" She laughed. This was a hundred percent useless. Not even bubbly affirmations could make working at the Clam Strip Café more appealing. She should do something truly meaningful . . . like quit.

Instead, she checked the clock on her nightstand—4:45 p.m.—and kicked into gear. Scurrying around the room, she stabbed the darts back into the bulletin board and grabbed her work uniform.

The navy-blue polyester miniskirt lay in a heap by the bed. As she yanked on the skirt, shiny gold anchors danced along the hem. She found her white sailor blouse hanging off a chair, smoothed out the wrinkles, and sat down to pull on her tights.

Waitressing was temporary, a hiccup in her new life. Her post-Frank rebirth, she corrected. Working at the Clam Strip paid her bills—and she couldn't let this crazy sailor outfit crush her mojo.

Rain pelted against the apartment windows as Maya put on red rubber boots and a purple windbreaker. She hurried down the outside stairs to the backyard. Her landlord had squeezed two rental units into this weathered old house—one upstairs, one down—and living on the top floor was a real workout.

She climbed into her ancient Corolla and headed north on Highway 101, the Oregon Coast Highway. The windshield wipers smeared fat raindrops across the glass and moisture spritzed onto the car seats. At the next traffic light, she adjusted the duct tape holding up the driver's window and gave the cracked dashboard a loving pat. Still kicking. Unlike her brief marriage to Frank. *Get over it,* she told herself firmly. *He's history.*

Two blocks later, the northbound lanes flared with red taillights. She slammed on her brakes and the Corolla jolted to a stop behind the broad backside of an RV. Tourists invading town already?

In the long line of vehicles, horns bleated.

Nobody moved.

Maya craned her neck to see what was going on. People had gotten out of their cars and were staring at something in the road. She quickly followed them.

Oh my God. Three bicyclists lay sprawled in the wet street, their mountain bikes next to them. Blood coated their faces and pooled around them in watery pink puddles. One biker wore a bright yellow jersey, a splash of neon against the gray, stained pavement.

"Are they dead, Mommy?" a little boy cried. He clung to his mother's hand, looking wide-eyed and worried.

"No, sweetie. They're pretending." She turned away, pulling the boy after her. "Don't look. It just encourages them."

Encourages them? Maya was rushing to help the bikers when she saw the yellow-jersey guy casually brush a raindrop off his nose. Her gaze swung past the prone bodies to the gathering crowd. On the far sidewalk, two girls with long blonde hair were marching around, holding hand-painted signs that read, "Wider? Over my dead body!" and "What's wrong with a few curves?"

A grizzly bear of a man, heavily bearded, held his own sign. It read: "Save our streams! Say NO to Straightening Highway 20." Underneath the words was a green circle with the letters CD inside.

The Coast Defenders? With a sudden ping of comprehension, Maya looked back at the street. She admired the first biker's toned muscles, which were well defined in his snug yellow jersey and bike shorts, before her gaze stopped on the second cyclist. He wore a blue helmet, with brown hair straggling out the back, faded hiking pants, and a mud-encrusted t-shirt. A tattoo of Poseidon holding a trident snaked up his left arm. His face was dotted with fake blood and his eyes were shut.

"*Harley?*"

He didn't respond. Maya made her way toward him, and nudged his foot with her rubber boot. "Harley! What are you doing here?"

He squinted up at her. "Protesting. Want to join us?"

"Sorry, I'm heading to work."

"It's for a great cause." Harley waved his arm at the road. "We don't need bigger, wider highways—or the whole coast will look like this."

She glanced up to see four fast-food restaurants, two car dealerships, a seedy motel and a gas station. "It's hideous, all right. But couldn't you say that without jamming up traffic?"

"Then nobody listens." He closed his eyes.

Maya rolled her own eyes skyward. How had her brother gotten sucked into this? "Occupy" was a passé term by now, but the Coast Defenders hadn't gotten the message.

It was hard to believe Harley had once claimed points for nailing crows with his BB gun. After joining the Coast Defenders last year, he'd started acting like a born-again—a zealous worshipper in his new eco-religion. Even getting arrested for logging protests in the Coast Range hadn't fazed him. He'd spent a few days in jail and earned his own probation officer. No big deal, according to him.

Police sirens wailed nearby. The three bikers stirred, but they stayed put while the bearded man grabbed their mountain bikes. He heaved them one-by-one into the bed of a black pickup truck. The blonde girls tossed in their protest signs and marched themselves into the front cab.

As the wailing sirens grew louder, the three bikers scrambled to life, rising like phoenixes from the road. The guy in tight bike shorts raced toward the pickup and hoisted himself into the truck bed. *Sweet view.*

But where was Harley?

Maya walked back to her car and found him waiting for her, bike helmet in hand. "Can I ride with you?" he asked. "You can drop me off by the Clam Strip. It won't take any extra time."

She shot him a dubious look. His clothes were damp, covered in mud and grit, and his backpack was ripped. Several days' worth of whiskers sprouted on his chin. And—to top it off—the fake blood was now dripping down his face and arms, making him look like a zombie. If he weren't family . . . "Get in," she muttered.

He grinned and jumped into her Corolla, just as two police cruisers pulled up to the intersection, their roof lights flashing red and blue through the rain. Her heart beat faster. Lights and sirens: they meant business.

She slid into the driver's seat. "Looks like trouble in Coast Defender land."

"Yeah. The cops are gunning for us again." He tossed his bike helmet on the car floor and ran a hand through his hair. Wild swirls of brown stuck up in all directions. Grabbing a wad of her tissues, he scraped the fake blood off his face, leaving bits of white on his fledgling beard. He found her old hoodie in the backseat and slipped it over his t-shirt. "Perfect. It's like I was never at this protest."

Maya bit her lip. After so many years apart, she had to tread a precarious line between big sister and mother hen. She couldn't slam him with advice. *But I don't want him to get arrested either.*

A uniformed officer approached the Coast Defenders' black pickup. After talking to the protesters, he made them all get out. They stood next to their truck, heads high and defiant, arms linked into a human chain. Another police officer walked down the string of stopped cars and scrutinized the occupants.

Harley turned his face away from the window. "I can't get taken in today."

"Just today? What about the other 364?"

He hesitated. "There's some . . . stuff happening. Stuff I need to do tonight."

"That's sufficiently vague." She couldn't keep the disapproval from her voice.

"Trust me. You don't want to know."

Trust you?

The officer moved closer to her Corolla, leaning down to talk to a driver. At last, traffic started to move and the RV inched forward. Maya followed it.

As they drove north on Highway 101, Harley kept his head down, looking furtively into the side mirror until the protest was a distant dot behind them. "The cops have it in for me. And I haven't done anything wrong. Not recently."

Maya laughed. "C'mon. You were just in the middle of the highway, blocking two lanes of traffic."

"We protest for good causes," he reminded her. "And, by the way, I've got an affirmation for your self-improvement plan. How about 'I'll fix my own life before I meddle in my brother's.' That's worthy of a dart, isn't it?"

"Nice one." Maya reached over and flicked his temple. Her pink Post-it notes were a crutch, but they helped. Sort of. The past seven months—getting over Frank's betrayal—hadn't been easy.

"I'm actually surprised the Coast Defenders are out in public," she needled back. "I thought you'd all gone into hiding after that fishing boat exploded."

"We didn't set the trawler on fire." Harley grimaced. "But our fearless leader, Tomas . . . he thought we'd better give the Newport P.D. something fresh to focus on, besides charred boats."

"And missing Coast Defenders." She frowned. "Have you heard anything more about Sara?" She'd met Sara Blessing once, briefly, but her photo was plastered everywhere. Maya felt like she knew her.

"I just heard," Harley said. "They called off the search."

"Already? She's only been missing two weeks." Maya glanced over at her brother. His jaw was clenched tight. "Are you doing okay?"

"Why wouldn't I be?"

Her hands tensed on the steering wheel. "Because you knew Sara. She was in the group with you."

"She knew a lot of people," Harley said.

Maya stared at him. "Well, what do you think happened to her?"

"Nobody knows." He gazed intently out the car window, as if he were taking in breathtaking scenery instead of strip malls and supermarkets.

"Someone has to," she insisted. "Women don't just vanish." They get hurt. Kidnapped. Murdered. Had the police given up on finding Sara alive? A chill passed through her.

"Thanks for rescuing me today," Harley said. "I appreciate the ride."

"But—" With a sigh, she gave up. She was still struggling to understand her brother. Still making up for lost time. When they were kids and their parents had split, Dad had fled to Newport with Harley while Maya stayed in Sacramento with Mom. She hadn't seen Harley for the next eight years.

Maya frowned as she pulled into the Clam Strip Café parking lot. The dashboard clock read 5:15. *Late, late, late.* Willy would be on the warpath. Quickly, she inspected her hair in the rearview mirror. Rain had plastered her wet bangs onto her forehead and kinked her brown curls into a frizzy mess.

She jumped out of the car and slammed the driver's door behind her. "Come inside," she told Harley. "I'll spot you for dinner. The seafood special, even." She hustled toward the restaurant, raindrops speckling her face.

"Forget it," he called after her. "I'm not going in there."

Surprised, she turned back. "What? How come?"

"Never mind." He grabbed his bike helmet and slung his backpack over one shoulder. "I've got something to do tonight. Something I can't miss." He took off jogging down the sidewalk.

What was he up to?

She reached for the restaurant door and her gaze flicked over the tattered paper taped to the glass. The color photo showed a smiling young woman with matted blonde hair and two tiny silver nose rings. The text read: *Have you seen Sara Blessing? Missing since February 27th.*

Maya's breath tightened. Sara wasn't a young girl. She was twenty-two years old and a trained Coast Defender. Nobody understood how she could vanish overnight, or why, after two weeks of searching, they hadn't found a single clue. Was she alive or dead?

Did her brother—and the rest of the Coast Defenders—know more than they were saying?

Three

Maya tried to breeze past the cash register, but Willy O'Brien held up a hand. He stared at the bar clock. Red crab legs chased time, their angled claws showing 5:20 p.m.

Uh oh.

"Late again, I see." Her boss wore a green top hat and a matching green polo shirt, stretched tight across his beer belly. Beads of sweat coated his face and damp circles darkened the shirt around his neck and armpits.

"Sorry." Maya tugged on her miniskirt, hoping to lengthen it a few millimeters. "I hit bad traffic." She started to sweat, too. The restaurant felt like a freaking sauna. Steam fogged the windows, and odors of fried seafood, damp coats and overcooked broccoli mingled in the muggy air.

He harrumphed. "You shouldn't park in the lot. It's for customers. And you used the traffic excuse yesterday."

"Well, today there were three bikers in the road, pretending to be dead. They shut down 101."

"You're kidding."

"I wish I was." Her eyes narrowed on his plastic top hat, which trumpeted "Kiss Me! I'm Irish!" in green cursive. Behind him, cardboard leprechauns dangled from the ceiling and sparkly shamrocks glittered across the windows and walls. Holiday décor run amok.

"Getting an early start on St. Patrick's Day?" she asked.

He broke into a crooked smile. "Celebrating holidays makes people happy. They eat more, drink more. I make money—and you get bigger tips. It's all good." He looked out the front window and his smile vanished. "I saw Harley get out of your car. You tell him he's not welcome in here."

Her eyebrows rose. "Why?"

Willy didn't meet her gaze. "You know, it's not smart to hang out with people who torch fishing boats."

"He's my brother. And he didn't set any boat on fire. In fact—"

"Better get to work." He angled his head toward the dining room. "My Shamrock Specials started tonight. Two-for-one seafood platters and slumgullion for a buck."

Whoa. Only a buck for Willy's famous clam and pink-shrimp chowder? Maya glanced over. Every table was occupied, creating a din of conversation and clanking silverware. Busy, she liked. Crowded with cheapskates, she did not.

"Look at you," he said, flicking the collar of her sailor blouse. "Your shirt's wrinkled and you're wearing rain boots and . . . "

It was *so* time for a new job. She tuned out the rest of his lecture, her gaze roaming past the low-hanging fishing nets, complete with miniature starfish, to the striped lingcod on the front wall. Waitresses bustled back and forth from the tables to the kitchen.

Crystal, her arms loaded with dirty dishes, gave Maya a sympathetic look as Willy rambled on. Crystal had probably never received this speech—not with her platinum-blonde hair and Beach Barbie figure.

Behind the bar, the "Clam" bulb was still burned out, leaving the word "Strip" glowing in pink neon. When Willy stopped talking, Maya pointed to the sign. "How about getting that 'Clam' light fixed?"

He beamed. "Hasn't hurt business one Budweiser."

Great, all we need is a pole. She pressed her lips closed, reminding herself of rent, and scooted past him. In the restroom, she exchanged her rubber boots for comfortable Skechers from her bag and dried her frizzy curls under the electric hand dryer. She took a quick look in the mirror. Hair: wild. Eyes: tired. Skirt: too short. Shirt: too tight. To her eternal surprise, the men frequenting the Clam Strip didn't seem put off by her keep-the-hell-away frown—or the extra pounds on her hips.

"I *love* my job," she said to the mirror, somewhat fiercely. "Every challenge is a fresh opportunity!" With a deep sigh, she walked back into the restaurant.

Barely an hour later, her jerk-radar twitched as she headed toward the window booth. Oh, no. Her least-favorite regulars had chosen a table in her section. The two men browsing their menus were as messy as toddlers and lousy tippers. Even worse—despite their receding hairlines and worn plaid-flannel shirts, they'd convinced themselves they were hot. Sexy-and-I-know-it hot. *Ick.*

She stopped at their booth, getting a heavy whiff of sweat and brine. They must have come straight from work, processing seafood on the Bayfront. "Ready to order?" She held her pad in one hand and faked a smile.

"Oh good, our serving wench has arrived," the chubby one drawled, his gaze roaming her skimpy uniform.

Double ick. Maya gritted her teeth. These guys reminded her of Frank, and there were plenty of reasons he was an ex. "What can I get you two?"

"Yellow Snow IPAs. The buck-ninety-nine special."

"And for dinner?" She put a hand on her hip. This wasn't happy hour.

He set down his menu and gave her a lazy grin. "Still deciding." His buddy nodded, dismissing her.

As she walked away, one of them whispered something, too quietly for her to overhear. She turned back to find them checking out her ass.

Maya fumed as she filled their pints from the beer tap. After Frank, she was done with this breed of loser. She had a new life in Newport. Moving on.

She placed the Yellow Snow ales, a local brew, on the tray.

Crystal made a beeline for the bar, her blonde hair and hips swinging as she sashayed across the room in platform heels. She stopped next to Maya. "Hope you're keeping an eye on that brother of yours."

"Why? What'd he do now?"

"Check out today's paper." Crystal reached under the bar and handed her a cell phone. "It's in the 'Rants and Raves' column." When Maya didn't immediately react, Crystal said, "Gawd, I forget what a dinosaur you are." She grabbed the phone and brushed a finger across it. "Here. When are you gonna enter this century?"

Maya laughed. "I use computers at the library. There's no need to keep one glued to my hand." *And no need to remind myself of how naive I was about Frank.* If phones were so *smart* these days, shouldn't they have known that picture of him was meant for his mistress, not for me? She was sticking with her cheap prepaid cell: no photos allowed.

"Di-No-Saur." Crystal rolled her eyes. "You're missing out, girl."

Maya fluttered her eyelashes. "You'll keep me up-to-date on the Hollywood gossip, won't you? Who's in rehab and all. I'd hate to miss any essential tweets." She glanced down. The web page's headline read: "Vandalism or Eco-terrorism? Let the FBI Decide." *Oh, shit.*

Crystal picked up the tray with the beer glasses. "I'll cover your table so you can read it. Guys in the window booth, right?" She fluffed her blonde curls.

"Beware of cavemen," Maya said. Crystal trotted away with a smile. The girl had been working here three long years. Maya would be lucky to last three months.

YOUR RANTS AND RAVES
Vandalism or Eco-terrorism? Let the FBI Decide
By Reginald Miller, Concerned Citizen

It's a good thing the police are finally bringing in the FBI. In the past five months, vandals have broken windows at the Oceanfront Bliss Hotel, spray painted "Tourists Go Home" at the Fish Fry Fridays restaurant, and set a bulldozer on fire at the DreamCoast Condos construction site. Last Thursday's explosion of the trawler Lady Littoral *is the last straw.*

Until now, the Newport P.D. hasn't taken these violent incidents seriously. Chief Johnson claims they're "keeping an eye" on the Coast Defenders, our local eco-activists. Well, did they keep an eye on the group's purchases of arson supplies, too?

Maya swallowed hard and kept scrolling.

. . . sources tell me the FBI will soon be investigating the explosion on the Lady Littoral. *Maybe the feds won't treat our homegrown terrorists with kid gloves—they can use the Patriot Act and lock them up. For good.*

She set the phone down with a quaking hand. Harley would be high on the FBI's watch list . . . and these days, they didn't exactly require proof to haul people in.

Crystal returned, slamming the empty tray down on the bar. "Those douchebags want more cheap beer. No food order. And one of them asked me out. *As if.*"

"Told you." Maya hid a grin as she returned the phone.

Crystal smacked her gum. "It'd be sweet if the 'men in black' came to town. Do you think they're like those guys on TV, with their hard bodies, dark suits and mirrored sunglasses?" She licked her lips. "Yummy."

Maya stared at her. This wasn't a Lifetime movie. It was a reality show—starring her brother as prime suspect.

Crystal saw her face. "Oh. Sorry." She brightened. "Maybe they can figure out what happened to Sara Blessing while they're here."

"Harley said the police called off the search."

"Yeah, talk about priorities. A woman vanishes, and the cops are freaking out about broken windows." She peered at Maya. "Did your brother have anything to do with this crime wave?"

"Absolutely not." Her stomach twisted. *Hopefully not.*

Crystal blew a pink bubble and popped the gum with a snap. "Everyone in the Coast Defenders claims to be as innocent as little lambs. Somebody's lying. You'd better hope it's not him."

"Ladies!" Willy's booming voice intruded. "While you're chatting, customers are waiting. Get to work."

Crystal saluted him and hustled off, saying over her shoulder, "You should talk to Allison about this. Harley could be in trouble. Huge trouble."

I know. Maya poured another pair of Yellow Snow ales and set them on the tray, her mind whirring. Allison was a fellow waitress—her friend and Harley's girlfriend. They both wanted him to leave the Coast Defenders, but Allison's passive approach wasn't getting results. This might be their shot to convince him. Still . . . what about this thing tonight he "couldn't miss"? Was the FBI already in town, watching him?

She tried to put her brother out of her mind as she delivered more beer to the Booth of *Ick.*

It didn't work. All evening, Maya moved robotically through the motions of waitressing while she fretted about Harley's plans. Could she convince him to leave the group?

She watched the front door anxiously. Allison wasn't working tonight, but she'd mentioned stopping by. Maybe she knew what Harley was up to.

At last, her quarry strolled into the Clam Strip. Allison looked like a gypsy in her white tunic, turquoise tiered skirt, and dangling earrings. She greeted the regulars warmly as she wound past their tables.

Maya rushed over. "Can you meet me in the restroom? We need to talk."

Allison flicked her long hair over one shoulder and studied Maya's face. "Let me guess. Does this have something to do with your red aura tonight?"

"If red means worried," Maya growled. "Intensely worried."

"Remember how I suggested centering your feelings? Holding peace inside you."

"Uh huh." Nothing disturbed Allison. Damn Pollyanna.

Yet today . . . Maya glanced at her friend. On the surface, Allison appeared as tranquil as usual, but something was smoldering underneath. "Things good with you and Harley?"

Allison stiffened. "Everything's great. I'll see you in a few." She headed toward the bar.

O-kay. Maybe it's not my business. Maya delivered a slew of two-for-one seafood platters to her tables before scooting to the restroom.

Allison stood next to the sink, gazing into the mirror. Seeing Allison's smooth golden hair and tall, lean body, Maya felt an unexpected surge of envy. Even if she started an exercise program, she would never look like a Victoria's Secret model. Too short. Too round. Too wild-haired.

Allison stopped admiring her reflection. "What's up?"

Maya checked the stalls—empty. "Did you see the *News-Times* web page today? There's an editorial about the Coast Defenders."

"No." Allison chewed her lip. "What did it say?"

"That the FBI's coming to Newport to investigate the fishing boat explosion. Look, do you know what Harley's plans are tonight?'"

"He's meeting me at the brewery later."

"No, I mean with the group. I'm worried about him. Does he know how big this is? The FBI . . . " Maya ran a hand through her tangled curls, knowing it was futile. Her hair did what it wanted—just like Harley. She thought for a moment. "What if I met him tonight instead of you? I could talk to him. If you'd cover my shift."

Allison hesitated. "My uniform's in the car, but—"

"Please? Think of the tips you can earn. And the boss'll be thrilled to get his favorite waitress."

"I haven't agreed yet."

"Look, we both know Harley needs to take a break from the Coast Defenders. I'll ask him to lay low for a while. At least until they're done investigating the boat."

"Lay low? I've tried that line."

"Your subtle campaign isn't working. On my way to work, I found him in the middle of the highway, protesting road construction. It's a miracle he wasn't arrested."

Worry flickered across Allison's face.

"Neither of us wants him locked up," Maya urged. "And I can convince him to leave the group. Promise." She held up two fingers in a loose approximation of Scout's honor. "He has to listen to me. I'm his sister."

"Okay, okay. I'll finish your shift." Allison took a choked breath. "You don't think he's involved in anything . . . dangerous, do you?"

Four

Maya dodged a beeping forklift in the Rogue Ales Brewery warehouse and climbed the stairs to the second-story pub. She stopped in the doorway, surprised to find a nearly deserted room. Wood tables lined the far wall, with rustic benches for seating. A surfboard hung over one window, and a bulletin board displayed snapshots of customers and their dogs. Behind the bar was a long line of taps, all Rogue brews.

Harley, the one remaining customer, was hunched over a table in the corner, typing on his phone's keyboard. Two pint glasses sat in front of him: one full, the other half gone.

Maya headed toward him. He'd cleaned up since the protest, and in his black t-shirt, clean jeans and high-tech rain jacket, he could pass for a college grad. If only he could see his potential, beyond the Coast Defenders.

When she slid onto the bench across from him, he set down his phone. "What are you doing here? I'm supposed to meet—"

"Allison's not coming." Maya reached for the full pint and took a sip of thick, brown brew. *Aaah.* Her favorite, Shakespeare Stout. "Good thing we share the same taste in beer."

Harley frowned. "What'd you do with her?"

"She's finishing my shift. I needed to talk to you." Maya had stopped at home to change out of her uniform and she was ready to forget about the Clam Strip. She took another sip of beer and gave a happy sigh.

"Talk to me? What did I do wrong now?"

She winced. Was she really that bad a sister? "Well, that depends . . . what have you been up to since the protest?"

His cell phone buzzed and he answered it quickly. "I told you I'd be there," he said to the caller. "And I will." He hung up and slid the phone into his backpack.

"Who was that?"

"A friend." Harley stirred on the bench. "I'm actually glad you're here." He unzipped his pack, pulled out a small velvet box with a gold clasp, and set it on the table. "I picked this up today. I wanted you to see it first."

A ring? For Allison? Maya tried to mask her apprehension. They'd only been dating a year.

"Open it." Harley pushed the box closer.

Slowly, she undid the clasp. The box held a delicate gold band with three gemstones: a diamond and two sapphires. It was engraved "Love Always." Maya gasped. She knew this ring. On the day of their parents' divorce, it had disappeared from Mom's finger. When Maya had asked about it, her mom had walked out of the room crying.

"Dad kept it all these years?" Her eyes watered.

"I found it in his dresser after he . . . passed away." Harley concentrated on taking off his rain jacket and laying it on the bench. She looked away, too. Their dad had died last summer in a motorcycle accident. Maya had come to Newport for the funeral and grieved alongside Harley. Even if she'd barely known her Dad—his birthday cards had ended once she turned eighteen—he'd done a good thing in raising her brother.

She pulled the ring from the box. "The sapphires are new." *Where had Harley gotten the money to buy them?*

His face softened. "Blue is Allison's favorite color."

She tried to smile. Her own marriage to Frank had imploded and now Allison would get the family ring . . . With a sidelong glance, Maya slid the gold band onto her finger, admiring it. "You weren't going to ask her tonight, were you?"

"Oh, no. I need time to plan things. Allison and I—"

The bartender appeared at their table. "Another round?" He noticed the empty velvet box and the ring on Maya's finger. "Hey, congratulations!"

"It's not mine." She wrenched off the ring. "I mean, this is my brother. And, yes, thanks. I will have another stout."

"I'll take one, too." Harley glowered at her as the bartender retreated. "You don't look very happy. Don't think I should get married, huh?" He replaced the ring in the box, snapped it closed, and slipped it into his pack.

Maya couldn't decide how she felt. She adored Allison, but maybe she wasn't the right person for Harley. Their blend of tranquility and firebrand seemed destined to fail. "Marriage is hard. It takes commitment. It's forever." She scowled. "Or it's supposed to be."

"I *love* Allison."

She picked up her beer. "Sometimes love isn't enough."

"This isn't about you and Frank." Harley looked pained. "What he did was brutal, but—"

"Which part? Dumping me for his yoga instructor? Their baby?" She gulped beer and set the glass down hard. "Or the $6,000 debt he ran up before walking out on me?"

She'd never forget that day. When she'd returned home after a long day at the office, Frank had been waiting in their living room, his face set for confrontation. Before she could even kick her shoes off, he'd blurted, "I'm moving in with Miranda. She's having a kid. *We're* having a kid." Not much to say after that.

"So Frank was a real bastard." Harley's voice penetrated her musing. "You can't spend the rest of your life being pissed off at men. Or marriage."

Maya didn't trust herself to speak. She wasn't opposed to weddings—not at all—but Harley should understand why she bristled at any mention of her ex. And he knew how painful it'd been when their parents had split up brother and sister as casually as a set of dishes. You couldn't rely on people. Too often, they left you.

"Can you give Allison and me a chance?" he asked.

Maya stared at the Poseidon tattoo on her brother's arm. The moody Greek god could use his trident to bring calm seas and safe voyage, or to deliver storms and shipwrecks. Poseidon was like family. Unpredictable.

But she was touched that Harley wanted her approval. "Of course you have my blessing. I'm really happy for you."

"Great." He smiled. "So what did you want to talk about?"

"Um, can I see your phone?"

He got it out and slid it across the table, watching with amusement as she tried to get online. "What are you looking for?"

She handed it back to him. "The 'Rants and Raves' page. The headline is 'Vandalism or Eco-terrorism.'"

His brow furrowed, but he found the editorial and read it. "Pot stirring," he announced. "The feds won't come to Newport. They've got bigger fish. Besides, we haven't done anything wrong."

"The FBI doesn't need proof to arrest people. They could already be tapping your phone, reading your texts. You'd better take a break from the group, at least until this blows over."

"I can't leave. I'm in the middle of something important."

"More important than staying out of a federal penitentiary?"

"Yep." He grinned. "You may even see me on the news. This is huge."

Oh no. It was worse than she'd imagined. He wasn't dabbling in the Coast Defenders—he was embedded.

The bartender delivered fresh beers. She waited until he'd left before saying, "You don't want to get on the FBI's shit list. Last I heard, they're still prosecuting people for arsons that happened more than ten years ago. They don't mess around with eco-terrorism. Not these days."

"It's eco-defense," Harley corrected. "And we're nothing like The Family or Earth First! We're your friendly environmental conscience. We don't destroy property."

"The owners of the Oceanfront Bliss Hotel and Fish Fry Fridays might disagree."

"The group didn't do that. Someone's trying to frame us."

Her eyes widened. "Really. Who?"

"I don't know." He took a long sip. "We weren't involved in that boat fire either. Just saying."

She waited for him to set his beer down. "You haven't mentioned the bulldozer." He fidgeted. "The bulldozer?" she repeated.

"Oh, all right," he admitted. "I set the damn thing on fire. Somebody had to stop DreamCoast. But I didn't do this other stuff. None of us did."

"Jesus, Harley." Maya's mouth dropped. "You set a fire? What happened to peaceful protesting?"

"It doesn't seem to work."

"Well, neither did burning up a bulldozer. The developer's going ahead with his condos. You didn't stop him. Who else knows about this?"

"Nobody. It was a spur of the moment thing. I was there at the site and saw the bulldozer and . . . anyway, I stayed around to make sure nothing else burned." He gave her an innocent look. "How was I supposed to know an old dozer costs thirty grand?"

"You're not even sorry."

"Sure I am." He smiled. "Call it a 'youthful indiscretion.' Everybody's got one of those."

"It was less than six months ago."

"Well, Alan Kingston deserved it. That man is evil."

Maya played with a cardboard coaster, spinning it under her finger. She'd known Harley hated the development, but sending a bulldozer up in flames? Good God. "If someone *is* trying to frame the group, that's even more reason to leave. You might get swept up in a police investigation."

"I can't leave. Not now." He fidgeted again. "I got someone involved and . . . something bad happened. I need to make it right."

"Is this about Sara?" Maya leaned in close. "Because she proves my point. Belonging to the Coast Defenders is not only risky, it's dangerous. People disappear." She shuddered. How could the police have given up their search already?

Harley picked up his jacket, looking ready to flee. "This thing I'm working on . . . it's much bigger than Sara."

"Wait." She held up a hand, mentally shifting gears. "If you leave the group, you'll have more time to spend with Allison, your future fiancée. You could keep working at the food co-op and start taking classes at the community college. They offer marine biology and ecology. Think about it, okay?"

He set down his jacket with a sigh. "Who needs more school?"

"You might. You're not going to be an eco-activist forever."

His face darkened. "My work for the group matters. I'm doing something I believe in. How many people can say that?" He pointed an accusing finger. "And you're not exactly putting that old college degree to use at the Clam Strip, are you?"

Ouch. He knew why she was living in Newport, killing time at the restaurant. And to bring it up now . . . "You can't do much with a liberal arts major," she protested. "And I'm getting by fine."

"Getting by?" He studied her. "There's more to life than that."

"Maybe for people who know what they want to do." She couldn't chase away her unease. Why was he talking about *her* life, her choices? She just needed time to heal. This was about him. "It's not only Allison who wants you to have a better future," she said. "Mom thinks—"

"She gave up on me long ago. A lost cause."

"No. She really cares about you."

"Then she has a funny way of showing it." His jaw clenched.

Stalemate.

The bartender appeared, check in hand. "Can I bring you anything else?"

Translation, Maya thought, *please leave so I can close.*

"No, thanks," Harley said. "We're done."

The bartender slid their check onto the table. Harley reached into his pocket and pulled out a wad of crumpled bills. He peeled off two and tossed them on the tabletop. "My treat."

Maya smoothed out the bills and handed them to the bartender. She added a generous tip from her own pocket, an apology for staying so late. Harley stood and put on his jacket. He picked up his backpack, with their mother's wedding ring tucked inside. The ring for Allison.

She stared across the table, feeling as if the Grand Canyon had opened up between them. Not only had she failed to convince him to leave the group, he sounded almost proud of setting that bulldozer on fire.

"Don't look so depressed," he said. "Let me show you what the Coast Defenders do."

Five

In the parking lot, Harley headed for his mountain bike. "I need to grab a few things from my bike before we head upriver. There's a skiff at the marina we can use."

Upriver? Maya suppressed a groan. Exploring nature in the dark was her worst nightmare. Add a boat, and it was *The Blair Witch Project* meets *The Perfect Storm*. But maybe—if she knew exactly what Harley did for the group—she could make a better case for him quitting. "Sure. I love boating at night."

"Oh, you'll be fine." He gave her a wicked grin. "I do this all the time."

Harley had a rainbow of bumper stickers covering his bike bags: *One Less Car . . . Nature Bats Last . . . Friends Don't Let Friends Eat Farmed Fish . . .* and a bright red *Remember BP: Ban Offshore Drilling*. Ever passionate, her brother.

He pulled a wadded-up rain poncho out of one bag and handed it over. Maya slipped the huge camouflage-print monstrosity over her head and slid her hands through the armholes. They walked across the boat ramp to the South Beach Marina and he ushered her down to the dock. Mist in the air mixed with spitting raindrops for a cold, damp stew.

He walked briskly, glancing at each boat before he stopped next to a palatial yacht named *Spring Fever*. Maya was admiring the luxury cabin cruiser when she saw him step into an aluminum dinghy in the slip beyond it.

The dinghy's engine cover was coated in duct tape and its hull mended with sloppy patches. A puddle of rainwater sloshed in the center. "Hop in," Harley said.

Maya eyed the decrepit boat. Would it sink? Reluctantly, she climbed inside, dousing her shoes in the puddle.

He handed her a bulky life vest. When she sat down, moisture seeped into her jeans. Rain dripped through the poncho's gaping neck hole, drenching her thin cotton shirt. She pulled up the hood. Could tonight get any more miserable?

Harley yanked on a cord, but the engine merely coughed in reply. After three more yanks, it finally started. He pushed the boat away from the dock and steered past the breakwater into Yaquina Bay. Lights on the Bayfront sparkled through the mist. Sea lions barked in the distance, arguing over prime space on the docks.

As the boat passed through the bay, dank smells rose from the mudflats: salt, seaweed and muck. Low tide. The night sky was filled with ominous clouds, and puffs of wind raised frosted whitecaps on the water's surface. Harley seemed unconcerned. He was cocooned in his sturdy jacket, and every time the dripping rain got heavy, he shook water from his hair like a dog.

Maya clutched the side of the boat. "Where are we going, anyway?"

"Rocky's Marine Service."

"To fix the engine?"

He laughed. "The engine's fine. I want to check something out."

"Why there?"

"We've heard reports of oil slicks on the river. There's a good chance it's coming from them."

Their boat hit the choppy water with a slap and her stomach roiled. She tightened her grip, hoping Harley knew what he was doing. She'd rather not toss her beers—or drown. No other boats dotted the bay. No one else venturing out on a night like this.

Soon, the water narrowed to a channel and the engine strained against the river's current. Maya turned to Harley, her face half-covered by the poncho hood. "I haven't been in a boat this small in years. It's terrifying."

"You didn't used to be scared of anything," he said. "Not when we were kids. I remember that summer you talked every kid on our block into a lawn-mowing strike—just because Mr. Rourke wouldn't pay girls the same rate. We all looked up to you. You were so brave."

"Well, I guess that girl's gone."

"Temporarily. You know, I could throttle Frank for how he treated you, but it's been seven months. You're still floundering. What I said earlier, about your job—"

"Enough with the psychoanalysis," she snapped. "I'd like to enjoy this lovely boat ride." Of course she was *floundering*. Her husband had left her, making it clear she had nothing to offer. Maya swallowed hard. Harley didn't have a clue what happened when people got married. He'd have to discover that on his own. She turned her back to him, feeling the full brunt of wind off the river. The dampness had now bled through her jeans to her underwear and her socks were soggy.

After a few silent minutes, he handed her a cut-open milk jug. "Mind bailing? It's getting pretty deep."

She shoveled water over the side. "I can see why Allison was reluctant to give up her date," she said between splashes. "You certainly show a girl a good time."

"You're the one who asked about the Coast Defenders."

So she had. She continued bailing until the water inside the boat was once again a puddle. "Harley, why did you really set that bulldozer on fire?"

"To see what would happen. See how Alan Kingston would react."

"That fire was the first incident, wasn't it? No vandalism happened before then?"

"I never thought of it that way." He got very quiet. So was the river. The only sounds were their chugging boat motor and an occasional vehicle speeding along the Bay Road that traced the north bank.

The rain had slowed. Thin clouds flitted across the moon.

When they passed a spot where rows of wood posts stuck out of the water, Harley spoke at last. "Oyster farm," he explained. "Those posts hold pallets underwater so the oysters can grow without sinking into the mud."

She nodded, breathing in the river's musky scent. There was so much to learn about this place—her new home.

Rocky's Marine Service was closed for the night when their boat nudged against the dock. Harley cut the throttle and they drifted in the sluggish current. He used an oar to pull them in and tied off the line to a cleat.

The dock was dark. But on shore, a lamppost highlighted a small shed and the silhouettes of several boats on repair racks. A crane hovered over the water. At the far end of the dock, floodlights lit up a white sign: *Rocky's Marine Service. Posted: No Trespassing. Violators will be prosecuted.*

Harley followed her gaze. "Don't worry. Nobody will be here at night." He tugged a black stocking cap low over his forehead, rummaged through his backpack, and pulled out a heavy-duty flashlight and what appeared to be lock picks.

"Burglary tools? I thought you said we were checking out an oil leak."

"Among other things." He leapt onto the dock and grabbed the supplies, sliding his phone into a pocket. "You wanted to know why I do this crazy stuff, right? This is your chance." She didn't move. "Stay in the boat if you want," he said. "But the river's running high, lots of debris."

That decided it. The water was inky dark. She wasn't going to sit alone in this rust bucket, waiting for a stray log to slam into it. Besides, she was curious. Maya climbed out of the boat and tossed the life vest onto the seat.

Harley was already well up the dock, kneeling next to a fuel pump. He brushed his flashlight beam across the water and showed her a streak of oil staining the river. "See. I knew it was them."

Maya stared at the thin streak. "That's not much. And it's a big river."

Harley's jaw dropped. "If everyone said that, we could kiss our oyster farms goodbye. Every ounce of pollution accumulates. If we all contributed 'a few drops,' we'd *destroy* the entire river ecosystem."

Uh oh. She hadn't meant to instigate a lecture. "You're right," she said. "Glad you're on top of things."

He pointed to the oil. "Leaks and spills do happen, but these guys should have a boom in the water to catch the oil. This is just sloppy. Let's go on shore, see what else they're doing wrong. I've heard rumors."

"Rumors?"

"From the group. We've been talking about Rocky's." They headed up the ramp.

Harley moved cautiously through the dark, his flashlight beam pointed at the gravel-covered ground. They passed two boats propped high on repair racks before he stopped at the shed. He handed her the flashlight and started working on the padlocked door with his picks.

"Next time, you should bring bolt cutters. It'd be a lot faster." Her damp clothes had chilled her skin, raising goosebumps.

He kept fiddling with the picks. "No property damage, remember?"

"Uh huh. With a special exemption for bulldozers."

He didn't respond. The lamppost provided ample light for him to work, so Maya swung the powerful flashlight toward the boats on repair racks. Most of them were fishing vessels, but there was one sailboat, its mast lying flat across the cabin. Her eyes widened. "Harley, check this out." She tapped his shoulder.

When he turned to look, he dropped the picks. "What the—" Grabbing his tools, he followed her.

The lone sailboat sat high above the other boats, propped up with cement blocks and metal rods to make room for its keel. A ladder leaned against the boat's side.

It looked like someone had gone crazy with an ax. Jagged cuts sliced into the sailboat's hull and deck, and the cabin windows were smashed. On the other side of the boat, spray paint decorated the hull below the waterline: a green "CD" surrounded by a circle. The Coast Defenders logo.

"Huh," Maya said. "I guess someone else didn't get that memo about property damage."

"This wasn't us." His voice hardened. "Can you point the light there?" He snapped several pictures with his phone. "I'm gonna find out who's doing this. It needs to stop."

A light flashed through the trees. Maya looked over and gasped. There was a vehicle on the south river road, heading toward them. She flicked off the flashlight, sending them into sudden darkness. Moments later, the headlights turned onto the site. A truck?

Harley pulled her behind the sailboat's keel, motioning her to stay low. She dropped to a crouch. Her heart thudded as the tires crunched across gravel. The glow of headlights brightened, washing over the shed.

"What are we going to do?" she whispered. "They'll see your boat at the dock."

"It's dark." Harley leaned close. "But if they do see it, I'll distract them. Can you find your way down there? You can take the boat and leave."

"Leave? What about you? We're miles from anywhere."

"I'll be fine."

Right. She wasn't going to abandon him. Maya peered around the keel. The truck sat mere yards away, its engine idling and headlights on. The driver's door hung open. A large man was peering into the shed windows.

"There's only one guy." She took a cautious step forward.

Harley's hand shot out to stop her. "What are you doing? Wait 'til I can distract him."

"*I'll* distract him." She took off the enormous camouflage poncho and handed it over. "Head down to the boat, get in, and hide under this. I'll be there as soon as I can."

He took the poncho. "But—"

"Go. I don't want you to get arrested. I'll think of something."

The powerful beam of light swept across the gravel in front of the shed. It moved toward their hiding spot. Harley eased back behind the keel.

It was up to her now.

Six

Maya started toward the light. "Excuse me!" she called.

"Who's there?" The man marched toward her, his flashlight beam waving wildly from side to side. He stopped about fifteen feet away, using the high-powered bulb to spotlight her body against the shed wall. "What are you doing here? It's the middle of the night."

"Um . . ." She squinted into the bright glare. He was a giant, well over two-fifty. The owner Rocky, or hired security? Had they discovered the damaged sailboat? Over the loud *puh-puh-puh* of his diesel truck, she could hear Harley's footsteps crunching toward the dock. She shuffled her feet in the gravel to cover the sound.

"Don't move!" The giant stepped into a wide-legged stance, still pinning her inside the flashlight beam. With his other hand, he pulled a gun out of a holster and pointed it at her chest. "Western Security," he barked. "We keep properties safe and sound."

"Whoa, take it easy." Her voice shook. There were too many stories about people being shot by anxious rent-a-cops. She raised her arms in the air slowly, showing her hands were empty. "Can you please put down the gun?"

He moved two steps closer, still aiming the weapon at her. "This is private property. And I asked what you're doing here."

"I was looking for . . . a restroom," she improvised. Her heart pounded. Far behind him, a shadow crept across the dock. Their tiny boat was barely visible. The shadow stopped next to it and got in.

The man waved his gun around. "Why are you out at night? Are you alone?"

"Yes. But my family knows exactly where I am." She tried not to look toward the damaged sailboat. If he discovered that . . .

"I don't see a car." He brushed his light around. "How'd you get here?"

"My, uh, boat had some engine trouble. I stopped to check it out." *What am I saying? Now he'll look for the boat.*

She held her breath as he turned and peered through the darkness at the dock. Even she could barely see the dinghy. Maybe this would work.

"I'll take a look at the engine," he said.

Oh, shit.

"I wouldn't want you to get stranded here." His tone carried a hint of menace. "This ain't no place for a woman alone. Especially at night."

"Thanks, but I'm sure the engine's fine now." *Or it will be once I get out of here.*

"I insist." His gun hand dropped and he holstered the weapon, turning toward the dock. "I'll walk you down."

"Really, there's no need." She scooted away from the shed, moving briskly. She had to get to the boat first.

"What's your hurry?" He fell in step beside her. "I said I'd look at the engine."

"It's *fine.*"

He ignored her.

Maya speed-walked toward the dock, her apprehension building. Was the poncho big enough to hide Harley? Maybe she could hop in the boat and just take off— *No.* This guy had a gun. A big gun.

He walked close, matching her stride like they were in a three-legged race. His bulk made the dock quiver with every step. "I really don't need help," she reiterated. "Everything's fine now."

He stopped next to the boat. "This your piece of junk?"

"Actually, it's my brother's." The camouflage fabric remained motionless and Maya stood where she could block the man's view of the lump underneath. *Oh, no.* Was that the tip of Harley's shoe showing?

"Try starting it." He set his flashlight on the dock. "Let's see how it sounds."

"Ok-k-aay." Maya climbed carefully into the boat and yanked hard on the cord, like she'd seen Harley do. The motor coughed, then died. She pulled the cord again, more slowly, but the engine still didn't catch.

"Let me have a go." The man reached toward the boat.

Desperate, she pulled again and the engine sputtered to life. "Thanks for your help," she said, putting the engine in gear. It whirred but the boat went nowhere.

"You forgot this." He untied the line from the cleat and tossed it in.

Maya held her breath until the dinghy caught the current and started downstream. The man watched for a moment, then headed up the dock toward shore.

"Is it safe?" the lump under the poncho whispered.

"I think so," she whispered back.

Harley eased out from underneath the poncho, just as the boat engine coughed. The sound boomed through the night air and the watchman aimed his light at the water. He thundered down the dock toward them, yelling.

"Let's get out of here!" Harley scrambled for the tiller.

A long time passed before her heart slowed. She couldn't stop shaking, as much from adrenaline as from cold. Harley took off his high-tech rain jacket and handed it over. "Trade you."

Maya put on the coat and buried her chin into the collar. She passed him the flimsy poncho in return.

"That was amazing!" he said. "I can't believe that guy followed you down to the dock, and we still got away. Thanks to your quick thinking."

"He saw you. He'll find the sailboat and tell the cops," Maya said. "They'll blame the Coast Defenders for the damage." *Or blame me.*

Harley waved a dismissive hand. "Not to worry. You deserve an honorary membership in the group for that stunt." He sounded gleeful. "Can we sign you up?"

"No way. You're acting like you have eight lives to spare." But excitement shot through her. Tonight had been an adventure. An adventure she didn't ever want to repeat. Still . . .

"None of us took an ax to that sailboat," he said. "I know that much."

"Don't you guys keep things in cells so one hand doesn't squeal on the other?"

"It wasn't us. With all the attention the group's getting, we aren't taking any unnecessary risks."

"How can you say that?" she cried. "That rent-a-cop could have hauled us to jail . . . or shot us. Sara Blessing disappeared into thin air. And now the FBI is painting a target on your backs. If that's not risky—"

Harley turned away. "I know what I'm doing."

"Do you?" Maya gave his back a baleful stare. "Then why . . . never mind."

As the boat chugged downriver, she bailed milk jug after milk jug, splashing water over the sides. She took a deep breath. Thanks to this wild, reckless evening, she felt more alive than she had in months. Maybe she should stop thinking of Harley as her little brother, a kid in need of direction. His passion for the environment obviously kept him feeling alive.

He tapped her shoulder. "Sorry for dragging you into that mess. I didn't expect anyone to be there tonight."

"It *was* kind of exciting," she admitted. Maybe Harley was right— she should find her own passion.

"We could use more people like you—calm under fire."

"Do you guys really think you can stop the coast from changing?

Stop people from moving here? That's a long, bitter battle. You'll wear yourselves out."

"I won't." His voice was forceful. "I just think about the salmon. With everything we've done to their habitat, they persist. Some fish in the Columbia River cross *eight* dams to reach their spawning grounds. And I've watched coho fling themselves up and over waterfalls to return to where they were born. They don't let obstacles stop them."

Maya liked that image. Wild salmon were powerful and determined. "But don't they die after they reach their spawning stream?"

"The point is they don't give up. Ever." He nudged her in the shoulder. "We could all learn from them."

She snorted. "Thanks for the fable, Mr. Aesop."

They returned the boat to the marina and walked up the ramp to shore. Harley headed toward his bike. Her teeth wouldn't stop chattering. She felt chilled to the core.

"You'd better head home," he said. "Get warmed up."

She started to take off his jacket, but he stopped her. "Keep it for tonight." He checked the time on his phone. "I've gotta run. I'll get it from you tomorrow."

"Somewhere you have to be?"

He nodded. "A meeting."

Now? She looked up at the arching Yaquina Bay Bridge, which he'd have to cross to get anywhere in town. It had no bike lane, only a narrow sidewalk. And he was at least fifteen miles from his house. "Do you want a ride somewhere?"

"That's okay." He slipped on his backpack and pulled the camouflage poncho over the top. He put on his helmet and flicked on the Trek's red and white flashing lights. "I'll be careful."

Before he left, he squeezed her in a tight hug. "It's great to have you in town, sis. Maybe we can do this again sometime—once you're ready for another adventure."

She smiled. "Don't count on it."

Seven

Fire engine sirens screamed into the morning hours. Groggy, Maya gazed out her apartment window. To the south, smoke billowed dark and thick. Something burning.

She shuddered. Hopefully not another fishing boat or the cops would be all over the Coast Defenders. Maybe the FBI would join in, too.

She slugged down two cups of coffee and put on her Clam Strip uniform. Despite her fatigue, a strange exhilaration buzzed through her. Last night's adventure—the newfound closeness with Harley—had given her fresh energy.

She was more than a waitress. She had goals. Dreams.

But what were they, exactly?

. . . .

At the restaurant, everyone was chattering about the blaze, and Maya was relieved to learn it had nothing to do with the fishing docks. A brand-new business on the Bayfront, Newport Nature Tours, had caught fire overnight, nearly taking out the seafood processing plant next to it.

The restaurant's front door opened, letting in a blast of damp. Maya gawked as Allison entered. What had happened to her future sister-in-law? Allison's eyes were rimmed in red and her mouth pinched with anxiety. She'd pulled her hair back into a tight braid, making her look severe.

Maya rushed over. "What's wrong?"

"Harley never came home." Allison's face crumpled. "Did he crash at your place?"

"No," she said slowly. "He's not with me." *Oh, no.* The security guard must have discovered the vandalized sailboat. The cops would have rounded up the Coast Defenders for questioning. Maybe they'd interviewed Harley and—

"You met him at the Brewery?" Allison asked. Maya nodded. "Did he say where he was going after that?"

"He had a meeting." *Was he heading to the Bayfront?* Fear shot through her. Surely he didn't have anything to do with that fire. He couldn't have. "He left around midnight."

"Midnight? Rogue closes at ten. What were you two doing?"

"We, um . . . went for a boat ride."

Allison stared at her. "Boat ride?"

"He wanted to show me something." No need to mention trespassing, vandalism or the gunslinging rent-a-cop. Allison was already agitated. "Maybe it was too rainy to ride all the way home. I bet he crashed at the Coast Defenders' house." *Either that—or he's talking to the cops while we speak.*

"So he's still with the group." Allison frowned. "What about your sisterly talk?"

"I planted the seed. We need to give it time to grow."

"You said you could talk him into leaving."

"I tried." Her mind raced to a new possibility: Harley had been arrested. "Maybe you should check the holding cell. Just in case."

Allison's eyes narrowed to slits. "Where exactly did you go on that boat ride? Did it have anything to do with Sara?"

"With Sara? No." What was Allison talking about?

Willy hustled over. His knit shirt was stretched so tight, the blue stripes were distended across his stomach. "Save the discussion for later, please." He turned to Allison. "Glad you made it in. Table seven needs refills." When she didn't move immediately, he nudged her toward the dining room. As if she were hypnotized, Allison obeyed.

"Get back to work," Willy said to Maya. "Your orders are ready."

"I'm all over it."

"Hope so." He pointed two chubby fingers at his eyes and then at her chest. "Cause I'm watching you."

Her stomach knotted as she delivered breakfast plates to her tables. She tried to smile. It wasn't her customers' fault that she was having a rough morning.

Around the dining room, the buzz of conversation seemed louder than normal, with everyone gossiping about the Bayfront fire. It had destroyed the Newport Nature Tours building, a business so new its grand opening wasn't scheduled until next week.

Maya listened halfheartedly. Her earlier exhilaration had dissipated, leaving behind slow-motion replays of last night and worries over Harley. She approached a booth along the front windows and held up a full pot. "Coffee?"

The man nodded. "What's all the chatter about today?"

"The fire on the Bayfront. I'll be back in a sec to take your food order." As she filled his mug, a police car drove into the Clam Strip lot.

She returned the coffee pot to the kitchen, feeling uneasy. Rob was working the griddle and Juan washed dishes while Crystal held court. "Everything's hush-hush," Crystal said. "But I heard there were some cans of fuel and—" Willy walked into the kitchen and she shut up.

Maya pushed through the swinging door to the dining room. Her stomach churned even more. Too bad Willy didn't believe in sick leave—not unless you were in a coma. She walked back to the man's booth. "Sorry for the wait. Can I take your order?"

"Number three, eggs over easy," he said. "That comes with bacon, sausage and hash browns, right?"

"Sure does. And buttered toast." Maya wrote H.A.S.—waitress code for Heart Attack Special—on her order pad.

The noise of conversation dimmed suddenly. She glanced toward the register and saw Willy directing two men toward the back of the Clam Strip. Make that one young, dark-haired cop and one older . . . priest? The second man had almost no hair left, and he wore a long, dark coat with a clerical collar. He trailed behind the uniformed cop, who was moving through the restaurant with a determined stride. Ominous.

A hand waved past her face. "I'll take some orange juice, too," her customer said.

"Sure." Maya wrote OJ on her pad and glanced up again.

The two men were walking straight toward Allison.

Maya's mouth dropped. "Excuse me. I'll be right back." She flew across the room, drawing close to eavesdrop.

"You're Allison Rafferty, right?" the young cop was asking. His name tag read Espinoza.

Allison nodded. A vein pulsed in her neck, and her arms quivered as she held the order pad in one hand. Her other hand flew to her neckline to finger a dangling crystal.

"We need to talk to you in private," the cop said. When Allison didn't move, he took her elbow and steered her toward the kitchen. The priest grabbed a chair and carried it after them.

Maya started to follow, but the cop waved her away. "This doesn't concern you."

It had to be about Harley. What kind of trouble was he in? She looked back at the register—Willy was occupied—and followed the trio through the swinging door into the kitchen.

"Give us some space, please," the cop told Rob. The cook's eyes darted to the police uniform and he scuttled off to the dining room, taking

Juan the dishwasher with him. The priest settled Allison into the chair he'd brought.

The cop—Espinoza—saw Maya hovering. "Like I said, we need privacy."

"She's my friend," Allison murmured. "Let her stay." Maya stepped forward and grabbed Allison's hand. She felt herself shaking. Dread gathered in her throat, a hard lump she couldn't swallow away.

"We're here about Harley Rivers," the cop said.

Her insides twisted. What had he done?

Officer Espinoza focused on Allison. "We know you've bailed out Harley several times. You live together, right?"

"Yes." Allison blanched. "Has he been arrested?" She clung to Maya's hand.

"I'm very sorry," he said. "I have bad news."

Maya stared at him. *How bad?*

"We discovered a body this morning at the Bayfront fire," he continued. "And we believe it's Harley."

"What?" Her head jerked up. "No!" They'd made a terrible mistake. Harley wasn't dead. She'd just seen him last night.

Allison pulled her hand away and buried her face in her palms. She started keening, and the shrill sound sliced through the kitchen.

Stop! Maya clamped her hands over her ears. Her vision tunneled. The police were wrong. It wasn't her brother in that building. He hadn't said a word about Newport Nature Tours. About fire. About danger. A wave of dizziness washed over her. "It must be someone else," she whispered. "It has to be."

Espinoza was leaning solicitously over Allison. He handed her a glass of water and urged her to take a sip. The loud keening stopped. Allison's face was white and her hands trembled as she tried to take a drink.

"It might not be him," Maya said, swallowing hard. "With a fire, you couldn't identify . . ." Her voice dropped. "It's just a guess, right?"

The cop turned away from Allison. "I'm sorry. It *is* him."

"But how do you know?" She felt dazed, unable to get her mind past this.

"We've done a visual identification," Espinoza said. "Harley was . . . found away from the heat of the fire. We'll confirm with dental records, but there's really no question."

Maya gave a strangled cry. Her chest felt so tight she could barely draw a breath. Harley was *gone*?

The cop motioned to the other man, who stepped forward. "This is our police chaplain, Chaplain Jones," Espinoza said to Allison.

The chaplain patted Allison on the shoulder. "Is there anyone I can call for you?" he offered. She began to weep. "Or perhaps you'd like to pray. God can help in these difficult times."

Maya took a gasping breath. Harley couldn't be dead. He'd been so full of plans for the future. She bit back a sob. "I can't believe this. Last night, he told me . . . "

"You knew him?" Espinoza's brown eyes scoured her face. "You saw him last night?"

"Of course I know . . . knew him. I'm his sister, and last night—" She stopped.

"His *sister*?" Espinoza turned as pale as Allison. "I'm sorry. We didn't know he had a sister in town." He took a few steps backwards, drawing her away from Allison. His voice lowered. "A man found Harley there, not long after the fire started. He was walking by and tried to drag him out of the building. That man's in the hospital now."

Maya started shaking. Someone else had gotten hurt?

"What was Harley doing at Newport Nature Tours?" Allison wiped a tear from her eye. "He never said a word about going there."

The chaplain patted her shoulder. "Nobody knows. Not yet."

"Looks like arson," the cop added. He paused, letting this new idea linger. "It's possible he . . . set the fire and then got trapped."

"Oh my God," Allison said.

Inside Maya, a slow, fiery rage grew. "My brother would never burn down a building," she cried. "He could've gone in there to try and stop the fire. You're just looking for someone to blame and you think because he has a record, you can claim he's an arsonist and—" She wobbled on her feet, seeing the kitchen through a dense fog.

The chaplain leaned toward her. "Miss? Do you need to sit down?"

"No." She brushed him away and moved toward Allison, whose chest now heaved with gasping sobs. Maya leaned over and tried to hug her. Allison's slender body stiffened but Maya hung on, clinging to the only connection to her brother she had left.

Eight

Harley couldn't be gone. But he was.
And now Maya had to say goodbye.

Before she'd left the Clam Strip on Monday, the police had "invited" her to the station for a grilling. There, in a haze of disbelief, she'd told them about Harley's final hours—at least the brewery and boat trip. She couldn't bring herself to mention Rocky's. It was bad enough everyone was calling Harley an arsonist. If the police knew he'd been at Rocky's, they'd surely blame him for the vandalism. *All* the vandalism.

Detective Rawling, a heavyset cop with a stern face, had laid out the facts for her. The firefighters had spotted signs of arson, he'd said, ticking them off on his fingers. "Multiple points of origin. Presence of accelerant. Thick black smoke." It appeared Harley had died of smoke inhalation, but they were waiting for the report. Trent Lindberg, the local fisherman who'd tried to save Harley, had lung damage from smoke inhalation, burns, and other injuries.

Afterwards, Maya had slunk home. She hadn't left her apartment for the next two days, in hiding from everyone. She'd let her calls go to the answering machine, ignored the pleading reporters who "just wanted her side of the story." She'd spoken with Allison and her mom several times, but hadn't seen them.

Until now. The funeral.

In the sky above the cemetery, somber gray clouds bulged with moisture, lobbing fat raindrops. The grass was damp, the dirt around the newly dug grave turned to mud after last night's rainstorm.

Maya stared numbly at Harley's coffin, already lowered into the pit. Her brother would have hated this scene. They should have scattered his ashes in the ocean or at his favorite spot in the woods, held a memorial hike in his honor. Instead . . .

The cemetery's grass was a brilliant shade of green—and probably laden with pesticides. His marble headstone had a cherub on it. A bouquet of red plastic roses sprouted from the vase. *Plastic roses?* What had her mother been thinking?

Maya fought back tears. She and Allison had been so dazed, they'd let Maya's mom—aka the Tornado—take over. She'd cruised into town from Sacramento, badgered the medical examiner into releasing Harleys's body, and told "the girls" she'd arrange everything. Not to worry.

So here they were. No minister. No other guests. Maya's hand shook as she held the paper where she'd written out a poem for Harley. She glanced over at Allison. Did she, too, think this was wrong? "I can't believe the Coast Defenders didn't come," she whispered to Allison. "They should've been here. Harley died for their cause."

Her mom overheard. "I told them not to show up. If they had . . . reporters would've come, too." She gave Allison's arm a little squeeze. "It's better this way, don't you think? Quiet and personal. Just the three of us?"

Allison nodded solemnly.

Maya turned back to the gaping rectangular hole. It felt like an equally big hole had opened in her heart.

. . . .

The next day, she was resting on the couch when a knock sounded on her apartment door. It couldn't be her mom. She'd bailed for California this morning, muttering about Newport's depressing rain and the need to rescue her cat from the kitty motel.

Maya opened the door, surprised to find Detective Rawling, one of her interrogators from the police station. Her heart sank. They must have found out about Rocky's.

Rawling was puffing hard from the hike up her stairs. He carried a thin notebook in one hand. "Sorry to bother you, Miss Rivers. I have a few questions. Mind if I come in?"

Hell, yes, she minded. The cops had "convicted" Harley without a trial. They'd made her brother sound like a terrorist. Irredeemable.

Rawling waited.

"I guess it's okay," she said, opening the door enough for him to slide inside.

Detective Rawling settled onto her futon couch, giving an "oof" as his hefty stomach rolled over his waistband. She brought in a hard wooden chair from the kitchen, sat down across from him, and crossed her arms.

Rawling opened his notebook and pulled a mechanical pencil from his shirt pocket. He creased the page flat. "You were the last person to see Harley that night."

A shiver slid down her back. "I wasn't anywhere near the Bayfront."

He gave a slight smile. "I didn't suggest you were. I said you were the last person to see him."

She sat up straight. "No, I wasn't. I told you at the station. He was on his way to meet somebody."

Rawling tapped the pencil on his notebook, seeming deep in thought. *Tap. Tap. Tap.* "And what was the purpose of this . . . meeting?"

"Harley didn't say."

"We've found no sign of another person being there, other than the man who tried to rescue him, Trent Lindberg."

"Well, that's what Harley told me." *He'd lied about other things. This, too?*

Rawling leaned forward, his gaze intent. "He never said who he was meeting?"

"No."

"Could it be . . . drug- related?"

"Absolutely not." Her face heated. "He didn't do drugs. Or are you suggesting he was dealing? Gee, what else can you accuse him of?"

"I'm just gathering information." Rawling scribbled something in his notebook.

She edged closer. He'd written: STILL CLAIMS MTG. *Claims?*

"Tell me again about this boat ride with your brother. Where'd you go?"

"Oh, just . . . sightseeing." She fidgeted in the chair. "Enjoying the scenery."

"Not much to see in the dark." His pencil went *tap, tap, tap* again.

"Actually, the river's lovely in the moonlight. Peaceful. Low boat traffic. It's the nicest time to be on the water."

He quirked an eyebrow and scribbled another note.

Was she going to get in trouble for lying to the cops? Really, it was more a sin of omission. Her gaze landed on the framed photo on her bookshelf. Harley and her. Allison had taken it the day Maya had moved into this apartment, both siblings sweaty and tired from endless trips up and down the outside stairs. But still, they were beaming. The move had meant a fresh start for Maya—and the chance for them to get to know each other again.

She swallowed hard.

Rawling started to set his notebook on her coffee table—two cardboard boxes covered with a thrift-store tablecloth—then reconsidered. "So you and Harley headed upriver on this boat ride?"

"Yes."

He cleared his throat. "We received a report of vandalism at a place called Rocky's Marine Service. Have you heard anything about that?"

His expression made clear he already knew the answer.

"No." Her voice quavered.

"Did your brother say anything about it?"

"Nothing." She shook her head. "Nothing at all."

He gave her a probing look. "We took a report from a night watch-man who'd talked to a young lady at the site. She was there with another person. In a boat. Sound familiar now?"

Maya smiled weakly. "I'm not sure what you're talking about."

Another probing look. "It's normal to want to protect your brother . . . and to stay out of trouble yourself. But in this case—" He stopped. Waited.

Should she tell him what Harley had said about the vandalism? That he'd believed someone was trying to frame the Coast Defenders? She stared at Rawling, noting the deep lines around his mouth. So stern. Unforgiving. He'd already documented her lies and omissions and judged her guilty. Just like he'd judged her brother. She wouldn't say anything about Rocky's.

Their eyes connected.

His steely gaze moved away, and she relaxed a little. Maybe the cops were letting the vandalism slide.

But then Rawling started talking about Newport Nature Tours. The fire department had confirmed the arson finding. And Harley's Trek mountain bike had been found across the street, locked up in a rack. His bike bags had contained traces of fuel and accelerant—lighter fluid—along with rags and a lighter.

How could that be? Harley's panniers *had* been stuffed full when she'd seen them at the brewery. But he'd taken the rain poncho from one bag, and she hadn't smelled any fuel on it. Unless he'd picked up supplies on his way to the Bayfront.

Rawling continued. "That same accelerant was used at the site." He closed up his notebook and attached his pencil to it. "I'm sorry to say this, but your brother was definitely the arsonist."

"If that's so, why didn't he leave after the fire got going?"

"I'm sure he didn't expect it to burn so quickly. He wouldn't have been able to carry much fuel on his bike. But the owner of the business had stored some boat fuel near the building, getting ready for their tours. The blaze burned out of control. Smoke can be pretty disorienting."

Maya let this image sink in. "How, exactly, did my brother die?"

"We have the ME's report," Rawling said. "Like we told you, the cause of death was smoke inhalation." He paused, fidgeted with his pencil. "He got a little banged up in the fire, too. A bump on his head."

Maya stared at him. "What do you mean by a bump?" Nobody, not even the funeral director, had mentioned any injuries besides the burns. The coffin had been closed.

"Oh, small bumps and bruises aren't significant," Rawling said. "It may have happened when Trent Lindberg tried to pull him out. Or during the fire itself. It's quite common for people to get those kinds of injuries. I'm sure you can imagine."

Not that she wanted to. She didn't want to think about Harley trying to escape the flames and running into a wall, or having a chunk of ceiling fall on him.

"The cause of his death was smoke inhalation," Rawling reiterated.

Maya nodded. "Is this man, Trent Lindberg, doing all right?"

Rawling frowned. "He's still in the hospital. Still in intensive care. The Fishermen's Wives are taking up a collection."

Maya started sobbing and Rawling looked stricken. He reached over, handing her a handkerchief from his pocket. "It's clean." She blew her nose on the soft fabric.

"If you think of anything else you want to share about that night, or about Rocky's . . . " He picked up his notebook and stood. "I guess it doesn't matter now."

She started to hand him back the handkerchief, but he waved it off. Through a veil of tears, she watched him walk across the room and open her front door. He turned back to say, "Sorry for your loss."

. . . .

On Saturday morning—six endless days after Harley's death—Maya slumped on that same futon couch, pecking at a piece of dry toast. She'd barely left her apartment all week, not even going to the library to read the news on the computer. She didn't want to know what people were saying about Harley.

Her stomach lurched at the sight of the empty Chianti bottle on her coffee table. The vino had served as last night's dinner, along with a pint of Ben and Jerry's ice cream—a foul combination. Grief and guilt battled inside. Why hadn't she talked him out of leaving the group? Why did he have to die?

Harley had lied to her. He'd gone through that whole charade about the Coast Defenders not damaging property—and then torched a freaking building. The group's actions had destroyed a local business and nearly killed Trent Lindberg.

Her gaze slid across the Moving Day photo of her and Harley to the picture of Allison next to it. Allison was sitting on the front steps of the house she and Harley rented in Toledo, a mill town upriver from Newport. Allison held their gray cat in her lap, and both cat and girl looked supremely content.

Harley had let them both down. But at least he died doing something that mattered, Maya thought bitterly. Isn't that what he'd said at the brewery?

With effort, she forced herself off the couch. It was time to face reality. Go to the Bayfront and see what he'd done.

Sliding her driver's license and a few dollar bills into her jeans pocket, she rummaged through the closet for a windbreaker. Instead, she encountered Harley's jacket: the perfect choice for this land of dripping rain. His jacket smelled like a damp night in the woods. She clutched the fabric in her hands, remembering his grin as they'd escaped Rocky's Marine Service.

If only she could take back her criticism that night. Her lack of acceptance. What kind of sister was she? Her last words to him had been "Don't count on it." Brushing away a tear, she pulled on his jacket and zipped it up.

Something prodded her in the side. She took the jacket off and patted the lining. She hadn't noticed anything that evening, not in all the excitement. But Harley had apparently slipped something inside here, then closed the seam with safety pins.

Maya carefully undid the pins, reached in, and pulled out a sealed white envelope. She ran her finger under the flap and her mouth dropped. A stack of crisp fifty-dollar bills?

She counted out two thousand dollars. Oh my God. Harley couldn't possibly have saved that much money, not working part-time at the food co-op. He'd carried cash in an envelope and a diamond-sapphire ring in his backpack . . . Where was that pack? And where had all this money come from?

Maya fingered the bills. He'd known this was in his jacket, yet he'd given it to her to wear home. Maybe he'd also known the fire would be dangerous. Was this a brotherly gift?

No, her conscience whispered, *It doesn't belong to you.*

She'd better talk to Allison. Frowning, she slid the fifties back into the envelope, hid it in her underwear drawer, and put on Harley's jacket.

Nine

Maya drove past the charred Newport Nature Tours building. A chain-link fence blocked access to the property, and strips of crime-scene tape flapped from the wire. Behind the fence, workers were dismantling the building's skeleton and several spectators had gathered to watch.

She slowed the car, her attention caught by a white banner draped over the fence: *Whale Watching Tours! Guided Kayaking Trips! Oregon Coast Trail Hikes! Coming Soon!* Why had the Coast Defenders wanted to destroy this business? It sounded so eco-friendly.

With spring break starting up, the streets were crowded and the nearest parking spot she could find was well past the fishermen's docks. She walked back along the boardwalk, gazing out at the boats with their names such as *Challenge* and *Persistence* and *Perseverance*.

The wind off the bay bit through her jeans and goose bumps rose on her skin. She pulled a stocking cap low over her ears, shoved her chilled hands into the pockets of Harley's jacket, and kept walking.

But before she got to the arson site, she saw another crowd of spectators, this one accompanied by loud splashes and yelling. She stopped to watch. Three men wearing bright red, bulky suits with hoods had just jumped into the bay and were swimming toward a life raft in the water. When all three men had scrambled inside the inflatable raft, their feet sticking in the air, everyone on the boardwalk cheered. Another three-some—this one included a woman—lined up on the dock and unrolled their red suits. They seemed to be waiting for a signal.

"What's going on?" Maya asked a spectator.

"It's the Survival Suit Races. The guys are hoping to win cash prizes—and bragging rights. See, they're getting timed."

A horn sounded. On cue, the three people on the dock hustled into their red hooded suits and flung themselves into the water.

Maya remembered now. Harley had mentioned these races, said the Coast Guard cadets and young fishermen had a strong rivalry, but the purpose was to practice putting on their survival suits before the deadly ocean-fishing season.

"If you're visiting," the woman continued, "you should check out the building down the block. An eco-terrorist tried to blow it up and two people died."

Maya edged away. She might need her own survival suit to get through the next few days. The arson story must be enlarging with every telling. Unless . . . had Trent Lindberg died? *Please, no.* It was already bad enough.

She continued down the boardwalk, noticing the signs advertising the Blessing of the Fleet this afternoon. All week, she'd grieved in private. Now that she was out among people, she missed Harley even more. He would have loved the Survival Suit Races, the crowds, the fishing boats. He loved Newport. Everything he'd done—even the protests and the bulldozer—had been because he wanted to preserve the coast exactly the way it was. Which made the group's choice of Newport Nature Tours all the more puzzling.

On the Bayfront, tourists thronged the sidewalks, stores and streets. Forklifts lurched in and out of the seafood processors' open bays, shuttling plastic tubs from one door to another. Workers stood around in waterproof overalls and rubber boots, waiting for their next load.

Maya passed Dock One with its barking sea lions—and more tourists—before she joined the people standing outside Newport Nature Tours. As a backhoe lifted charred debris into a truck bed, the crowd murmured and pressed closer, like vultures circling the building's carcass.

On the left side of Newport Nature Tours sat a seafood processing plant with black streaks down its corrugated-metal walls. On the other side, a vacant lot held stacks and stacks of crab pots. With different neighbors, the fire could have spread through the Bayfront. Maya latched on to the only positive she could find: the damage could've been much worse.

She jostled through the crowd until she reached the chain-link fence. A few bedraggled bouquets, mostly carnations and mums, were woven through the wire, along with several "Get Well" cards for Trent Lindberg. The only homage to Harley was a laminated photo someone had twist-tied to the fence. It showed him chained to a logging-road gate along with several other protesters. The Elliott State Forest protest?

She looked more closely. That was Sara Blessing next to Harley. Why had he sounded as if he barely knew her?

"You'd think environmentalists could appreciate nature tours," a low voice said behind her. "What's so terrible about watching whales?"

Maya turned. The man who'd spoken was around sixty, and a woman with fluffy hair hung on his arm, a tote bag dangling from her shoulder. A tiny rat-dog poked his head from the tote and yipped at Maya.

"No barkies, Peanut." The woman pushed his head back down.

"Have you heard anything about Trent Lindberg, the man who got hurt here?" Maya asked the couple. She held her breath, waiting for their answer.

"Still in the hospital," the man said. "But it sounds like he's doing better."

Her relief was short-lived.

The woman broke in with, "It's a shame the police didn't throw that arsonist in jail sooner, along with the rest of his group. What a bunch of lunatics."

"I guess the jail's too crowded," the man said. "The Coast Defenders can deny this all they want. Everyone knows they did it."

The group had denied setting the fire? The crowd pressed close around her. She hadn't heard that. Maya grasped the fence for support. *How could they deny it?*

"You okay, honey?" the fluffy-haired woman asked.

Maya couldn't respond. Tucking her head down, she plowed through the crowd to the open sidewalk. Of course the Coast Defenders had denied the fire. They'd abandoned Harley. He'd take the blame and they would stay out of trouble. They could claim he'd done *everything* the group had been accused of. He was their fall guy.

She climbed into her car as the first raindrop hit the windshield. Then the dark skies opened. She sat in her beat-up Corolla, soaked in misery and fury. Her vision blurred, tears fusing with the rain outside. Harley had given three years to the Coast Defenders' mission. He'd given his life.

And there was no way he'd set this fire on his own. The group had coaxed—or bullied—him into doing it.

Then she thought about the incinerated bulldozer. The $2,000 in his jacket.

How well did she really know her brother?

Ten

Maya marched up the steps to the yellow house. The Coast Defenders might be telling the cops it was all Harley's fault, but they owed her the truth.

The group's house in Nye Beach was small and bedraggled, its wood siding beaten by wind and weather into faded amber. The roof was missing several shingles, and a sizable crack angled across the front window, covered with tape. Still . . . where had the Coast Defenders gotten their rent money? In this neighborhood, even fixer-uppers cost mega bucks.

She rang the doorbell. Behind the glass panes, shadows moved but no one approached. She pressed the bell again.

This time, the door opened wide enough for a face to peer through. "Whaddya' want?" the face snarled.

Maya stared. The girl was probably eighteen or nineteen and her black hair spiked from her head like porcupine quills. Three silver hoops punctured her lower lip. She wore a black turtleneck, black jeans and heavy boots. Thick eyeliner. Dangling black earrings.

Maya took a closer look. Spider earrings. How *goth*. "I'm Harley's sister."

"Really?" Goth Girl's eyes thinned to slits.

"Can I come in? I have a few questions for the group."

"Wait there." The girl pointed toward the tattered wicker loveseat on the porch and closed the door.

The lock shot home with a loud *snick*. Maya stood by the wicker seat and listened to the muffled voices inside. The smell of smoke wafted across the porch. Their chimney was working overtime, belching gray curls into the moist ocean air. Smoke reminded her of fire . . . and fire of Harley.

Nobody appeared at the door.

She leaned on the bell again. Goth Girl eventually returned, this time accompanied by a heavyset man with broad shoulders, a barrel chest and massive arm muscles. He was exceptionally hairy, with a thick beard and sideburns. Dense fur coated his arms.

It was the bearded guy she'd seen at the highway protest.

He wore pants with ripped knees, a faded orange t-shirt that said *Earth Day is HOT & Getting Hotter*, and flip-flops displaying very hairy toes. "Tomas Black," he said. "The group leader."

"I'm Maya. Harley's sister."

"Yeah." His eyes lingered on the too-big rain jacket, obviously recognizing it. "What do you need?"

"I'm hoping to . . . get some closure on my brother's death." *Get some answers.*

"Closure?" He grimaced. "I guess I can spare a few minutes."

Maya bristled. Harley had been a dedicated activist and he'd given his life for the group. They should be mourning him, too. And they definitely owed her the real story behind the fire.

Frowning, she followed Tomas inside. Goth Girl took up the rear, dogging her heels, and Maya had the distinct feeling she was being escorted through the house.

Large framed photographs lined the front hall—vivid images of old-growth forests that dripped with moss, waterfalls splashing onto wet boulders, and crimson sunsets over the ocean. In one shot, the photographer had captured the eerie light of a storm as thunderheads rolled toward the jetty.

Maya stopped. "Who took these? They're amazing."

Tomas turned. "Sara Blessing."

She couldn't hide her surprise. Sara had been a gifted photographer.

"That's her there." He pointed to the framed newspaper photo to the left of the prints. It was the same one she'd seen on the Bayfont—the timber protest, with Harley and Sara chained to the logging-road gate.

"Have you heard anything more?" Maya asked. "I mean, after they called off the search."

"There's no news."

A shiver passed through her. How come nobody knew anything? The cops should keep looking for Sara. It was their job.

Tomas continued walking and she followed. His flip-flops slapped on the floor ahead of her, while Goth Girl's boots clomped behind. The whole house smelled smoky and something was making a steady grinding noise.

They escorted Maya through French doors into the house's former dining room, where an elegant chandelier still hung from the ceiling. She stared—now the smoke and grinding noises made sense. A fire raged in the fireplace, fueled by a man with a shaved head and soul patch. He was tossing papers from a cardboard box into the flames.

A girl with long blonde hair fed her own box of papers into a shredder, while an elderly lady with a snow-white perm sat at a computer, presumably sending files to the cyber landfill. Goth Girl hurried over to her.

Maya's gaze traveled past the cardboard boxes and metal file cabinets to the scratched wooden desks with their prehistoric PCs. Greasy papers lay on the desktops, displaying remnants of fish and chips—or more likely, tofu and chips. Between the smoke, congealing food, and sweaty bodies, the air smelled foul. She tried to take shallow breaths.

"This is Harley's sister," Tomas announced. The white-haired lady gave a little wave and smiled. Everyone else grunted "hi" and returned to work.

"What's going on? Are you shutting down the office?" Maya asked.

"Darn close," Tomas growled. "Thanks to your brother."

"What do you mean?"

"He's made a world of trouble for us. Everyone's calling us eco-terrorists now." He shook his head in disgust. "The family of the man who got injured is threatening to sue the group, even though we didn't set the fire. We didn't have anything to do with it."

"Oh, c'mon," Maya said. "Harley was working for you. He had been for years."

"Sure he was." His face darkened. "Until he went rogue."

She'd been right—denial was their survival strategy. Of course they didn't want to get blamed, not with one person dead and another hurt.

The shredder stopped whining momentarily while the blonde girl dumped the bits into a sack. She grabbed the full bag and left the room. Tomas took over, shoving papers into the machine.

Over the whine, Maya said, "That's a lot of trees. Have you considered going electronic?"

"Maybe when we figure out a way no government agency can hack into our network." He fed the shredder again. "Green is the new red." At her blank look, he added, "Surely you've heard of McCarthy and the Red Scare. Well now it's the green scare. Guilt by association."

Maya could barely hear him over the paper-chewing motor. She raised her voice. "I was just down at the Bayfront. People are having a tough time understanding why the Coast Defenders wanted to destroy Newport Nature Tours. They think you should *promote* nature exploration."

"It's not that simple." Tomas turned off the shredder. "But the short answer is . . . we didn't ask Harley to burn down that building. He did it on his own."

"Is that what you meant by 'going rogue'?" Maya's anger surged. They were carrying this charade too far. "He's dead—so you let him take the blame."

"He was freelancing. Nobody here knew about his plans." Tomas looked coldly at her. "We've spent the last year trying to get people to take our group seriously. Not to be known for illegal, violent shit like arson. We don't destroy property." His voice came out as a hiss.

It was the same line Harley had fed her. "And what about the fishing boat? The hotel's broken windows? The spray paint at Fish Fry Fridays?"

"That wasn't us," Tomas said firmly. "Our mission is to educate people about the natural environment. Change their attitudes. Change policy. We don't encourage extremists to join. I'll show you what I mean." He guided her to a vacant computer and opened up the group's web page. The tagline read, *Defending your coastline for future generations.*

There were two rows of photographs, with the first row showing scenic shots of Northwest rainforests and beaches. The second row showed clear-cuts, a construction site with heavy erosion, and a cormorant with a fishing net twisted around its neck.

"Kelsey set up our page." Tomas angled his head toward the black-haired Goth Girl. He clicked on a link called Action Alerts and pointed to an article about a proposed golf resort on the southern coast. "See. We let people know about land use issues, ask them to get involved and support our cause. The last thing we need them thinking is we're eco-terrorists. Setting buildings on fire won't earn us respect."

Neither will blocking traffic on the highway. "Well, if the group is so . . . innocent, why are you destroying your files?" Maya waved a hand at the charred paper in the fireplace and the whining shredder.

"Thanks to Harley, the cops are focused on us. And when the FBI arrive, I'm sure they'll join the party. Even innocent words can be twisted by the Gestapo."

Maya thought for a moment. "What kind of work was my brother doing for the group? He told me it was something important. Something 'huge.'"

"Uh, when did he say that?" Tomas asked.

"The day he died."

"He didn't tell you what it was?" His eyes probed hers. "No details?" She shook her head.

"Then I'm not sure what he meant. Anyway, we need to get back to work. I'll see you out." Tomas herded her toward the nearest exit, a back door off the kitchen, and practically nudged her onto the steps. "Forget what your brother told you," he said. "I'm sure it doesn't mean anything."

The door swung shut.

Maya walked down the steps, both annoyed and puzzled. *He didn't like her asking questions? Tough luck.* She gulped fresh air, glad to breathe again after the rank-smelling room. She felt eyes on her back and turned. Goth Girl stared at her through the kitchen window, then ducked out of sight.

Parked in the driveway was a black pickup truck. Smoke puffed from its exhaust pipe, smelling of French fries—obviously biodiesel. It looked like the same truck she'd seen at the protest. And leaning against the side was one of the three mountain bikers. The hottie, Mr. Yellow Jersey.

"Were you causing trouble inside?" His brown eyes crinkled as he smiled. "We don't usually send visitors out the kitchen door."

She almost smiled back. "Guess I got special treatment."

He eased himself off the truck and walked toward her. "You're Maya, aren't you? Harley's sister?"

"Yes." This guy knew who she was?

"I was so sorry to hear about the fire. We're gonna miss Harley a lot. He was a great guy."

After Tomas' hostility, this small dose of sympathy broke through her defenses. Maya swiped at her eyes with a hand.

"Are you doing okay?" he asked.

She nodded, her throat too tight to speak. Would this ever get easier? Every time someone mentioned Harley's name . . .

She looked up. The mountain biker's straight, dark hair hung sloppily across his face and trailed over his collar. He brushed it aside. Wow, he was even more good looking than she had remembered. She'd always been a sucker for guys with long hair. An armchair psychologist would probably guess she was searching for someone who resembled the dad who'd abandoned her—and perhaps they'd be right.

Her gaze traveled over his green fleece jacket and Levi's. His build was lean, but muscular and . . . *Hold everything.* Her brother had just died and she was checking out some guy? A Coast Defender, no less.

Seconds later, a cell phone burst out in song. He reached into his jacket pocket and checked the number, but didn't answer it. "I need to run, Maya. Just a second."

He leaned into the truck, wrote something down, and offered her a piece of paper. She stared at it, confused. A carryout menu from a Thai restaurant?

"Other side," he said.

She flipped over the menu to see a phone number and his name: Nick.

"Maybe we can get together sometime, share our memories of Harley," he said.

"Sure. I'd like that."

He gave her a long, soulful look before he climbed into the truck and waved goodbye. It pulled away, still emitting pungent smoke. The bright red bumper sticker on the back was the same one Harley had on his bike bags, *Remember BP: Ban Offshore Drilling*. Maya stood in the Coast Defenders driveway until the sticker became a tiny red blur in the distance.

She walked back to her Corolla. As she opened the car door, Goth Girl stalked down the front steps of the yellow house. "What were you and Nick talking about?"

"Harley, mostly."

"Just so you know, Nick isn't available." The girl shook her head emphatically as she spoke, but her stiff black spikes barely stirred.

"All right." Maya clasped the paper with his phone number in her palm. "We were just talking."

"He's taken," Goth Girl insisted. "And if you're interested in what Harley was up to, you'd better be careful. Look what happened to Sara."

Maya watched in disbelief as the girl flounced up the steps to the house. The front door slammed shut behind her.

She climbed into her Corolla. Nick hadn't acted "taken." Or maybe her emotions were so jumbled she'd read too much into his kindness. He was probably just being nice to a grieving sister.

What had Goth Girl meant about Sara, anyway? Maya knew of no connection between the missing girl and Harley, beyond that timber protest they'd both attended.

She stared back at the Coast Defenders house. If the group really hadn't targeted Newport Nature Tours, as Tomas claimed, it didn't make sense for Harley to burn down the building. He'd admitted to the bulldozer, but he'd been adamant the group hadn't destroyed the fishing boat or broken any windows. He'd appeared shocked by the sailboat at Rocky's.

But . . . if the Coast Defenders weren't doing this vandalism, who was?

She tried to remember their conversation at the brewery, but only vague phrases came to mind: Harley had mentioned "something important," "something bad happened," and a thing he had to "make right."

He'd said he was on his way to a meeting. Who had he met? And why hadn't that person come forward after the fire?

Eleven

Late that afternoon, Maya pushed open the door to the Clam Strip. She was dreading the long shift after so many days off. Even more, she dreaded telling Allison that her boyfriend had hidden two thousand dollars inside his jacket. No doubt *that* would go over well.

The "Missing Woman" flyer, showing Sara with her silver nose rings, still hung on the glass door. A new flyer had appeared next to it: Crime Stoppers had offered a $1,000 reward for information leading to the arrest of the *Lady Littoral* arsonist. Maya tensed. The cops probably hoped to pin that on Harley, too. He couldn't defend himself.

The restaurant smelled of fried seafood and grease. Allison was across the room, waiting on a table. When Maya waved, Allison gave a listless wave back and walked in the opposite direction. Maya stared after her. Harley's death should be pulling them closer, not driving them apart.

Crystal trotted over, her blonde curls swinging as she bounced from one foot to the other. "How are you holding up, girl? Is your mom still visiting? Is she staying with you?"

Maya shook her head. "She left after the funeral. And she camped out at the Sylvia Beach Hotel while she was here. Apparently she needed to 'soak up inspiration' from the Hemingway Room."

"Oh." Crystal leaned in. "How come I wasn't invited to the service? I could've sung a ballad. I've done funerals before, you know."

"It was just family. We didn't have any music." Maya's mouth turned down. She should have stood up for Harley. "I wish you'd come. My mother—"

"I totally feel your pain," Crystal squeezed Maya against her ample chest. "I mean, if I found out that my brother was an arsonist, and then someone nearly *died* trying to save him. What a downer."

Maya pulled away. The girl meant well, but . . .

"I'm heartbroken for you," Crystal added. "After all those years apart, you two were finally getting close. And then, boom—just like that—he's gone."

Maya fled for the bathroom, trying hard not to cry. Whatever Harley was guilty of, she still loved him. He hadn't known a man would get hurt trying to rescue him. She patted her face with a damp paper towel. Harley had been a good person. A loving brother. She just had to get past the arson.

When Maya headed behind the bar to stash her bag in a cupboard, Willy patted her shoulder awkwardly. "How're you doing?" Without waiting for a reply, he started stacking beer glasses. "Looks like table five's ready to order."

She was relieved for the chance to keep busy.

More than once that first hour, she caught Allison's eye. Each time, Allison turned away.

On her break, Maya slouched at the bar, picking at a basket of fish and chips. The next time Allison hustled past without a word, Maya intercepted her. "Got a minute?"

"Not really. I need to get my order in." Allison's face had broken out with acne and her eyes were smudged with dark shadows. She looked fatigued, years older.

"What's wrong?" Maya asked. "Why are you avoiding me?"

"I'm not." Allison bit her lip. "I can meet you in a few minutes. The usual spot?"

Maya nodded. She dumped her uneaten fries into the trash, checked her tables, and headed to the restroom.

Seconds later, the door flew open. Allison stopped well across the room. "I don't have much time."

"Why are you so mad?"

"*Why?*" Allison's eyes watered. "I just lost my best friend. My soulmate. And thanks to you insisting on talking to Harley that night, I didn't even get to say—" She broke off with a sob.

"I didn't get to say goodbye either," Maya murmured. Did Allison think she'd pushed Harley into setting the fire? Was she blaming her for his death? Oh, God. She couldn't lose Allison, too.

"I was down at the Bayfront earlier." Maya's voice quivered. "I heard someone say the Coast Defenders denied setting the fire." Allison nodded. She'd obviously heard that, too. "So I went by their house, and Tomas Black pretended they didn't even know about the fire. He tried to tell me Harley was 'freelancing.' Can you believe it?"

"Maybe they're right."

"What?" Her mouth dropped. "The arson had to be group business. Why would Harley set a fire for no reason? He's their scapegoat."

Allison flinched. "I'm not so sure. In the past few weeks, he was acting really strange. He was agitated about something, but he wouldn't tell me what." She dabbed her eyes with a tissue.

"Did he mention the Bayfront? Newport Nature Tours?"

"No." Allison slumped lower on the wall.

"Maybe he was upset about Sara's disappearance," Maya suggested. "He seemed to take that hard."

Allison blanched, her face turning so pale that Maya thought she might faint. "He didn't talk about *her* with me. I don't know anything about her disappearance."

"And why would you?" Maya felt a sliver of unease, reminded of Goth Girl's parting words. Why did people keep mentioning Harley and Sara in the same breath?

Allison looked away. "Forget I said anything."

Maya stared at her. "You seem kind of . . . stressed. Are you doing all right?"

"I haven't been sleeping well. Someone keeps crank-calling the house."

"What does your Caller ID say?"

"Pay phone. It's the one on the Bayfront, next to the Barge Inn." Allison grimaced. "I called back and some drunk guy answered. Apparently my nighttime caller found the last pay phone in the universe."

"What do they say?" Another sliver of unease. Were they harassing Allison because of the fire? Because of Harley?

"They don't say anything. They just breathe and hang up, like they're checking if I'm home. It's freaking me out, now that I'm living there by myself."

"Have you kept track of the calls?"

"And what am I supposed to tell customers here?" Allison burst out. "I don't know why Harley burned down that building. Now you're saying the Coast Defenders don't know either?"

"So they say. But why would he set a fire, if not for the group? He told me he was going to a meeting. He didn't say anything about committing arson." Maya's voice cracked. "In fact, he made a point of saying 'no property damage' all evening." *Except for that bulldozer . . .*

"Harley's been known to bend the truth." Allison blew out a long breath. "And he *was* acting weird recently. Jumpy. Anxious."

"Maybe he was nervous about proposing."

"Proposing?" Allison jerked in surprise. "To me?"

"Of course to you. That's what the ring was for."

"What ring?"

Maya started. *Allison didn't know?* "The one in his backpack. Didn't the police give it to you? It was my mother's ring, but he added two sapphires to the diamond, because blue is your favorite color."

"Really?" Allison's face lit up. "I haven't gone back to the station yet. They said they had his bike, but they didn't mention a pack. I hope . . . " Her face twisted.

Maya finished the thought: *I hope it didn't burn up*. Was the ring gone?

"I can't believe this." Allison looked shell-shocked. "You say he had a ring—and then everyone's telling me he set this fire and destroyed a business. And that poor fisherman, Trent Lindberg, who tried to save him." She put her face in her hands. "That's not the Harley I knew."

"It's not the Harley I knew either. The Coast Defenders are hiding something. They've denied all the vandalism. Seems a little convenient, don't you think?"

Allison was silent for a moment. "I would've spent my life with him—if he'd asked. I loved him. Really loved him." She looked down at the floor. "But you've got to admit he had issues. He went ballistic when people did anything he thought would hurt the coast. He was extreme. You know that."

Maya choked back a tart response. This felt like betrayal. If the situation were reversed, if Allison had set the fire, Harley would be defending her to everyone—not condemning her "issues" and "extremism." What'd happened to love—for better or for worse?

"He committed arson," Allison said, nailing the coffin closed. "I've accepted that now. You need to accept it, too."

Maya crossed her arms over her chest. "I'm not accepting a damn thing. Not until I know exactly what happened at Newport Nature Tours. Why was he there? Why that business and not another one?" Frustration strummed through her body, giving heat to her voice. "Who did he meet that night? Was it another Coast Defender? Nobody's even asking these questions."

"Easy." Allison put a hand on her arm. "Holding in that much anger, it's not healthy."

Maya shrugged her off. "Forget healthy. Harley was—"

"Yo." Crystal bustled into the bathroom. "You girls okay? You should get back to work before Willy notices. We've got a full house."

Allison tossed her wet tissue in the trash and hurried to the door. "Thanks," she said over her shoulder. "I feel better now."

I don't.

Maya followed Crystal out of the bathroom, profoundly hurt by Allison's easy acceptance of Harley-as-lone-arsonist. She hadn't mentioned the $2,000 cash she'd found in his jacket. Now she didn't want to.

For the next half hour, she fought tears. The customers were nice enough—none of them mentioned Harley directly, or asked why he'd done it. But too often, when she arrived at a table, the conversation would halt. And when she left, the buzz started up again.

She carried a tray of ice waters toward a window booth and stopped abruptly, dismayed to see one of the guys from the other night. The chubby one. Sitting next to him was a woman in skinny jeans and a tank top. Her lacy shrug barely covered her cleavage. The man slipped an arm over the woman's shoulder and smirked at Maya.

Please don't start, she thought. *I can't take it tonight.* She forced herself to walk toward the couple's table. The tray wobbled in her shaking hands. Ice cubes clinked. Water sloshed.

The man watched her closely. When she finally arrived, he said, "Perhaps you should set that tray down, sugar, so we don't end up wet." His smirk widened. "Not that I mind a wet crotch," he added in a stage whisper to the woman.

Maya's emotions boiled over. "Oh? Then you'll enjoy this." She grabbed a glass of ice water and dumped it on his pants.

He squealed as the cold liquid soaked through the fabric. The woman leaped up, her oversized breasts jiggling. "What's your problem? He wasn't talking to *you*."

"The problem is you shouldn't let your man out of his cave," Maya said. "He's not civilized." She turned to flee and bumped into Willy. He grabbed her elbow. Hard.

"Sorry," she mumbled. *Oh, God. What had come over her?*

"Dinner's on the house," Willy said to the couple as he guided Maya behind the bar. He put his hands on her shoulders and his eyes burned into hers. "What just happened? How did that man get all wet?"

She winced. "I . . . uh, spilled ice water in his lap. Klutzy me."

"Spilled?" His eyebrows rose.

"Okay. I did it on purpose. But he *said* he liked 'wet crotch.'" She stuck out her chin. "I can't work in a place like this. I quit."

"Don't be so dramatic," Willy said. "You've had a hell of a week. You shouldn't be making rash decisions."

Hell of a week was right.

"You're grieving, honey," he continued. "You just lost your brother. It takes time to deal with that."

Maya wilted. Harley had been her rock, the one person she could count on . . . *No. I'm not going there.*

"I'm sure you didn't mean to dump the water," Willy said, giving her an out.

Yes, I did. But a small voice inside reminded, *This job pays your rent. You have no money. No choice.* "You're right," she choked out. "I didn't mean to. Not exactly. But I can't let that crude remark slide. Will you say something to him?"

Willy motioned toward the booth, where the man sat with his arm looped over the woman's shoulder. "He's a regular."

"So?"

"All right," he said, a bit grudgingly. "I'll have a word. I can see you're too wound up to be out front." He thought for a moment. "Rob could use a hand. Finish your shift in the kitchen."

As Maya headed toward the kitchen door, Willy walked over to the couple. He'd actually been nice. Surprisingly tolerant, really.

She looked back, hoping to see her boss pointing the man to the door. Instead, he was sitting in the booth across from the couple. They looked in her direction, and the three of them laughed.

Twelve

When Maya shoved through the swinging door, Rob glanced up, then turned back to the fish fryer. His sandy brown hair was shorn close and a baseball cap, worn backwards, served as a hair covering. Grease from the fryer and sweat from kitchen heat made his skin shine under the fluorescent lights.

"To what do I owe this great honor?" He kept his back toward her, tossing fish sticks into the bath of hot oil. It sizzled and spattered.

"Willy asked me to give you a hand." Despite her dwindling tolerance for the male species, Maya tried to be friendly. Not that Rob's back noticed. He'd been chilly ever since she'd turned down his sly flirtations, two days into the job.

"How about chopping those onions into rings?" Rob waved his tongs at the counter, where three large onions awaited. "Juan never showed. Hopefully he didn't get deported," he muttered to the fryer. "Don't know what I'm supposed to do without a prep cook or a dishwasher."

Maya sliced into the first onion and her eyes immediately teared up. To her horror, the dripping tears became a waterfall. Everything—Harley's death, Allison's aloofness, that horrible couple in the booth—it was too much. She rubbed her eyes on her sailor blouse, leaving a wet splotch on one shoulder.

Rob bustled over. "Hey, step away from those onions. We don't need you dripping on them. If your eyes are sensitive—"

"It's not that," Maya said.

He placed a tentative hand on her shoulder. "I'm sorry about your bro." When she stiffened, he removed his hand and motioned toward the fish fryer. "Timer's gonna go off soon." He wiped his sweating brow, the skin pitted and scarred from old acne. "I'll chop. You do the fish."

Not the fryer. Please. Grease spatters coated the nearby walls, and the oily residue had permanently stained Rob's apron. "Um . . . " She thought fast. "Willy wants me to keep my uniform clean, in case he needs me out there later."

"Figures," Rob grumbled.

The door swung open and Crystal popped her head in. "Are my orders ready?"

"Uno minuto!" he said.

The fryer's timer buzzed just as a pot on the stove boiled over with a loud hiss. Rob pulled the fish basket from the bubbling oil and yelled over his shoulder, "Get that pot, will ya?"

Maya scooted around the thundercloud of steam, removed the pot lid, and turned the burner down. The broth bubbled furiously, coating her face with hot vapor.

Rob handed her an apron. "You can clean crabs without getting your uniform dirty. I need a half-dozen or so."

Maya searched the walk-in's shelves for the cooked Dungeness crabs, gigantic beasts with monstrous white-tipped claws. She loaded six of them into a plastic tub and carried it to the counter by the sink. One crab landed belly-up. *Hold on.* She turned the others over. "Rob, come here." She pointed at the crabs. "Those two are females."

He leered at her. "You're an expert in crab sex, huh?"

The kitchen door opened again. This time, it was Allison. "What's the hold-up? I need my orders!" she hollered. Her eyes widened when she saw Maya, but she didn't say anything.

"Soon," Rob yelled back. He added under his breath, "Don't get your panties in a wad."

Allison left without a word to Maya.

She pointed to the shells again. "You can't keep female crabs, Rob. There's a huge fine if you do." Harley had taken her crabbing off a Bayfront pier. In the drenching rain, she'd accidentally moved a female from the trap to the bucket. He'd gone on and on about protecting breeding crabs to keep the population going. Her shoulders slumped. She'd gladly hear that lecture now.

"They're already cooked," Rob said. "It'd be a waste not to use them."

Maya picked up a male crab, broke apart its shell, and turned on the sink. Under the running water, she pulled out the meat. "Where does Willy get his seafood from?"

"Different places."

"Well, who delivered this batch?" She tossed the crabmeat into a bowl. "It's illegal as hell."

At the word illegal, Rob twitched. "Don't go down that path. It won't lead to no good." Sweat beaded on his upper lip and he rearranged his baseball cap. "Around here, you gotta act like those three monkeys. See nothin'. Hear nothin'. Say nothin'. Just forget about the crabs."

Right. She tucked her head down and kept extracting meat as Rob hovered behind her. She never had learned why Willy didn't want Harley in here—but if Harley had discovered her boss was messing around with illegal seafood . . . "Do you have any idea why Willy was pissed off at my brother?" she asked.

"Maybe he don't like arsonists," Rob growled. "I'll do the crabs."

She handed him the bowl and turned to face him. "I'm talking about before Harley died. Before the fire. You ever hear him and Willy arguing?"

Rob gave her a sharp glance. "Maybe."

"When?"

"A week, week and half ago."

"What were they talking about?" She crossed her arms over her chest.

"Told you, I mind my own business."

"Sure. The three monkeys."

"How 'bout less talk and more work." Rob reached in front of her and set a few peeled carrots on the counter. "I need these sliced up for salads." He carried a load of meals to the service counter and dinged a bell. "Order up!"

Crystal poked her head into the kitchen. "It's about time!"

Rob muttered something under his breath. Maya stared dully at the carrots and let her thoughts swirl. What if the crabs were part of a bigger problem? Rob had basically admitted he and Willy didn't care about illegal seafood. Maybe Harley had accused her boss. Maybe that's why they'd argued and—

A knife landed on the countertop with a crash. She jumped.

Rob pointed to the carrots. "I said, 'Get slicing.' And you'd better put something over your hair." He eyed her unruly curls. "Health department rules." Brushing past her, he slipped out the back door, a pack of cigarettes in hand.

Since when had the health department become a concern of Rob's? Still, Maya grabbed a paper hat from the cupboard and tucked her hair up before she re-washed her hands and started cutting. What had Allison meant about Harley acting strange? And him not talking about Sara? Allison was as bad as the Coast Defenders—abandoning Harley when times got rough.

After he returned from his smoke break, Rob seemed hyped up. His rants on various topics flowed out of his mouth without brakes, ranging from "those damn unreliable Mexicans" to "those assholes in Congress" to "liberals stealing my Second-Amendment rights." Thankfully, he didn't mention Harley or the arson, or she might've beaten him up.

After a few minutes, her head throbbed, and she was relieved every time a server interrupted his nonstop commentary.

As he rattled on, she made the occasional "Mmm hmm." It seemed all the encouragement he needed, and it gave her a chance to think. If Harley had discovered Willy's indifference to sustainable seafood, he'd have been angry. But angry enough to confront him? Maya sighed. Absolutely. Her brother wouldn't have let that go.

"And then," Rob said, "We went target shooting near Elk City. You know that spot?"

"Mmm hmm."

"I nailed five cans of Silver Bullet," He raised his arms like he was holding a rifle and demonstrated. "Pow. Pow. Pow. Pow. Pow. Five of 'em. In a row."

"Amazing," Maya said, and his monologue continued. She counted the minutes until her shift ended—and she could escape hell's kitchen.

She no longer felt guilty about the ice water. This was true punishment.

At five minutes to ten, Willy breezed into the room. "Quitting time," he said. Rob tossed a baseball jacket over his dirty apron and skulked out into the restaurant.

Finally. Maya pulled off her own apron and the paper hat. Folding them neatly, she left them on the counter.

Willy watched her closely. "Stovetop clean?"

"Sparkling." She displayed the black grease under her fingernails. "You got a minute?"

"Not really." He tilted his head toward the dining room. "There's a few stragglers left. Can't leave them unattended or they might steal the fine china." He guffawed at his lame joke and started toward the kitchen door.

"Wait." She'd have to get to the point. "Why did you tell me Harley wasn't welcome in here?"

Willy turned around slowly. "I don't know what you're talking about."

"On Sunday, you said—"

"That had nothing to do with the Clam Strip," he said firmly and walked out the kitchen door.

I didn't say it did. Maya stared after him for a moment before she followed him into the dining room. One couple lingered in a corner booth.

"When did Allison leave?" she asked.

"About an hour ago." Willy frowned. "She said she felt sick, so I sent her home."

And she couldn't take thirty seconds to stop by the kitchen and say goodbye?

Maya went behind the bar and retrieved her bag while Willy shooed out the last two customers. She rummaged for her cell phone and flipped it open. Almost out of juice, but enough for a call. Willy returned to the kitchen, probably heading for his office at the back.

Maya dialed. The phone rang and rang—six rings before voice mail kicked in. "Hi, you've reached Allison and Harley," the message said. "Give us a shout and we'll call you back." Her brother's low timbre. Maya's throat tightened. She hung up without leaving a message and checked the crab clock. 10:05. Allison was a night owl—she never went to sleep before midnight.

Her phone beeped at her: out of battery. Maya glanced at the kitchen door before she walked over to the restaurant phone and dialed. Still no answer at Allison's house. Where was she? Toledo was a long drive, but not that long. She should have arrived home forty minutes ago.

Willy came out of the kitchen. "You're still here? Go. I'll close up." He moved to the register.

"See you later." Her shoulders slumped as she walked out the door. The parking lot was empty—Willy must have left his SUV around back. He was always chiding the waitresses to leave the lot spaces for customers.

Obediently, she'd parked the Corolla down the block. It was pitch black outside and the streetlight was burned out. Mist had rolled in from the ocean, giving the night a ghostly feel.

A pickup truck was idling at the curb, the driver hidden in shadows. Maya glanced toward the vehicle several times. It didn't move. She picked up her pace. As she passed the truck cab, its headlights flicked on.

Heart racing, she hurried to her car.

Thirteen

As soon as Maya got into the Corolla, she locked the doors. That truck was still idling at the curb, a few vehicles behind her. Were they waiting for someone? She puffed out a breath. Ever since Harley's death, she'd been anxious and unsettled.

Her fingers drummed on the steering wheel. Maybe she should drive out to Toledo and check on Allison. What if she were seriously ill? Nobody was at her house to take care of her. Maya winced. They'd both depended on Harley.

She could stop by to see Allison and still get home by midnight. She turned the car south, heading toward the Bayfront by habit. Given the choice between the quicker route on Highway 20 and the quiet, winding road that traced the bay and Yaquina River, the peaceful drive always won.

On the Bayfront, the shops and restaurants were all closed. Light spilled from the windows of two bars, the only sign of nightlife. The street held a handful of parked cars. Maya averted her eyes as she passed the burned remains of Newport Nature Tours.

Allison—along with everyone else—seemed convinced Harley had set the fire by himself, without the Coast Defenders' urging. The police and fire departments had investigated, found the evidence he'd committed arson. Strong evidence. So why couldn't she accept what he'd done? Grieve for him and let go.

Maya stared out at the dark road. Because it didn't make sense. There was more to this fire than the Coast Defenders were admitting. Without a push from the group, Harley had no reason to destroy a building. They had to be involved.

The city lights soon gave way to country darkness. Misty fingers of fog dipped low, blurring her vision. She concentrated on driving. This winding road hadn't been the best choice, not when she was so drained she could barely keep her eyes open.

Harley was no casual arsonist. Impulse and passion had driven him to set that bulldozer on fire. But how could he be against Newport Nature Tours? Nobody could find fault with kayaking or guided hikes. Was it the whale watching? Was he worried tour groups would harass whales? Or maybe the owner also had a second business, like a timber company. Otherwise, it just wasn't logical.

So why was she the only person who seemed to think that?

The Bay Road wound through the darkness, the few houses and businesses set miles apart. She kept a firm grip on the steering wheel. She'd have to watch those twisting curves along the river, especially with the wet pavement.

Maya glanced in her rearview mirror and saw headlights.

Unanswered questions nagged at her. Where had that $2,000 in Harley's jacket come from? Could someone have paid him to burn down the building? *No.* She refused to believe he'd do that for money. Had he met up with another Coast Defender, who'd helped him set the fire? *Maybe.* That could explain why it'd burned so quickly, trapping him inside.

She should lean harder on the group. Thinking about her encounter with Nick, her pulse quickened. He'd said he wanted to talk about Harley.

A yellow "S" sign warned her of winding curves ahead. As she slowed down to take the first turn, the headlights behind her zoomed up close, filling her car with a bright glow.

Startled, she checked her rearview mirror. The headlights shone high—a pickup truck or SUV. The driver—surely a male—flashed his lights and pulled within a few feet of her back bumper. It was a crazy move in the darkness.

Her hands tightened on the steering wheel. The road ahead veered sharply, following the winding riverbank. There wasn't anywhere to pull over; this impatient driver would just have to wait his turn.

The mist got denser. Maya could barely see the lines on the pavement. She had to slow down—the shoulder was only a foot or two wide and the riverbank steep. Deep brown water waited on the other side.

Another round of curves. The tailgater stuck close.

Too close.

Before heading into the next bend, Maya tapped her brakes in warning. Just ahead were the worst curves—where the road twisted toward the river, then away, then angled back sharply.

The truck's horn blared and the driver turned on his high beams.

She squinted against the brightness, flicking the rearview mirror up so she could see the road. What was his problem? It wasn't safe to go any faster.

The horn blasted a second time and the truck's engine revved, a roar so loud it sounded like a freight train.

Her heart thumped wildly. Maya pressed on the accelerator, forcing the tired Corolla to its limits. With the truck bearing down, the car slid through another sharp turn. The river and slough met here, turning the road into a narrow ribbon of land with water on both sides. No room for error.

She had no choice. She braked.

The heavy vehicle rammed the back of her Corolla. Their bumpers collided. Metal screeched. One of her tires slid onto the narrow gravel shoulder and the car started to spin. Maya screamed in fear as she lost control.

The Corolla jackknifed across the oncoming lane, spun around, and sideswiped a tree trunk, coming to an abrupt stop. Her head whipped forward and bounced off the steering wheel.

Oh my God. Her heart beat in a rapid tattoo. What had just happened? She turned to look, and pain arced through her neck. She gasped. The truck was right there, behind her car. Its headlights bathed the Corolla's interior with an eerie glow.

At least the driver had stopped.

Maya started to get out of her car. As she did, the truck swerved around her and drove off at high speed. Red taillights subsided into the fog and disappeared. All she'd seen was a dark-colored vehicle with a mud-splattered license plate.

Maya jumped back into the Corolla and locked the doors. Her breath came out in panicked gasps. If she'd hit that tree head-on—or her car had spun toward the river—she could have been killed. And the driver had driven away as if nothing had happened.

Were they drunk? Was it road rage? An accident?

She needed to call the police.

Maya pulled out her cell and flipped it open. The phone was dead, not even a whisper of juice.

Okay, think. She could call from Allison's house. At least she wouldn't have to wait here, alone in the dark, for the police to arrive.

Maya felt moisture on her face and swiped at it with her hand. The skin turned pink with blood. Her body wouldn't stop quaking. A lump had formed on her forehead, sure to become a bruise. She rubbed the back of her neck. Ow. Not for the first time, she cursed the thieves who'd stolen her airbags a few years back.

Still breathing hard, Maya took stock. The side of her car was pressed against the trunk of a massive Douglas fir. The hood was dented. Underneath the bent metal, the engine clanked and rattled, sounding dangerously close to a breakdown.

Would the truck come back?

Heart pounding, she shoved the Corolla into reverse and backed away from the tree. Despite the worrisome engine noises, her car seemed drivable. She didn't need a tow. *Thank God.*

Cautiously, she pulled out onto the road. Just two or three miles to go before reaching Toledo . . . two or three miles of fog-laden driving, the desolation broken by only a handful of houses along the river. She gripped the steering wheel hard as her eyes searched the night. Had that truck been black? Blue? Dark green?

Was it waiting for her somewhere?

As her car climbed the big hill, the engine clattered and the dented hood gave off a puff of steam. She'd never been so relieved to see glowing lights in the distance. The sprawling mill complex, well lit at night, made the tiny town of Toledo look like a booming metropolis.

She took a sharp right turn onto Main Street. The quaint cafés and antique stores were all closed, every darkened storefront reinforcing her isolation.

When she turned up Allison's street, the Corolla strained to climb the steep hill. She parked outside the tiny beige house with its overgrown shrubs and leggy rhododendrons. The lights were off inside, but Allison's Subaru was in the driveway.

Maya stepped out of her car gingerly, her muscles already stiffening. The lump on her forehead was tender, and dried blood crusted around her nose. She could check out the damaged car later.

She rang the doorbell. No answer.

After a moment, she pounded on the door with her fist. "Allison, it's me." Now that the adrenaline had worn off, she felt suddenly exhausted. Her muscles quivered. She dropped her hand.

Where was Allison?

Maya examined the porch under the dim, flickering light. A dark, reddish-brown stain colored the floorboards near the door. She'd just leaned down to take a closer look when she heard a scraping sound inside the house.

The locks clicked and the door opened partway. Allison, her long hair tousled, wore pink pajamas under a silky bathrobe. Fluffy pink slippers adorned her feet. A gray cat twisted around her ankles, mewing and rubbing against the slippers. Hence the cat's silly name: FuzzyBear.

"*Maya?*" Allison cried, opening the door wider. "What happened?"

Fourteen

"A truck rear-ended my car." Maya's voice rasped as she pointed to the crumpled Corolla. "Probably a drunk driver. Or road rage. They thought I was going too slow . . . I don't know. Maybe they just hate California plates."

Allison stared at her. "Are you all right?"

"I'll survive," Maya said. "But I don't feel so hot. Neither does the car."

FuzzyBear headed for the porch stairs, ready to prowl. "No, Fuzzy! Stay here!" Allison grabbed the cat, motioned Maya inside, and locked the door behind them. "You said it was a truck? It didn't follow you here, did it?"

"No. He just bounced off my bumper and drove away."

"A hit-and-run?" Allison's face tensed as she inspected Maya's injuries.

"I haven't called the police yet. My phone was dead."

Allison turned the deadbolt and pushed a tall-backed chair in front of the door.

"What's with the security measures?" Maya pointed to the chair.

"I don't like living alone."

Those crank calls sure had her freaked out. Maya kicked off her shoes. Her Clam Strip uniform felt coated in sweat and kitchen grime.

"It's late." Allison smoothed her robe. "Why'd you drive all the way out here?"

Maya bit her lip, giving irritation the chance to wane. "Willy said you went home sick, and you left without saying goodbye. I didn't know if you were seriously ill. You didn't answer your phone."

"Sorry," Allison mumbled at the floor. "It's been a rough evening. Rough week."

"That it has." Maya walked into the living room and sank onto the couch. She propped a throw pillow behind her head and leaned back, wincing at the pain in her neck and shoulders. The room seemed starker than usual. Then she realized what was missing—Harley's recliner, the one he'd inherited from their dad. Cracked leather with a few historic cigar burns. "Where's the chair?"

Allison avoided her eyes. "It's in the basement. I'm doing some house clearing."

"Cleaning?"

"*Clearing.* Getting rid of negative energy. I want to bring the space back into harmony." As she talked, Allison paced back and forth across her living room rug.

"Oh." Apparently harmony meant banishing all signs of Harley, especially grungy old chairs that Allison had never liked. "Why are you so jittery?"

"I'm not." Allison stopped pacing, sat down on the couch, and crossed her legs. Her foot jiggled.

"Did you get another crank call?"

"I don't know." The foot jiggled again. "The ringer's off."

"That reminds me. I'd better call the police." Maya went to the hall to grab her wallet. They'd need her insurance information. She pulled out the card and stared at the expiration date. *Oh, no.* Her insurance renewal was sitting on her kitchen table, in a small stack of bills waiting for her bank account to stabilize. She could get in big trouble for driving without liability insurance.

She returned to the living room. "I'll call in the morning." *After I get that bill in the mail.*

It's probably for the best," Allison said. "The police won't be happy you left the scene."

"I wasn't going to wait there in the dark by myself, just praying another driver would come along and loan me a cell phone."

Allison nodded.

Maya reclined onto the couch. *Now there's a puzzle—Ms. Responsible doesn't want me to call the police. Why?* "It's not like I have much to tell them," she agreed. "I can't describe the driver or the truck. I can't even say what color it was."

Allison leaned in. "It was definitely a truck that hit you? Not an SUV?"

"A dark-colored pickup." Maya sat up again. Apparently she wasn't going to get any sympathy here. "Do you have an ibuprofen?" She wanted the old Allison back—the caring angel who'd dispensed peace and tranquility—not this callous twin.

"I'll look." Allison set the cat down.

Maya couldn't help shivering. She really could have died tonight.

While Allison was gone, Maya roamed the living room, trying to settle her nerves. Harley's chair was missing, but there was a new glass bowl holding agates and a basket with small paper rectangles. She picked one up. It had a cutesy drawing of an angel and one word: *Accep-*

tance. She picked up another. *Serenity.* Her hand shook as she dropped the angel cards back into the bowl. *If only it were that easy.*

When Allison returned, she handed over a glass of water, one pain pill, and a damp washcloth. There was a loud howl outside the house—a cat in heat?—and Allison nearly leaped out of her skin.

Maya swallowed the pill and chased it with water. Allison appeared wide-awake, her eyes bright and her pajamas unwrinkled. Though she was dressed for bed, she hadn't been sleeping. "Tell me what's going on. Please."

"I . . . can't." Allison's voice trembled.

"Yes, you can." Maya pushed aside the living room curtains. Her eyes slowly adjusted to the dark yard and street. Nothing moved outside. No headlights crept up the hill. No cigarette glowed near the rhododendrons. "There's nobody out there. You're safe. Now tell me."

Allison rearranged the curtains so no light would shine outside. "When I got home tonight, there was a dead—" She took a choked breath before continuing. "A dead squirrel on my porch. It was all bloody, its little paws splayed out, the stomach ripped open."

"What?" Maya stared at her, shocked. That explained the stained floorboards. "What'd you do with it?"

"It's in a shoebox on the back porch. I want to give it a proper burial." Allison closed her eyes. "It reminded me of a . . . pet I had when I was a kid. A rat. He got out of his cage and got mauled by the tabby next door. It was awful."

Maya glanced over to the couch, where Allison's gray cat was curled up. "I can't believe FuzzyBear massacred a squirrel. She looks so sweet."

"It wasn't her," Allison said heatedly. "She can't even catch a mouse. Besides, cats don't leave notes." She reached over to the table and handed Maya a folded-up paper. "This was tucked underneath."

The paper had brownish smudges on it—squirrel blood? Holding it with her fingertips, Maya unfolded the note and read the typed words:

SECRETS AND LIES.
EYE FOR AN EYE.
DON'T TELL ANYONE OR . . .

Or what? She let the note flutter to the floor, her heart racing. "The squirrel and note were here when you got home?"

Allison nodded.

Creepy. Was it from someone angry about the fire? Were they trying to scare Allison—or punish Harley? "What aren't you supposed to tell?" she asked.

"Beats me. It's the second note I've gotten."

"The second?" Maya's mouth fell open.

Allison picked up the note, rubbing her fingers on the creased white paper. "At least the other one didn't come with a mutilated squirrel."

"Don't touch that. Maybe the police can get prints off it."

"I'm not calling them." Allison set the note on the table. "This says 'Don't tell anyone.'"

"I'm sure that doesn't mean—"

"Ever since Harley died," Allison pressed her palms to her face, "I feel like someone's tracking my movements. It's freaking me out. The phone calls in the middle of the night. A weird feeling I'm being watched. They'll know if I go to the police. I can't take that chance."

"*They'll* know? Did you see someone?"

"Nothing I can say for sure. Except . . . twice when I was sitting on the front porch, this huge gold SUV—maybe an Escalade or a Yukon—cruised up my street. It slowed down when it passed the house. I thought I saw a man looking through the window. It's probably nothing, but . . ." Her face paled.

A gold Escalade? They weren't common, not in Toledo. "I don't like that 'eye for an eye' bit," Maya said. "It sounds like a threat."

Allison started shaking, and Maya mumbled soothing words as she rubbed her back. What she'd thought was distance and hostility had been fear. Allison was terrified. "They can't scare you anymore," Maya said. "I won't let them. Besides, you don't know any 'secrets and lies' about the fire." She hugged Allison tightly.

"It might not mean the fire," Allison whispered. "I think that note's talking about Sara." She twisted out of Maya's arms and fled from the living room.

Maya's jaw dropped. *What?*

She found Allison in the bedroom, sitting on the queen-sized bed. A purple batik bedspread covered the down comforter, and Allison was clenching handfuls of the thin cotton. Maya sat next to her. "I don't understand how you get 'Sara' from that."

Allison walked over to the dresser and yanked open the top drawer. "See for yourself." She pointed. The drawer still held Harley's socks and boxers and one tie, a gift from Allison. Her finger nudged a carved wooden box in the corner. "Open it."

Slowly, Maya lifted the lid. The box held a folded piece of paper—the Missing Woman flyer—along with a stack of photos and a few news articles printed off the web.

She picked up the photos first. Feeling Allison's intent gaze on her, she flipped through them. They started with snapshots of Allison and Harley horsing around at Yaquina Head Lighthouse. Harley was beaming in every shot.

Maya kept flipping. Broken windows? It must be the Oceanfront Bliss Hotel, and those spray-painted words, the restaurant. Harley had also snapped pictures of the *Lady Littoral*, its blackened hull floating at the dock. "Why do you think he was documenting the vandalism?"

"Keep going," Allison said.

Maya stopped on a photograph of a small, dilapidated cabin. The photo was dark and grainy, the background obscured. Why had he saved this? The next two images showed tree stumps and a white truck with half a business logo showing on the door panel. She squinted but couldn't read it. Harley had also taken blurry shots of something brown. Dirt?

"Keep going," Allison repeated.

Maya turned to the next picture and her hands shook. *Sara Blessing.* The missing girl stood next to a stream. She was wearing hiking clothes, carrying a backpack, and holding the collar of a panting Dalmatian.

Maya glanced up at Allison. The look on her face was fierce.

She returned to the photos. There was Sara, smiling at the photographer. In the next picture, Harley's arm rested on her shoulder. The image was slightly crooked, as if they'd propped the camera on a log. Ancient trees loomed tall in the background. When had Harley taken these? He obviously knew Sara well. Why hadn't he said so?

Maya unfolded the three news articles and scanned the headlines: "Young woman vanishes." "Police search coast for missing woman." And, "Police have no leads in missing woman case."

"He was following the investigation," she said.

Allison bit her lip. "He was obsessed with Sara. When she disappeared, he couldn't let it go. I found that 'shrine' after he died."

Maya returned everything to the wooden box. Worries shot through her, but she tried to downplay them. "Everyone was upset about her disappearance."

"He hid those photos from me. And he wasn't just upset, he was *obsessed*." Allison closed the drawer hard. "That's why he was acting so strange recently."

She sat down on the bed, her hands twisting the batik fabric. "In the last couple of weeks, whenever I tried to talk to him, he seemed distant. His mind was somewhere else. Now I know why." She let go of the bedspread and stood up. "He was thinking about *her*."

It couldn't be true. Maya closed her eyes, unable to watch the pain on Allison's face. If Harley were here to defend himself, he'd be down on one knee, proposing to her. Everything would be all right again. Instead . . .

"So he kept pictures of another girl," she said softly. "He kept pictures of you, too. He loved you."

Allison's gaze shifted to the box. "Then what was he doing with Sara in the woods?"

Good question.

Fifteen

Maya placed the non-Sara photos on the bed. The white truck, cabin, and tree stumps didn't seem related to the vandalism—but he'd chosen to print these shots. Why? She pointed. "Do any of these places look familiar?"

"The vandalism sites. But not the others."

Maya picked up the pictures. "Do you think it was a project for the group?"

"Or something with Sara," Allison said glumly.

"Sweetie, there's nothing to be jealous about. We'll get you that ring from his backpack and you'll see. Harley loved you. It was all about you."

"I guess." Allison wouldn't meet her eyes.

Maya set the photos down with a sigh. "I wish I knew what happened at the Bayfront that night."

"Didn't the police tell you? They found the same accelerant in Harley's bike bags as inside the building."

"Sure, they gave me the facts. But they haven't explained why he set the fire. How could Harley dislike a business that exposes people to nature? Apparently the cops don't give a rip about motive—it's enough that he was there."

"The fire department investigated, too. It was definitely arson."

"I know that," Maya said. "But maybe the police went into their investigation with their minds made up. They'd already decided Harley was their arsonist, that he'd acted alone. Didn't they say that at the restaurant? They couldn't have known at that point. All they knew is they had a body—and a suspicious fire. And when the detectives interviewed me, I *told* them Harley was heading to a meeting, but they weren't interested." She prowled the bedroom. "Think about it. If Harley *was* there with someone else . . . that other person could have helped set the fire."

"What are you talking about?" Allison hunched forward. "Nobody else was there."

"He said he had a meeting."

"Well, I doubt he'd tell you, 'I'm heading off to commit arson now, sis.'"

"He didn't have to lie, not to me."

"Sure he did. He admired you, wanted your approval. He wanted you to think he had his shit together, even if he didn't. I can see him feeding you a line."

Really? Harley looked up to me? "It wasn't a line," Maya said. "And it's quite possible another person *was* there. I have an idea." She paused. The pieces had been falling into place all day—finally they'd clicked. "Harley thought someone was trying to frame the group. Maybe they wanted to frame him, specifically. Suppose they offered him money to show up on the Bayfront that night, thinking they'd set a fire and he'd get blamed. The plan was to call the cops—and get Harley arrested. But something went horribly wrong. The fire grew too fast, and he died instead. And now they can't admit they were involved."

"And you're basing this theory on what?"

Maya took a deep breath. "Harley had a wad of cash. And—"

"Cash? How much?"

"Two thousand dollars."

"New fifties in a white envelope?" Allison brightened. "Where did you find it?"

"Inside his new rain jacket. But . . . how did you know?"

"It was my savings," Allison said. "He asked for a loan and I gave him two thousand dollars." She looked relieved. "I'm glad to know it's safe."

"Yeah. It's at my apartment. I'll get it to you." Too bad—that cash would have been nice. And there went her theory.

"You honestly believe he didn't set the fire?" Allison asked.

"I don't know what to believe. But this doesn't feel right. We should look into it." She motioned to the stack of photos. "These pictures might give us somewhere to start. Or maybe we could talk to Trent Lindberg, the guy who tried to rescue Harley. He might've seen Harley talking to someone on the Bayfront." A strange thought popped into her head. What if the fisherman had been the person Harley was meeting? Did it have something to do with illegal seafood?

"Forget it." Allison put a hand on her arm. "You can't bug a man who's in the hospital healing. Especially not when your brother's actions put him there."

"I won't 'bug' him. And of course I'd wait until he was feeling better. But—"

"No," Allison said firmly. "Digging into this will just open a can of worms."

"But what if I could show that Harley didn't set the fire by himself . . . or at least explain why he did it. Don't you want to know?"

The doorbell rang.

They stared at each other. It was nearly midnight, long past visiting hours.

"I don't think anyone delivering dead squirrels would ring the bell," Maya said.

Allison winced. "Should we answer it?"

"Not yet." Maya ran to the living room window and peeked outside. A big, beefy guy stood on the porch, his face partly covered by the hood of his sweatshirt.

The doorbell rang again. Insistent.

Maya pulled the chair back from the doorway, its legs scraping loudly on the hardwood, and looked through the peephole. The person was wearing dark clothes and a black hoodie. A beard and sideburns masked his face. "It's Tomas," she told Allison, then yelled through the door, "What do you want?"

"Is this Allison?"

"No. It's Maya." She peered through the lens again. Had he left the squirrel here?

"Maya, Harley's sister?" He muttered, "I should have known." He pulled off the hoodie, exposing his bearded face. "Open the door."

"Maybe we shouldn't," Allison said.

"Let's find out what he wants. It's the quickest way to get rid of him." Maya flung open the door and Tomas jerked backwards. She stared past him at the curb. A truck was now parked behind her Corolla, their bumpers kissing. A black truck. The group's truck—the one she'd seen at the protest and the Coast Defenders house.

Was it the truck that had hit her? She stared at him. But Tomas didn't seem to even notice her bruised face. He was too focused on Allison. And why would he hit her car, anyway?

"What are you doing here?" Allison asked.

"The lights were on, and I was in the neighborhood."

"That doesn't explain why you're here," Maya said.

"Oh, right. I came by to get Harley's files."

Allison cowered behind her. "I don't have them."

"They belong to the group," Tomas said.

"Says who?" Maya glared at him. "Is this the same group that ditched my brother after the fire?"

"I haven't found any files yet." Allison drifted away, leaving Maya standing in the doorway alone.

Tomas took a step closer, as if he planned to come inside. She blocked him. "She doesn't have the files. So beat it."

He didn't move. "I really need them. Has she searched the whole house?"

Maya shrugged. "Papers aren't like vampires. They don't disappear in the daylight. If you want them so desperately, come back at a decent hour. Call first."

She closed the door in his face, locked the deadbolt, and replaced the chair. She hovered by the window as he slouched down the walkway and climbed into his black truck. He made a U-turn and headed down the hill.

Maya watched him go. It was too dark to see if his front bumper was dented.

Moments later, Allison returned to the hall.

"Harley kept 'files' about his Coast Defenders work?" Maya asked. "I wonder where they are."

Allison smiled. "Oh, I found them. But you think I'd tell Tomas that?"

Sixteen

Allison led the way down steep, narrow stairs to the basement. "He had a room down here where he kept things."

"What kind of things?" Maya ducked down the last step, yelping as her feet hit the concrete floor. Even with tights on, it was frigid cold.

"Papers, mostly." Allison pulled on a string, and the bare bulb cast a faint light around the unfinished space. Despite the oil furnace, the basement was drafty and damp. Cold air leaked through the single-pane windows. FuzzyBear stuck close, brushing up against their legs.

Maya spotted Harley's missing recliner in one corner. *Oh, right, the spatial harmony.* Her throat closed up.

Allison walked toward a wall of shelves that held camping equipment. She grabbed a rolled-up sleeping bag and tossed it on the floor. "The room's behind here." She lifted a camping pad and a frame pack off the shelf and added them to the pile. "He built this barricade a few weeks ago."

"It's well hidden," Maya commented, reminded of the cash in his jacket. "How come Harley borrowed so much money from you?"

Allison stopped heaving equipment. "He was talking about signing up for classes at the community college. Marine science, I think."

"Really?" Then why had he brushed off her idea? Why had he sealed the money inside his jacket? "I didn't know you could pay tuition in cash."

Allison picked up a foam pad and tossed it on the floor. "He said he needed money for school."

"Okay." Maya lugged a backpack onto the pile of camping gear. Why had Harley really wanted that cash? Not for the ring—he already had that.

As the hill of gear grew into a mountain, a door emerged behind the metal shelf. They pushed the shelving unit to one side and Allison pulled on the knob. The door creaked open.

"This is it?" Maya said. It wasn't even a room; more of a dusty closet. The space held a mountain bike wheel with a flat tire, an assortment of rusty tools, and four cardboard boxes, overflowing with loose papers.

"Yep." Allison carried a box into the main basement and set it down.

Maya followed her until they'd removed all four boxes. "Is his laptop in there?"

They searched the small room thoroughly, but didn't find it. "He may have had it with him," Allison said.

Maya shook her head. "He didn't have it at the brewery. And he wouldn't have left it in his bike bag. No chance anyone's been down here?" As soon as the words came out, she wished she could take them back. With dead squirrels on the porch and late night visitors, she didn't need to plant any more fears.

"I sincerely hope not," Allison said. "He must have left it somewhere."

Maya settled cross-legged on the living room floor and surveyed Harley's so-called files. The four cardboard boxes sat in the middle of the rug, with papers flowing out of them and spilling onto the floor. "Before we dig in, we need a plan," she said. "I'll look for anything related to Newport Nature Tours. And you—"

"Could we do this tomorrow? I'm beat." Allison curled up in a corner of the couch and spread a crocheted afghan across her lap. "And I'm working early. I picked up Crystal's shift to make up for missing so many hours after . . . " her voice trailed off.

Maya nodded. The words were hard to say. So final. She rubbed her bleary eyes, not too thrilled about digging through these papers now either. But they might explain why Harley had gone to Newport Nature Tours—didn't Allison want to know?

The first handful she grabbed provided pages and pages of her brother's scrawled notes, so messy they might as well be in hieroglyphics. Tucked among them was a receipt for toilet paper, dated six months ago.

"Find anything?" Allison asked from her comfortable nest on the couch. She rearranged the afghan to cover her toes, closed her eyes, and breathed deeply.

"You're right, this can wait 'til morning." As Maya shoved papers back into the box, her gaze caught on a colorful brochure. She pulled it out. A marketing pamphlet for DreamCoast Condos? "Don't miss a day living out your dreams," it promised. "Luxury residences available soon. Enjoy city comforts in a country setting!"

"Check this out." She waved the brochure at Allison. "Think Harley secretly wanted a condo?"

Allison's eyes flicked open. "You know he hated DreamCoast. He thought Alan Kingston was pond scum."

Maya wondered if Allison knew about the bulldozer. "Ha. He'd probably consider that an insult to pond scum." She studied the developer's photo on the brochure. Alan Kingston had unforgettable blue eyes and wavy blond hair, trimmed short and dotted with gray. "It's hard to believe he's that evil. How come Harley disliked him so much?"

"The guy's a 'tree butcher, habitat destroyer and wildlife exterminator,'" Allison said. "Take your pick."

"Got it." Maya opened the brochure to find a glossy photo of a forested hillside, with the ocean in the distance, and a map of the proposed complex. The three condo buildings were named *Forest Glen*, *Oceania Crest* and *Windswept Pines*. The condos surrounded a community garden, rec center and playground. It sounded idyllic.

"I didn't realize Harley was still working on DreamCoast," she said.

"He wasn't. After Alan Kingston started chopping down trees, Harley gave up. I think it broke his heart."

Maya tossed the brochure into the box, then pulled it out again. There was a name scribbled on the back: Jonah. It was circled multiple times, as if Harley had been doodling. A local phone number was written below it. "Who's Jonah?" She showed Allison.

"I have no idea. We'd better get some sleep." Allison pulled the afghan up. FuzzyBear jumped onto her chest, curled into a small gray ball, and started purring.

"The police didn't mention having Harley's cell phone, did they?"

"No." Allison settled deeper into the couch. "If he had it with him, it probably didn't survive the fire."

Along with the ring? "Do you have his email password?"

"I used to." Allison hesitated. "After he died, I tried to log in at the library—to let his friends from out-of-town know. The password I had didn't work."

"I might be able to figure it out."

"Good luck." Allison sounded bleak. "After a year together, I thought I knew him. Guess I was wrong."

Maybe he had to change his password, Maya thought. "Why do you think he was so upset about Sara's disappearance?"

Allison sat bolt upright. "Do we have to go there again? Because I don't want to say negative things about him. You seemed to think he was perfect . . . I'd hate to destroy your illusions."

"Illusions? I know he had flaws. Plenty of them. And what I meant about Sara—"

Allison held up her hand. "The night she disappeared, he was out. All night."

Unease shot through her. "Out doing what?"

"I don't know. He left that afternoon and didn't come home until the next morning. When he finally strolled in, he asked if I'd say he'd been here with me."

Maya gulped. What was Allison suggesting? "He never told you where he went?"

"He said he couldn't tell me. And now he's *dead*. So I don't have a clue where he was, or what he was doing. If he was with Sara."

Her mouth went dry. "You don't think he was cheating—"

Allison closed her eyes. "Or he had a guilty conscience."

Disbelief struck. "Allison." Maya forced her to look up. "You've been living with Harley for the past four months. Do you seriously think he made Sara disappear?"

Allison didn't say anything.

Believing he'd set the Newport Nature Tours fire was one thing, but suggesting he'd kidnapped Sara or worse . . .

At last, Allison spoke. "I guess I don't picture him hurting anyone."

Not exactly a vote of confidence. Maya bit back her anger. "I'd better let you get some sleep," she said. "Mind if I take these boxes home?"

Allison gazed at the papers cluttering her living room. "Please do."

"Have any other Coast Defenders asked about them? Besides Tomas?"

"No. This guy Nick called to ask if Harley had left anything for him, but I had no idea what he was talking about."

"Nick?" Her interest piqued. He'd offered to get together, talk about Harley. She should follow up on that invitation.

"He joined the group last fall. Harley introduced us," Allison said. Her lips pinched tight.

Maya picked up a cardboard box and carried it into the front hall. She pushed the chair away from the door. Allison was still lying on the couch, looking bereft. Looking frightened. Maybe she should cut her some slack. It hadn't even been a week. They were still navigating their new friendship, the one without Harley as glue. "Do you want me to stay?" she asked.

Tears glistened in Allison's eyes. "Will you?"

Maya nudged the chair against the door and set the box on it. "Of course."

Allison pulled sheets out of a basket in the closet and tossed them onto the living room couch. She added a pillow and the crocheted afghan, then went into the bedroom to get an old t-shirt of Harley's and a pair of her own yoga pants. She handed them to Maya, hugged her goodnight, and left the room.

Maya pulled off her Clam Strip uniform and slipped on the borrowed clothes. She lay down. The clock on the bookcase ticked loudly. One a.m. One-thirty. Two a.m.

Her whole body ached. As she struggled to find a comfortable spot on the lumpy couch, she thought about Harley. As soon as she'd convinced herself he hadn't set the fire—not by himself—new worries emerged. Did he really have something going with Sara, as Allison suspected?

What had he been doing the night Sara disappeared . . . and why had he asked Allison to lie about it?

Seventeen

Maya awoke to the intruding beep of an alarm clock. Morning already? *Beep. Beep. Beep.* With her eyes scrunched closed, she flung aside the sheets and sat up. Ouch. Overnight, the lump on her forehead had been joined by a sore neck, achy shoulder muscles and a deep-rooted headache. Images from last night flooded back—the harrowing drive along the river and smashing into that fir tree. Allison's fear. Tomas and his black truck. The photos of Sara.

Maya pushed that last image away. She refused to think about Sara. *Beep. Beep. Beep.* She padded into the bedroom, following the beeps to the alarm clock, and turned it off. The bedcovers were tangled, but the sleepyhead she'd expected was gone. The shower was running.

Maya walked into the kitchen and pulled out Allison's coffeemaker. Before long, the scent of brewing coffee filled the room. She stretched her arms and winced as pain rolled from her neck down her back.

"Oh. You're up." Allison walked into the kitchen, toweling off her wet hair. Her white sailor top looked crisp over the navy-blue miniskirt and tights, but dark shadows had taken up residence under her eyes.

"How'd you sleep?" Maya poured a mug full and handed it over.

"As well as anybody can in five hours." Allison set the mug down without drinking and returned to the bathroom.

Maya rummaged for breakfast, eventually settling for stale Cheerios with milk. When Allison returned, she filled her own bowl with dry cereal and started munching.

"Still feeling sick?" Maya watched her, worried.

"I'm fine." Allison grimaced at the kitchen clock. "Great. It's already time to leave for work." She set down the bowl, walked into the front hall, and put on her coat.

Maya accompanied her. "I'll follow you into town. I just need to get dressed."

"I can't wait, but stay as long as you want." Allison picked up the file box from the chair so she could open the door, and the cardboard bottom fell open. There was a loud thump as an object hit the floor, followed by an avalanche of loose papers.

"What was that?" Maya pushed aside the papers and they both stared. It was a bone. Big, whitish-yellow, and lined with cracks. An old bone.

Allison recoiled. "Is that human?"

"I doubt it." Maya touched the surface tentatively, then picked it up. Surely human bones weren't this long. This heavy. "Not unless you're talking a giant."

Allison ran out of the hall. The bathroom door closed, but it didn't cover the sound of retching. Maya set down the bone and knocked on the door. "Are you okay?"

Allison came out, dabbing her face with a wet tissue. "Maybe now you understand why I'm concerned about Harley. Apparently, he's been hiding bones in our basement."

"It's probably deer or elk. I bet he found it in the woods." She tried to reassure herself—it was perfectly normal behavior to keep old bones around, right?

Allison opened the front door. When she saw the dried bloodstain on the porch, her hands flew to her mouth. She rushed outside. Seconds later, she leaned over the railing and vomited into the bushes.

Maya rushed over. "Please don't work if you're sick. I'll cover for you."

Allison straightened up and wiped a hand across her mouth. Her eyes were bloodshot and face ashen. "I have to work. I need the money. Besides, it's nothing contagious. I'll feel better soon—a few more weeks."

Maya stared at her. "Are you saying . . . ?"

"Ten weeks yesterday."

Maya squealed and gave Allison a bear hug, then immediately backed off. "I didn't hurt you, did I?" She stared at Allison's belly. Still flat. "Wow! I can't believe I'm going to be an aunt. That's so exciting! The best news ever."

Allison rested a hand on the porch railing. "Forgive me if I'm not so thrilled."

"What do you mean? It's Harley's baby and . . . Oh." She got it: the single mom thing, money worries, no dad in the picture. "I'll help out, and so will my mom. I'll even babysit."

Allison blanched. "Please don't tell your mom about this. Or anyone else."

"I understand. It's early."

"Harley and I didn't plan this," Allison said. "And I'm not . . . sure what I'm going to do. I can't think straight right now."

"But you'll keep the baby."

"I have a doctor's appointment in two weeks," Allison mumbled in the direction of the bushes. "An ultrasound. I'll decide then."

Maya bit her lip. *This baby was all they had left of Harley.* "Are you feeling okay to work? I don't mind taking your shift. Not at all."

"I'd better get used it. And I'm late. You know Willy hates that. Just lock up when you leave." She flew down the walkway and jumped into her Subaru.

Maya leaned against the doorframe, watching her drive off. A baby! Her niece or nephew was probably the size of a split pea, but she already felt tender toward it. Would it be a girl or a boy? She smiled. A new family member. For the first time since Harley had died, she felt the promise of the future.

She closed the front door, her gaze dropping to the large bone on the rug. What the heck was her brother doing with this?

Maya re-taped the cardboard box, tossed the papers inside, and set the bone on top. After carrying the other three boxes into the hall, she went into Allison's bedroom.

She sat on the queen bed holding the carved wooden box, with its mementos of Sara and photos of vandalism. *I'm sure there's an innocent explanation for all this. He told me he didn't know what happened to her.* Doubts crept in. *He hadn't wanted to talk about it, either. Just like he hadn't said anything about the arson.*

No. Maya chastised herself. Everyone else had abandoned her brother. She couldn't give up on him. Too many things felt wrong here—the vandalism that nobody would claim, Sara's disappearance, the inexplicable arson. It was possible Harley had kept this stuff about Sara and the vandalism because he was interested in investigating it, not because he was involved.

She would prove to Allison that Harley had been a good, worthy partner. Her future niece or nephew shouldn't grow up under a cloud of rumors. Another clench of doubt. What would her digging reveal?

Maya debated for a moment before leaving a note saying she was taking the wooden box.

After a long, steamy shower to soothe her sore muscles, she reluctantly put on her dirty Clam Strip uniform. The bruise on her forehead was getting darker and more swollen. More painful.

She stopped in the kitchen and picked up the phone, wanting to call the police about the accident. But the fear in Allison's voice—and her own fresh doubts about Harley—stopped her. Maybe it was better to keep the cops out of it for now. It wasn't like they could find the fleeing driver—or make her car whole again.

She carried the boxes of papers and carved wooden box out to the porch. When she returned for the bone, she stopped to inspect the bloodstain. Did the squirrel and cryptic note mean somebody was angry about what Harley had done? What secrets didn't they want revealed? She reached under the flowerpot for the spare key, locked Allison's door, and returned the key to its hiding spot.

In the morning light, her battered Corolla looked even worse than she'd remembered. In addition to the dented hood, the back bumper and one side of the car were damaged. When the engine started, she gave heartfelt thanks.

Maya drove home along the river, listening anxiously to the engine's rattling. It was a beautiful morning. Sunshine reflected off the rain-soaked road and yellow daffodils covered the hillsides, along with the occasional vivid pink of flowering currants. Last night's drive seemed a distant, surreal dream. But when she passed the tall Douglas fir, she saw the gouge she'd left in its bark. And when a pickup truck pulled behind her, coming up fast, her breath quickened.

It roared past.

At her apartment, she heaved the boxes upstairs and went back for the bone. Her downstairs neighbor, Emma, came rushing out her own apartment door, her crazy-curly hair pulled into a knot on top of her head. "Hey, is that a *bone*?"

"Yep." Maya tucked it under one arm.

"I'm heading to Seattle this afternoon." Emma eyed her speculatively. "And my gerbil sitter just fell through. Would you mind?"

"All right." Maya laughed. "But I'm probably not your best choice. I can barely keep a Chia Pet alive."

"Oh, gerbils are easy. Just give 'em food, water and something to chew on." Emma ran back inside her apartment and came out carrying a ten-gallon aquarium. "I owe you."

Maya took the aquarium, setting the bone on top of the mesh lid. "Do I pet them?"

"Better not," Emma said. "They bite."

Maya carried the unwieldy glass cage upstairs and set it on her kitchen table. The two gerbils, which had been snuggling inside their house, were now running around frantically. Emma handed her bags of bedding and food. "Have fun! I'll be back in six days."

Maya stared at the tiny, energetic animals. So much responsibility. She had to keep these things alive and happy for almost a week? She didn't know anything about gerbils—they didn't even let you have them in California.

At least they were cute. Allison would probably adore them. *Allison, who had dead squirrels appearing on her porch.*

Maya's stomach dropped. She'd tried to picture the driver of that truck as a guy with too many beers in him, impatient at her slow speed. But maybe it hadn't been an accident. What if it was somehow tied to the squirrel on Allison's porch—or to that gold Escalade she'd seen driving by her house? Was someone watching Maya, too?

She walked into her bedroom and stashed Harley's bone in her underwear drawer next to his cash—make that Allison's cash. When she returned to the hall, she saw the red light blinking on her answering machine.

Maya smiled. Her elderly landlord had insisted on including a landline with the apartment, for "a young lady's safety." He'd handed her an old white phone with a curly cord and an equally ancient answering machine.

She plugged in her cell phone to charge and pressed the button on the answering machine. One new message, from last night.

"Hi, Maya, this is Nick." *Really? Nick had called?* She listened with interest. "It's late notice, but do you want to grab a cup of coffee tomorrow? I usually head over to Octopus Coffee on Sunday mornings, around nine." He paused. "Hope you can join me."

Her smile spread. She was dog-tired and achy, her neck muscles so sore she could barely turn her head—but this sounded promising. Her list of questions for the Coast Defenders was growing, and having coffee with Nick would be a lovely way to ask them.

She pulled on jeans, a red scoop-neck sweater and big silver hoop earrings. Not that this was a date or anything. The past seven months—aka "the drought"—had left her too eager. She'd better get her life together before she went looking for a guy.

Maya ran down the stairs, holding the paid insurance bill in one hand. As she slipped the envelope into the mailbox, she wondered why Nick wanted to meet. How had he gotten her phone number, anyway?

Eighteen

Maya glanced around Octopus Coffee as she waited for her latte. The walls displayed framed collages made from pastel-tinted pasta and buttons. The artwork closely resembled craft projects she'd done in kindergarten, and she was shocked by the $125 price tags.

Most of the customers sitting at the tiny café tables were engrossed in books or typing away. But in the coffee shop's back corner was a communal table, its surface a gigantic slab of driftwood. Five Coast Defenders were sitting there, huddled around a single laptop.

The group was here? Obviously she'd misunderstood Nick's invitation.

Maya sipped her latte as she walked toward them. Tomas, Goth Girl, the bald man with the soul patch, and the two blondes were here, but the friendly, white-haired woman was missing. And, mysteriously, so was Nick.

She stopped behind Goth Girl, who was seriously working the vampire look with her pale skin, all-black clothes and spiky black hair. Maya peered over her shoulder at the laptop screen. "What's Fossil Fools Day?"

The girl quickly closed the computer. Five pairs of eyes narrowed on Maya's paper coffee cup. Oh, yeah. She was supposed to ask for a ceramic mug.

"Did you bring me Harley's files?" Tomas' massive shoulders strained against the fabric of his t-shirt. The back of the shirt read, *Hike Naked. It Adds Color to Your Cheeks.*

Hike naked? She couldn't help smiling. "No, I didn't."

"Then what are you doing here?"

"Yeah, what do you want?" Goth Girl echoed.

"Is Nick around?" Maya asked. "He said he'd be down here."

The girl's eyes flashed. "When did you talk to him?" She glared at Maya.

"Chill out, Kelsey." Tomas looked up, his facial expression masked by the heavy beard. "Nick isn't around, and if you didn't bring me the files, why did you come?"

"I, uh . . . have some questions about the fire."

"Was I not clear yesterday? The Defenders weren't involved."

"But—"

"When exactly did you talk to Nick?" Goth Girl interjected.

"He called me at home last night," Maya said, now thoroughly confused. "He invited me to join him here. I thought—"

The girl jumped up. "He'd never!" She scampered toward the front door, pulling a phone out of her pocket and texting furiously as she left the building.

Maya watched her go. Where was the animosity coming from? Nick was just being friendly. She said to Tomas, "You've lost two members of your group in two weeks. You must have questions about the fire, too." When he didn't respond, she added, "Don't you care about what happened to Harley?"

"Of course we care."

"Then why won't you talk with me?"

"Fine." He angled his head at the blonde girls and the soul-patch man. They immediately picked up the laptop and moved to another table.

Maya sat down in a vacated chair. She could now see that the front of Tomas' *Hike Naked* t-shirt read "Drift Creek Wilderness." It was a popular hiking spot in the Siuslaw National Forest, and a place Harley had promised to take her once the weather improved. For a moment, she lost direction. She'd never see that wilderness with him now—or hear his usual trail advice: "Take only pictures. Leave only footprints. Kill only time." Tears stung her eyelids.

"Do you know why my brother would want to burn down the Newport Nature Tours building?" she managed to ask.

"He wasn't working for us. I told you that."

"You said the group didn't target the business. But why do you think Harley would?"

"I don't have a clue." Tomas' gaze flicked over her before it moved to a pasta-button collage on the wall. He tilted his head, studying the crude artwork as if it were a Picasso.

"No one in the group ever talked about Newport Nature Tours? Or setting a fire on the Bayfront?"

He crossed bulging arms over his chest. "Nope."

Apparently she wouldn't get answers about the arson here. But maybe . . . "What kind of projects did Harley and Sara work on together? Anything recent?"

Tomas' eyebrows shot up and his mouth opened, but no words emerged.

Kelsey returned to the table, sending the hard edge of a chair into Maya's hip. "I texted Nick," she announced. "He's on his way."

The interruption had given Tomas time to compose himself. "I can't talk about group business with you," he said firmly. "You're not a member."

"You can't even tell me what my own brother was working on?"

"Sorry."

"Info is power." Kelsey gave her a snarky grin. "You never know who you can trust." She and Tomas shared a long look.

Oh, these two were impossible. Maya stood up. "I'm sure I can find what I need in Harley's files." Tomas whipped his head around. "Oh, yeah, I've got 'em," she said.

He jumped to his feet. Before she could retreat, he grabbed her wrist with a thick, hairy hand. "Let *go*," she cried.

His grip tightened. "You'd better give those files back."

"Why should I?" She tried to break loose, but he kept her tethered.

"You have no right to them." His voice rose sharply. "They belong to us."

By now, several people were giving them curious glances, but nobody stepped in to help. Maya debated—if she tried to jerk away, she might re-injure her neck. Could she talk him down? "You said my brother wasn't working for the Coast Defenders anymore. You said he was freelancing. So I guess those files don't belong to the group."

He leaned forward, putting his face inches from hers. "They're ours."

"What are you going to do? Leave another squirrel on Allison's porch?"

His face twisted. "What the hell are you talking about?"

"Dude!" A male voice carried through the coffee shop. "Let her go."

As Nick barreled toward them, Tomas loosened his grip, but not enough for her to escape. "What are you doing?" Nick said. "Get away from her."

Slowly, deliberately, Tomas' hand dropped to his side. He sauntered back to the table and sat down, displaying the *Hike Naked* slogan across his broad back.

Maya stepped closer to her rescuer. Despite Nick's ripped jeans and ratty t-shirt, he looked proud—as if he'd battled the forces of evil to save her. In fact, he looked like a pirate with his long, dark hair in a ponytail. The thought made her grin. Captain Jack to the rescue.

After a moment, he smiled back. "I didn't think you'd come today."

Kelsey walked over and curled a possessive hand around his arm. "Hey there."

"Hey." Nick didn't shrug her off. He gave Maya an apologetic look.

What was up with that? She drained her latte and tossed the cup into the trash. "Thanks for protecting me from the coffee shop bully. Not that I needed help."

"I'm sure you didn't. You had things under control."

"I did." Irritated, she wound through the maze of tables and went outside. She opened the door to her car.

"Wait up, Maya." Nick appeared next to her—without Kelsey. "I'm sorry I wasn't here. I overslept. I meant something different when I called, but the whole group decided to come down. They were worried the house could be bugged."

"*Bugged?*"

"I know. It's crazy paranoid." He saw her Corolla's dented hood. "Uh, what happened to your car?"

"It ran into a tree last night."

He gaped at her. "Really? Are you okay?"

"Sore muscles and ugly bruises." She lifted her overgrown bangs to show off her mottled forehead.

"Ouch. Did you get that bump checked out?"

"It's not as bad as it looks." She glanced up the street and her eyes narrowed on a dark blue, mud-splattered pickup. Her heart started to gallop. Was it the truck from the Bay Road?

"What's wrong?" Nick asked.

"Last night there was—" She stopped. Talk about crazy paranoid. Half of Newport drove pickups. It could have been anyone driving that road. "Is that your blue truck?" She pointed.

"No. I rode over." He waved a hand at the battered Schwinn in a bike rack by the coffee shop.

"So that wasn't your truck yesterday, at the house?"

He shook his head. "You mean old Black Beauty? That belongs to Tomas."

Who had showed up in Toledo last night. "He doesn't seem too fond of Harley," she said.

Nick hesitated. "They butted heads a lot. After the group got blamed for the hotel vandalism, there was one meeting . . . well, they almost brawled."

A brawl? That didn't sound like Harley. "Over what?"

He shrugged. "Those two were oil and water. Tomas likes to plan everything, evaluate every possibility before moving ahead. Harley would get hot about something and jump in. It drove Tomas crazy." He laughed awkwardly. "It drove all of us a little crazy."

She gulped. Harley was impulsive, but he'd liked the group members—and she'd thought they had liked him. She put up a hand to rub her sore neck.

Nick stared intently at her wrist, where faint bruises were starting to form. "Did Tomas hurt you?"

"It's fine. I bruise easily."

"What an asshole." His hands clenched at his sides.

Uh oh. After her experience with Frank, she should probably go for a nice, mild guy. Not one who made her heart race. Not someone like Nick.

"Have you seen Harley's laptop around the Coast Defenders' house?" she asked. "Allison's looking for it."

He shook his head. "But I can ask around. How's she holding up? This must be tough on both of you."

Maya leaned back against the car. *Tough* was right. But she didn't want to think about that. Because if she got started . . . "Allison's doing okay," she said, swallowing the lump. "We're hanging in there."

"I shouldn't have brought that up. I'm sorry." Nick's dark hair had slipped from the ponytail, and he tucked the loose strands behind his ears. "You look like you could use some time off from your troubles. I'm going crabbing later. Want to come?"

Tempting. She'd gone twice since arriving in Newport—both times with Harley—and she'd loved pulling up the crab pot to see what was crawling around. But that was the problem—she'd gone with Harley.

"So?" Nick nudged her. "You up for it?"

"I wouldn't be good company." *Too many memories.*

His face fell. "Are you free for dinner tonight? I'd really like to talk to you."

"I'm . . . " Her mind whirred with indecision. Why had he invited her to the coffee shop today? "I don't think Kelsey would like that much."

"Kelsey?" He looked confused. "Oh, you mean what happened inside?" She nodded. "She kinda . . . has a thing for me," Nick said. "I didn't want to hurt her feelings." His gaze met hers and she felt a jolt of electricity pass between them. "Asking you to coffee . . . well, you seemed sad when I saw you yesterday. I thought it might cheer you up."

"You know what?" Maya said. "Dinner tonight sounds great." They made plans to meet. She climbed into her car and Nick waved goodbye.

As she drove away, her gaze caught on a storefront nearby. The sign read Walter's Big Bucks Taxidermy. Maybe she could give Allison one less thing to worry about.

Nineteen

Thirty minutes later, she returned with Harley's mysterious bone. She'd wrapped it in a t-shirt, but the bone was so long, the knobby ends stuck out on both sides.

The taxidermy shop had the Missing Woman flyer posted on its front door. Maya averted her eyes. First she'd had to worry about Sara vanishing . . . now she had to worry whether Harley had known something about it. The thought made her cringe. Allison was wrong about this. Completely wrong.

Maya pushed the door open and a small metal bell clanged over her head. The shop smelled of stale cigar smoke, musty old animals, and fresh paint. A high-pitched whine that sounded like a dentist's drill came from the back room.

There were plenty of dead animals to enjoy while she waited. One wall displayed elk and deer heads, interspersed with bleached-white antlers. The back wall was dedicated to birds, including green-headed mallards, their wings spread for flight. A third wall displayed fish of all sizes. Faded photographs dotted the spaces between the mounts, showing triumphant hunters standing next to their trophies.

Near the cash register, a furry black bear stood at full height, his front claws scraping the air. She set Harley's wrapped-up bone on the dusty counter, next to a hawk in its own glass case. Three flies lay belly-up in the dust and a few more stuck to the flypaper dangling from the ceiling. *Whoa.* This place was trapped in a time warp. The frame around the dollar bill on the wall explained why: the taxidermist had had started his business in 1968. Eons ago.

"Hello? Is anyone here?" she called.

The shrill whining sound stopped. "I'll be right with you. I'm just finishing up." The whine started again.

She checked out the glassed-in case below the counter. More dead animals, including a gray rabbit posed mid-hop next to a tuft of grass, a tiny chipmunk holding an acorn, and a stiff-looking squirrel. She immediately thought of Allison's bloodstained porch. What kind of sick person mutilated squirrels?

Still waiting, Maya started to read the yellowed newspaper clipping taped onto the register. The headline read "Local Taxidermist Uses

Beetles to Help His Business," and the photo showed a stooped, elderly man with tufts of white hair. He was holding an animal skull.

"I've worked on everything from a lady's pet Chihuahua to prize-winning bucks," said Walter Dearborn, who has been tanning hides and running a thriving taxidermist business out of his Lincoln County home since the 1960s. It's a family business, one he inherited from his father . . .

"Sorry for the wait. What can I help you with?"

She blinked. The guy who'd walked out of the shop's back room wasn't old at all, maybe early thirties. He wore an army-green t-shirt with a rip on one shoulder and a black stocking cap. His muscular arms were inked with colorful tattoos, so dense she could barely see his skin.

"You're not Walter," she said, gesturing to the article.

"What? I don't look like him?" He laughed. "I'm Dan. Walter's my uncle. I came to Newport to help out, keep his business going while he has some medical treatment."

"I'm Maya." Too bad he was just visiting. He probably wouldn't know about local wildlife—or their bones.

"What can I help you with?" He leaned his elbows on the counter.

She unwrapped the t-shirt bundle. "Can you tell me what kind of bone this is?"

Dan picked it up and his face sharpened with interest. "Where'd you find this?"

"I got it from a friend."

He studied the knobby ends and ran a hand down the surface. "It's very unusual." He stepped back, holding the bone hostage. "Where did your friend find it?"

"I'm not sure." Her heart skipped a beat. Hopefully "unusual" didn't mean human. "Do you know what kind it is?"

"It's too big for deer or elk." He set it on the counter. "Must be moose."

She stared at the bone. "Are you serious? I don't think moose live in Oregon."

"Doubting me, huh?" He raised his eyebrows. "There *are* moose here. Not on the coast, but there's a small herd in northeastern Oregon, near the Wallowa mountains. Still . . . "

"What?"

"Well, you're right—there aren't moose in Newport. And I think only the Nez Perce and Umatilla tribes have the right to hunt the herd."

"Really?" Maya didn't know anything about tribal treaties, but she was relieved it was an animal bone. Allison could stop being so suspicious of Harley.

Dan studied her. "So the real question is, how did this bone get to Newport?"

"I have no idea," she murmured.

"Well if you find out, let me know. You've got me intrigued." His smile transformed his face, and she realized he was a good-looking guy under all that ink.

"Thanks for the info." She took the bone and re-wrapped it in the t-shirt, then motioned to the animals on the walls. "Did your uncle stuff all those?"

"Oh, dear God, if you come back when he's here—please don't call them stuffed." He smiled again. "They're mounted."

"What's the difference?"

"A few decades of craftsmanship. They used to stuff rags or straw inside the animal's head or body. Now we use forms. If you want to come in back, I can show you what I mean."

She hesitated. He seemed eager to chat, no surprise if he was new to town. It could take a while to make friends here. She knew that firsthand.

"All right." Curious, she followed him into the back room. The space was stark, with a long, narrow counter covering one wall and several tall shelving units, filled with plastic jugs and bottles. The countertop held an assortment of tools and more bottles, along with a blue towel. On it was a dead duck, the body sliced open. Next to the duck was an animal hide, the underside showing fatty pink flesh.

Dan picked up a piece of yellowed foam, the size of a small turkey breast. "This is the form. After I flesh the duck and dry it out, I'll put this inside to hold the shape."

She stepped closer. "I never thought about how taxidermy works. I just pictured some guy in overalls sawing off the deer's head and . . . sorry."

Dan jabbed a pretend knife at his chest. "I'm wounded. Taxidermists are *artists*, you know." He pointed to a mounted duck-in-flight at the end of the counter, with an array of colored paints and slender paintbrushes next to it. "My Uncle Walter is a sculptor, a woodworker, a tailor, and a painter—a true Renaissance man."

"Did he teach you?"

"It's the family business. My grandpa started it, and then my uncle took over. Even as a kid, I was fascinated. Whenever I came to Newport, I spent hours watching them work in their studio. I even studied wildlife biology in college."

"So that's how you knew about the moose."

He laughed. "Glad my education's good for something."

"Is your uncle coming back soon?"

His face clouded. "I hope so. He's in Tijuana getting cancer treatment. Oxygen therapy or ozone . . . something like that." He shrugged. "Nobody knows if it'll work. I'm staying in Newport until he returns, living the high life in his oceanfront condo."

"Lucky you."

"Actually, I've barely seen the ocean. It's been too misty. He's basking in sunny *Me-hi-co*, while I'm chatting up his retired neighbors and staring at the fog. And then I have this wonderful old shop to care for." He swept an arm around the workroom.

"You seem to be enjoying it just fine."

He grinned. "Guess my secret's out." He pointed to the hide on the counter and picked up a tool with a metal disk on one end. "If you have time, I can show you how to flesh a deer cape."

"Uh, that's okay. I've got to get going. Thanks for the info about the bone."

"Glad I could help." He walked her to the front door and held it open. As she passed through the doorway, he said, "It's funny. My uncle said somebody else asked about a bone."

"Really? Who?"

"I don't know. I just remember him mentioning it."

She got into her car and set the bone on the seat, wondering why Harley had saved it. When she pulled out of her parking spot, she glanced into her side mirror and saw a black truck. Someone following her?

Just in case, she ran a yellow light and left the truck behind.

. . . .

When she unlocked her apartment door, the phone was ringing. She rushed inside, leaving the door open, and set Harley's bone on the table. "Hello?"

"Maya?"

"Oh, hi, Mom. What's up?"

105

"I'm working on a new poem—a tribute to Harley—and I felt the need to *connect* with family. Do you have a few minutes?"

"Sure." She was dying for a nap, but it'd be quicker to go along. "I've got time."

She must have let a sigh escape because her mother huffed, "Well. If you're too *busy*, we can do this later."

"No, it's fine." It was daytime, plenty of light outside, but the gaping front door made her feel exposed. She tried to walk over to shut it, but was trapped by the phone's curly cord. She stretched it out as far as it would go. On the porch, tucked most of the way under her mat, was a slip of white paper. A note. Her mouth went dry.

Mom said, "Have you thought about moving down here? You could stay with me for free, save on your rent."

"Uh huh," Maya murmured, her focus on the white paper. She unfolded it and read the typed words in disbelief. STOP ASKING QUESTIONS.

Stop asking questions? This *had* to be from the Coast Defenders—or maybe not. She scanned the small porch. No dead animals. Maya stared down at the backyard, mostly dirt and patchy grass. Somebody had walked up her stairs to leave this note outside her door. They knew where she lived. "Mom, I have to go," she said.

Her mom kept talking. Maya pulled her front door shut and a shiver passed through her. The note felt damp. Had it arrived last night, at the same time as the squirrel at Allison's? No, she'd made several trips up and down today—she'd have found this.

"So you'll come?" her mom asked.

"Come where?" Maya set the note next to Harley's bone. She carried the phone over to the door and checked the locks.

"To Sacramento. To live with me."

"*What?*" Maya nearly dropped the phone. "I'm not moving back to California. My life is here." Her heart twinged. Obviously, her mom was lonely.

"There's nothing keeping you in Newport. You're working that dead-end job and living in that run-down apartment, and Harley is, well . . . no longer with us. Why *can't* you leave?"

Maya chewed her lip as her mother continued, "I ran into Frank the other day with that woman, the yoga teacher. They were pushing a stroller with the cutest newborn inside. I couldn't resist a peek."

So Frank and Miranda had their kid. Maya exhaled a heavy breath. How could she convince Allison to keep Harley's baby?

Her mom prattled on. "It's a boy. He had the sweetest face— and Frank's eyes. Of course I started thinking about grandkids. I'm counting on you." She trilled out a laugh.

"Sorry, Mom. My biological clock isn't even turned on. Besides— never mind." She'd better change the subject before she spilled the news. "Guess what? I'm going out to dinner tonight. With a guy." *No need to mention he's a Coast Defender.*

"Wonderful!" her mom gushed.

"Maybe I'll drop into the conversation how much my mother craves grandchildren. I'm sure that'll be the highlight of his evening."

"That's not what I meant," her mom said firmly. "You sound funny today. Is something wrong?"

Five minutes into our conversation and she finally asks about me. "I didn't get much sleep last night. I got in a car accident and spent the night on Allison's couch. All this strange stuff is happening. She's really stressed out—and so am I."

"A car accident? Well, you do sound·worked up. Be sure to take your B vitamins. If I have time, I'll send you a fabulous smoothie recipe. It's got bee pollen and green tea and two protein powders. All organic. It's great for stress."

"Sounds tasty." Maya couldn't help laughing at her mother's ability to ignore anything unpleasant. "I really have to get going. Love you."

"Love you, too, sweetie. Enjoy your date." She paused. "I hate to say this, but you were looking peaked when I saw you. I hope you'll make an effort tonight."

"Uh huh." *Goodbye.* Maya hung up. She picked up the phone again to call Allison about the moose bone, but remembered she was working at the Clam Strip.

Maya headed to the kitchen. She refilled the gerbils' food bowl, but they seemed lethargic, uninterested in the fresh food. *Maybe I should get Allison to take them. She'd be better at this.* But no, Emma had asked her. Maya stared into the aquarium, willing the tiny creatures to open their eyes. She tapped lightly on the glass and one gerbil jumped to attention. Good. Still alive.

She headed into the bedroom and set the note on her nightstand. Idly she tossed two darts toward the bulletin board and read her latest Positive Thought for the Day: "I take satisfaction from a job well done!" and—a little joke—"I *love* being a waitress!"

These Post-its were useless. She'd never be happy at the Clam Strip.

Harley had been right. She needed to get her life going again. Maya closed her eyes, fiercely reminded of everything she'd lost. She and Harley had just been getting to know each other. And now they never would.

Before she pulled down the window blinds, she scanned the barren backyard. For once, she was glad to live on the second floor, especially with Emma out of town.

She picked up the note and read it again.

STOP ASKING QUESTIONS.

Twenty

Maya awoke groggy and disoriented. She was trapped in her comforter, rolled up like a burrito with her arms pinned at her sides. The room was dark, the blinds closed. She must have slept for hours.

Her gaze dropped to the note on her nightstand. If anything, people telling her not to ask questions made her more determined. But who'd left this note? Tomas, who didn't want her digging into Coast Defenders' business? Another group member—say, the hostile Kelsey?

Or maybe it was someone upset over the arson. Could it be from the family of the injured rescuer, Trent Lindberg? *No.* They shouldn't care if she asked questions. Unless there was a reason he'd been on the Bayfront that night . . . a reason they didn't want people to know.

Could he have been the person meeting Harley? Had the police investigated that possibility? Rawling hadn't said a word.

Maya jumped out of bed and checked the clock on her nightstand. Nick had offered to borrow a friend's car and pick her up around seven p.m. It wasn't much time for the work she had to do.

She needed to figure out the connection between Harley and Newport Nature Tours. If she couldn't find the answers in his files . . . would Nick tell her?

In the living room, she picked up one file box and dumped the contents into a heap. Loose papers flew everywhere, but no more bones appeared. Thankfully.

She dug through the pile, glancing at each page before sorting it. After fifteen minutes, her "worth a closer look" stack held only two items—a brief article about a timber protest and the DreamCoast brochure where Harley had scribbled the name Jonah. Why did Tomas even want these files? They were worthless.

There wasn't anything here about Newport Nature Tours. She'd have to do some research at the library, find out the owner's name. See if there was anything more to "nature tours" than the business suggested. She turned back to the heap of papers and sighed deeply. So far, the contents of Box One were a packrat's hoard.

There had to be a better way to get information, such as going through Harley's laptop or phone. But his phone had probably been destroyed in the fire and Allison didn't know where his laptop was. Nick hadn't seen it either.

Maya picked up the timber protest article and skimmed a few paragraphs. Nothing useful. The photo showed a group of protesters huddled in front of a canvas shelter in the forest. They were holding banners painted with anti-logging slogans. Her eyes narrowed. That was Sara Blessing in the middle, the girl in a knit cap. Harley was standing next to her. Again.

Apparently she wasn't going to be able to forget about Sara.

Maya opened the carved wooden box and read the three articles Harley had saved about her disappearance. According to one article, a witness claimed to have seen her riding a mountain bike south of town, along Highway 101, but her bike hadn't been found. The cops had questioned her boyfriend, a Redd Harrison. *Redd?* Didn't that have something to do with salmon eggs? The crazy names people came up with around here. Her amusement died quickly. They probably thought the same thing about Harley—who'd been named after a motorcycle.

She set the articles down. This was a waste of time. Sara's disappearance didn't have anything to do with the Newport Nature Tours fire. But the vandalism might.

She pulled the rest of Harley's photos from the wooden box. The stumps, white truck, and dilapidated cabin meant nothing to her. She glanced through the rest, then grabbed a piece of paper and scribbled down a timeline:

DreamCoast (bulldozer fire)—October
Oceanfront Bliss Hotel (broken windows)—January
Fish Fry Fridays (spray paint)—February
Lady Littoral (boat explosion)—March
Rocky's Marine Service (damaged sailboat)—March
Newport Nature Tours (arson)—March

After the bulldozer, there'd been a lag. But March had been a busy month, the vandalism escalating. If someone was trying to frame the group, why? What did they hope to achieve?

Maya glanced outside. The sun was dropping fast, and she was no closer to answers. Her last hope was Nick.

After changing into a lacy bra and matching thong—even though nobody would see them—she added dressy black pants and a green sweater, and attempted to tame her frizzy curls. This wasn't a date, but she could still look nice. It was the first time she'd gone out with a guy since Frank.

Maya studied her appearance in the mirror, critical of every flaw, both the ones she could see—like her too-curly hair and her too-plump hips—and the flaws she knew were inside. The reasons Frank had left her. She just wasn't . . . enough for him. Pretty enough. Good enough. Grr.

Maya reached into her wallet and got out twenty-five dollars. She slid the bills into her pants pocket. Nick wasn't taking her out. They'd split the tab.

She fed the gerbils before starting to tidy the living room. As she reached down to scoop papers off the couch, Harley's DreamCoast brochure slid to the floor. She stared at the name Jonah.

Grabbing her cell phone, she dialed his number. It was Sunday, so she wasn't surprised it went to voice mail. "You've reached Jonah Bishop. Leave a message and I'll get back to you." She hung up. Now she had a name: Jonah Bishop.

A knock sounded on her apartment door.

Nick was early.

"Just a sec!" She surveyed the mess of boxes and papers. Quickly, she pushed the wooden box with the photographs and articles under the couch. There wasn't time to clean up the rest—she'd meet him at the door.

Outside, rain dripped. Drops of wet beaded on Nick's fleece jacket, and his long hair was damp. He was wearing the same ripped jeans and grungy t-shirt he'd had on at the coffee shop. Despite having told herself this wasn't a date, she felt a pang of disappointment.

"Hey, Maya." His gaze moved behind her to the tiny living room. His eyebrows shot up. "Are you moving?"

"No, just sorting through old papers." She didn't mention they were Harley's, and wondered if Tomas had.

Twenty-One

As the car coasted down the hill from the Yaquina Bay Bridge, her heart sank. And when Nick pulled into the parking lot—their final destination—she sucked in air.

"Something wrong?" he said.

"I should have asked where we were going." She stared at the sign on the warehouse: *Rogue Nation World Headquarters*. "I came here to the pub with Harley the night he died."

"Seriously?" Nick stared at her. "We can go somewhere else."

"It's okay. I'll be all right." She tried to believe it.

He turned off the engine. "Are you sure? I figured we shouldn't go to the Bayfront. But I didn't realize . . . You saw him that night?"

"Just a few hours before he died." Her voice shook.

A dark-colored pickup passed through the brewery lot. She spun around, straining to see it in the dusky light. The truck stopped near the bridge posts, too far away to identify the driver. Maya chewed her lip. What, she was going to flinch every time she saw a dark truck?

Nick craned his head. "What are you looking at?"

"Nothing important." If she told him the truth, he'd think she was crazy.

"Okay." He opened his car door. "If you're sure you're fine going here . . . "

She nodded, unable to speak.

They passed through the red silo and walked into the warehouse, neither of them commenting on the Missing Woman flyer tacked to the door. As they hiked upstairs, Maya fought a lump in her throat, and she was immensely relieved when Nick suggested the restaurant instead of the pub.

The room was packed with families, but the hostess somehow found them a window table. She beamed at Nick as she handed him a large, multi-page menu. Almost as an afterthought, she offered Maya a menu, then turned back to Nick with another blinding smile. "Let me know if I can get you anything. Anything at all."

After the hostess left, Maya said, "You certainly get personal service here. Maybe you should ask for a free beer."

"Oh, she's just being nice."

Maya smiled to herself. Nick seemed oblivious about his looks, a refreshing change from Frank.

Their metal-topped table overlooked the marina, reminding her of the midnight boat ride with Harley. The cops hadn't returned to her apartment with any more questions. Were they letting the Rocky's incident go? She stared at the dark docks and even darker water. The marina's tiny, sparkling lights looked like the Milky Way in a black sky. That night, Harley had . . .

Nick tapped her arm. "Sure you're okay being here?" His eyes searched hers. "You seem preoccupied."

"Sorry, I was thinking about Harley." Oh no, she wasn't going to cry, was she? She flipped through the menu, focusing hard on the words. Beer-battered halibut or the black bean-quinoa salad? A dark beer? A light beer?

Nick was still watching her closely. In the end, she ordered pasta with chipotle chicken and a Chocolate Stout beer. He seconded her order, saying, "Hey, great taste."

Their pints arrived quickly and Maya took several sips, trying to get rid of the lump in her throat—the one that seemed to grow every time she thought about Harley.

Nick didn't seem bothered by the restaurant full of loud kids. Another contrast with Frank. He'd be raging at the parents, informing them if they couldn't control their "spawn," they didn't deserve to have them. *Utter irony.* Now he was a dad himself.

Worry flickered through her. How would Allison survive as a single parent? She'd need plenty of help—and Maya was prepared to offer it. But . . .

A red crayon hurtled into the air from the next table and bounced off Nick's forehead. He looked irritated, but he picked up the crayon and handed it back to a little girl with braids. "Your plane must have missed the airport," he said. "It landed on me instead." The girl giggled and continued coloring on her kids' menu.

Nick sat back down.

He was *nothing* like Frank. Maya relaxed her guard. In fact, Nick was so nice, she almost felt bad using him as her Coast Defenders source. But she couldn't pass up this opportunity. She leaned in, resting her arms on the table. "Do you know much about the work Harley was doing for the group? I'm trying to figure out why he went to Newport Nature Tours that night."

"I thought you saw him. He didn't tell you?"

"No, he never even mentioned the place." She sipped her beer. *If only he had. Maybe she could have talked him out of it.*

"I don't know any more than you do." Nick set down his glass. "That fire must have been quite the shock."

"It sure was. I still can't understand why he'd burn down a building. Especially a business that's all about introducing people to nature."

Nick shifted in his chair. "It is an odd choice."

"And Harley wouldn't destroy it without a good reason. For the life of me, I can't imagine what that reason would be. And if the Coast Defenders don't know either . . . " She looked up expectantly.

Nick was silent for a moment. "Tomas mentioned you'd been asking a lot of questions about the fire, and I understand why. It was a huge blow to all of us. But digging into what happened, trying to figure out why Harley did it, well . . . it can't bring him back."

"I know." Nick was right—but that sounded like a prepared speech. Was he the Coast Defender designated to get her to lay off?

Silence fell over the table. Maybe she *was* being delusional, trying to prove Harley's innocence. But she owed it to him to try. She owed it to Allison. To their baby. And she really had nothing to lose. If she couldn't prove Harley had set the fire with someone else's help, she would at least learn *why* he'd done it. She couldn't forgive him until she knew that.

Their waiter hustled past, apologizing over his shoulder for the kitchen's delay.

"I don't understand," Nick said. "Are you thinking Harley didn't set the fire? Because the cops had all that evidence."

Maya flicked him a glance. "It's probably time for me to accept what happened." Nick's loyalty was to the group, not to her brother. She wasn't going to say any more.

After an awkward moment, he said, "So where did you grow up? Harley said you weren't from around here."

"No. Sacramento." She told him a few stories from her childhood, realizing belatedly she'd gone on and on about herself. Nick was a great listener.

By the time their meals arrived, she was ravenous. She dug into her spicy pasta with gusto. "Where did *you* grow up?"

"I'm a California kid, too. My parents had an avocado farm near Fallbrook. Talk about a dull place to grow up. More trees than neighbors." He brightened. "I've only been in Newport a few months, but I love it here. There's always something happening."

"You think you'll stay?"

"Who knows? It's hard to picture living in one place forever."

"I know what you mean." How old was Nick? Twenty-three? Twenty-four? Or was he closer in age to Goth Girl? Maya sobered up quickly. "So . . . what's the deal with you and Kelsey?"

"We're just friends." He took a bite of pasta.

Friends with benefits?

"We hung out for a few weeks last fall," he admitted. "But it's over. She's having trouble accepting that. She's got a . . . jealous side." Under the table, his knee pressed gently against her leg. "Please don't worry about her. I want to get know *you*."

His touch awakened long-dormant sensations, and a pleasant buzz spread through her body. Maybe this wasn't a date—but it sure felt like one. "What do you want to know?"

"I'm curious why you and Harley grew up in different states." His gaze was warm, and a bit intense.

"When our mom and dad split up, they were . . . estranged." She paused. Calling her parents "estranged" was like saying terrorists were "cranky." The last year of their marriage had been an all-out brawl.

She realized Nick was waiting for her to continue. "*Anyway.* Harley moved up to Newport with my dad, and I stayed with my mom. We didn't see each other for years."

He pushed his half-finished meal to one side. "So you moved here to find Harley?"

"Oh, I knew where he was. We'd just lost touch. And then when my marriage ended . . . " Maya stopped. He didn't press for details and she was relieved. A promising chemistry was bubbling here, and she didn't want to hammer him with drama.

She leaned back and pain shot through her neck. A moan escaped. "What's wrong?" he asked.

"A bad case of whiplash. From my car hitting that tree last night."

"You just ran off the road?"

"Oh, no. A truck rammed my back bumper. I lost control and sideswiped a Doug fir." He gaped at her. "At the time, I thought it was a drunk driver. But I keep seeing dark trucks everywhere I go. And when I saw one drive through the parking lot here, tonight—call me paranoid, but it freaked me out."

"You're talking about the truck by the bridge?"

"You saw it, too?"

"That was Tomas." His face darkened. "He must have followed us here." Nick leaned forward. "And followed you last night. I can't believe he shoved your car off the road. I bet he's trying to frighten you. He's upset that you're asking so many questions about the fire, worried you'll try to pin it on the group."

That note on her porch. If the Coast Defenders hadn't been involved in the arson, her questions shouldn't bother Tomas. "He doesn't scare me. It takes a lot to frighten me off," she said, more bluster than truth.

"He's such a bully. When he grabbed you in the coffee shop . . . " Nick traced his finger along the dark smudges on her wrist.

Maya tried to smile. Forget Tomas. All she could think about was Nick's hand touching her skin. How good it felt.

Outside, the parking lot had emptied. She checked: the black truck was gone. Her body sagged with relief. She and Nick exchanged a glance. He'd noticed, too.

"We could go out on the dock," he suggested. "It's a nice night."

"Sure." As they strolled onto the fishing pier, traffic whirred on the bridge above them, and waves slapped gently against the shore. The foghorn blew once, a mournful sound. He took her hand and squeezed it. His palm felt warm and comforting, and she let herself relax. Finally.

They stopped at the end of the pier. Across the water, lights glittered in the windows of the Coast Guard station and back along the Bayfront.

"Maya?"

She turned to him. Nick put an arm on either side of her and leaned her back against the railing. His lips touched hers tentatively. When she responded, his kiss deepened.

Something hard inside her thawed. Nobody had wanted her for so long. Not Frank. Not anyone. She clung to him.

He pulled back first, breathing hard.

Twenty-Two

On the tiny porch outside her apartment, he kissed her again. "I hate to leave."

"Then don't." Maya unlocked the door, glancing down to see if there was another note. But the porch was bare.

She kicked the door open and pulled Nick inside. Desire swept through her. She led him into the living room—her very messy living room. "Excuse the disaster area," she said, motioning to the papers. "I wasn't expecting you to come in."

"Neither was I." He leaned down to kiss her.

After a few lovely moments, she pulled back. "There's really nothing going on with Kelsey?"

He whispered softly in her ear, "You think I'd be here with you if there was?"

Relief shot through her. The worry had been nagging at her all day. She was no boyfriend poacher.

She moved to the couch, shoving the loose papers to the floor. He sat down next to her, so close their thighs were touching. Her skin prickled with anticipation. "So here we are," he said.

Here they were. Maya melted into the couch as his lips moved back to hers. His hands moved with purpose over her sweater, awakening sensations she'd kept buried for months. She could hardly think. "Oh my," she murmured.

"What?" His hand paused mid-stroke, just below her breast. "Should I stop?"

"Don't you dare."

His fingers moved again, closing in on her nipples. Soft lips traveled to her neck, nuzzling and nibbling. Maya gave a breathy sigh.

"Happy?" His hand slid lower.

"Ummm-hmmm." She could hardly believe it—her seven-month drought ending with such pleasure. She'd never slept with a guy on the first date. What the hell. It was time to get over Frank.

Nick's hands tugged at her sweater. When he saw her lacy black bra, he smiled and reached in back to undo it. She arched upwards, moaning as his fingertips traveled along bare skin.

Something vibrated against her hip.

"Whoa, talk about bad timing." Nick sat up, wrestled a cell phone out of his jeans pocket, and checked the screen. "I'm really sorry. I have to answer this. I'll be right back." He walked into her kitchen.

Maya lay there, stunned. He was talking urgently into his phone. In the kitchen, the gerbil wheel squeaked while the critters ran laps, and the sound blurred his words. With effort, she pushed herself to sit up. What kind of a guy answered a phone call in the middle of foreplay?

A jackass. Heat burned through her as she reattached her bra, searched the floor for her sweater, and yanked it on.

She could no longer hear him talking on the phone. He was back.

His face was tight, mouth set in a frown. "I'm sorry. I had to answer that—it was family. An emergency."

A family emergency? She searched his face for the truth. He didn't look too upset.

"I'm really sorry," he repeated. "Where were we?"

"I think you were on your way to the door." The statement came out harsher than she'd intended, and she clapped a hand over her mouth.

It took him a second. "Oh. You want me to leave?"

She nodded, not trusting her voice. Tears pricked her eyelids.

"I should've told you I was expecting a call. Like I said, it was family." He waited a beat. "But I'll go, if that's what you want."

She nodded again. *This is what happens when you rush things.*

"C'mon, Maya, don't be mad. We'll be at the coffee shop again tomorrow morning if—"

"*We'll* be at the coffee shop? You and the Coast Defenders? Or you and your cell phone?" She pointed toward her front door. "I think you'd better leave."

He stared at her for a second before he turned to go.

She shut the apartment door behind him and marched into the living room, picking up Harley's papers and shoving them into boxes. She slapped the cardboard lids closed and sank onto the couch, closing her eyes. Nick hadn't wasted any time walking out. Was it really a family emergency . . . or had he wanted to go?

By two a.m., her t-shirt and shorts were damp with sweat. Her throat was dry and her neck ached. Three hours of lying in bed, attempting to get comfortable, had provided about thirty minutes of restless sleep. She could feel every pore on her skin, every breath that pulsed through her lungs. Her nipples stood at attention. Dammit. Her body had awoken from months of celibate hibernation only to discover snow drifts outside.

She kicked the covers down with her feet. Maybe that phone call was actually a blessing—because she would have slept with Nick. No question. And if he was the kind of guy who'd answer his cell in the middle of sex, he wasn't worth it.

Her betraying body didn't listen.

Confusion swept through her. She'd told him to leave, sure, but he'd given up so easily. *He* had invited her out, paid for dinner. He'd kissed her on the pier, hinted that he wanted to be invited in. And then, right in the middle of action, he'd jumped up to take a phone call.

What had she been thinking? She didn't even know Nick's last name. And he was a Coast Defender. *And* her brother had just died. She'd seriously gone crazy, ignoring all that. Stupid hormones.

A noise came from the kitchen. The gerbils were running around their cage, playing on the wheel, and gnawing on wood. So loud. Did they ever sleep?

After another half hour of churning mind and tossing limbs, she finally dozed off.

Scratch. Thunk. Maya awoke from her erotic dream reluctantly. Nick's hand had been about to—her heart thumped. What was that sound? She reassured herself. It was probably Emma downstairs, bumping around her apartment after a hard night partying.

Another thud. This one sounded closer . . . and Emma had left town. These noises weren't coming from downstairs. They were coming from her own apartment.

Was it the gerbils? She climbed out of bed and tiptoed to the bedroom door. Slowly, she opened it, waiting in the doorway. Her pulse beat rapidly.

No lights.

No sound but her own heavy breathing.

Then, a loud thump.

Definitely not a tiny rodent. She grabbed a piece of driftwood off her dresser—a beachcombing find—and crept into the dark living room. Harley's boxes cluttered the floor. One box had tipped over on its side, spilling papers onto the rug. Maya set down the driftwood and reached for the papers.

Something moved behind her.

The intruder wore a mask, dark fabric covering his head.

She screamed for help as gloved hands reached around her and held her in a vise grip. She struggled to break free, her fingers scrabbling for the driftwood on the rug. The intruder got there first.

Her head exploded with pain and the world went black.

Maya rolled open one eye. Dust bunnies under a futon couch? *Her* couch. She was lying on her stomach in the middle of her own living room. She meant to get up, but she was so tired . . .

Eventually, music awoke her, a faint sound coming from the bedroom. She stirred. Her face was pressed against a piece of paper, wet with drool. Her fingers found worn carpet as The Stones sang *Emotional Rescue*. Oh—her clock radio.

When her mind finally kicked into gear, she panicked. Was the intruder still here?

Maya rolled onto her hands and knees, then stood up, wobbling. A spasm of pain shot down the back of her head. She touched the spot. Very tender. She remembered reaching for the driftwood and the pain that followed. That masked person—a man?—must have whacked her over the head.

She listened, heart racing. All was quiet. Nobody was in her apartment—or so it seemed. She flicked on the living room light and checked every corner of the room.

The chunk of driftwood was gone.

Her eyes widened. So were most of Harley's files. Last night, there'd been four cardboard boxes in her living room. Only one box was left. It was tipped onto its side and papers spewed across the carpet. Her gaze bounced to the iPod and cell phone still sitting on her bookshelf. Someone had wanted Harley's files. The Coast Defenders did. She'd announced to Tomas she had them, waved a cape in front of the bull, and he'd apparently helped himself. It had to be him—the intruder had been strong, trapping her in a tight grip.

Tiptoeing down the hallway to her bedroom, she eased the door open. Nobody there. Nobody was hiding in the closet. She ran over to the dresser. *Thank God.* The cash and moose bone were still at the back of the drawer, undisturbed.

Maya cocked her head, listening. Was that water running? She hurried to the bathroom. The shower curtain was closed. Behind it, a steady drip-drip-drip.

Holding her breath, she flung the curtain to one side.

The tub was empty.

Baffled, she returned to the hall and examined her apartment door. Locked. Nobody had climbed in through her second-story windows. They had to have come through this door. But if the intruder had picked her lock, how had he re-locked it when leaving?

Maya gasped. Harley had kept a spare key to her apartment on his key ring. Could he have left his keys at the Defenders' house? Had Tomas found them?

She needed to report this—and tell the cops about the threatening note he'd left on her porch and the car "accident," likely caused by his truck.

But first, she'd pay a trip to the Coast Defenders. Before getting the police involved, she should try to get the files back on her own. Maybe someone in the group would trade her silence for information.

She returned to the living room. Tomas had left one box behind—after hitting her, he must have panicked and fled. She righted the box and started stuffing papers back into it. Half buried near the bottom, something shiny and silver caught her eye.

It was an oval-shaped pendant. A locket missing its chain.

Maya held it in her palm, noticing the delicate leaf pattern engraved into the silver. With her thumbnail, she eased the locket open. Inside were two miniature pictures, women with dated hairstyles. She didn't recognize either of them.

Maya closed the locket. Was it Allison's?

She got dressed for work, her outrage building with every yank of the uniform. It was frightening to think about intruders in her apartment. But if Tomas expected her to cower in fear, he thought wrong.

She still had Harley's photos and this remaining box of files. And . . . she reached under the couch for the carved wooden box.

Still there.

Twenty-Three

A black Ford truck sat outside Octopus Coffee, with a red *Remember BP* sticker decorating its back end. She inspected the front bumper—not a dent on it. Maya cupped her hands over the window glass and peered inside. There weren't any stolen files in the cab, but "Say NO to Straightening Hwy 20" signs littered the front seat.

Tomas was here.

Last night, Nick had blamed him for driving her off the road. And although this truck's bumper didn't show any damage, Tomas *had* followed them last night to the brewery. He'd probably used Harley's keys to get into her apartment, waiting for nightfall to invade her home. She shuddered. Better do something about that lock.

A gusty wind whipped down the street, whistling through the thin fabric of her miniskirt and sailor blouse. The weather this morning certainly matched her mood: cantankerous and unpredictable. Dark clouds vied with snippets of blue sky, and raindrops splattered on one side of the street while sun shone on the other.

Maya marched into the coffee shop and scanned the back of the room.

Today, only three people were sitting at the big driftwood table—Tomas, Kelsey, and an older, clean-cut guy she hadn't seen before. As usual, Kelsey had a laptop in front of her. Maya glanced from side to side. Nick wasn't here.

She headed toward their table. "I guess you took what you wanted," she said to Tomas. "Was it worth breaking in?"

He swiveled, showing off his t-shirt: *You Can't Scare the Green Out of Me.* "You again? What do you want now?"

"I'd like Harley's files back."

He stroked his beard with one hand. "His files?"

"The ones you stole last night."

Kelsey's gaze flickered over Maya's work uniform. "That's a lovely sailor outfit," she sneered. "And by the way, Harley's files belong to us. He was working for the cause."

"Were you there? Did you steal them?" Maya stepped closer to the table. "Did you copy his keys?"

"Tell me what's going on," Tomas said.

Her eyes narrowed. Did he think she was stupid? "Someone broke into my apartment last night and stole several boxes of papers. Harley's papers. As a parting gift, they conked me over the head."

He paled. "What time was this? How many boxes did they steal? What was in the papers?"

"I think my head will be fine," Maya said. "Thanks for asking."

"I don't understand. How did this person get into your apartment?"

"This person?" She stared at him in disbelief. "*You* asked about his files yesterday, I refused to hand them over, and now they're gone."

"I didn't do it." Tomas turned back to the table. "John? Kelsey? You know anything about this?"

The clean-cut guy shook his head. Kelsey smirked at Maya before mouthing, "No."

"Seems you're barking up the wrong tree," Tomas said.

I don't think so. Kelsey seemed awfully smug. Could she have broken in, brought another Coast Defender with her? Maybe even this guy John. Or was Tomas bluffing?

"This wasn't a random crime," Maya said. "The thief knew what he wanted. The only thing stolen was Harley's papers."

Tomas' brow furrowed. "Did he take all the files?"

She nodded, not wanting to give them an excuse to break in again, then stared around the table, meeting each person's gaze. "I *will* find out which one of you did this." She turned and marched out of the coffee shop, ignoring a wolf-whistle from one of the tables.

Outside, she leaned her head against the car. It'd be tough—impossible?—to figure out the links between the arson and Harley and between Sara and Harley without the Coast Defenders' cooperation.

"Hey," a familiar voice said.

Maya looked up. Nick broke into a sunny smile, as if nothing were wrong. As if he hadn't walked out on her last night, leaving her hanging.

"How's it going, Maya?" He gave her cleavage an appreciative glance. She crossed her arms over the sailor blouse. "Fine. Couldn't be better."

His smile faltered. "I don't know what to say. I apologized for taking that call. My mother was waiting for some news from her doctor. It was bad news." He blew out a breath. "She has breast cancer."

Maya felt her stomach drop. Oh my God. How awful. Why hadn't he explained that last night? He'd barely mentioned his mother. "I'm so sorry," she said.

"Her surgery is scheduled for next week." His mouth turned down. "It's been really, really tough."

"I feel terrible. I was upset last night and . . . I'm sorry." She rubbed the back of her head, wincing as her fingers encountered the tender lump. "I hope she'll be okay."

"I hope she'll be okay, too." He studied her. "Still hurting from that car accident?"

"Not exactly." She wasn't sure how much to tell him. "After you left last night, somebody broke into my apartment."

"Are you kidding?" He blew out a shocked breath. "How'd you get hurt?"

"They clubbed me with a piece of driftwood."

His brown eyes widened. "I should have stayed. I would have protected you."

"Not unless you wanted to go *mano-a-mano* with your friends. It was probably a Coast Defender."

His mouth dropped. "One of *us?*"

"Yes." It had to be. Nobody else would want those files. She climbed into the Corolla. "I'm really, really sorry about your mom."

"Thanks." He leaned over, looking bereft. "Can I call you later?"

Maya nodded and closed the car door. Harley's death had turned her into such a small-minded, suspicious person. She'd acted like a bitch last night, making Nick leave just because he got a phone call from his mom. His mom who had breast cancer.

But I didn't know that, she reminded herself. And maybe she was justified in being cranky. She'd had two nights of bad sleep. Her neck still hurt from the accident. Her car looked like it had participated in a demolition derby. She had a painful bruise on her forehead and a matching lump in the back—a walking wreck.

She turned the key in the ignition. Worst of all, in forty-five minutes she had to be at the Clam Strip, wearing a smile on her face.

She'd better get to that police station fast.

As Maya pulled onto the street, she saw Dan walk out of the taxidermy shop and head down the block. Was he going to Octopus Coffee? Too bad she only had time for one stop.

Twenty-Four

Maya's footsteps slowed as she walked up the steps to City Hall. Hopefully this visit wouldn't be as traumatic as her last one—the grilling after Harley's death. The long white building with its clapboard siding and huge paned windows looked like an old-fashioned schoolhouse. Which it actually had been . . . before becoming government offices and the police station.

She paused at the door. How much should she report? Allison wouldn't want her to mention the squirrel, but the police should know about the car crash, the note on her own porch, and the break-in. Maybe she could nudge them in the Coast Defenders' direction. Nudge them toward Tomas.

Inside, Maya admired the abundant artwork, including several paintings and a glass case holding a shimmery kimono, before she headed down the hall to the police station. "I need to report a break-in," she told the receptionist through the window. "But I'm on my way to work. Will it take long?"

"No. I'll see who I can find." The woman checked her computer.

Maya paced the carpeted hall, bracing herself for a macho police officer—or the stern Detective Rawling who'd come to her apartment. But the person who arrived was short and slender, with a freckled face and long reddish hair in a braid down her back.

"I'm Detective Gloria Ames," the woman said. "How can I help you?"

"I need to file a report. Somebody broke into my apartment last night and stole some things."

"Things? Can you be more specific?" Detective Ames' gaze traveled to the sailor blouse and skimpy skirt. Her eyebrows rose.

Nobody takes me seriously in this silly outfit. "They stole papers," Maya said.

"Let's go in back." Ames gestured to the purpling bruise on Maya's forehead. "How'd you get hurt?"

"Uh, a fender bender." She'd better start with the break-in and work back.

Ames led her to a small, cluttered office and waved her to a chair. She poised her pen over a form. "I'll need to get some information, starting with your name and date of birth. Got ID?"

Maya pulled out her driver's license and handed it over. A California license—she hadn't yet updated—and she hoped Ames wouldn't press the issue.

The detective asked for her current address and handed the license back. "So, Maya, any relation to Harley Rivers?"

"He's—he was—my brother."

"Yes." Ames set down her pen. "Tell me about this break-in. What happened?"

"I woke up in the middle of the night last night and heard a noise in my living room. So I went to check it out and someone attacked me. They hit me over the head with a piece of driftwood. And then—"

Ames put up a hand. "I thought that bruise was from a fender bender."

"It was." Maya pointed to the back of her scalp. "They hit me here."

"Have you seen a doctor?"

"It's just a lump." Maya waved it off. "And what they stole is more important. Three boxes of files that belonged to my brother."

Ames perked up. "Oh? What was in them?"

"I didn't get the chance to look through."

"So this thief hit you over the head with a chunk of driftwood and stole your brother's papers," Ames said. "But you've still got your purse? Cell phone? iPod?"

"Nothing was taken except the boxes." Didn't Ames believe her? It did sound a little bizarre—unless you were a Coast Defender.

The detective tapped her pen on the desk. "How do you suppose this intruder got in? Do you live alone, or with a partner?"

"Alone." Maya hesitated. "And that's the thing. I locked the door, and there's not even a scratch on the lock. So I was thinking someone might have keys. My brother had an extra set." Ames' face clouded as Maya continued. "It's possible the Coast Defenders found his keys and used them to get inside."

Ames leaned forward. Her eyes took on an excited gleam. "You have evidence they did it?"

"Not exactly," Maya admitted.

"Too bad." Ames eased back into the chair. "Still, we need to investigate. This is serious. Someone attacked you. They burglarized your apartment."

"I'm not trying to get anyone in big trouble. I just want the papers back."

Ames studied her. "You were assaulted inside your home. Usually I find victims are very, very concerned when that happens." She rummaged around in her desk drawer and pulled out a brochure, setting it facedown on the desk.

"I just want the papers back," Maya repeated.

Ames gave her a long look. "You should report the assault. We don't have to mention the stolen items." When Maya shook her head, Ames flipped over the brochure and nudged it closer. The title on the front read, "If he's hitting you, we can help."

"Nobody's hitting me," Maya said.

Ames gave her a skeptical look. "Well, it's your call. You've gotten pretty banged up. But if a victim doesn't want to press charges . . . it makes our job a little tougher."

I'm definitely not describing the car crash now. She'd never believe me. "Really. Nobody's hitting me," Maya said again.

Ames frowned. "All right." She typed on the computer keyboard and checked the screen. "Like I thought. We have your brother's mountain bike in the property room. We're done with it. Do you want to take it with you? You're next of kin."

"Sure. What about his backpack? Do you have that, too? I'm looking for his phone." *And his house keys.*

Ames consulted her computer. "I don't see any mention of a pack."

"There's nothing?" Not only were his keys missing, but so was her mother's wedding ring. The ring for Allison. "Can you check if anyone else here, or the firemen, saw a backpack that night? I know he had it with him."

"It may have been damaged." Ames pointed to the screen. "The only property we have listed is a bicycle."

Would the pack have burned completely? She thought for a moment. "Have you guys made progress in identifying the person Harley was meeting that night?"

"Progress?" Ames looked blank. "We've closed the case."

Maya shot to her feet. "You mean you decided Harley's guilty, so you're done?"

"I understand how distressing this must be. But the arson . . . the evidence . . . it was pretty straightforward."

Straightforward? If you only knew. "Could you, uh, answer a few questions for me about the fire?"

"I can try," Ames offered. "Espinoza, the officer who worked the scene, is on family leave. He'll be back later this week. And Rawling isn't in today."

"I was in such a fog after my brother died," Maya said, sitting back down. "The details about his . . . last moments didn't sink in."

Ames checked her watch. "I've got a few minutes." She typed quickly and scanned the screen. "It looks like the fire was called in at 3:06 a.m."

Almost three hours after Harley had left her. It shouldn't have taken him more than twenty minutes to bike to the Bayfront. What was he doing all that time? Meeting someone? Helping to set up the arson?

Ames continued, "A man passing by, Trent Lindberg, saw smoke coming from the building. He ran inside and tried to pull your brother out." She gave Maya a dark look. "He's still in the hospital. Just got out of intensive care."

Maya winced. She'd promised Allison not to do any "bugging," but maybe Trent Lindberg had seen something important. Maybe he even knew why Harley was there. She hunched forward. "Was Harley dead when Trent Lindberg found him?"

"Apparently." Ames continued in a gentler tone, "Often, arsonists do escape fires they set. But in this case, with the heavy use of accelerants, the fire burned very quickly." She consulted her computer. "Your brother died of smoke inhalation. There were blunt trauma injuries as well, but the smoke was the cause of death."

Maya jerked to attention. Rawling had mentioned a "bump on the head," but blunt trauma sounded way more serious. "What caused the injuries?"

Ames turned away from the computer. "It's possible something fell on him, like a beam, or he hit his head on the floor. These injuries are quite common in fires."

Were they really? Why didn't anyone think this was important?

"How did the investigators decide that Harley set this fire . . . not someone else?"

"Well, the firefighters did find him at the site." Ames pressed her fingertips together and returned to reading the screen. She summarized with, "The investigator found traces of the same accelerant inside the building and on the frame of Harley's mountain bike. There were arson supplies in his bike bags, too."

"Anyone could have planted those things in there." Maya leaned forward in her chair. "You found his bike on the street. And he told me he was going to a meeting. The person he met could've set the fire. Not him."

Ames frowned. "According to our report, you were the last person to see him."

"Did you interview the Coast Defenders?"

"We did. The case was thoroughly investigated. There wasn't anyone else there, except for Mr. Lindberg, who happened to be walking by."

Sure about that?

Ames stood. "I'll go get the bike for you."

"Wait." Maya held up a hand to stop her. "When Harley left me that night, he had a small velvet box with a diamond-sapphire ring in it. A family heirloom. It was in his backpack."

Ames sat back down and gave Maya a speculative look. "Was the ring insured?"

"No." Maya caught the implication and bristled. "It's not replaceable. It was my mother's wedding ring."

"The report doesn't mention a ring. That could mean—"

"It's 'gone missing,' along with the rest of his stuff?"

"Or no one found it." Ames jotted a note on a sticky pad. "I'll check into it when Espinoza's back." She passed the notepad to Maya and asked for her phone number.

Maya wrote it down. She noticed Ames staring at the bruises on her wrist. "I *know* Harley had the ring with him," she said.

"I can do a supplemental report," Ames offered.

"Don't bother." *A report wouldn't bring the ring back.*

Ames pushed her braid behind her shoulder. "Truthfully, arson scenes are messy. The fires are meant to burn quickly and cause maximum damage. And when firefighters arrive, they drag hoses through the building and chop out escape routes. There's charred wood, foam and dripping water everywhere. If the backpack burned, something small inside it—like a ring—could have dropped into debris on the pier and gotten lost. Soft metals like gold can even melt. Or someone could have simply missed seeing it."

She shuffled some papers on her desk, clearly wanting the conversation to end. "We don't have an exact time of death. After he left you, it's possible your brother met a friend and dropped off his backpack and the ring *before* going to the Bayfront."

"He wouldn't give away his house keys—and they won't melt," Maya persisted.

"Not all the way," Ames agreed. "I'll check into it. And I can get the word to Rawling." She stood up, handing Maya the brochure. "Don't forget this."

"I'm really not a victim of domestic violence. I'm just accident prone."

Ames pressed her lips closed. She'd heard that line before.

Not wanting to make things worse, Maya took the brochure. "Have you guys really shut down the search for Sara Blessing?"

"Yes." Ames' face pinched. "After a certain time, we can't justify the resources."

"So her case is closed, too?"

"Oh no, it's an open investigation. We *will* find out what happened to her. We can't have women vanishing around town."

Amen to that. At least they took some of their police work seriously. Ames walked Maya out to the hall. "I'll go get your brother's bike."

While she waited, Maya read the papers posted on the bulletin board: Town Hall meeting, classic movies at the library, a recruitment announcement for the police department, and a huge poster titled *Alcohol, Energy Drinks, and Youth: A Dangerous Mix.* Her gaze moved to a flyer in one corner of the board. She froze.

The flyer said, *Missing Since February 27th.* Unlike the blurry, tattered photocopies she'd seen around town, this one was crisp. The image showed Sara Blessing with her matted blonde hair. And something she'd never noticed before. Nestled into the v-neckline of Sara's sweater was a silver oval hanging from a thin leather cord—a silver locket with a delicate leaf design. The same locket she'd found in Harley's files this morning.

Maya's heart stopped. Thank God she hadn't mentioned the locket to anyone.

Ames appeared, wheeling a mountain bike. "There you go." She saw Maya's face. "Are you okay?"

"I'm fine." Her stomach heaved. Was it possible Allison had been right about Harley and Sara?

"Sure you're okay?" Ames stared at her.

"Yes. Thanks for the bike." She reached for it blindly.

"Wait, you've got to sign the form."

Maya scrawled her name and handed it back. Without looking at Ames, she pushed the bike down the hall.

As she wheeled the Trek down the front ramp, she let a moan escape. As much as she tried to suppress the idea that Harley knew something about Sara's disappearance, connections kept popping back up. He'd saved articles about the police investigation and photographs of Sara. He was out and about the night she vanished.

He'd asked Allison to lie about it. And now he'd hidden Sara's jewelry in his files?

Shaking, she leaned the bike against her Corolla and reached down to flip the quick-release lever on the front wheel. The car keys jingled in her hand.

There was no way Harley had cheated on Allison. She'd *seen* his face when he talked about proposing. There must be an innocent explanation for the locket.

There had to be.

Because otherwise . . . everything she knew about her brother was wrong.

Twenty-Five

Maya carried the mountain bike up the flight of stairs to her apartment. She leaned the Trek against the wall and poured herself a glass of water, gulping it down as she walked into the living room. Sara's locket was sitting on the futon couch where she'd left it.

Hand shaking, she set the water glass down. She couldn't give this locket to the cops. Her fingerprints were all over it. Harley's prints would be, too. And if she wiped it clean, she might erase other evidence that could help them find Sara.

She sank onto the couch and pressed her face into her hands. Where had Harley gone the night of February 27th? Had he and Sara been together? Would Sara's boyfriend know anything? How could she get answers?

Her gaze dropped to the locket. It was wrong to keep this. But until she knew why Harley had it . . . Maya used a tissue to pick up the locket and put it in a plastic sandwich bag, working hard to convince herself it was okay to keep it. The police had already called off their search for Sara.

But the investigation was still open. Harley could still be named a suspect in her disappearance, still get crucified by the media. And that would put Allison over the edge. Maya sighed. Maybe it already had.

She hid the plastic baggie in her closet. *Just a day or two*, she promised. *Then I'll turn you in.*

The phone rang in the hall and she raced to pick it up.

"Where the hell are you?" Willy sounded ticked.

Oh, no. She checked the clock. How could she have forgotten her shift? "I'm *so* sorry," she told him. "I lost track of time. I'll be there in five minutes."

"Don't bother," Willy said. "I'm tired of you not taking this job seriously. You're fired."

"But—" *Slam.* He'd hung up.

She held the receiver, listening to the silence.

. . . .

Thirty minutes later, Maya hurried through the Clam Strip's front door, trying not to stare at the locket dangling from Sara's neck in the Missing Woman flyer. She needed to break the news, but Allison was going to freak when she heard.

The dining room was surprisingly busy for a Monday morning. Waitresses were flying around the room, holding full plates in both hands. The specials board said Willy was offering a Spring Break Brunch with seafood cioppino, corn muffins, wild salmon chowder, and marion-berry waffles.

"Could I get some coffee, please?" A customer waved at her and she stared blankly at him. "Miss? Coffee?"

Maya looked down. Whoops. She'd rushed out of the house in her Clam Strip uniform. She grabbed the coffee pot and poured him a cup. "I'll find you a server."

Crystal bustled toward her. "You're not supposed to be working, girlfriend. You got fired."

"Uh, where'd you hear that?"

"From Willy."

Maya winced. "Well, I'm hoping to change his mind."

Crystal pursed her lips. "He says you're always late. He says you don't appreciate this job. That you're not career-focused."

Career-focused? Maya tried not to roll her eyes. It was a service job. As long as she didn't bark at the customers, what difference did it make what her long-term goals were?

Crystal rambled on. "In fact, Willy says—"

"Is Allison working today?" Maya interrupted. "I need to talk to her."

"She's here." Crystal looked around the restaurant. "Or I thought she was. Maybe you should try the restroom. She's spending a lot of time in there recently." Her face lit with excitement. "Oh! We had some drama earlier. Willy—"

"Wow. They look desperate for coffee at the window booths." When Crystal glanced over, Maya hurried off to search the ladies' room. No Allison.

She walked back toward the bar and saw Crystal aiming for her again. Maya turned to escape and bumped into Willy's substantial body. "That was quick," he said. "I just left a message at your apartment, asking you to come in."

"Did you un-fire me?"

"No." He frowned. "Let's go in my office. We need to talk."

Men supposedly dreaded that four-word phrase, but Maya felt equal trepidation. She stalled, searching the room one last time. "Is Allison here?"

"That's what we need to talk about." Willy pushed open the kitchen door and motioned her inside. Reluctantly, she followed him. As she passed through the kitchen, Rob tsk-tsked her with his wooden spoon.

Willy was already in his office, but Maya paused on the threshold. On the wall behind his desk hung a calendar. The photo showed a red-haired Miss March lazing on a tropical beach, with palm trees leaning over white sand. Miss March was naked except for one artfully placed seashell. *Eeeew.*

Willy eased his bulk into the desk chair. "Have a seat."

Her gaze moved to the recliner in the corner of the room. She gasped aloud. Allison was curled up on the chair, eyes closed, with a plaid fleece blanket covering her legs. Her face was very pale. Maya rushed over, relieved to see her chest rising and falling.

"She's sleeping," Willy whispered. He shut his office door. "Come sit down."

Maya glanced back at Allison before she moved to the extra chair. The girl must be exhausted. She sat down gingerly. A thick layer of dust coated Willy's desktop, the chair's upholstery was a dingy gray, and wispy cobwebs dangled from the ceiling. "Is Allison all right?" she whispered back. "How come she's sleeping?"

"I was hoping you could tell me."

She pressed her lips closed. If Allison hadn't mentioned the pregnancy, Maya wasn't going to spill the news.

"You're her friend. You must know what's going on. Why she lost it."

"Lost it?" Maya wished Willy would throw her a lifeline for these cryptic comments. Was she supposed to know what he was talking about?

Willy scowled. "She was fine when she got here. And then . . . "

"Then?" Maya leaned forward.

"She dropped two plates," he said, still whispering. "Eggs and bacon everywhere, grease all over the floor."

"Accidents happen."

Allison stirred, and they both looked over. Was she waking up? No. She sighed softly and kept dozing.

Willy's eyes darkened. "I told her to clean up the mess and she started to . . . but then she asked why you weren't here, and I said I'd fired you. She dropped the mop on the floor and told me to 'F' off." He drew air quotes, as if Maya needed protection from swearing.

She smiled. *You go, girl. Tell it like it is.*

Willy gave her a stony look. "It's not funny. She's never done anything like that before. I had to fire her, too."

She was still smiling, imagining the scene, and his words took a second to register. "*What?* You can't fire Allison. She's one of your best waitresses," Maya said. "She's reliable. Never late. Everybody loves her."

"If I don't fire her, I'm asking for sass. Insubordination. If news gets around . . ."

And trust me, it will.

"It's just that—she's . . . I don't know if . . . " his voice trailed off.

"What's the real issue?" Maya asked.

His scowl deepened. "Right after she said that, she almost fainted. She turned all pale and woozy looking. I thought she was going to drop to the floor in front of me."

"Oh my God." Maya jumped up and ran over to the chair. Allison's eyelids fluttered, but she didn't wake up.

"Don't worry. She's fine now," Willy said. "Ten seconds later, she was totally normal. Talking, smiling. I told her to wait in my office. It got busy, and when I finally came back, she'd crashed out." His face softened. "I didn't have the heart to wake her."

Willy had a heart? "So you won't fire her." Maya walked back to his desk.

"Being sick is no excuse for what she said. After that episode, I have no choice." He shrugged. "Maybe you two can hunt for jobs together."

She paced the carpet. Allison couldn't lose her job. Not now. Especially not now.

"I need you to take her home," Willy added. "That's why I called you. I can't send her out on the road like this." He pulled two envelopes out of a drawer and tossed them onto the desk. They skittered across the metal, stirring up dust. "Final paychecks, for both of you."

Maya gulped. She was now unemployed. But she could find another job, unlike Allison. Nobody would hire someone who was vomiting and fainting everywhere. Even if it passed in a few weeks—Allison needed security. She couldn't get overwhelmed by anything else. Maya couldn't let that happen.

Willy motioned to the envelopes. "I said, 'final paychecks.'"

She sat down again. "It's sure busy out there," she tried. "Customers waiting for their food, waiting for their coffee. And you've fired two servers. Risky move."

"I know." Willy's fist slammed the desktop, creating enough breeze to ruffle the Miss-March-with-a-seashell calendar on the wall. "Dammit," he growled. "I hate to lose Allison. She's one of my best waitresses."

"Then keep her," Maya said.

"Sorry. No can do."

"She's a hard worker. Experienced. Loyal. You've never had any complaints. Therefore, you can't fire her. It's discrimination."

"Now you're her lawyer?" Willy scoffed. "Too bad you don't understand the law. Not only *can* I fire her, I already have."

They were both kicked to the curb. Unless . . . She locked eyes with him. "What were you and Harley arguing about before he died?"

Willy shifted in his chair. "Nothing, really."

"Then why didn't you want him to come in here? Because of the illegal seafood?"

A muscle twitched in his cheek. "I don't know what you're talking about."

"I found female crabs in your kitchen. I took pictures with my cell phone." She improvised quickly. "I'll post them on my blog with the headline 'Clam Strip Owner Taken Down in Seafood Sting.' It could go viral."

"You don't have a blog," Willy said. "Besides, *I* haven't done anything wrong. I'd never buy illegal seafood. That'd piss off the fishermen— my suppliers."

It sounded like the truth. Maybe the crabs were Rob's doing. Maya thought for a moment. "I could call up the Coast Defenders anyway. Ask them to protest out front, march around your door every evening. I'm sure a *few* customers wouldn't mind crossing a picket line."

He frowned. "But I didn't do anything."

"Well, someone here did. And I'm sure you don't want the government breathing down your neck while they investigate." She rested her hands on his desk. "Keep Allison. Tell people she has the flu, and the fever made her lose her temper. She apologized and you accepted. She assured you it would never happen again."

Willy stared at her. "All right," he said, laughing to himself. "I guess it's better her than you. You sucked as a waitress."

Did he *need* to add the slam? "Newsflash. You didn't win boss of the year either."

Allison stirred again, and this time her eyes opened fully. They widened as she took in the room and Maya's presence. She sat upright. "What are you doing here?"

"C'mon, girl. We're outta here. You need to get home and rest." She helped Allison from the chair and turned back to Willy. "Thanks for doing the decent thing," she said. "I'm kind of going to miss you."

He harrumphed. "You'll miss sparring with me." He escorted them through the kitchen into the restaurant. "I'll have somebody drop off her car later today."

Just before they reached the front door, Allison started to gag, and Maya veered her quickly toward the women's restroom. "I got you your job back," she said as she helped Allison navigate the heavy bathroom door. "Willy said you could stay."

Allison looked awful, the worst Maya had ever seen her: a pasty complexion, puffy cheeks, and limp, greasy hair. She put a hand over her mouth and ran for a toilet stall, vomiting.

It wasn't the best time to tell her about Sara's locket.

Twenty-Six

Maya tucked Allison into bed and drove home from Toledo. How had everything gone so wrong? In one short week, she'd lost her brother, been robbed and attacked in her apartment, and gotten fired. Yet things could still get worse. She'd chickened out on mentioning Sara's locket, the theft of Harley's files, and the missing engagement ring to Allison, not wanting to shove her over a cliff. Not wanting her to decide that Harley's baby wasn't worth keeping.

Pain washed through her. That baby was all they had left of him. But it wasn't her choice to make.

Maya climbed the stairs to her apartment and stopped on the porch. No threatening notes. She let out the breath she'd been holding. Maybe it had been a one-time thing. They'd vented—it was done.

In her bedroom, she yanked off her Clam Strip uniform and tossed it into a corner, sliding on jeans and a comfy sweatshirt in the sailor outfit's place. Thank goodness she'd never have to wear that stupid miniskirt again. Her shoulders slumped. Of course, no uniform also meant no income.

She headed for the hall, dialing her landlord's number to make sure he was okay with her adding a chain to the door. He thought it was a fine idea. She hung up, relieved. After borrowing a power drill from her neighbors across the street, Maya installed the brass chain she'd bought at the Toledo Hardware Store. She checked to make sure it worked—the slim chain didn't look very solid, but at least she'd hear it if someone broke in.

The gerbils were making their usual racket in the kitchen. They needed both food and water. Maya frowned as she closed up their cage. All morning long, that reference to Harley's "blunt trauma" had been nagging at her. There was a big difference between Rawling's "bump on the head" and Ames' description. Did the head injury mean anything? Did Allison know about it?

She dialed the police station and asked for Ames. When the detective came on the line, Maya said, "You know that medical examiner's report you mentioned? Could you tell me exactly what it says about Harley's head injury?"

There was a long pause. "You should probably talk to Rawling. This was his case. He'll be in tomorrow."

"I just want to know if my brother suffered," Maya pleaded.

"All right, all right. Give me a minute."

Maya waited anxiously for Ames to pull up the report.

"Here it is." The detective summarized as she read. "Blunt-force trauma, hairline fracture, bruising in the brain." She stopped. "Do you really want to hear this?"

"I want to know how he got hurt."

"That's anyone's guess." Ames gave a little sigh. "Like I told you, blunt-trauma injuries are common in fires. I wouldn't put much stock into it. In your brother's case, there was a clear cause of death, the smoke inhalation. So even if he had another injury . . . "

"You don't think it's important?"

"I'm sure the medical examiner just wanted to be thorough," Ames said. "But if you have questions, ask Rawling. I'll give you his direct line. He's back tomorrow." She rattled off a number.

"Thanks." Maya hung up. Had anyone investigated this head injury? Or had Rawling ignored it, convinced Harley was there alone?

A blow to the head could knock you out, as she'd learned during her close encounter with the driftwood. Harley's injury might have been an accident, caused by the fire . . . or he might have been whacked in the scalp and left there to die.

She considered this new possibility. A person would have to be desperately angry to kill Harley. They'd have to bring arson supplies to the site and know how to set a fire. They'd have to lure him inside the building—someone he trusted. Unless he'd gone there expecting to meet a friend . . . and the killer showed up instead.

Too bad Trent Lindberg—the only potential witness—was off-limits in the hospital.

Maya paced the hallway. Nobody else was going to follow up on this. The police had closed their case. Allison didn't have the energy. And the Coast Defenders would just try to hide the truth. She stopped pacing. It was up to her. She had to figure out why Harley had died—and if his death had anything to do with Sara vanishing.

But where to start? There were so many potential paths to follow. Could she get a list of his phone calls, access his emails and texts, with help from the police? *No.* That wasn't the best plan. Not unless she knew what those records would reveal. He and Sara might have made plans for February 27th.

Maya went back to pacing. Harley had Sara's locket; therefore, he'd known something about her disappearance. She really should talk to

Sara's boyfriend, Redd Harrison, and find out what Sara was doing before she vanished.

Grabbing her jacket, she walked down the stairs to her Corolla. When the engine started, it clanked at her. Maya prayed it would hold on for a few more days. With no job, how was she supposed to come up with the money for repairs?

. . . .

At the library, she nabbed a one-hour Internet station and found an article about Sara—the one that mentioned her riding her bike south of town. She grabbed a piece of scratch paper and a stubby pencil from the library stash and jotted down Redd Harrison's name. Unfortunately, whitepages.com didn't offer an address or phone number.

Neither did a thorough cybersearch. There were similar names on Facebook and Twitter and Google+, but none of them lived in Newport. Redd Harrison didn't seem to exist outside the news articles. Either Redd was a nickname—or he lived well off the grid.

Discouraged, Maya went to Gmail, hoping to guess the password for Harley's account. After her first few tries didn't work, she got locked out. A job for another day.

She checked her own email and found a message from her best friend, Lydia, in Sacramento. Lydia was getting married in five months, and she wanted to make sure Maya would be there—to wear the "hideous chartreuse gown" Lydia had chosen for her maid of honor. Maya laughed out loud. "Absolutely," she wrote back. "But only if I can pair it with my purple stilettos and a matching headband."

She was about to log off the computer when she noticed a headline on a local news site: *Environmental Firm Hired to Supervise Arson Cleanup.* She skimmed the article, reading about how the owner of Newport Nature Tours had hired an environmental consulting firm to oversee the demolition work and make sure no burned debris polluted the bay.

The photo showed two men standing on a pier. The caption identified them as Doug Sammish, the owner of Newport Nature Tours, and Curt Klein, with Bishop Environmental Consulting. Any relation to the mysterious Jonah Bishop? Maya added the two names to her scratch paper, then typed *Bishop Environmental Consulting* into the search engine.

Their webpage had a staff directory, but no headshots. Jonah Bishop was indeed listed as the owner, and he had five employees, including this Curt Klein. She wrote down the business phone and address.

Their "Clients" link included a short, glowing write-up about DreamCoast Condos that described how the consulting firm—BEC for short—had advised Alan Kingston throughout the planning and development process. *That project again.* If Jonah Bishop's firm had worked on DreamCoast, with Alan Kingston as their client, that would put Jonah and Harley on opposite sides of the fence. Yet Harley had apparently called him. Why?

She stared at the computer screen.

"Are you done?"

Maya jumped. A scruffy-looking man was standing right behind her. He pointed to the blank screen, which had logged her out. Her time was up.

"It's all yours." She rose to her feet. Before she'd gotten distracted by Sara's locket, she'd wanted to talk to the owner of Newport Nature Tours. Maybe Doug Sammish knew whom Harley had met that night. Maybe he could tell her about Bishop Environmental Consulting.

. . . .

Maya walked briskly along the Bayfront. Sea lions barked loudly, quarreling on the narrow docks. Despite the gray clouds that threatened rain, spring break crowds were out in full force. Busy traffic. Busy shops.

She stopped outside the chain-link fence that still blocked access to the Newport Nature Tours property. The impromptu flower memorial and the rubberneckers were now gone, along with most of the charred building.

A horn honked behind her. She turned to look. A minivan had stopped, backing up traffic while a stream of kids jumped out and ran over to the sidewalk. Her eyes narrowed. In the line of vehicles behind the van was a black pickup truck. Was it Tomas?

Maya turned back to the fence, feeling uneasy. On the pier, a man wearing a hard hat and safety glasses was talking on his cell phone. He couldn't be a construction worker—his yellow hat was shiny new, his jeans pressed, and his boots free of dirt. When he hung up, she waved. "Excuse me!"

The man walked over. "Can I help you?" he said through the chain link.

"I'm hoping to talk to Doug Sammish."

"You've got him." He slipped the phone into his pocket and took off the safety glasses. "What do you need?"

"I have a few questions about the night of the fire."

He studied her through the metal gate. "I've already 'shared my story' for half a dozen reporters—and the insurance company investigators. What's your interest in it?"

"Harley Rivers was my brother."

"I'm sorry." His mouth thinned. "But what exactly do you want?"

"I'm starting to think he didn't set the fire."

"What do you mean he didn't set it?" Doug Sammish blinked. "The building is *gone*. It was obviously arson. The police showed me the evidence. Your brother carried the accelerant on his bike."

"There's a bigger story here. The police don't know all of it."

He gave her a disbelieving look. "Sorry, I don't have time for this."

She clasped the fence's cold wire. "Someone else was here with Harley that night and—" A diesel engine rumbled behind her, and she and Doug Sammish both turned to look. A mammoth white pickup had parked a few feet away.

"Excuse me," he said briskly. "I have a meeting."

A tall, lanky man climbed out of the white truck and walked toward them. He gave Maya a curious glance as the owner let him onto the site and locked the gate behind them. She'd been dismissed.

She crossed the street and sat down on a bench. On the pier, the two men seemed deep in conversation. The visitor's white truck was a company rig, a Dodge Dakota with a green logo on its door. And she recognized that logo—the circle with evergreen trees silhouetted inside. Harley's photo had captured a partial design. But now she could read the small letters underneath: Bishop Environmental Consulting. BEC.

What luck! Harley had photographed a white BEC truck in the woods. He'd kept a phone number for Jonah Bishop. Now an employee from that same business was here at Newport Nature Tours. These weren't coincidences.

Maya continued watching the two men, her view obscured by the traffic crawling past on Bay Boulevard. Several black trucks passed, and it gave her an idea.

She jogged back to her Corolla, parked in a loading zone where she could see the white truck clearly, and waited for the man from BEC to finish talking. Before long, he walked out the Newport Nature Tours gate and climbed into the truck cab.

As he headed east, Maya followed. She trailed the vehicle past Dock 5 and Dock 7, past Englund's and the Embarcadero. He drove along the north edge of the bay and upriver a couple of miles. Just past a curve, he turned right without signaling and pulled into a gravel parking lot.

Maya drove another hundred yards and parked her battered Corolla in a pullout on the shoulder. She jogged back. The BEC lot was empty except for the white truck, a brown Hyundai sedan, and a gigantic SUV. The man took something out of the SUV and headed toward the building.

Maya ducked behind his supersized vehicle, snickering at its "hybrid" label. This beast? And then she realized it was a Cadillac Escalade. A gold Escalade . . . like the one Allison had mentioned cruising her street.

She peeked out from behind the vehicle. The BEC building was one story, painted gray, with a red sign that said *Bishop Environmental Consulting*. Next to it, a squat wooden building perched on the edge of the Yaquina River, probably a storage shed.

The man entered a narrow corridor between the main building and the shed and tossed something into a dumpster. He strode toward BEC's front door.

She waited until he went in before she scuttled to the dumpster, raised the lid, and peered inside. *Pee-uw.* The stench of overripe garbage mingled with tangy smells as she searched for whatever he'd thrown into the mess. That banana peel? The crumpled paper towel? Something important? She didn't know.

"What do you think you're doing?" a voice growled behind her.

Twenty-Seven

Maya dropped the lid with a clang and spun around.

Tomas stepped forward, trapping her between the dumpster's metal side and his dense body. "Digging for treasure?"

"You scared the crap out of me!" She tried to sidestep toward the open parking lot. "What are you doing here?"

With a quick move, he blocked her exit. "You're messing in things that aren't your business. It's causing trouble for us."

His muscular body seemed as impenetrable as a wall. Maya forced herself to take a breath, fighting the tightness in her lungs. "What do the Coast Defenders have to hide?"

He folded his arms over his chest. Unmoving.

She glanced behind her. No boats on the river—nothing but gray water and low-hanging clouds for company. No windows on this side of the building either. Would any BEC employees hear if she called for help?

"You shouldn't be here," Tomas growled.

"Neither should you."

His mouth pulled taut. He reached for her arm but she jerked away. "Oh no, you don't. Look what happened at the coffee shop." She displayed her bruised wrist. "I bet you clocked me in my apartment, too, right before you stole Harley's files. I could go for assault charges." Ames would love that.

Tomas glared. "I already told you. I didn't hit you—or take the files."

"Then who did?"

He shrugged.

"I went to the police station earlier," Maya said. "I didn't mention the possibility it was your truck that rear-ended my car. Not yet." She rubbed her neck. "I'm still feeling whiplashed."

Tomas blinked. "My truck hit your car?"

"Like you don't know." She rubbed her neck again. "A black, mud-splattered truck that bullies small Corollas off the road in the pitch of night. Sound familiar now?"

He stared at her. "That wasn't me."

"So you say." She didn't know. The pickup she'd inspected outside the coffee shop hadn't shown any damage, but bumpers could be replaced. And it hadn't hit her very hard. The Douglas fir tree had caused most of the Corolla's dents.

Tomas scooted closer to her.

"*Back off,*" Maya snapped.

To her surprise, he stepped away. "I didn't mean to hurt your wrist." He looked worried. "But why do you keep asking us about the work Harley was doing? You should leave things alone or—"

"Oh, please. A threat?"

"Take it easy, Maya. I'm not threatening you." He took an exaggerated step backwards and flung up his arms. "See, hands off."

"Then why are you following me?" The misty moisture had seeped through her clothing, leaving her damp and frozen.

"It's for your own good." He watched her closely.

"Bullshit. And if you don't stop stalking me, I'll tell the police you broke into my apartment. I'll say you were trying to get your hands on Harley's files and when I refused to hand them over, you assaulted me."

Tomas' mouth hung open. "But I didn't."

"Then you can explain that to the cops. I'm sure they'll believe you . . . after hours of questioning and a night in the cell."

"Nice, Maya. Just throw me under the bus. You know they're already gunning for the group. For me, the leader." His face twisted. "What'll it take to get you to lay off?"

Oh. He wanted to bargain? "You could answer my questions. Then I might develop amnesia and forget the bruised wrist. The hit-and-run. The beating in my apartment." Moisture dripped from the sky and ran down the dumpster's sides. She waited.

"What kind of questions?" he said finally.

"For starters, what does Bishop Environmental Consulting do?" She gestured to the building.

"Environmental consulting." At her dirty look, he added, "Water sampling, soil sampling, wildlife inventories, plant inventories, and land use studies. They have a small chemistry lab, too."

"How do you know so much about them?"

"They worked on DreamCoast."

"Doing what?"

"They helped Alan Kingston get his permits." Disdain laced his voice. "Thanks to BEC calling the property 'unproductive forest,' everyone decided it should be developed. Why not transform tree lots into luxury condos? We can never have enough of those."

She pictured the DreamCoast brochure, with the three large complexes. "Did you guys think you could shut down the whole project? That seems ambitious."

"We just had to delay things. If Kingston couldn't make his payments on the property, no more condos."

"He *financed* DreamCoast?" That was a surprise. She'd pictured Kingston as a One Percenter.

"He had to. Some of his Colorado investments went belly-up right before he moved here." He smiled at her questioning look. "It pays to research your enemies."

"Is anyone from the Coast Defenders still trying to shut it down?"

"No." Tomas scowled. "But you'd better stop poking your nose into things. It'll just get you in trouble."

"One more question." She shifted in place. "Who do you think damaged the hotel and boat?"

"I don't know. It wasn't us." His gaze shifted back to the river. "It's a waste of time to break windows and chop holes in sailboats. That won't solve anything."

As his words sunk in, Maya froze. She'd meant the *Lady Littoral*, not the sailboat. There'd been nothing in the news about Rocky's. With Harley dead, the only other person who'd know about it was the person who'd done the damage. Well, plus the marine service staff, the rent-a-cop, and the real cops. But they weren't talking.

"How did you hear about the sailboat?" she asked.

"Uh, Harley mentioned it."

"Oh." *Wait—if Harley had gone from the brewery to the Bayfront, how had he "mentioned" the sailboat to Tomas? Unless they'd seen each other that night.*

Her heart felt like someone had closed a fist around it and squeezed. Could Tomas have set the fire? Absolutely. Maybe he was the real vandal, and Harley had found out and confronted him . . . That explained why Tomas didn't want her asking questions. She took a shaky breath.

"Maya?" He nudged her. "Did your brother say anything about a special project he was working on? Something with Sara?"

"Not a word." *Oh, God.* She really needed to talk to Redd about the locket. How could she get in touch with him? "Have you met Sara's boyfriend, Redd?"

He gave her a suspicious look. "Why?"

"I want to . . . offer my condolences. But I couldn't find his phone number."

"He lives on a boat. Try the El Capitan Marina. The *Lucky Charm*." Tomas folded his arms over his chest, emphasizing his bulk. "And if you're smart, you won't call him Redd. He hates it. Goes by Ryan."

That's why she couldn't find him online. He wasn't using his real name.

"Just a friendly warning," Tomas said. "Keep digging and you could end up like Sara. She's probably at the bottom of the ocean by now."

Maya flinched. *What did he mean by that?*

"Anyway, no more questions. I've gotta run." He headed for his truck.

After Tomas drove off, Maya jogged back to her car. Forget the dumpster. She was getting closer to the truth. BEC owned that white truck, but she still didn't know where Harley had photographed it. Or why.

As she turned the key in the ignition, she shivered. Tomas' remark about Sara and the "bottom of the ocean" was seriously creepy.

Did he *know* she was dead?

Twenty-Eight

At home, Maya dug out the baggie with Sara's locket. It was time to tell Allison everything.

"I'm glad you called," Allison said when she picked up the phone. "Do you want to come over for an early dinner? I've got something to talk to you about."

"Oh . . . me, too." Maya glanced at the Trek taking up space in her hall. "I picked up Harley's bike from the police station. Should I bring it with me?"

There was a long pause before Allison said, "You can keep it. You may need cheap transportation, now that you're . . . unemployed."

It was obviously an excuse: Allison was trying to erase every sign of Harley.

"See you soon," Maya said through gritted teeth. She hung up, eyeing the gerbils in her kitchen. They were suffering under her haphazard care. They needed someone who knew about pets. Emma would want the best. And maybe it would help Allison, too, by taking her mind off Harley.

Feeling guilty at her incompetence with animals, she carried the glass aquarium and the locket to her Corolla, set them on the front seat, and placed a towel on top. Now she just had to convince Allison to take the gerbils.

. . . .

When she arrived at Allison's, Maya slid the baggie with Sara's locket into her jeans pocket. She left the aquarium in the car and ran up the steps. The bloodstain was gone, the porch boards scrubbed clean. Before she could knock, the door opened.

Allison waved her inside. "Great timing. I was just about to make tea." Maya followed her into the kitchen and Allison pointed to three colorful boxes on the counter. "Do you want 'Relax Your Mind,' 'Stress Relief,' or 'Women's Balance'?"

"Too bad they don't make a tea called 'Get a New Job,'" Maya said with a laugh. "But if we're talking stress relief, how about a margarita?"

"Sorry. Even smelling alcohol makes me nauseous."

"I guess I'll have 'Relax Your Mind,' then."

Allison filled the kettle with water and set it on the stove.

"I have something to show you. I'll be right back." Maya ran out to her car and returned with the ten-gallon aquarium. She set it on the kitchen table, ripping off the towel with a flourish. "Ta da!"

"What the heck are those?" Allison peered through the glass.

"They're gerbils. My neighbor Emma left them with me."

"Emma left you in charge of her pets?" Allison smiled. "She obviously skipped the background check."

"She was desperate. Her sitter fell through. How could I say no?" Maya gave Allison a pleading look. "But I'm sure they'd be much happier with you."

Allison hesitated. "I don't know anything about gerbils."

"Neither do I. But what I've learned is they eat like they've been on a hunger strike for weeks and they chew everything. I had no idea how much responsibility they'd be. I'm worried they're going to die on my watch."

Allison peeked into the aquarium again. "They're darling. Look how they snuggle up together."

Maya crossed her fingers behind her back. Allison was a born caretaker. And it wasn't too big a leap from snuggly gerbil to snuggly baby, was it? "They're very sweet," she said. "And they hardly make any noise." *Except between midnight and four a.m. It's perfect training for having a newborn.*

"I don't know. With FuzzyBear around . . ."

Maya tapped the aquarium's mesh top. "Solid glass and a tight lid. No cat's getting in here." When Allison didn't object further, she ran to her car and retrieved the gerbil supplies. By the time she returned, Allison was cooing at the cage.

"Here's their food and bedding." Maya handed them over.

"So you knew I'd take them off your hands."

Maya grinned. "One can always hope."

The kettle whistled and Allison poured steaming water over the tea bags. She pressed a button on the stove. "I'll just top-brown the enchiladas."

Maya carried her mug into the living room, taking a cautious sip as she walked. *Bah.* "Relax Your Mind" tasted like dandelions, and she didn't feel one bit tranquil. Every time she thought about the news she had to share, her nerves jangled all over again.

Allison sank onto the couch, pulling FuzzyBear onto her lap. "Thanks for bringing me home earlier—and for saving my job. I'm really sorry you got fired, though."

"I can get another job." Maya sipped the nasty tea. "I'm not too worried."

"Maybe you should be. We're in the middle of a recession."

"I'll get by." Maya smiled grimly. "That's one lesson I learned from Frank."

Allison leaned forward. "You should probably make some plans. Do you have enough money saved? Have you considered where you might apply?"

"Easy, girl. I'll be fine." Obviously Allison was worried about money herself, projecting that onto Maya because she was anxious about having a baby to support. Understandably so. "I'm sorry. I didn't think to bring the cash you loaned Harley. I'll get it to you."

"Great." Allison sighed and her voice flattened. "I can't believe he told me he needed that for school. Why do you think he really wanted it?"

"I don't know." Maya didn't even want to head down that path. "I saw a gold Escalade today," she said quickly. "It was parked outside a business called Bishop Environmental Consulting, BEC for short. Did Harley ever mention them to you?"

"No. It probably wasn't the same SUV that drove by here."

"Why not? They're pretty rare. When was the last time you saw a gold Escalade cruising around Toledo? That's a city ride."

"It's spring break. People are visiting the coast."

Maya persisted. "Apparently BEC has been helping Alan Kingston develop the DreamCoast Condos site. And you remember that phone number I found on the sales brochure? It's for the owner, a Jonah Bishop. Listen to this. A white truck pulled up to Newport Nature Tours today. I recognized the logo from Harley's pictures, so I followed the truck to BEC . . . and that's where I found the Escalade."

To her disappointment, Allison didn't seem at all interested. "I'd better check the enchiladas," she said, just as the smoke alarm went off.

They rushed into the kitchen. When Allison opened the oven door, black smoke poured into the room. She grabbed the casserole dish, set it on the stovetop, and slammed the door shut. She turned off the broiler. "There went our dinner."

"I'm not starving." Maya carried the gerbils out of the room.

"I *am*. I've hardly eaten all day." Allison gazed at the charred food and burst into tears.

Maya dug through the refrigerator and pulled out a packet of slightly expired tortillas and a hardened stub of cheddar. "We can have burritos. Got beans?" Allison shook her head. "Quesadillas, then."

Allison wiped her eyes and sniffled. "Sorry for the waterfall. Everything feels so discouraging right now."

"Give it time," Maya soothed as she placed cheese slices on tortillas and set the plate in the microwave. "Between Harley's death and the pregnancy, your world's been turned upside down." *And I have to rock it further.* She patted her jeans pocket. *Why did this locket need to show up?*

The microwave beeped. When they sat down at the table, Maya took a bite. Yuck. Her quesadilla tasted like cardboard with a topping of grease. She washed it down with lukewarm tea. "Relax Your Mind" was not doing its job.

Allison placed a white envelope on the table.

"What's that?"

Allison turned it around so she could read the return address. The business name was *From Your Heart to A Good Home.* "I'm thinking about adoption," she said.

Adoption? Allison wanted to give away Harley's baby, just like his easy chair and his bike? Maya bit her lip as she read the letter. Allison had already consulted this agency, already set up an appointment to "discuss options."

"Maybe . . . I could adopt the baby," Maya offered.

Allison's mouth dropped. "You? The woman who thinks gerbils are too hard?" She stared at Maya, seeming astounded at the idea.

"I used to babysit. People trusted me with their kids."

Allison shook her head. "I have a . . . different image in mind. What this baby needs is—"

"Let me guess. Two parents. The dad's a doctor or lawyer. A nice house with a picket fence, maybe a golden retriever in the backyard."

"Stop joking!" Allison cried. "I want the best for my child. And I'm not sure I can provide that right now."

Maya pushed bits of hardened tortilla around her plate with her fork. Her heart was breaking. What was next? Was Allison looking to discard her, too? She folded up the adoption agency letter and shoved it back into the envelope. Before Allison made any big decisions, she needed to understand about Harley's death.

"The police haven't been able to find Harley's backpack," Maya said.

"Really?" Allison's face scrunched with concern. "It's gone?"

"According to them, it never existed. Which is odd, because a backpack shouldn't burn up completely. Not the metal zipper or his house keys inside. Not your engagement ring, either." *A not-so-subtle reminder.* "Most likely, the person who was with Harley stole his pack. The person who really set the fire."

"This again?" Allison pushed her plate away. "There wasn't anybody else there."

"How can you be so sure? We should ask Trent Lindberg that question." Maya ignored Allison's frown. "Because the missing pack means someone was with Harley. And I think it was Tomas." She explained about the vandalized sailboat. "Either he did the damage himself—or Harley told him on the Bayfront. Right before the fire."

Allison gripped her mug. "Tomas isn't the most socially gracious guy. But he wouldn't . . . "

"Socially ungracious? He's a brute. Look what he did." Maya showed her bruised wrist. "And he threatened me, too. He said, 'If you keep digging, you could end up like Sara.'"

"Maybe he's worried about you." Allison pursed her mouth. "You're running around accusing everyone of setting the fire. Everyone *except* Harley."

Maya took a deep breath. "I have something else to tell you. It may be hard to hear, but you need to know." Allison stared at her. "The detective I spoke to earlier today . . . " Maya took another breath. "She told me Harley had a blunt-trauma injury. A hard enough blow to fracture his scalp."

"I thought he died of smoke inhalation." Allison's lips trembled.

"He did. And supposedly, it's common to get banged up in a fire. But it's also possible another person hit Harley over the head and left him there." Maya held Allison's gaze. "The police have closed their case. They're not going to look into this. So we have to."

Allison wrapped her hands around her stomach. "Great," she muttered under her breath. "Another wild theory to chase down. You're just like Harley."

"Is that a bad thing?" Maya's fork clattered to the plate.

"You and him—you never give up. It's one conspiracy theory after another . . . Do you think the world's out to get you?"

Maya felt truly wounded. She'd been trying to protect Allison, but . . . she took out the locket baggie and set it on the kitchen table.

"Where'd you find that locket?" Allison turned ashen. "It looks like Sara's, the one in the flyer."

"It is. And it showed up in Harley's files. Those boxes you gave me."

"*What?*" Allison wore a serious deer-in-headlights look. "Where did he get it? Why didn't he take it to the police?"

"I don't know where he found it. But he probably kept the locket because he wanted to know why Sara disappeared. Maybe he thought the police wouldn't help him. And since he can't follow up . . . it's up to us."

"Forget it," Allison said. "You're out of your mind."

Maya held up the baggie. "The cops aren't doing anything. They're done searching for Sara. And if we could figure out what happened to her, every woman in Newport would be relieved. Doesn't it terrify you that she just vanished?"

"Let the police do their job. It's not our business."

Maya tapped the locket. "It is now."

"You can get rid of that," Allison said. "Toss it in the ocean."

"Harley's dead. The cops can't hurt him any more."

"I'm talking about the media," Allison snapped. "If they hear about this, they'll destroy him. Call him a kidnapper. A violent murderer. I can't go through that again."

"Harley didn't kill anyone. And this locket might tell us if Sara's disappearance is linked to his death. It could tell us why he died." Her voice cracked. "Don't you want to know?"

Allison rubbed her palms over her cheeks. "You're like a kid who can't stop picking at a scab. Every time my wounds start to heal—every time I make peace with who Harley was, what he did—you rip that scab open again. You must enjoy watching me bleed."

"*What?*" Maya frowned. Allison didn't understand. This wasn't about her. It was about believing in Harley, trusting in him. Knowing he was worthy of their love. She shoved the baggie into her pocket. "I take it you're not going to help me."

Allison shook her head. "Just go."

"What do you mean? Go where?"

Allison pointed to the front door. "Get out. And take that damn locket with you."

Maya stared at her, shocked to the core, before she walked outside. She tossed the bag into the Corolla's passenger seat, feeling her armor already falling into place. That same hard shell had gotten her through the pain-filled weeks after Frank's betrayal. *I don't need her. I can figure this out on my own.*

153

Twenty-Nine

The sky was rapidly turning to dusk when her Corolla rattled across the gravel parking lot of the El Capitan Marina. Maya peered through the fogged windshield. Unlike the busy South Beach Marina, most of the slips were empty. Of the five boats moored, only one had lights on. Hopefully it was the *Lucky Charm*.

The Corolla's engine was still clanking, and she prayed it wouldn't conk out. Not in the fading daylight, with those alders casting long shadows across the gravel.

She stared back down the road. No sign of Tomas' black truck, but the swollen river reminded her of what he'd said about Sara. *At the bottom of the ocean.*

Maya climbed out of her car and breathed in cool air, trying to settle her rapidly beating heart. This marina was so desolate. She should have told someone where she was going. Not that Allison wanted to hear.

As she walked down the dock toward the one lit boat, a dog started barking—loud, hoarse woofs that echoed across the water. Waves slapped gently against the wooden boards. The dog's barking grew louder. Maya slid a hand into her jacket pocket and touched the tiny locket in its plastic baggie. If Ryan Harrison was here, she'd have to decide if she dared show it to him.

As she walked, she checked the name on each boat hull. *Glory Days. Wild Ransom. Dreamcatcher.* Her footsteps slowed. It was crazy to come here alone.

She stopped next to the lit-up sailboat.

The *Lucky Charm* was obviously old, but well tended. Sails were tied neatly along the boom, and ropes coiled on deck. Two surfboards leaned against the mast. She breathed a sigh of relief. Surfers were usually young, carefree guys. Right?

Maya stood on the dock, wondering what to do with no doorbell. "Hello?" she called. No answer.

She grabbed a post on the boat deck and swung herself on board, landing on her knees. As she struggled to her feet, the hatch to the cabin opened and a person appeared in the gap.

"Who the hell are you?" he shouted. "Get off my boat." Below deck, she could hear a hound barking furiously. It sounded like Cujo.

Her heart raced. Before she could reply, the man went down into the cabin. When he reappeared, he had a shotgun cradled in his arm. "I said, *get off* my boat."

"I'm, uh, sorry to bother you," she stammered. "I'm Maya, Harley Rivers' sister . . . from the Coast Defenders. I just want to talk to you. Are you Ryan?"

He nodded but kept holding the shotgun, his gaze darting from her to the deserted dock. "You don't have a camera, do you?"

"No camera." She held up her hands to show they were empty. "I didn't know how to reach you by phone. I'm trying to figure out why my brother died and . . . never mind." She turned to hop down.

"No, stay." He stepped out of the shadows. He was younger than she'd thought, probably early twenties, and wore a black stocking cap over his hair. "I knew Harley," he said, unsmiling. "Sara introduced us."

"Really?" She slipped a hand into her pocket and touched the locket bag. Ryan didn't sound like he was burning with jealousy.

"I assumed you were another damn reporter," he grumbled. "They don't seem to have any boundaries. One of them even tried to break into the boat. My neighbor caught him and gave him a good thumping."

Oh, boy. "I'm definitely not a reporter."

"You can come down, then." The dog woofed from the cabin and Ryan waved a hand toward the noise. "Domino doesn't like to be cooped up. It's criminal to keep him on a boat, but he belongs to Sara. I can't let him go." He climbed down into the cabin.

Maya hesitated. Ryan seemed friendly now, but her heart was still galloping. And it was never smart to descend into an enclosed space with a stranger.

"Aren't you coming?" he called.

She took a last, wistful look at the open deck before she followed him into the cabin. He'd tied the dog to a cupboard with a leash. She'd seen this Dalmatian in the photo with Sara, and he wasn't as fierce as he'd sounded from the dock. When she petted him, his tail wagged vigorously.

"People know I'm here," she murmured. Ryan laughed.

The cabin provided tight quarters, but it was scrupulously neat— except for the shotgun lying on the counter. He saw her looking. "Don't worry. That's just for show."

Uh huh. "Sara's a great photographer," Maya said, admiring the scenic prints covering every inch of wall space. "The Coast Defenders have her picture of the jetty. It had amazing lighting, with that storm rolling in."

"She's talented all right." Ryan opened a small fridge and removed two beer bottles. He flipped off the caps and, without asking, handed her one: a Kiwanda Cream Ale from the Pelican Pub. He took a long swallow.

"Thanks." She sipped her beer to be polite, then sat down at the table.

"I was sorry to hear about Harley's death." Ryan slid onto the bench across from her. "Sara always liked him."

"They worked together in the group?"

"On DreamCoast, last fall. Sara was pretty fired up about that project. I remember her mentioning him."

She did? "Harley stopped working on DreamCoast a while back."

He nodded. "Sara, too."

On a shelf behind him were several snapshots. The locket hung around Sara's neck in each one. Maya wanted to ask, "Was she wearing that when she disappeared?" but she wasn't ready. She took another sip of beer, this time for courage. "Harley was really upset about Sara's disappearance. But whenever I asked him about it, he didn't say much. I was hoping you could . . . clarify some things about that night."

Ryan gave her a look. "You think your brother knew something?"

"No. I just think it's strange that, within two weeks, both of them die—" She broke off, wincing. "I mean, Harley died and Sara disappeared." Her gaze darted around the cabin, looking anywhere but at Ryan. Sara possibly *was* dead, but to say that aloud was cruel. "I'm so sorry."

"I keep hoping . . ." He looked across the room at Domino, who'd settled onto the floor. "I didn't see her that night. I worked late, picked up an extra shift. We were saving up for a road trip to Santa Cruz this May. Planning to take our boards and explore the coast."

He took a long sip, draining his beer bottle, before continuing. "When I finally got home, Domino was pacing the boat. He'd peed everywhere. And I was—" He stopped. "I was furious at her for not letting him out. I waited up until six in the morning, getting angrier by the minute. And then she didn't come home at all."

Pain flooded his face. He stood up. "*Shit.* This not knowing . . . it gnaws at me." He pulled another beer out of the fridge and uncapped it. "I've spent the past two weeks visiting every place she might have gone. She took her mountain bike, so she couldn't have ridden far. But the search-and-rescue crews have looked everywhere. There's no sign of her."

"Did the police say what they think happened?"

"They don't have a clue. And after I told them she'd gone out on Coast Defenders' business, they started huffing about the 'illegal nature of her activities.' Like she got what she deserved."

"She said it was for the group?"

"It had to be." Ryan sat back down and stared at his fresh bottle of beer. "She took a bunch of stuff from the boat with her. Her backpack, headlamp, a camera. A folding shovel and her army knife. You can imagine what the cops said about that." He picked up the bottle and drank.

"What did she do for the Coast Defenders, besides work on DreamCoast?"

"This and that. She protested some timber sales and got arrested a few times . . . " His voice trailed off. "She didn't talk about the group much. She knew I didn't approve. I got tired of bailing her out."

Maya bit her lip. Is that how Allison felt, too? Maybe that's why she was so mad at Harley. "Did Sara ever say anything about Tomas Black? How she felt about him?"

"She kept things to herself."

"But you said she liked Harley."

"I got that impression." Ryan sighed. "I'm sorry I can't be more help."

"Well, did she ever mention Newport Nature Tours to you?"

"No." He picked up his beer and drank.

"How about Bishop Environmental Consulting, or BEC?"

Ryan stared at her. "Interesting you should mention that." He drained his second beer and clunked the empty bottle on the table. "She didn't take her phone with her that night. I found it later, buried under a pile of clothes. Right where you're sitting."

Maya looked down. The wood bench had a thick blue cushion, covering a storage space. "Her phone never rang?"

"She'd turned it off. I went back and checked her calls, in and out. There were a dozen from me, and some from friends. Then I checked the dialed numbers, and called the ones I didn't recognize. One of those was Jonah Bishop's direct line—he's the owner of Bishop Environmental."

"You don't say." She took a sip of beer to cover her excitement. Sara and Harley had both tried to contact this Jonah person at BEC? Her hand trembled as she set the bottle down. "Why do you think she called him?"

"No idea. I went to their office and tried to talk with him, but he said he'd never spoken to her. He wouldn't tell me anything." Ryan slammed his palm on the table. "If I ever find out who did this to her, I'll destroy them. Take everything they care about, like they took Sara from me."

Well, that settled it. She couldn't trust him with the news of the locket—or of Harley being out that night. "Did you tell the police about her phone call to Jonah Bishop?"

"I'm sure they know." His voice turned bitter. "I didn't tell them any more than I needed to. They've treated me like a suspect."

"Do you remember anything else about the night she disappeared? Anything unusual?"

Ryan thought. "Not then . . . but a week or two before, she came home super excited." He reached into a cupboard behind him, pulled out a shoebox, and set it on the table. "Apparently she gave this to a neighbor a few slips down for 'safekeeping.' After she went missing, he brought it over." He tapped the box. "She must have figured I'd know why it was important."

Maya lifted the lid. Inside the box was a piece of cotton cloth wrapped around something. Her hands shook as she unrolled the bundle. A bone. It was much smaller than Harley's and gnawed on both ends. "Animal?"

"Yeah, probably deer."

She picked up the bone. "You don't know where she got this?" He shook his head. "Harley had a bone, too," she told him. "But his was from a moose."

Ryan's eyebrows rose. "I didn't think moose lived in Oregon."

"Apparently there are some. In the northeast corner, near the Wallowas. According to Dan, a biologist I met." Maybe he could identify this bone, too.

"Who knew?" Ryan took Sara's bone back, wrapped it up, and tossed the box into the cupboard. When he saw her staring at the portrait of Sara on the shelf, he slid it across the table. "I took that last fall. It's the same shot they used for the flyer."

Her gaze went straight to the silver locket. "That's a beautiful necklace." She nearly choked on the words.

"Her grandma gave it to her. It has pictures of her grandma and her mother inside. Sara *loved* that locket, but she thought it was old-fashioned. She always wore it on a leather cord instead of the silver chain it came with."

Maya felt faint. "Did she wear it often?"

Ryan held the photo in his hands. He gazed fondly at Sara's image, as if it really were his living, breathing girlfriend. "After her grandma died, that locket was precious. Sara never took it off. Ever."

Maya's breath caught. The tight quarters of the boat got even tighter. Making a feeble excuse that she needed fresh air, she clambered past the dozing dog and ran up the ladder to the deck. Breath wheezing, she gulped for air.

Ryan followed, eyeing her nervously. "Something I said?"

"No. Maybe it's a dog allergy." She gasped another breath. "I should probably get going."

A phone rang, trilling loudly in the still evening. "Hold on a sec." He pulled a cell phone out of his pocket, checked the screen, and put it away. "I don't know who that is."

Maya had seen the hope surge on his face. But it wasn't Sara calling. Poor guy. "Thanks so much for talking with me." She jumped down to the dock.

"Wait!" Ryan called. "How can I reach you?"

Maya rattled off her phone number and fled for shore.

Thirty

She drove toward home on autopilot, the words repeating over and over in her mind: *That locket was precious. Sara never took it off. Ever.*

Harley and Sara both had an interest in Bishop Environmental Consulting, Jonah Bishop specifically. Both of them had kept an animal bone. But Maya couldn't ignore the most damning connection of all: If Sara never took that necklace off, how had Harley gotten it?

Was it possible Sara was still alive? Probably not, or she would have contacted Ryan. Harley must've found that locket somewhere—or found her body. Dread coursed through her. Why hadn't he told anyone?

A few blocks from her apartment, Maya stopped at a stop sign. The Corolla's engine sputtered once, then died. She cranked the key in the ignition, pumped the gas pedal, let the clutch on and off. Nothing worked. Finally, she let the car roll downhill to the curb. She parked it, wheels askew, and walked home in the dark.

On the bottom step was a muddy footprint. Heart thudding, she followed the muddy trail up the stairs. When she got to the top, the footprints turned and headed back down. Maya searched for other signs of intruders, but didn't find any. There wasn't a scratch on the lock. Still, she held her breath until she'd gotten inside and fastened the new chain behind her.

Her apartment felt very quiet. Isolated. She flipped on every light. Maybe she should've kept those gerbils. They were a pain, but they were also company. Maya grimaced. Great—if she was calling gerbils "company," her social life could be summed up in one word: pitiful.

The light on her answering machine blinked with a message. It was Ryan.

"That phone call I got was the cops," he said. "They found Sara's bike in the bay. Tomorrow, divers will search for—" His voice strangled with emotion, and the message cut off abruptly.

Maya closed her eyes. They'd found Sara's bike in the bay? That sounded a lot like "the bottom of the ocean." She'd better tell Ryan what Tomas had said.

She used *69 to reach him. His phone rang several times before going to voice mail, and she left a message, asking him to call her.

Seconds later, her phone rang. She tripped over Harley's mountain bike as she lunged for it. "Hello? Ryan?"

The caller didn't say anything. "Who *is* this?" she snapped.

"Maya, it's Nick." Then, "Who is Ryan?" His voice was gruff.

"Just a friend." Was Nick jealous? Despite what he'd said at the coffee shop this morning, she hadn't expected to hear from him so soon.

"Oh." A long pause. "I was calling to see if you wanted to go out tonight."

"*Tonight?*" Her breath caught. She couldn't go out—not picturing lockets and bones and Sara's bike at the bottom of Yaquina Bay. "I'm sorry . . . I can't."

"What's wrong?" he asked.

Maya drew a ragged breath. "Did you hear about Sara?"

"No." His voice turned sharp. "What about her?"

"A diver found her bike in the bay."

"In the *bay*? What do they think happened?"

"I don't know. I just heard from her boyfriend. That's who I was expecting on the phone."

Nick was silent. When he finally spoke, he sounded just as distressed as she was. "I can't believe this," he said. "I was on those search crews. We looked everywhere. But the bay—" His voice choked off. "I just can't believe it."

"I know. It's awful."

"Is it all right if I come over?" he asked. "I just need someone to talk to."

Maya gulped. She did want to see him, and he really sounded miserable . . . but tonight wasn't the best plan. She was feeling too fragile, too likely to reveal things better left unsaid. She couldn't tell the Coast Defenders about Harley and the locket. She just couldn't.

"Maya?" he said. "Is that okay?"

"I'm sorry. I . . . can't. Not tonight."

"How about tomorrow? I'd really like to see you."

Her defenses dropped. "All right."

"Dinner? Around seven-thirty?"

"Sure. I'll see you then." She hung up.

According to Ryan, Sara had been *wearing* that locket when she disappeared. Hearing that she never took it off—it rocked Maya's faith in Harley. Of course he hadn't hurt Sara, but the locket proved he knew something about her disappearance. Why had he kept it a secret?

She walked into the kitchen and dug out the tequila bottle. Ever since that awful microwave quesadilla with Allison, she'd been craving a margarita. Too tired to blend one, she poured liquor and margarita mix on the rocks and downed the drink.

She took the locket baggie out of her jacket. Where had Harley found this? He must have stumbled onto it while helping to search for Sara. But then, why hide it? He didn't trust the police, sure, but the locket could have helped them find Sara. Or find the person who'd harmed her.

Her fingers closed around the bag, trapping the locket in her palm. If she turned this in now, would they arrest her for withholding evidence?

Maya desperately wanted to talk this through with someone, but Allison didn't want to hear it. She couldn't trust the Coast Defenders, not even Nick. She couldn't tell Ryan. She'd never felt so alone.

Did anyone else know that Harley had this locket? She froze. Maybe that's why the intruder had broken into her apartment. Why Tomas wanted the files. He'd been trying to find this.

Maya chugged the last drops from the glass and crunched on an ice cube. If the Newport Nature Tours fire had been intended to take Harley out of the picture, it might not relate to the vandalism at all. Perhaps he'd witnessed—or discovered—what had happened to Sara, and the person responsible had silenced him.

Maya set the glass down hard. This was too much to think about. In the morning, after a good night's rest, she'd decide what to do. She hid the locket under a stack of folded blankets in her closet.

Before getting into bed, she triple-checked the door chain and searched for a weapon to replace the driftwood. Feeling a bit silly, she got a large frying pan from the kitchen cupboard and set it on her nightstand.

Eventually, she fell into a restless sleep, the dark corners of her mind grasping at strange, jumbled dreams. She awoke, sweating, then dozed back off to nightmares. Bones jutted out of the ground and a locket lay in the dirt, its leather strap tangled. A menacing man climbed out of a white truck and strode toward her. Tomas grabbed her neck and squeezed. "You don't belong here," he said. "You're going to end up like Sara."

She ran for her life as a black truck chased her along the riverbank. The faster she ran, the closer it came. In front of her, a dead squirrel lay in the road, surrounded by a circle of blood.

A noise penetrated her dream, and she awoke abruptly. What was that creaking? Heart pounding, she listened. Something clattered against the apartment's siding. The wind must be howling. This old house groaned with every gust—amazing it was still standing.

Another loud creak. Giving up on sleep, Maya climbed out of bed, carrying the frying pan with her into the kitchen. Everything seemed normal. Quiet, except for the wind.

She returned the pan to the cupboard, poured herself a glass of milk, and sipped it slowly, wishing Emma was back from Seattle.

There was a thump outside her front door.

Milk glass in hand, she tiptoed through the hall and put an ear to the wood. The chain was in place, blocking entry, but still . . . were those footsteps? Coming up or going down?

There was no eyehole to look through. All she could do was listen.

Another footstep. Closer.

Should I get the pan?

Step. Step. Step. They weren't trying to mask their presence.

The doorknob turned slowly. Right, then left. Someone with a key? Her eyes darted to the flimsy chain as the knob rotated again.

Giving a sharp cry, Maya dropped the glass of milk. It shattered on the floor, and white liquid splashed everywhere. She reached for the porch light and flipped it on.

Heavy footsteps thudded down the stairs.

She stood there, breathing hard, and put her ear to the wood again. No sound.

Leaving the chain in place, she opened the door a crack and peered out. Nobody was on her porch or the steps. Heart hammering, she undid the chain and opened the door wider.

Fresh muddy footprints led down the stairs to the yard.

With a gasp, she slammed the door closed. She cleaned up the glass shards and milk residue and got the pan back out of the cupboard. When she returned to bed, sleep eluded her.

. . . .

Morning came too quickly. The scent of stale alcohol filled her nostrils and the creases of her lips were lined with cottonmouth. Maya dragged her body out of bed. Memory returned, unwelcome. The cops had found Sara's bike and Harley had her locket.

She stared outside. Rain dripped down the kitchen windows and the dark clouds hung so low, everything appeared muted. The morning called for strong coffee, and she was chagrined to find the bag empty.

163

Desperate, she shook a few loose grains onto a spoon and licked it clean. It wasn't enough to chase the fuzz from her brain.

What had that person wanted last night? Why had they climbed her stairs?

She ran to the hall and opened the front door. The muddy footprints on the treads were gone, washed away by rain. She stared down at the barren yard. In the mud was the faint outline of a bike tire. Left over from when she'd brought Harley's bike home—or her nighttime visitor?

Shaken, Maya went back inside. She paced the apartment for a few minutes, then decided that keeping busy would be the best way to shake her restlessness. She reached for her iPod, blasting an old Bonnie Raitt song, "Angel of Montgomery," as she did the dishes, scrubbed the kitchen counters, and scoured the bathtub ring. She belted out the blues, refusing to think about intruders and stalkers. Refusing to think about how Harley had gotten Sara's locket.

She moved into the bedroom to pick up her dirty clothes and found her closet door ajar. Before shutting it, she looked inside. She'd put the locket in here, but the folded blankets now lay on the floor in a messy pile. Had they fallen overnight? Her heart thumped rapidly as she leaned down and moved the last blanket aside.

The silver locket was still there.

Feeling even more troubled, she re-stacked the blankets, then checked her dresser drawer. Everything was fine—her underwear and bras, Harley's photos in the wooden box, the bone, and the envelope of Allison's cash. All here.

Nobody's been inside your apartment, she told herself. *They got what they wanted the first time.* Unease rippled through her. If Tomas suspected she had one box of files left, he might assume she had the locket, too.

She couldn't stop thinking about his "friendly" warning. Had he really known where they'd find Sara's bike—or was "the bottom of the ocean" a wild guess? He kept showing up wherever Maya went. Maybe she should check her car for a GPS receiver. No. Her broken-down car wasn't going anywhere today.

She gave herself a shake. Tomas wasn't going to scare her off. All these strange things happening—it meant she was close to finding the truth. And Harley was her *brother*. He'd never stopped caring about her, even during their years apart. He'd found her this apartment when she'd moved to Newport, promised to kick Frank's cheating ass if he ever came to town. Harley had been there for her. It was her turn. She couldn't abandon him.

But where should she start? Maybe she could figure out why he and Sara had both tried to contact Jonah Bishop. BEC seemed like a vortex that lured in Coast Defenders. Sara had called Jonah, then disappeared. Harley had taken a picture of their truck, possibly called Jonah, and then died. And the moment she'd arrived at their building yesterday, Tomas had showed up and told her to butt out.

Maya couldn't find the brochure with Jonah Bishop's direct line—stolen along with the files?—so she grabbed the scrap of paper from the library and dialed the business number.

"Bishop Environmental Consulting." The woman sounded sour, as if it were a major imposition to answer the ringing phone.

"I'd like to speak with someone about setting up an appointment with Jonah Bishop." Maya held the phone tightly.

"One moment."

"Bishop here." His voice was curt.

Oh. She hadn't expected the owner himself. Flustered, she blurted out, "Sorry. Wrong number."

Click. He hung up before she could.

Maya took a deep breath and dialed the business number again. "Jonah Bishop, please."

He came on the line, sounding just as busy and impatient as before. "Bishop."

"My name is Maya. I'm Harley Rivers' sister."

Silence. Then, "What do you want?"

"My brother had your name and phone number. I'm wondering if he talked with you about anything, before he died."

A longer silence. Eventually, he said, "Harley did contact me, but we never had the chance to talk."

So he *had* called this guy. "Could I meet with you?"

"I'm horribly busy. We're short-staffed. Just lost an administrative assistant."

"Would later in the week work?"

"I doubt I could be any help."

"But—" She was speaking to air. He'd hung up.

The BEC connection was a real puzzle. Jonah claimed he hadn't met Harley, but what about Sara? Surely the police had followed up on her cell phone records. And then there was the man who'd met Doug

Sammish, the owner of that gold Escalade. But why would he drive by Allison's house? What did all this contact with BEC mean?

Maya paced her apartment. *No money. No job. Plenty of free time.*

Then a bold idea popped into her head. Jonah Bishop had said they were short an administrative assistant. What if a qualified employee showed up on his doorstep, job hunting?

It wouldn't work for her to be Maya Rivers, Harley's sister and a former Clam Strip waitress. She'd have to become someone else.

Thirty-One

Maya knew exactly who to call—her friend Lydia in Sacramento. And Lydia was not only home, but excited to help. "I see something called 'Omega Environmental' listed. But their web site is pretty bare-bones. I can't even find their phone number."

"That sounds perfect." Maya filled her in on the plan.

"I miss you," Lydia said. "When are you going to leave that rain-soaked fishing village and return to sunny California?"

Maya laughed. "Newport's not as bad as my mom makes it sound. You should come visit sometime."

"I ran into her the other day, you know. She wants me to lobby you to move back home. She thinks you could be roomies."

"Sheesh, what a depressing thought."

"You're coming for the wedding, right?" Lydia said. "I'm counting on you to keep me sane."

"I'll be there." As Maya hung up, she realized how much she missed her longtime friends. She'd fled to Newport seeking a fresh start, a chance to reconnect with Harley and heal her wounds from Frank. But now . . . what *was* holding her here? Allison, who was barely speaking to her. Her memories of Harley. And, of course, that little baby she really, really wanted Allison to keep.

She couldn't give up yet.

Maya waited a half hour, then called BEC again, claiming to be Laura Miller, a brand-new arrival in town. She made an appointment for an informational interview with Jonah Bishop for three o'clock this afternoon. It was charming how he'd suddenly become available when she didn't mention Harley's name.

The dripping rain had turned into a downpour by the time she jogged down the stairs from her apartment, and her Corolla was parked three long blocks away. As if they'd heard her complain, the dark clouds unleashed their fury. Maya was drenched when she reached the car, only to find the engine still wouldn't start.

She sprinted back home. In the bathroom, she hung her wet clothes over the shower rod and put on a wool sweater and dry jeans.

Harley's mountain bike was taking up space in her hall. Maya looked at the rain pounding the windows and back at the bike.

. . . .

She rode on the sidewalk next to Highway 101, squinting into the wind and envying the warm, dry occupants of each car that passed her. The mountain bike's tires whirred across wet pavement, flinging water up her back. Raindrops dripped off her nose. As she rode past the taxidermy shop, she considered stopping in to say hi to Dan. But she probably looked like a drowned rat, and it was already 10:30 a.m. She needed to put her plan into action.

At the drive-through espresso, she counted out tip money from her final shift at the Clam Strip, treating herself to a large coffee and a cranberry-hazelnut scone. Now for the disguise.

The antique mall netted her a pair of vintage tortoiseshell-frame glasses. At the grocery store, she added a box of "Dark Chocolate" hair color—and a bag of the local Killer Coffee.

Her last stop was Cheap Cutz. Maya had to wait twenty minutes for an open chair, plenty of time to question her bold plan. She picked up *People* magazine and tried to relax, humming along with Kelly Clarkson singing "Stronger" from the salon's speakers. *That's right. What doesn't kill me . . .*

When it was finally Maya's turn, she told the hairdresser, a woman named Tammy, she wanted something "short and professional." Eyeing Tammy's blue-and-purple-streaked hair, she decided she'd better clarify. "Nothing shorter than here." She held a hand to her jaw.

"That'll look good on you," Tammy said. Maya climbed into the chair and stared in the mirror. Her bangs hung low over her eyebrows and shaggy curls obscured her cheekbones. She closed her eyes as Tammy started spritzing her hair with a spray bottle to dampen it.

The hairdresser ran a comb through Maya's gnarled curls, then pinned up a section and started cutting. Inches of hair fell to the floor. "So why the drastic change? Your boyfriend just became an ex?"

Maya laughed. "My husband. But that was months ago. I'm over it." *Maybe she was.* Frank had barely entered her thoughts in the last twenty-four hours; she'd been too caught up in the mysteries surrounding Harley's death. Thinking of Sara and the locket, she frowned.

Tammy stopped cutting. "Too short? I don't want any tears."

"No regrets," Maya said firmly. She sat up straighter in the chair, and they made small talk until the blow dryer overwhelmed conversation.

"Spunky," Tammy pronounced. "I like it."

Maya stared at her reflection. The overgrown, frizzy curls were gone. In their place, a chin-length bob, with soft waves brushing her cheeks and wispy bangs over her forehead. Pleased, she left a large tip.

She rode home, puffing as she carried Harley's heavy bike up the stairs to her apartment. After a quick porch inspection and making sure no intruders were inside her apartment, Maya raided the cereal cupboard, eating Captain Crunch out of the box while listening to a phone message. Her elderly landlord had called to "remind" her that rent was due soon.

She paced her tiny kitchen, three steps one way and three steps the other. The math was simple. She didn't have enough money for both rent and car repairs. Except for the thick envelope of cash sitting in her dresser drawer. *Which isn't yours*, her conscience chided.

She walked into the bathroom and opened the box of hair color. After reading the instructions, she put on gloves, tossed a towel over her shoulders, and scrubbed in the dark dye.

Could she really pull this off? She'd never met Jonah Bishop, so he couldn't possibly recognize her as Harley's sister. But so many things had to fall into place. He had to believe her resume. He had to want to hire her. She needed to transform herself into an irresistible employee.

Maya fretted. Maybe she should reveal everything to the cops and let them handle it. *No.* They probably wouldn't believe her. And it was police bungling that had gotten Harley in trouble. She could do this alone. She'd just have to be careful. The other two people who'd tried to talk to Jonah were *gone.*

Maya blow-dried her hair and studied the new style in the bathroom mirror. She didn't look anything like herself, not with this dark shade and the sleek waves. When she turned her head to one side, the strands swung neatly into place.

She excavated her closet, searching for work clothes from the days before low-cut sailor blouses and miniskirts. After putting on black slacks and a purple turtleneck sweater, she applied makeup to cover the bruises on her forehead and wrist.

Maya practiced in front of the mirror, slipping on the glasses from the antique mall. "Hi, I'm Laura Miller. Nice to meet you." The prescription on the glasses was strong, and she had to squint to see. She took them off.

Her bulletin board was still plastered with pink sticky notes that verged on the ridiculous: *Hurrah for waitressing! A satisfying career!* Maya

169

threw a few darts for fun and then pulled off the notes and tossed them into the wastebasket. Goodbye, Clam Strip.

The view from her window showed the rain had slowed, but the wind still blew hard. No sign of letting up. She couldn't ride Harley's bike miles and miles to her interview, or she'd arrive looking like a wind-whipped seagull.

She hesitated before grabbing a stack of fifty-dollar bills out of the envelope in her dresser drawer. *I'll pay Allison back every penny.*

Thirty-Two

Maya hiked over to Highway 101, heading for Rent-A-Dent. Flapping blue-and-white flags marked the edges of the lot, while bundles of yellow balloons whipped around with each wind gust. To her disappointment, the Rent-A-Dent lot was nearly empty. Only two vehicles were left—a 15-passenger van with a cracked front windshield, and a Buick Skylark, circa 1970s, in bubble-gum pink.

Maya walked over to the Skylark. It looked hand painted, as if someone had spilled a bottle of "I Luv Pink" nail polish over it and smeared it around with a brush.

The rain had softened, leaving behind misty air, a few puddles in the lot, and steam rising off the pavement. Her carefully straightened hair started to curl.

The Skylark was ugly and way too big. She eyed the sales price on the sticker—$1,600—and the note that said it was available for rent for "only" sixteen dollars a day. A fluorescent green tag on the passenger window read "CREDIT CARD REQUIRED FOR RENTAL."

Too bad it didn't say "no credit, no problem." This had been a hassle ever since Frank went on his spending spree. Maya was living without credit cards for the moment.

As she turned to walk away, a salesman came jogging out to greet her. His comb-over stood straight up in the wind, and he reached up to flatten the wisps into place. He wore navy slacks and a polo shirt, with a forest-green jacket that read "Ted" in cursive lettering. The jacket, like the Rent-A-Dent vehicles, had seen better days.

"Well, hello there!" Ted took her hand and pumped it up and down. "I mean, Konnichiwa."

She raised an eyebrow and retrieved her hand.

"I was in the middle of my online lesson," he said. "Japanese. I'm hoping to travel to the islands this summer."

"Well, Konnichiwa back."

"If you're looking for a car, you've come to the right place." His smile displayed bleached-white teeth. "I'm Ted. And you are?"

"Laura." She tried out the name.

"You ready to buy, Laura?" He gave the Skylark a tender pat.

"Actually, rent. Is this all you have?" She gestured toward the Skylark's scraped door. Pink wasn't exactly the color for keeping a low profile.

"Three cars went out earlier this week. What we have left is the van or this beauty." He smiled again. Another flash of blinding white teeth. "Let me show you its special features." He demonstrated the locking glove box, AM/FM radio, and automatic transmission before his sales pitch concluded with, "And what a sporty shade!"

"It's kind of, I don't know . . . garish."

Ted's face fell. The wind gusted, whipping his hair straight up again, and he smoothed it with both hands. "Tell you what, Laura. I'll knock five percent off the rental fee. With a license and a credit card, you can drive it off the lot right now."

She calculated the discount—a whopping eighty cents a day. What should she say about the credit card? Ted seemed anxious to get rid of the Skylark; maybe he'd be flexible. "How old is this car?"

He ran a loving hand across its flank, brushing off the water drops. "It's a classic, fourth-generation Buick. A powerful V-8. They don't make 'em like this anymore."

He opened up the hood and Maya obligingly admired the engine's tubes and wires. Maybe if she waited until the last minute, when they'd already filled out the paperwork, to mention her lack of credit . . .

He closed the hood, and she gazed down at the massive expanse of pink.

"So, Laura?"

Every time he repeated her fake name, she couldn't help wincing. Guess she'd have to get used to it. "You sure you don't have anything else? Something less bright?"

"No." He shook his head. "I shouldn't tell you this, but the Skylark's been sitting in the lot for weeks. Nobody seems to appreciate the color." He paused. "I'll make you a great deal. Ten percent off."

"How about twenty? I bet this thing really guzzles gas."

Ted nodded. "Okay. Twenty percent."

"Deal." Maya followed him into the trailer.

"Your license and credit card, please," he said. When she handed him her driver's license, he squinted at the ID. "This says Maya. Why'd you tell me your name was Laura?"

"It's . . . a nickname."

His eyes darted between the license photo and her now-dark hair. "This is out-of-state. And the picture doesn't look anything like you."

"They never do."

He gave her a suspicious glance.

"Look, I just dyed my hair." She leaned over the counter so he could get a whiff of chemicals. "It's me. Really." She made the same unsmiling face she had for the woman at the California DMV.

He scrutinized her again as he copied down her driver's license number. "Okay, MasterCard or Visa?" He looked up expectantly.

"I, uh, don't exactly have a credit card."

Ted pulled the paperwork back behind the counter. "Too bad." He tapped a small metal sign, engraved in capital letters. "We *require* credit cards for rental."

"Could I pay a cash deposit?"

He tapped the sign again. "Rules are rules."

"You said the car's been sitting here for weeks," she tried. "You might as well have it out and about making money." Ted didn't seem swayed. "Please?" she begged. "I need it for a job interview this afternoon. My own car got smashed in a hit-and-run."

He frowned. "You'd bring the Skylark back in good shape?"

"Of course." She nodded enthusiastically.

At last, he slapped the rental contract back onto the counter. "I suppose I can overlook the credit card, just this once, *Maya*. But I'll need a $400 cash deposit. And the rental will cost you an extra twelve bucks a day for insurance."

Oh, dear. If she spent four hundred dollars from the envelope, she'd owe Allison a chunk of change. And then, how would she pay for repairing her Corolla? But she desperately needed transportation. Jonah Bishop awaited. Once she got her own car fixed, she could return the Skylark and get the deposit back, minus the rental fee. It would all work out.

"Okay." She unrolled eight fifties from her pocketful of cash. Ted's eyes widened, but he accepted it. She took the keys. Two hours until showtime.

As she climbed into the Skylark, a black truck passed the Rent-A-Dent lot. She craned her neck to look. It was Tomas. Had he followed her here? Remembering her disguise and the unfamiliar car, she convinced herself it was coincidence. This place was pretty close to the Coast Defenders' house.

She swung the Skylark onto Highway 101, nearly taking out a compact car in the other lane. *Buckle up, baby.* She'd have to remember this Pink Beast turned like an oil tanker, or she'd never make it through the week alive. She checked the rearview mirror. Tomas' truck was nowhere to be seen.

Maya drove to the library, where she boned up on news stories about BEC and took a quick tour through their web site, as well as that for Omega Environmental, her so-called "former employer."

Outside the copy shop, she attempted to parallel park in a spot her Corolla would have fit into easily. She finally wrenched in the Pink Beast, too far from the curb.

Her resume took longer than expected. Should she claim laboratory assistant in her last job? No, that'd be tough to fake. She made herself an administrative assistant, but added a science degree. It wasn't often she got the chance to reinvent herself.

After the printer jammed twice, and the clerk insisted on reprinting her resume on "nice thick paper," Maya started to panic. She hustled out to the car, holding two copies of the resume she'd created out of thin air.

Other than its wide turning radius, the Skylark was a sweet ride— spacious seats, no duct tape holding up the driver's window, and the defroster actually worked. Maya fiddled with the radio until she found a palatable station and sank back into the grooved vinyl seats. A female country singer wailed a mournful "I got screwed and then he left me" ballad, one that made Maya's life sound pretty darn good in comparison.

Jonah Bishop was expecting her momentarily. The bait was ready. The only question was: would he bite?

Thirty-Three

A long line of cars crawled down Bay Boulevard. Every few feet, another minivan of tourists slowed to rubberneck at the ocean-scene murals painted on the walls of the seafood processing plants. Moms, dads and kids ambled across the street while dipping into bags of salt-water taffy or caramel corn. One by one, vehicles squeezed through the three-way stop, and then traffic stalled again for a parallel parker.

Maya gritted her teeth. Jonah Bishop had offered her only fifteen minutes to chat, and waltzing in late would make a horrible impression.

The Skylark was itching to go faster. She could feel its powerful, thrumming engine, but had to ride the brakes until she got through traffic. It was now 2:58. Maya sped along the Bay Road, following it upriver.

At the BEC building, she turned into the lot. Her car rocked over uneven ruts in the gravel and she slipped the Pink Beast between a black BMW and the gold Escalade. Beamers and Cadillacs? Environmental consulting must pay well.

3:05 p.m. Maya brushed her fingers through her newly short hair, put on the tortoiseshell-frame glasses, and grabbed the file folder with her resume and a slim notebook. "Go get him, *Laura*," she said and climbed out. She hurried toward BEC's front door. Maya might have doubts, but Laura was eminently qualified. Laura was going to get this job.

The toe of her shoe caught in the deeply rutted gravel. She stumbled and her tortoiseshell glasses fell to the ground. Before she could stop herself, her foot crunched down on the eyepiece. *Oh, no.* She picked up the cracked glasses and shoved them into her pants pocket, feeling naked without them.

Maya pulled open BEC's door and entered the lobby. Unopened mail cluttered the front desk, and there was no sign of a receptionist. Across the expanse of gray carpet, two doors beckoned, one closed, one open. She hurried toward the open doorway. The desktop was clear, the bookcase empty—a vacant office.

"Have trouble finding us?" a voice boomed behind her.

Maya jumped in surprise, and her arm flailed, connecting with rock-hard flesh. Startled, the man stepped back, rubbing his chest. He wasn't tall, but he looked athletic, like he spent weekends toning his body at the gym—or maybe kayaking. He wore khaki slacks and a royal blue shirt, both pressed with neat creases.

She choked back a gasp. She'd seen this guy in the Clam Strip before, talking to Willy. What if he recognized her?

"Are you Jonah?" Her voice came out in a squeak. Oh, she was nailing this so far—five minutes late, she'd whacked her future boss in the pecs, and now she was so edgy, she could barely speak. Maya took a deep breath and tried again. "I'm sorry about bumping you. And about being late. Traffic was horrible." She couldn't look straight at him; he might realize he knew her.

"Laura, I presume?"

She nodded. "Laura Miller." This time her voice came out stronger.

"I've only got a few minutes. Let's talk in my office." He walked her next door to a large room with a picture window overlooking the Yaquina River. Sunlight broke through the clouds, making the water glisten. His office had a modern, Scandinavian-style desk with matching shelving units. A huge flat-screen monitor sat on the desktop, with mountains of paper surrounding it.

As she sat down, her gaze caught on the newspaper sitting on top of his piles. The photo showed a diver in a wetsuit, and a bicycle being pulled out of the bay. Sara's bike? Her voice shook as she said, "I'd love to learn more about the work BEC does."

"Sure, I can tell you about our company."

Maya glanced at the newspaper photo again. *Forget about Sara. Focus.* "I'm actually hoping to find work as an administrative assistant. I used to work at a small lab in Sacramento." At least she didn't choke on the lie.

Jonah perked up. "Really? Which lab did you work at?"

"It's called Omega Environmental."

"I haven't heard of it," he said.

"It's a very small company. Not many people have. Anyway, when I moved to Newport and heard about BEC, I wondered if you had any job openings."

"We're not hiring. But I'd be happy to tell you about the work we do."

Not hiring? "I appreciate you taking the time."

He checked his computer screen. "We've got, oh, ten minutes." He leaned back in his chair and started talking. "A lot of our work involves helping developers plan their projects so they have less impact on rivers, wetlands and wildlife habitat. We provide scientific data to assist them in making smart choices. Balancing the need to preserve and protect the environment with the need for economic development."

"It sounds very green," she said.

"That's right." He turned a photo around on his desk so she could see it. Sure enough, he was kayaking at sunset, the arching Yaquina Bay Bridge in the background. "I grew up in Waldport, spent tons of time on the water. Protecting our resources is important to me."

If he was such a gung-ho environmentalist, why was he helping Kingston cut down a forest to build a huge condo complex? Why wouldn't he talk to Sara or Harley? Her eyes strayed to the desktop. No appointment calendar; he must keep things electronic.

"Does BEC ever get involved in controversial projects?" she asked.

His eyebrows rose. "Define controversial."

"Well, say a group tries to . . . prevent a development from moving forward."

"That happens. Lots of folks see the environment in black and white. But there's plenty of gray in between."

It was risky to ask, but she might not have another chance. "I heard BEC's been involved with DreamCoast. That must be quite controversial."

His gaze sharpened. "We've finished our work there." He leaned back in his chair. "For someone who's new to town, you're certainly well informed."

"It's mentioned on your web site." But Maya took the hint and shut up. Right now she needed to get herself hired. Once she got inside . . .

There was a subtle pinging sound and Jonah said, "Excuse me." He pulled a Blackberry from his pocket, checked the number, and slid the phone back.

He didn't seem shifty or dangerous. He said all the right things. But he *had* been reading about Sara's bike. Was it more than a casual interest?

Maya was about to start her pitch for the job when his phone pinged again.

"Sorry, I've got to take this one." He said hello. "I need to talk to you, too, but someone's in my office. I'll be done in a few minutes." He ended the call. "Anything else you wanted to know?" he asked her.

"Could I leave a resume with you, in case a position opens up?"

"Well, like I said, we're not hiring at the moment. But you can leave one."

Maya handed him a copy. After he perused it, he said, "Where have you been working since you moved to Newport?"

"Nowhere yet. I've only been in town a couple of weeks. I'd love the chance to put my skills to use." She leaned forward in the chair. *Remember: eager and qualified.*

Jonah tossed her resume onto an overflowing pile of paper. "You certainly do have a strong background. I'm sorry we can't help."

Maya bit her lip. What about your administrative assistant, the one who just left? Don't you need to replace her? But Laura wasn't supposed to know that. Maybe she'd blown it with her question about DreamCoast. Or maybe he was aggravated because she'd said this was "informational" and then hit him up for a job.

"Well, thank you for your time." She hated to leave. How else could she find out why Harley and Sara had contacted Jonah? What if it explained why Harley had gone to Newport Nature Tours that night?

He stood. Their meeting was over. "Good luck with your job search."

Reluctantly, she rose to her feet.

Maya was already in the lobby when an idea struck. She hurried back to his office. "Do you ever use volunteers here? I could help out while I'm job hunting."

Jonah shook his head. "Liability issues." He picked up her resume again, and drummed his fingers on the desktop. "Tell you what, Laura. I like your persistence." He smiled. "I'd planned to wait a few weeks before bringing someone new on board, but we *could* use help around here. I'll give Omega Environmental a call."

Her heart thumped with excitement. "I've got my supervisor's direct line right here." She pulled out her notebook and rattled off her friend Lydia's cell number.

He wrote it down. "You can wait in the lobby. Close the door behind you, please."

Yikes. He was going to call right now? She sat on a chair in the open space, her legs jiggling nervously. Hopefully Lydia would recognize the area code and remember to answer her phone with "Omega."

Jonah's voice rumbled from behind his office door, but she couldn't hear what he was saying. He and Lydia talked a long time. Too long. If Lydia ran out of details about Maya's supposed job responsibilities, she'd start making things up. *Risky.*

Moisture beaded on her forehead. She strained to hear.

His office door swung open. "Come in," he said.

She went inside. Jonah looked stern. Maybe he'd researched Omega Environmental and called their real phone number.

He picked up her resume. She perched on the edge of the seat, poised for flight. Something had gone wrong. He'd seen through her disguise. Maybe he'd even recognized her voice from her earlier phone call.

Jonah looked up, and she felt like a bug caught under a magnifying glass. "Are you all right, Laura?"

She wanted to flee, but she made herself stay. "I'm fine."

"Are you sure we haven't met before? You look kind of familiar." He leaned back in his chair.

Thirty-Four

The skies had cleared to an azure blue. As Maya drove away from BEC, she felt equally sunny. Starting tomorrow, she'd be the firm's newest employee. She couldn't wait to tell Allison . . . even if Allison had made no attempt to reach out since their fight yesterday.

The Clam Strip was bustling. Maya scanned the crowded dining room. A new girl was working today—a brunette with ultra-straight hair and a curvy body. Her replacement? Allison was serving a booth in the far corner and Maya started toward her.

Crystal came flying through the kitchen door and nearly bowled her over. "Oh. My. God," she squealed, "Is that *you*, Maya? I *love* your new haircut! You look super-fab with dark hair!" In response to Crystal's declaration, nearly every customer turned to stare.

Great. She'd blown her disguise. "Thanks, Crystal. Catch you later." She scooted past the bar and hurried over to Allison. "Hey, I've got big news."

Allison glanced around furtively. "Willy says you aren't welcome in here. He thinks you're a bad influence on me."

Maya was momentarily speechless. A bad influence? That hurt. "I'm a paying customer," she said, plucking a vinyl-covered menu from Allison's arms. She headed for the only vacant table in her section—a two-top in the middle of kitchen traffic—and sat down.

Allison rushed over. "He sounds pretty serious. He doesn't want us 'mingling' with you."

Heat shot through her. "When did you start taking social advice from Willy?"

"Since I needed this job." Allison's gaze darted around again.

"He can't ban me from the Clam Strip. I'll set him straight," Maya said. "And I'm here because I need to tell you about my grand plan. And the bones."

"Bones, plural? Harley had *another* one?"

"No." Maybe she shouldn't bring up Sara's bone. "Never mind."

"I like your new hairstyle," Allison said.

"Thanks. It's for my new job. I start tomorrow."

Allison's mouth dropped. "You got a job already?" She saw Maya's black pants and turtleneck sweater. "No uniform? Lucky."

"Well . . . the position's temporary. I'm going undercover."

"Undercover?" Allison croaked.

"Starting today, I have a whole new persona." Maya motioned to her hair. "My name is now Laura."

"What do you mean by, 'My name is—'"

A plump hand wrapped over Allison's shoulder. Willy's belly was squeezed into a brown shirt as tight as a sausage casing, and his hair was slicked back. His eyes narrowed on Maya. "Didn't I fire you?"

"She's eating," Allison said. "And paying. I'm taking her order."

Willy dropped his hand from her shoulder. "Go check on your other tables, please."

Allison gave her a "what can I do?" shrug before scurrying off.

Maya turned to Willy. "What's this? Now I'm not allowed in the Clam Strip?"

"Not if you're distracting the help."

"But I need to talk to Allison."

"Come back after the rush's over." Scowling, he held out a hand for her menu.

She pretended to misunderstand. "How nice that you're helping out. I'd love a cup of chowder and the Hefeweizen. Thanks."

He snorted. "Just chowder and a beer? Hardly worth taking up a table for that." He glanced at her hair, but lumbered off without commenting.

Minutes later, he returned with the chowder and a foamy pint. "Eat quick. We got real customers waiting."

She lingered, sipping her beer and savoring every spoonful of soup. She watched Allison and the other waitresses scurry back and forth, carrying food and clearing dishes. It was sure relaxing to be on this side—especially with Willy as her server.

But why didn't he want her in here? Harley had been banned, too, and she'd never found out why. When he returned with her check, she said, "Got a sec?"

"Nope." He picked up her chowder cup and empty glass.

"What are you hiding besides those crabs?"

Willy froze, dirty dishes in hand. "I'm not hiding anything. And I did what you asked. I kept Allison, even though she's a complete mess. She can barely finish a shift without breaking into tears."

"You'd better cut her some slack." Maya stood up. "Or I'll get that picket line going." She left a tip on the table.

"Don't you worry. She's staying," Willy said.

Maya felt suddenly powerful. "C'mon. Let's talk in your office. It won't take long." She breezed through the kitchen, expecting to see Rob. But there was a new cook leaning over the fryer.

Willy followed her, moving slowly. He waved her into his office and shut the door behind them.

"What happened to Rob?" Maya asked.

Willy sat down at his desk. "He's gone. What is it you want?"

Gone? She remained standing. "Tell me about those crabs."

Willy gave a long, weary sigh. "There's not much to tell. Rob did something behind my back, and I called him on it. He tried to say it was a 'mistake,' but that's bullshit. I fired him."

"Wow," Maya said. "You're certainly on a firing spree." But why was Willy still jittery around her? If it wasn't the crabs . . . what was he nervous about? She thought for a moment. "Why were you and Harley fighting?"

Willy moistened his lips. "We had a small misunderstanding."

Her heart leapt. Finally some answers. "About what?"

"He asked me for help." Another weary sigh.

"And?"

"He wanted to set up a meeting with someone. Someone who didn't want to talk to him . . . because of the Coast Defenders' reputation." He fidgeted in his chair. "I know this person, so Harley asked if I'd smooth the way."

"Which 'person' are we talking about? Jonah Bishop?" He'd said a *meeting.*

"How—" Willy's mouth dropped. "How did you know?"

"A lucky guess. And now you've confirmed it." Her satisfaction disappeared. "But you refused to help Harley, didn't you?"

He nodded. "I felt awful about it later."

"Sure you did. What did he want to talk to Jonah about?"

"He didn't say. And I didn't ask. I was in a hurry that day. Not that it's your business, but my girlfriend's son was in town. He was waiting out front, waiting for me to take him fishing."

Maya wilted. Willy had a girlfriend? If a slob like Willy had found somebody to endure him on a regular basis, what did that say about her own sorry love life?

"You should have helped my brother," she said. "It wasn't that much to ask."

When she left his office, Willy stayed behind.

Maya found Allison in the dining room. "How soon can you take a break?"

"Not now. I have to get some orders to the kitchen." Allison brushed past.

Confused, Maya stared after her. When Allison didn't come back, she headed for the register, waiting impatiently while the new girl fumbled her way through ringing up the bill. She pressed the wrong button so many times, Maya was ready to jump behind the counter and ring up her own meal. Finally, the girl figured it out and gave her change.

Maya stalked out the front door and headed for the Pink Beast. She climbed inside. She wasn't going anywhere, not until she talked to Allison. Her shift should be done in an hour.

Maya zipped up her jacket against the chill. Rain dripped down the car windows. Watching the drops fall, she fidgeted. Willy had just confirmed she was on the right track. Her new boss might appear benign, but there was that damning Sara-Harley-Jonah link. And Willy had admitted Harley wanted to set up a meeting with Jonah. On the Bayfront?

But she couldn't forget about Tomas. Sara's bike in the bay. The vandalized sailboat. The moment she'd first arrived at BEC, Tomas had showed up, too. Were he and Jonah working together?

And then there were the two bones . . .

The long day was catching up with her. Maya's eyelids drooped. She closed her eyes for just a second.

The next thing she knew, a car was honking. She jerked awake, stunned to see Allison's Subaru had peeled out onto Highway 101—nearly hitting a sedan—and was speeding south.

O-kay. Maya wasn't driving out to Toledo again. If Allison wasn't excited to hear her big news, she knew someone who would be.

Thirty-Five

She crossed the Yaquina Bay Bridge, glancing at the familiar blue-and-white sign as she came down the hill: ENTERING TSUNAMI HAZARD ZONE. The image showed a stick person trying to flee the huge, devastating wave behind him. She could relate.

Maya turned onto the road leading to the El Capitan Marina. The bay's mudflats were exposed, leaving shallow puddles of water near shore. Had the divers discovered Sara's body yet? Poor Ryan. Finding her bike there wasn't an uplifting sign.

In the dim afternoon light, the marina looked dreary. As Maya walked down the dock, something splashed in the water, startling her.

She stopped next to the *Lucky Charm*. "Ryan, are you here?" The boat appeared closed up and vacant. No barking dog. She climbed on board. "Ryan?"

He didn't answer.

The cabin was locked up tight, so Maya poked around the boat deck. One of his surfboards was missing. She glanced up. Metal cords pinged against the mast, but the flag at the top was barely fluttering. Maybe he'd taken advantage of the calm winds and gone surfing.

She'd been sure he would be here, waiting for news of Sara. Maya walked back to the Pink Beast and searched for a pen to leave a note. Of course the rental car was barren.

She was about to give up and head home when an old VW pulled into the parking lot. A long board was tied haphazardly to its roof, with the fin sticking up like a shark's.

When she walked over, Ryan did a double take. "Hey, I almost didn't recognize you." He started working on the straps tying his surfboard to the roof rack. His wetsuit was stripped down to the waist and his hair was damp. "What are you doing here?"

"Did you get my message?"

"Yeah." His eyes were bleak. "Sorry I didn't call back."

"That's okay. Thanks for letting me know about Sara's bike."

He grimaced. "Waiting around the boat today was killing me. I needed to get outside, so I headed over to Agate Beach. The surf was good."

"Have they found, uh . . . anything else?"

His face fell. "No." He turned back to the straps.

"Well, I wanted to let you know how sorry I am. About Sara."

"It wasn't your fault she disappeared."

"I still feel bad." She reminded herself of the other reason she'd come. "Remember I told you Harley had a moose bone? I could take Sara's bone—if you're willing to part with it—and find out what kind of animal it's from."

He pulled the surfboard off the VW roof and leaned it against the side. "What's that going to do?"

"Well, if we knew what kind of bone it was, maybe we could figure out where she got it. What she was working on. I know a guy who might be able to identify it."

Ryan opened the car door, grabbed a duffel bag, and dropped it on the gravel. "I don't really see the point, but if you want the bone, fine. Don't know what I'm going to do with it."

Maya picked up the bag and he took the board. When they reached the *Lucky Charm*, he dumped everything on the boat deck, went down the stairs, and came up holding the cardboard box. He handed it to her.

"Thanks. I'll let you know what I find out."

He shrugged. "Fine."

"Where's Domino? Isn't he your security system?"

"I left him with a friend. Someone who has a real backyard."

Boy, Ryan sure seemed beaten down—the past twenty-four hours must have been rough. "I have some good news," she said.

He looked at her, eyes dull. "What's that?"

"I met with Jonah Bishop this afternoon. He doesn't know I'm Harley's sister, so I got him to offer me a job. I'm starting work at BEC tomorrow. And once I'm there, I can find out why Sara wanted to meet with him."

Ryan's eyes blazed with interest, then the light disappeared. "That's not going to bring her back, is it?"

Maya felt awful pressing him when he was so obviously distraught, but she needed to know. "I'm sorry to keep asking questions, but did Sara ever mention any concerns she had about Tomas Black?"

His hands dropped to his sides. "I told you. She didn't talk about the group."

"So she didn't say anything about meeting another Coast Defender that night? Either Tomas or . . . Harley."

"No."

"I read in a newspaper article that someone saw her riding her mountain bike south of town. Can you think of any place she might have gone?"

Ryan's shoulders slumped. "I don't feel like dredging this up. Not now." He motioned to the shoebox. "You can keep the bone."

She thanked him and hurried up the dock to shore. He was staring out at the bay, his eyes focused on the rippling water.

. . . .

The sun hung low over the ocean as Maya drove south on Highway 101, leaving the city behind. After she passed South Beach State Park and the Southshore housing development, the highway became more rural, with only a few businesses and homes tucked into the trees. Most driveways on the ocean side had signs saying: *Private: No Beach Access.*

She kept driving. DreamCoast was south of town, but she didn't know how far. Was it bikeable? Sara had been heavily involved in that project, so she might have visited the site recently. And Harley *had* saved that brochure . . .

Maya spotted a wide driveway with an enormous billboard claiming "DreamCoast—Don't miss a day living out your dreams! Luxury condos available soon!" As she turned onto the paved road, she checked her odometer: a fair distance on a mountain bike, especially at night.

The road twisted east, climbing into the tree-lined hills. She drove about a half mile before she went around a curve and had to slam on the brakes. A swing-style gate blocked entrance, with a heavy chain and padlock holding it closed.

Maya parked off to one side, hiding the shoebox with Sara's bone under the car seat.

She climbed over the gate and started hiking up the road. Dark woods loomed on both sides, casting shadows across the pavement. Freshly poured pavement. The air was moist and misty, and her breath emerged in white puffs. Any vestiges of daylight were quickly masked by clouds.

She kept walking, glancing around nervously as she got farther from the car. Were there wild animals in these woods? It was kind of spooky here, especially being alone. Her heart pounded as she conjured up images from an old horror movie—campers screaming through the woods, tripping over tree roots as they tried to flee a giant, man-eating Sasquatch.

After a few more minutes of uphill hiking, Maya stopped. She still hadn't reached the construction site. Why had she come here, anyway? It wasn't like she'd stumble across some magical clue after hundreds of searchers had failed. And Sara's bike had been found in the bay, miles away from here.

Her breath was heavy, roaring in her ears. If she really wanted to see DreamCoast, she should come back in the morning, when things weren't so . . . quiet.

She turned around and walked down the hill. She wasn't leaving because she was scared. No—she had things to do: research at the library, maybe stop by the taxidermy shop to ask Dan about Sara's bone. Both places would close soon.

She'd better get going.

. . . .

It took numerous back-and-forths to turn the Pink Beast around on the narrow road, and Maya was sweating by the time she reached Newport. She drove by Dan's shop, disappointed to find it dark. She pulled over to read the hours. He closed at five? She'd have to bring him Sara's bone during her lunch break tomorrow. If BEC allowed lunch breaks.

At the library, Maya walked downstairs to the computer station. This was starting to feel like her second home. She plunked into a chair. Ryan's lack of enthusiasm about the BEC job was discouraging, but she understood. He was hurting. He didn't know if the bay was going to reveal Sara's body as well. Just like she didn't know what had happened to Harley.

Maya studied BEC's web site as if she were cramming for a test, scanning each web page and committing the facts to memory. She wanted to be prepared.

After she finished, she Googled "Sara Blessing." The lead story was about a recreational scuba diver who'd discovered her mountain bike submerged in the bay, not far from the public fishing pier. A team of divers was now searching for Sara's body around the pier and under the Yaquina Bay Bridge. Just in case she'd jumped.

It was possible. But that wouldn't explain Harley having her locket.

Maya logged off the computer. What did Tomas know about Sara and her bike? *Had* he been on the Bayfront with her brother?

Maybe it was time to track down Trent Lindberg and ask.

Thirty-Six

Maya parked in the hospital lot and hurried inside the building, hoping the visiting hours were still going. She stopped at the reception desk, bouquet in hand. "I'm here to see Trent Lindberg." She waved her flowers at the young, perky receptionist. Under this harsh light, her skin was a peculiar shade of orange-brown. Spray tan?

The orange-tinted receptionist started to say something, but her cell phone rang. She picked it up quickly. "O-M-G. You're kidding me," she said into the receiver. "No way. He really said . . ."

Maya paced in front of the desk, then tapped her fingers on the counter.

The receptionist continued her call. "O-M-G," she repeated. "Listen. I'm working a temp job? The hospital? And some lady needs something. Can you hold for a sec?" She set down the phone and asked Maya, "What did you want again?"

"Trent Lindberg's room."

The girl looked blank, then, "Oh, the guy from the fire?"

Maya nodded. Miss Chatty tapped her fingers on the keyboard and gave her a room number. "I don't think he's had any other visitors tonight." She turned back to her phone and squealed, "O-M-G!" a third time.

Lucky for her, the temp was free with patients' personal information.

At this time of evening, the halls were nearly empty. Detective Ames had said Trent was out of intensive care, so it should be no problem to access his room.

She passed a nursing station and held up the flowers. Her shoes squeaked on the slick floors and the air hinted of chemicals, something antiseptic.

The hospital was small, maybe thirty or forty beds. She passed two nurses speaking in hushed tones and then a heavyset woman with platinum-blonde hair who was using the drinking fountain.

Maya poked her head into Trent Lindberg's room. A man lay in the bed, his eyes closed. The sheet was pulled high. Beside the bed, a machine beeped softly, its lights flickering. She glanced around. The room was bursting with "Get Well" cards and floral arrangements.

"What are you doing in here?" The voice behind her was loud and authoritative. "Who are you?"

Maya turned, expecting a nurse. But it was the woman she'd seen by the drinking fountain. A relative of Trent's? She was wearing a sweatshirt and baggy sweatpants, and her hands rested on well-rounded hips.

"I came to say thank you to Trent." Maya held up the flowers. "Pay my respects."

"You and the rest of Newport." The woman's eyes narrowed. "I asked who you are."

"Maya Rivers," she admitted.

"Rivers? As in *Harley Rivers*?"

Maya nodded. "He was my brother." She motioned to the bed. "I've been wanting to thank Trent for trying to save Harley's life. I can't tell you how much that means."

The woman hesitated. "I'm Trent's wife, Melissa," she said finally.

"How is he doing? Is he recovering all right?"

"Better than he was."

Maya held out her mums. "These are for you." Under the stark fluorescent light, the bouquet looked cheap, a stem or two snapped, the tips of the flowers tinged dark.

"Thanks." Melissa took the bouquet and set it on a chair. The plastic crinkled.

"Is it okay if I talk with him for a couple of minutes?" Maya asked.

"He's resting." Her lips thinned. "I'll pass on your good wishes."

"But, I'd like to—" Maya slid her hands into her pockets. "Do you know why he went down to the Bayfront that night? Was he working on a boat or . . . "

Melissa frowned. "I'll pass on your good wishes," she repeated.

"I'm very sorry he got hurt. I know Harley would be, too."

"Because of that fire, because my husband could never ignore a person in need—he could be here for *weeks*." Melissa's eyes watered. "And I'm supposed to 'carry on' and pretend everything's fine. I've got a five-year-old at home who keeps crying for her Daddy—and these enormous medical bills . . . I don't know what we're going to do." She put her face in her hands.

"I'm so sorry." Maya's shoulders sagged. She should have thought this through. She shouldn't have come here and intruded on this family. If only she weren't so poor—maybe she could talk to Allison, see if there was anything they could do to help.

There was a faint noise behind then, and they both turned. Trent Lindberg's eyes had opened. Melissa rushed to the bed. "Oh, honey," she cried. "You're up."

"I'm sorry I bothered you," Maya said softly and left the room.

She slunk down the hall, feeling like weeping herself. Thanks to the fire, everyone hated Harley, and poor Trent was struggling to heal, his family devastated.

In the hospital restroom, she lingered by the sink. She'd come here for a good reason: to prove that the police were wrong about Harley. And if she understood who'd been at Newport Nature Tours with him that night—and why—she might be able to solve Sara's disappearance as well. And that would mean peace for Ryan, for Allison, for every woman in Newport who'd been terrified when Sara vanished in the night.

According to the police, Trent Lindberg was the only witness to the fire, the only person who could tell her if Tomas Black had been on the Bayfront with Harley.

She loitered by the vending machine, keeping an eye on Trent's door. When Melissa finally came out, Maya walked down the hall and scooted inside.

She stopped next to the bed. Trent's eyes fluttered open, but were unfocused. Was he awake? "Hi. I'm Maya," she whispered. "I'm really sorry to bother you, but did you see anyone else on the Bayfront that night? Anyone besides Harley?"

His eyes opened wide. Pain? Recognition? Remembering?

"Get out," a voice said behind her. "Leave him alone."

Maya turned. "I just had one question. I'm not trying to bug him. I—"

Melissa's face reddened and she shook with fury. "Security!" she bellowed, lunging for the phone on the bedside table. "I need security! Now!"

Maya fled.

When she left the hospital, the sky was dark. Fog had rolled in from the ocean, blanketing the streets with mist. It hung low, making every light look ethereal through the haze.

Visiting Trent Lindberg had been a terrible idea. She'd left Ryan's boat feeling hopeful, but now she just felt defeated.

When she reached her block, she stared through the fog. Vehicles packed both sides of the street. The only available parking spot was too small for the Skylark. She kept driving, passing a house that was blasting dance tunes. It had a "Vacation Rental" sign out front and every room glowed with light, showing silhouettes of people drinking and dancing.

She finally found a parking spot in the next block and walked back toward her apartment, carrying the shoebox with Sara's bone. As she passed the party house, a guy stumbled out the front door. He gave a drunken "Woo hoo!" and staggered back into the house.

She kept going. When she reached the corner, footsteps sounded behind her. She glanced back, but the fog made everything fuzzy.

She walked more quickly.

So did the footsteps. Her pulse quickened.

Maya searched the mist for her apartment. Both floors were dark. She tucked Sara's shoebox under her arm and picked up her pace until she was jogging. Panting, she raced down the sidewalk and up the stairs to her apartment.

The porch light was off, just the way she'd left it. She was two steps from the top when she realized someone was standing by her front door.

Waiting.

Thirty-Seven

"I've been here for thirty minutes," Nick said. "Did you forget about dinner?" His teeth chattered as he handed her a bundle of wilted red tulips.

Maya gasped for breath. "Sorry. I . . . spaced it." She juggled the shoebox and bouquet as she patted her pockets for house keys. "It's been a wild day. Thanks for the flowers."

"Why were you running in the dark?"

"Someone was following me . . ." She took another gasping breath. "You didn't see anybody on the sidewalk, coming up behind me?"

He looked at her like she was crazy.

"I did hear footsteps," she said. "It wasn't my imagination."

"It's okay. You're safe now." He shivered, his lips slightly blue. "But can we go inside? It's really cold out here."

"I'm sorry," Maya said again. She unlocked her front door and flicked the switch for the porch light. Nothing happened. She looked up at the porch ceiling. The bulb was broken; only jagged edges emerged from the socket. Eyes wild, she stared at Nick. "Did you—" She stopped herself. *Get a grip.* He invited you on a date. He brought you flowers. He didn't break your light bulb. But why . . .

"That was broken when I got here," he said.

"I'm glad you waited." Her voice was shaky. "And thanks again for the tulips."

He followed her inside, bumping into the Trek bike in the hall. "Is that Harley's?"

"Yeah. The police were done with it."

He rested a hand on the bike frame. "I learned something interesting today about Tomas' truck. I was in his room at the house, and I found a receipt for a local body shop. Looks like they did some bumper repairs recently."

"So it *was* him." Maya placed the limp tulips in a vase and set it on her kitchen table. She shouldn't be surprised. Tomas was a bully—and perhaps a murderer. A little car accident would mean nothing to him.

"Should I give you a few minutes to change?" Nick asked. "I can push back our reservation. Again." He moved closer, touching her hair. "I like the new color." His gaze was warm and teasing. Heat washed through her.

"I'll be quick." Maya hurried into the bedroom. She slipped the shoebox with Sara's bone under her bed and pulled on a camisole and short red jacket. Armed with a brush, she tamed her newly black hair into a semblance of its earlier sleekness.

When she returned to the living room, Nick was sprawled across her couch. Lounging around the apartment sounded awfully inviting— and she almost suggested they stay in. But her refrigerator was bare. And if they stayed here . . . she knew what would happen. They should take things slow, get to know each other better. She felt another rush of heat. Apparently her hormones weren't listening to reason.

She grabbed her coat. "Let's go."

"Do you mind driving?" Nick asked as they walked down the dark staircase. "I thought we'd have time to walk to the restaurant, so I rode over here." He pointed to the old Schwinn leaning against the house.

A bike? Her gaze dropped to the tires. No, they were much slimmer than the marks she'd seen in the mud last night. And too smooth. She let out a breath of relief. "I can drive, but we'll have to take my new pink car. That tree finally got the best of my Corolla. I should send the repair bill to Tomas."

"I can guarantee the jerk won't pay. He's always crying poverty."

They walked past the party house, which was blaring a rap song. Behind the lit-up windows, people danced to the beat, their arms moving in coordinated rhythm. Maya hummed along. For the first time in this stressful day, she let herself relax.

Nick whistled when they reached the Skylark. "Whew! This *is* pink." He ran a hand over the hood. "Good thing I'm comfortable with my masculinity."

"Good thing." She grinned.

When she pulled out of the parking space, his arm brushed against her thigh. She inhaled sharply. Ever since their interrupted date, her body had been primed. Seven months was a long drought, and she was more than ready for a refreshing downpour. *Deep breath, girl. You can't jump him in the car.*

"You seem a little distracted," he said.

She let out a sigh. *Was she ever.*

Nick directed her to an intimate Italian restaurant with white table-cloths, crystal wine glasses, and candles at each table. It was lovely, but as Maya studied the menu, her heart sank. Was it her turn to pay? She ordered butternut-squash ravioli, no salad, just water to drink.

"I'll have the lasagna," Nick told the waiter. "And we'll share a bottle of the Montepulciano."

The waiter said, "A fine choice, sir," and left.

Nick smiled. "Nice place, huh?"

"Sure." Another wave of worry. How much was the wine? Without a job, she had to be thrifty. Nick was still smiling at her. He'd shed his bulky parka and she could see he'd gotten dressed up: slacks and a blue shirt. His gaze met hers head-on. Suddenly nervous, she plucked a piece of focaccia from the breadbasket.

When their wine arrived, the waiter poured the glasses and left.

Nick swirled his glass. "Nice legs."

"Excuse me?" Maya stared at him.

"The wine legs. The way it hangs on the glass." He did the swirly thing again.

Was he trying to impress her? She picked up her own glass and drank. This place was not her style. Try fish and chips with a bottle of beer. But Nick was aiming for traditional romantic—flowers, a fancy dinner, wine. He continued to surprise her.

"I've been worried about your mom," she said. "Is she doing all right?"

"Yes." His face flashed with emotion. "She's trying to prepare for the surgery."

She waited for him to elaborate, but he didn't. Maybe he didn't want to be reminded. She bit her lip, unsure what to say.

Nick cocked his head, studying her with those deep brown eyes that reminded her of Harley's. "So a new haircut, new pink car. What's with the changes?"

"I'm trying to . . . get a job."

"Aren't you waitressing at the Clam Strip?"

"I got fired." Her mouth turned down.

"Well, I'm sure you'll miss those sailor outfits." He gave a laugh. "And I'll miss seeing you in them."

"Ha." One bonus of being unemployed—no more miniskirts. "Tomorrow I start temp work at . . . an office." She shouldn't advertise what she was doing, not to the Coast Defenders. A knot formed in her throat.

"Are you okay, Maya?"

No, she wasn't okay. It seemed like everyone, including Allison, had abandoned her after Harley died. Everyone except Nick.

"What is it?" he urged.

She bit her lip again. There wasn't much she could share. Nothing about Tomas or BEC, certainly. "I'm worried about Allison."

"Harley's girlfriend." He took a sip of wine. "Is she . . . pregnant?"

Maya stared. "How did you know?"

"I have an older sister with three kids. I thought I recognized the signs."

Allison had sworn her to secrecy, but if Nick already knew, did that count? "She's still hurting over Harley," Maya said. "She seems so fragile, and I'm worried about the baby. If she even keeps it. So many things can go wrong early in pregnancy . . . " her voice trailed off. Most guys would be shouting "TMI" by now. Nick was a great listener.

"I'm sure she'll be okay," he said. "But something else is bugging you. I can tell."

Was he a mind reader? She grabbed another piece of focaccia from the breadbasket. "How did you find that receipt? The one Tomas had for bumper repair."

"It was in his room, on his dresser."

"And you went in there looking for it?"

"Because you were so worried about the truck. I wanted to help." His eyes held her gaze. "And if you need anything else, just ask."

"Thanks." Maya felt a small crack in her emotional armor, but she mended it quickly. Could she trust him, or were he and Tomas buddies? Would he report back on her suspicions? "When did you first get involved with the Coast Defenders?"

"Oh." He looked startled. "Last fall. I read online about what the group was doing. I'd studied chemistry and biology in school, and . . . I've always been a huge environmentalist, so I moved up here to join. It's not what I expected, though."

"You don't sound very enthusiastic."

His face darkened. "I thought we'd be doing tree sits and peaceful protests, like the web site promised. Instead, we get blamed for setting things on fire and breaking windows. And then Sara disappears and Harley dies. I mean, hell, what's next?"

"Maybe murder."

Nick jerked in his chair. "What do you mean?"

She lowered her voice. "I found out from the police that Harley had a 'blunt-force injury' on his head. It could be the fire or . . . "

"You think someone *killed* your brother?" His eyes widened. "Who?"

"I'm just starting to put the pieces together."

"Wow." He sat back. "No wonder you're agitated. That's huge."

"Please don't tell anyone," she said. "I could be wrong." *But I'm not.*

"You've never even hinted about this. You must be freaking out." He seemed stunned.

The waiter arrived with their meals. After he left, Maya said, "Sorry. Didn't mean to dump that on you. Great date, huh?"

He took her hand. "Hey, I was the one who said, 'If you need anything, just ask.' And I meant that."

Maya let her palm rest in his. "Thank you." Her eyes filled. She was thanking him for more than he knew—being a person she could count on when she felt so alone. "We should probably talk about something else or you'll find me in tears."

"You've got it." He gave her hand a squeeze before letting go. While they ate, he told her stories about growing up on the farm and playing in the avocado groves—funny stories that kept her mind off Harley. She asked him about his science studies, and was surprised to find he'd been pre-med. He was wasting that education on the Coast Defenders.

After a while, he excused himself to use the restroom. Maya twirled her wine glass, smiling about the "nice legs." She and Nick didn't have that much in common, besides knowing Harley. But she needed this. She needed to put Frank's memory—his betrayal—to rest. Move on. She needed to set down Harley's burdens for a short while. Nick was kind. And hot. She imagined him sliding off that shirt and slacks. Hard muscles and hard . . . He returned to the table and she blushed.

He didn't sit down. "Do you want to get out of here? I can think of a dozen places I'd rather be with you right now."

She stared at him, again surprised by his ability to intuit what she was thinking. She jumped up so fast, she almost knocked over her wine glass.

The waiter rushed over. "Was everything fine with your meal?"

"Sure. We just remembered an urgent appointment." Nick handed the waiter several worn bills. "Keep the change."

As they hurried out the restaurant door, a wave of giddiness swept through her. "You want to head down to the beach? Go for a walk?"

He took her face in his hands and gave her a long, sensual kiss. "I was envisioning somewhere much more private."

Thirty-Eight

An hour later, Maya lay naked and sated on her bed. When they'd first rushed into the bedroom, Nick had started off with a sweet, tender kiss. Forget that. She'd pressed her lips into his, nipped at his tongue, demanded his full attention. He'd started panting—and things had moved quickly from there.

Now, Maya stretched across the sheets, grinning. She slid a hand up Nick's leg, exploring new territory.

He groaned in response. "You've worn me out, babe."

Babe? "Uh, can't you rest later?"

"I'm exhausted, but maybe I can lend a helping hand." His palm skimmed over her stomach, then glided lower. His fingers moved, searching for warmth, and she let out a moan. Oh, yes. Nick was very, *very* good. Before long, pleasure rolled through her. She dropped to the mattress with a happy sigh.

He flopped onto his back. Ready to crash.

Maya lay next to him. Did she want him to stay? She had to get up early for her job—the fake job. And it might be complicated to answer questions in the morning. "Uh, Nick?" She nudged him with her elbow.

"Whoa. Give me time to recover," he murmured.

Recover? Maya flung back the comforter to sit up and her elbow caught Nick in the face. "Ow!" he yelped, holding his hand over one eye.

"I'm sorry. Are you okay?"

He crawled out of the bed, still covering his face. "You bonked my eye. I have to make sure it's all right."

As he walked out of the bedroom, Maya stole a glance, admiring his lean body and the way his muscles rippled as he moved. Definitely a hottie. So why wasn't this easier? She felt so tentative around Nick— probably because Frank had left her traumatized. And then she'd been her usual klutzy self, ruining the mood.

She pulled on a robe and padded toward the bathroom. "Is there anything I can do?" she asked through the closed door.

"No. I'll be fine."

She headed back to the bedroom. After daydreaming about her chemistry with Nick, she'd had high expectations. Too high? He was a considerate lover. The rest would come with time.

When he returned, she apologized again. "I should've warned you. Klutz could be my middle name. Does it still hurt?"

He nodded. "A little."

She looked closely at his reddened eye. "I didn't know you wore contacts."

"Yep." He leaned down to pick up his jeans and slid them on, stuffing his boxer shorts into a back pocket. He picked up the spent condom and carried it to the wastebasket, looking a little sheepish. "I have to go."

"Really? Already?"

"Yeah." He leaned over for a lingering kiss. "This was great, Maya. When can I see you next?"

"Um . . ." she stalled. He was sure blowing hot and cold. "I'm not sure, exactly." She snugged the sash on her robe, suddenly uncomfortable being naked underneath.

After Nick left, she locked the apartment door and attached the chain. She'd expected fireworks, and things had started off with a bang. But then . . . Oh, well. They were still getting to know each other.

For some bizarre reason, her thoughts bounced to Dan and their easy rapport. He seemed so passionate about his work. Was he passionate about everything? She pushed the idea away. *The sheets aren't even dry, you hussy.*

The phone rang in the hallway, startling her.

"Where have you been?" Allison asked. "I stopped by your apartment earlier—after my shift ended—and your porch was all dark and your blinds closed. Where were you? You said you had big news."

"I do, but . . ." Maya bristled. *Now* she wanted to know? "I've been out. I went to visit . . . a friend, then to the library, and the hosp—I also had a date."

"A *date*? With who?"

"Nick."

Allison got very quiet. "From the Coast Defenders?"

"We've gone to dinner twice. Tonight, well . . ." Her cheeks burned. "Dinner went long. He just left."

"Oh my God. You *slept* with him? Do you even know this guy?"

"I'm getting over Frank," Maya said.

"But . . ." Allison stopped. "I thought Nick was seeing someone."

"No." Maya swallowed. "Why would you say that?"

"I saw him once with that girl from the group, the one with the black spiky hair."

"Oh, you mean Kelsey." Relief shot through her. "That's been over for a while."

"But I thought I saw . . . " Allison's voice trailed off.

"You saw what?" Her stomach churned. *Nick wasn't like Frank. Not at all.*

"I must've been mistaken," Allison murmured.

Maya shushed her doubts. Nick had told her that he and Kelsey were through. Allison must have seen the same thing Maya had—Kelsey trying to put her arm around him and Nick letting her. He'd said he didn't want to hurt her feelings.

And she wasn't going to ask for details, not when Allison was acting so disapproving about everything. Silence filled the phone line.

"So about that new job," Allison said at last. "Where will you be working?"

Maya explained about BEC. "I'm going undercover to see what I can find. They're the company working on DreamCoast."

"That's crazy," Allison said. "What if they learn who you are? It's risky, too. If people discover you lied to your employer, you may never get another job in Newport."

Maya winced. She'd spent the entire day working on her plan to get inside BEC—she'd succeeded—and all Allison could offer was *crazy* and *risky*?

She was about to end the call when Allison said, "I really don't want this strain between us. When you were at my house yesterday, I overreacted about Sara's locket. It was such an ugly surprise." She blew out a breath. "It's no excuse, but I'm so tired all the time, and I took that out on you. I shouldn't have."

"Thanks for saying that. I shouldn't have badgered you, either."

"You certainly are . . . determined," Allison said. "And I've been thinking more about what you said. I'd like to know why Harley was at the fire, why he had the locket. Can we meet tomorrow, sometime in the afternoon, to talk? I get off work at two."

Maya chewed her lip. "I'll be working then. How about later, around seven?"

"That's fine. I don't have any evening plans." Allison sounded morose.

Maya considered telling her what she'd learned by visiting Ryan, DreamCoast, and Trent Lindberg, but she felt seriously drained. She'd share the whole story tomorrow.

"Is there anything I can do between now and then to help?" Allison asked.

Maya thought. "Well, I still would like to know what happened to Harley's laptop. Nick hasn't seen it, but maybe one of the other Coast Defenders has. Stay away from Tomas, though."

"Sure." Allison's voice brightened. "I'll see you tomorrow at seven. Let's meet by the Coast Guard Station. We can walk over to that fish and chips place for dinner."

"Sounds great." Maya hung up. At moments like this, she missed Harley more than ever. But Nick was right. Nothing she could do, not even solving the arson, would bring her brother back. Maya squeezed her eyes shut, willing the tears not to start.

Before she got in bed, she leaned over and plucked a few hairs off her pillow. Long strands of straight dark hair. Nick's.

She dropped them into the wastebasket, then picked them up again. Weird. The very tips of the roots were pale, almost blond.

Thirty-Nine

Maya traipsed across BEC's parking lot, dying for some caffeine. She'd slept soundly for the first time in days, but getting out of bed had been a challenge. After hitting the snooze button four times, she'd chosen timeliness over coffee.

In retrospect, it wasn't a wise move. Her brain cells were lumbering along at half-speed. If she was going to pull off Laura Miller, the experienced administrative assistant, along with her own mission, she'd need to do some serious acting.

Maya entered the lobby and saw Jonah's office door was ajar. She walked toward it. When he glanced up, she said, "Reporting for duty."

Jonah smiled. "Right on schedule." He rummaged through the papers on his desk, muttering to himself. "Let's see. I know she left me with some paperwork. Oh, here it is." He handed Maya a piece of paper and a pen. "My office manager's out sick today, but she wants you to fill out this W-4."

Maya took the form. *Uh oh.* She hadn't considered this, but of course a new hire would require paperwork. She set the form down, her hand wavering over the signature line. Lying to the IRS? With a gulp, she invented a Social Security number and signed the form "Laura Miller." She handed it back, trying to smile.

"And your photo ID?" Her new boss held out his hand.

"Could I, um, bring that tomorrow? I misplaced my driver's license." With luck, she'd get what she needed today—before this all caught up with her.

"Tomorrow's fine." Jonah checked his watch and stood up. "Well, Laura, welcome to BEC. I'm sorry to rush off, but I have a meeting in a few minutes. Let me show you your work space."

He walked her next door to the vacant office—a whole office, just for her?—and pulled a thick binder off the bookshelf. "You can read this employee handbook," he suggested. "I have back-to-back client meetings all morning. I'm sorry to abandon you . . . we'll get started with the real work this afternoon."

"No problem." *Because the fewer tasks I have to do . . .* She set the bulky handbook on her desk. "When I finish reading this, I can see if anyone needs help."

"That'd be great. Check with Julie, our biologist, or Curt, the chemist. The rest of the staff's out in the field." He hurried off to his meeting, leaving her alone.

Alone was just fine.

She spent a few minutes exploring her new digs. The desk and recycling bin were empty and when she turned on the computer, it asked for a password. Maya flipped open the employee handbook to Page 1, Expectations for BEC Staff.

A. Dress professionally. *Check.*
B. Arrive on time. *Check.*
C. Follow all guidelines outlined in BEC's Ethics Policy. *Hmm, as long as they don't outlaw snooping.*

This was ridiculous. She wouldn't learn anything sitting inside this office. She needed more information about BEC—and DreamCoast. Would they have site photos or maps? Client reports? If she found something worthwhile, she could ask Nick to help her. Thinking of last night, she reddened. *I jumped into bed so quickly.*

She shut the employee handbook. Time to start sleuthing.

Maya strolled down the hall and found a small kitchen, where she happily chugged a mug of coffee and poured herself a refill before continuing her journey. There was a door labeled Biology Lab. She knocked and went in.

A petite woman was hunched over the counter, her back to the door. When Maya entered, she whirled around. "Oh, you startled me!" She held a pair of tweezers in her gloved fingers. "Are you Laura, the new admin?"

"I am." Maya smiled at her. The woman's hair was dyed a violent shade of red, the color of maraschino cherries. "And you must be Julie."

The woman nodded. "So what color is yours?"

Maya didn't understand what she meant until Julie motioned to her hair. Oh, she'd recognized the dye job. "It's something chocolate." With Julie's neon-red hair and fleece jacket and jeans, she wasn't at all what Maya expected when she thought biologist. Of course, Dan hadn't conformed to expectation either.

Julie pointed to a small, grayish lump on a tray. "Have you ever dissected owl pellets?"

"In middle school." Maya scooted closer. "I remember everyone freaked out about handling bird poop."

"This isn't fecal matter." Julie's expression was serious. "The owl regurgitates the hair and bones it can't digest. It hacks up the pellets through its mouth."

"That's right, I remember." Mr. Fisker had lectured the seventh-graders about their squeamishness and encouraged them to "dig in" like true scientists. "It's more vomit than poop," he'd said, generating a whole lot more screaming.

Julie returned to work, using her tweezers to break apart the lump. She started pulling out tiny white objects—long and thin, no bigger than toothpicks—and arranged them on a paper towel. She tweezed out a miniature white chunk. "There's a skull."

Maya leaned forward, fascinated. "Do you work a lot with bones?"

"Not too often. Once in a while, I'll find an animal bone at a site I'm studying. I love when that happens, because if I can identify the kind of wildlife that uses a site, I know what habitat matters most." She touched the owl pellet with her tweezers. "This is from a *Bubo virginianus*—Great Horned Owl—and he's been eating deer mice."

"Cool! You can tell what kind of rodent it is? And the owl species?"

Julie nodded.

"Have you ever found bones from wildlife that . . . don't belong there?"

"What do you mean?" Julie placed more miniature bones on the paper towel. "If an animal doesn't live in a particular habitat, it wouldn't leave bones behind. Unless scavengers brought them there." She stopped picking. "Did you find some bones?"

"No. Just curious." Maya let out a breath. *Probably shouldn't have brought that up.* She glanced around the room. On the far wall hung a large aerial photo labeled DreamCoast.

When Julie turned back to her pellet, Maya headed over. The photo showed a road winding up a hillside. In the center of the picture was a large clearing, a rectangular patch of dirt with forest on all sides. A few stumps lined the edges. Stumps, just like in Harley's pictures.

She leaned in closer. The photo was dated February 10th. Maya traced a finger along the road, the one she'd walked up yesterday. It ended at the clearing. But in this photo, the road appeared to be gravel—it had been paved recently. She should have kept walking; she'd been close to the construction site when she turned around.

"Laura?" Julie's voice intruded. "Did you hear me?"

Maya jumped. "Sorry. I was engrossed in this photo."

"It's an old one."

Maya took another quick glance. In one corner of the clearing was a small building. A roof view. Was it a construction trailer? House? She turned back to Julie. "Where are the condos? I thought they'd started building."

"They were supposed to." Julie grimaced. "It's been a crazy wet winter, lots of construction delays. And then Kingston . . . . " She stopped. "How'd you hear about DreamCoast? Jonah said you just moved to town a week ago."

"Everyone's talking about it," Maya said. "You can't help but hear. Has BEC done much work on the project?"

"I was involved in the early stages, before they harvested the timber, but Curt's spent enough time there, I wouldn't be surprised if he picks out a condo."

"Really?" Was Curt the man she'd followed from Newport Nature Tours, the driver of the gold Escalade? If he worked on DreamCoast . . .

Julie smiled. "Show him a speck of interest and he'll offer you one of these." She reached into her desk drawer and pulled out a sales brochure. It was the same one Harley had in his files.

"Now that the weather's improving, will they get back to building?"

"I'm sure they will. They paved the road recently. But then Kingston put things on hold . . . I'm not sure why. Maybe the soil needs to dry out more."

Maya winced. Or he needs a new bulldozer.

She walked back to where Julie was sitting and set her mug on the counter. "Do you need help with anything this morning?"

"I might later," Julie said, "Doesn't Jonah have work for you?"

"He was in a hurry to get to a meeting. He did leave me with the employee handbook."

Julie laughed. "You poor thing. Talk about dull reading. I can show you how the network's set up, so you'll be ready when he gets back. I know we have a bunch of reports that need editing."

Julie leaned over her Mac and clicked the mouse. The screen displayed two tidy rows of folders. "We keep most of our files on this main drive." She clicked on a few folders to demonstrate. "But some bigger projects—like DreamCoast—have their own drive. I doubt you'll be using that. It requires security access."

Maya glanced around the room. If she couldn't get into the computer files, how could she learn about DreamCoast? The aerial photo was the only related item she could see.

Julie put her Mac back to sleep. "So what kind of work does Omega Environmental specialize in?"

Maya dredged her memory. "Water testing and, uh, aquaculture."

"Aquaculture? Isn't Sacramento inland?"

"Yes. They . . . partnered with someone on the coast." Maya picked up her coffee mug. "I should let you get back to work. Thanks for showing me the network."

"Any time." Julie smiled at her and turned back to her pellets.

Maya eased out the lab door. She leaned against the hallway wall, sipping her now lukewarm coffee. Her hands sweated on the mug. It felt awful to deceive people—especially people as nice as Julie.

Maya reminded herself why she was here. There was something suspicious going on at BEC, something Harley and Sara had questioned. And it—quite possibly—was the reason they were both gone. She had to keep an eye on Jonah and the rest of the BEC employees, including Julie.

Maya washed out her cup in the kitchen and continued down the hall. She stopped by a door labeled STORAGE.

"What are you doing?"

She whipped around. It was the man from Newport Nature Tours. Curt the chemist? He had dark blond hair, tinged with gray, and an über-lean body that reminded her of a mountain lion, nothing but sinew and skin. His eyes drilled into her.

"I'm . . . Laura," she stammered. "The new employee. I was just . . . trying to learn my way around the building. See if anyone needs help."

"I'm Dr. Curtis Klein." He laughed, a short bark that held little humor. "And you're certainly efficient if you're roaming the halls to find work."

"Jonah's in a meeting." Even though she was telling the truth, her heart beat faster.

"That's my lab." Curt motioned to a door across the hall marked with colored diamond shapes. He walked over and held the door open. "Come on in."

Should she? He didn't seem to have recognized her from the Bayfront. And she could ask him about DreamCoast. She followed him inside.

The boxy machines on the counters were covered with buttons, lights, tubes and wires. A shower curtain hung from one wall, with an EYE WASH sign next to it. There were two refrigerators, three sinks, and a glassed-in area with a vent. Plastic jugs and glass bottles filled every countertop. She motioned to the equipment. "What kind of projects do you work on?"

"Anything that requires chemical analysis." Curt sat down at his desk, wiped his hands with a wet wipe, and bit into a bologna sandwich on white bread. "Mostly water and soil samples."

"At DreamCoast?"

"Among other places. Why do you ask?" A sliver of bologna stuck out the corner of his mouth.

"Just curious." She waited for him to offer her a brochure. He didn't.

Curt pointed to the molded plastic chair across from his desk. "Have a seat, Laura. I'd like to talk to you."

Could she bluff her way through an inquisition? Doubtful, if the experience with Julie was any indication. Maya edged closer to the door. "I'd better get back to—"

"Not so fast." He stood, sandwich in hand. "Jonah mentioned you'd heard about the work we did for DreamCoast. What do you think about that development?"

"I'm new to town." She feigned casualness. "I haven't thought about it much."

"Everyone has an opinion. And if you're working here, we should know yours."

"I'm sure it'll bring tons of money to Newport. That's a bonus."

"Not everyone agrees," Curt said darkly. "There's a group here called the Coast Defenders." His frown sent deep lines down his face. "They fought hard to stop Alan Kingston from getting permits, showed up at every land use meeting to squawk. And when they don't get what they want, they destroy something. One of them even torched a building on the Bayfront recently. You may have heard about that."

"Uh, no." Maya started backing toward the door. "But I'd better finish reading my employee handbook." She escaped into the hall.

Curt followed her. "Hold up, Laura."

What did he want? The morning's coffee churned from her stomach to her throat. If she made it through today, she deserved a Golden Globe for her performance.

She turned around to find him scrutinizing her, head to toe. "Have we met before?" he asked.

He must have recognized her from Newport Nature Tours. Maybe Doug Sammish had revealed she was Harley's sister, too. Maya looked down, letting her hair obscure her face. "I don't think so. I just moved to town." As she walked down the hall, she could feel Curt's eyes tracking her.

She returned to her small, warm office. Taking this job wasn't her brightest idea ever—she hadn't learned anything worthwhile yet. But the BEC staff were touchy about DreamCoast. That had to mean something.

Maya sat at her desk, staring at the employee handbook, her foot jiggling nervously. When Jonah returned from his meetings, he'd be right next door. She wouldn't be able to roam the building. In fact, she should look through his office now—see if she could find anything tying him to Sara or Harley. If he was still logged into his computer, she might be able to access his electronic calendar. Jonah could easily have met Harley on the Bayfront. She'd been sure it was Tomas, but it *could* have been her boss . . . if he'd lied about not talking to Harley.

Maya jumped up and headed next door. She put her hand on the doorknob to his office. It was locked.

She'd just turned away from the door when she heard footsteps coming down the hall toward the lobby. Blood rushed from her heart to her head. Jonah was back. Maya hustled to her office and flung herself into the chair. *Pretend you're reading the handbook.*

Seconds later, there was a rap on her door and Curt walked in. He carried a stack of papers, which he set on her desk. "You said you were looking for work, right?"

Her heart thudded, but she managed a nod.

"Good." He reached over her to type on the keyboard. She drew back, uncomfortable with him so close. "There. You're logged in. Start with this first report." He clicked to open a file. "And if you can't interpret my handwriting, ask. It's important you do this correctly." He pointed to the papers on her desk. They were covered in red ink, illegible scribbles with arrows darting everywhere: insert this, move that, replace with chart on page 92.

Maya's heart sank. This would be tough to fake.

After an hour of painstaking editing, she rubbed her eyes, weary with the strain of being Laura. She already missed the Clam Strip waitresses and their easy work banter. This lab was so sterile. And, with the exception of Julie, unfriendly.

She couldn't wait for her lunch break to start.

Forty

Maya was munching on a slice of cold pizza as she walked into Walter's Big Bucks Taxidermy. The bell on the door clanged and Dan called from the back room, "Just a sec."

While she waited, she browsed the newspaper article on the register, the one she'd started on her last visit.

. . . "We used to think the best way to clean a skull was boiling it," said Walter Dearborn. "But nowadays we use dermestid beetles. They're meat-eaters, always ready for a meal. They scavenge off the fat and muscle and clean the skulls right up." Walter said he feeds fresh meat to the beetles in his taxidermy studio every few days.

Dan walked out of the back room. "Is that you, Maya? You look so different." So did he. Now that he'd taken off his stocking cap, she could see his hair was short and bristly.

"I was reading about those meat-eating beetles." She motioned to the article. "It's kind of gross. Especially just after pizza."

He laughed. "It sounds awful, but dermestids do a great job of removing flesh." He leaned forward on the counter. "What brings you here today?"

"I have another bone for you."

He faked a swoon. "A woman who brings me wildlife parts. Be still, my beating heart."

She smiled and set Sara's shoebox on the counter. Dan unwrapped the bone while she admired the tattoos on his forearms. One showed an elaborate Celtic knot in shades of green and black.

He touched the bone's gnawed ends. "This'll be tough to identify, but we can try. I've got some books to look at. Come on back."

Dan set Sara's chewed bone on his workbench and pulled out a hefty reference book, flipping through the pages rapidly.

Maya wandered over to the shelves. They held dozens of containers, from pint and quart bottles to five-gallon jugs. She read a few labels and her eyes widened. *Bird Feet Injection Fluid, Relaxer-Degreaser, Bloodout, Odor Eliminator, Fish Tan, Hair Sheen, Brite Eyes.* On the bottom shelf sat a line of clear plastic bags, each containing a light-colored powder. No hint of what the powder was for.

"How's your uncle doing?" she asked.

"Pretty well. He should be home in two or three weeks." He glanced at her. "I'll be sorry to leave Newport, though."

Remembering how Dan had crept into her own thoughts last night, she flushed. "What, you'll miss the rain?"

He frowned and returned to studying the book. She shouldn't be so flippant. Dan was super nice. His only drawback was not having long hair.

He handed her the bone. "I'm sorry. The moose was obvious, but this one . . . it'd be easier if it weren't chewed. It could be deer, or maybe dog. If you want to leave it, I can ask around."

"That's okay." Her shoulders slumped. Deer and dogs were common, so Harley's and Sara's bones were probably unrelated. She'd hoped for a clear link, something that would suggest what to do next. But this bone was another dead end. That meant everything depended on BEC—and what she could find there.

Dan walked her back into the shop. "Where'd you say you were getting these bones?"

"I'm not sure where they came from originally," she said glumly. "I found them in basements. Boxes." She wrapped up the bone and returned it to the shoebox.

"People store the strangest things in their basements." Dan pointed to the bird sitting in its own glass case on the counter. "My uncle discovered that hawk at a garage sale. They'd kept it in a box downstairs for years. When they sold it to him for five bucks, I thought he was going to keel over in shock."

The mangy hawk was missing several tufts of feathers and its body was coated with dust. Five bucks sounded a bit steep. "What did he think it was worth, two?"

Dan's mouth dropped. "No way. That's a Victorian-age mount, late 1800s. See that white dust all over it?" She nodded. "My uncle had it sitting out, but I put it in a case. That's arsenic. Taxidermists used to use it to bug-proof their mounts."

"Pretty dangerous."

"It was a long time ago. They didn't know any better. My grandpa even used DDT to protect his work, until, as he said, the 'damn environmentalists and their damn regulations outlawed everything.'" He straightened the hawk's glass case. "His workshop used to smell terrible, this mix of chemicals, cigar smoke and dead animals."

"I can still smell the cigars."

"Oh, this shop is new." He waved a hand at the dated décor. "Well, relatively new. Before my uncle bought the oceanfront condo, he and my grandpa lived in the country. The condo's nice, but they don't allow animals. I had to leave my dog with a neighbor at home." His face brightened. "You have any pets?"

"Well . . . I was watching someone's gerbils, but I was worried I wasn't doing it right. I passed them on to a friend."

Dan looked amused. "You think gerbils are tough? You should try a real animal, like a dog."

"Gerbils are more complicated than they seem."

He leaned over the counter, laughing. "Oh, I know. I had a pair for about a year. They belonged to my sister, but she got pregnant and had to give them up. They can carry some virus that causes birth defects. And once she had a newborn, she didn't want them back. Too busy."

Maya gasped. "What do you mean, birth defects? In people?"

"Yeah. I can't remember what it's called, but pregnant women aren't supposed to have gerbils."

"Oh my God. That friend I gave them to—she's having a baby."

Dan's brow furrowed. "I didn't mean to worry you. As long as she wears gloves and a mask, and doesn't handle their bedding, it's probably just fine."

Maya sucked in a breath. "Can I borrow your phone?"

He handed it to her and she called Allison, who didn't answer. She left a panicky message, asking her not to touch the gerbils and to bring them with her tonight when they met.

"Is there anything I can do?" Dan offered.

"Thanks, but—" She glanced at the clock. "Oh, no. Is that the real time? I need to head back to work." She picked up Sara's shoebox. "I didn't realize it was so late."

"Wait," he said. "Would you, uh, want to go hiking or to the aquarium sometime?"

"I would like to . . . but things are hectic right now."

His face fell. "I get it."

"No, I mean my life is really crazy at the moment. Maybe in a couple of weeks?"

He brightened. "Sure."

Maya said goodbye and left the shop, wondering what she was thinking. She couldn't juggle two guys—but Dan seriously intrigued her. He always seemed so happy.

And somehow, he reminded her of Harley. Despite her brother's angst over the changes to the coast, he'd been an optimist at heart. She envied that.

Maya opened the door to the Pink Beast and leaned down to slip Sara's shoebox under the car seat. A shadow loomed over her. She stood up quickly, closing the door behind her. "Oh joy, it's my own private stalker. What are you doing here?"

Tomas rested a thick, hairy arm on the Pink Beast's roof. "I was curious about your new car. Saw you shopping at Rent-A-Dent yesterday."

So he *had* followed her there. A prickle of sweat slid down her back. "You should know why I needed new wheels. You totaled my Corolla."

"That wasn't me."

"I know you're lying. I've got proof." *Well, Nick does.*

"Right." His gaze flicked over her. "That's a nice haircut, Maya. Or should I call you Laura?"

Her heartbeat quickened. She'd given her "nickname" to the salesman Ted, but how had Tomas found out?

He leaned closer. "This car was parked outside BEC this morning. What were you doing there?" When she didn't answer, he said, "I thought I warned you to stay out of Coast Defenders' business."

"You did. I didn't promise to listen."

He crossed his beefy arms over his chest. "Have you heard about Sara's bike?"

Maya nodded, her throat too tight to speak. She moved around to the other side of her car, putting distance between them.

"If I were you, I'd be careful. Very careful," Tomas said.

"I'm sick and tired of your threats. Just stay away from me."

"You've got it all wrong. I'm actually looking out for you."

"Leave. Me. Alone."

"As you wish." He saluted her and left.

Maybe it *was* time to go to the police with her suspicions.

Forty-One

When she returned to BEC, only one vehicle was parked in the lot—the gold Escalade. The building was quiet, too. Was Jonah still gone?

Maya hurried into her office. Curt had set another stack of reports on her desk, plenty to keep her busy. She picked up the phone to try Allison again, but there was still no answer. She checked the clock. *Oh.* Allison was working at the Clam Strip until 2:00. Maya left another message, reminding her to bring the gerbils with her.

She leaned back in the desk chair, unable to concentrate on actual work. She wanted to have good news to share with Allison tonight. She still had no idea why Harley and Sara had contacted Jonah, or why they were so agitated about DreamCoast, beyond their obvious dislike for the project.

If Harley had taken his picture of stumps at the site, he'd probably photographed the white truck there, too—and possibly the cabin. Which meant he'd gone to DreamCoast recently. Had Jonah been driving that truck or Curt? Maybe even Julie. She couldn't cross anyone off her suspect list.

Jonah could return from his meetings at any moment. Maya got up and checked the lobby. Still quiet. Surely they hadn't left her here by herself. She walked to the front door and looked out. Just the Escalade. Julie must have gone out for lunch. This might be a good time to take a closer look at that aerial photo of DreamCoast—and determine whether the building in that photo was the same cabin Harley had photographed.

Maya walked down the silent hallway past the closed Chemistry Lab door and stopped outside the Biology Lab. She knocked twice.

No answer. Her heart beat rapidly as she pushed open the door. The lab was empty.

Maya hurried over to the photo, but she couldn't tell if the small building was a cabin, not from its rooftop. She glanced around the room. Perhaps Julie stored photos from the DreamCoast site on her computer—if they weren't on that drive that required special access. Quickly, Maya poked her head into the hallway. Nobody around. She sat down at Julie's desk and opened iPhoto.

She started scanning the photo library. It held thousands of photos, most of them showing shrubs, trees and forested hillsides. One big mass of green. Maya scrolled down to the recent albums. About fifty photos later, she found a cabin with a red door. Nothing indicated where it had been taken. She zoomed in on the picture, trying to memorize the visual details: gingerbread trim on the eaves, peeling paint, a moss-coated roof. She was ninety-nine percent sure it was the cabin in Harley's photo, but she'd have to compare them to be positive. Could she print this shot?

The lab door opened and Julie walked in.

Busted. Maya leaped up from the chair. Her heart was hammering so hard, it felt like it would jump out of her chest. Hand shaking, she reached for the mouse and closed iPhoto.

Julie stared at her. "What are you doing in here? Why are you sitting at my computer?"

"I, um, needed . . . some information," Maya stammered. "For a report."

"You should have asked me." Julie gave her a pointed look.

"I'm sorry. You're right. I should have." Maya angled toward the door. "I'll come back another time." Julie's mouth was set in a thin line. "I'm really sorry." Maya fled the room. Julie's angry gaze drilled into her back.

She hurried down the hall. She'd been caught red-handed. What if Julie said something to Jonah?

In her office, she opened up the next report for Curt and tried to work. Her mind kept returning to that cabin.

When she came back to her office after a quick bathroom break, Jonah was sitting in her chair. Maya gasped.

At the sound, he turned toward her. His gaze was chilly. "My office manager had a question about you," he said. "So I had the opportunity to follow up with the owner of Omega Environmental. We had an interesting chat on the phone."

Oh, no.

"Surprisingly, they'd never heard of you. And they don't have a supervisor named Lydia, either. So whom did I speak with the other day?"

"A . . . friend of mine." Her body vibrated with tension.

"I should have been more thorough in checking your references," Jonah said. "As my office manager so kindly pointed out."

She looked down at the floor.

"And then I got to thinking," he added. "Someone called me the other day, asking if I'd spoken to her brother. I assume that was you. Maya Rivers?"

She nodded, miserable. "I'm sorry I didn't tell the truth. But there's a reason I needed to be here." Jonah didn't say anything.

Could she trust him? What if he was the person responsible for Harley's death? She took a deep breath, considered her slim options. The BEC door was closing. If she wanted information, she had to take the risk. "Harley wanted to meet with you," she said. "That's why I'm here."

"He and I never even talked." Jonah ran his hands through his hair. "I can't believe this is happening."

She couldn't either. "I don't know what Harley wanted to say to you, not exactly. But I do know he didn't set that fire at Newport Nature Tours. He was silenced—murdered—because of something he knew. Something that relates to BEC, possibly DreamCoast. An employee here is involved."

Jonah stared at her as if she were speaking Swahili. "What are you saying? Which employee?"

"I don't know."

Jonah frowned. "Do you have any evidence?"

"I can get some. I'm in the middle of researching it."

"Do you realize how ludicrous this sounds? When I heard from Omega, I wanted to give you the benefit of the doubt. I really did. But you lied to me about who you are, lied about your work experience. Lied about your reasons for being here. We could press charges."

"I'm telling the truth now." She swallowed hard. "My brother was concerned about something here. I just don't know what."

His face tightened. "I'm sure it was terrible shock, losing a family member so suddenly, and I understand that you're grieving. Sometimes that makes people act in . . . irrational ways."

"You don't understand. Harley found out about this thing—and now he's *dead*. Her voice wavered. "Sara Blessing found out about it, too, and she's gone. I'm certain that someone here is involved."

Jonah rose to his feet. "When you start flinging accusations about my business, my clients and my employees, you'd damn well better have evidence to support them." He pointed to the door. "It's time for you to leave."

Forty-Two

Maya grabbed her belongings and slunk out BEC's front door. Fired again—for the second time this week. In the parking lot, the Pink Beast awaited. She kicked the front tire hard, letting off steam, before climbing inside. She'd finally told Jonah the truth—and it had gotten her nowhere.

Maya drummed her fingers on the steering wheel. Now what? She turned the key in the ignition and the engine growled to life. Okay, she sucked as an undercover agent. But she couldn't let this setback stop her—she still needed to know the truth. She and Allison both needed to know.

It was getting closer to that adoption agency appointment every day—and Maya hadn't heard Allison say a single "after the baby comes" or "the baby and I."

As Maya drove back to Newport, she decided today hadn't been a waste. With the photos, she'd established a connection between Harley and BEC. But what exactly *was* that link? And who was involved?

Julie didn't seem a likely criminal. That left Jonah, Curt, or some BEC employee she hadn't met. She was pretty sure Jonah had been dumbfounded by her accusations. He didn't fake that. But Curt . . . Julie had said he'd spent so much time at DreamCoast, he might buy a condo there. He certainly seemed dedicated to the project. Was it possible he was working with Kingston? Getting kickbacks for referring people to the development? She sighed. That'd be a conflict of interest, but not necessarily illegal. Unless Curt had lied to potential buyers. But about what?

. . . .

Maya raced up the stairs to her apartment. Inside, she was surprised to see the light on her answering machine blinking. Three messages?

The first was Nick, saying how much he'd enjoyed their date, and could they get together soon. He'd left a second message asking if she'd gotten the first one. Maya almost laughed. Nick had seemed in such a rush to leave last night, and now he was hounding her to call him back.

The third message was from Detective Gloria Ames. Maya held her breath as she listened. "I promised I'd call you after talking with Espinoza," Ames said. "Nobody saw your brother's backpack or any ring at the arson site. Just wanted to let you know. I'm sorry we couldn't be more help." She paused. "Take care."

Maya set down the phone. Harley's backpack was gone. Proof that someone else had been at the Bayfront with him. Was it Tomas—or an employee from BEC?

She retrieved Harley's photos from her dresser drawer and took them to the kitchen, anxious to confirm that the cabin she'd seen in Julie's iPhoto library was the same one Harley had photographed. She studied the picture. His shot was so dark and grainy, it was hard to tell.

She glanced at the other photos: the tree stumps and the forest behind the white BEC truck. It could be DreamCoast. The shot of brown dirt could have been taken anywhere. There was a blurry white blob in one corner. She set the photos down.

The only way she'd know for sure that Harley's pictures had come from DreamCoast would be to drive out there herself. And she wasn't going there alone. Could she talk Allison into accompanying her?

Maya slumped against the table. To convince Allison—or the police—that BEC and Alan Kingston were involved in something illegal, she'd need more damning evidence than a few photos Harley might have—or might not have—taken at the construction site.

Jonah had made that clear.

She left the photos on the table and retrieved the envelope with Harley's cash from her dresser. She needed to give this back to Allison tonight. She'd hung onto the money long enough.

In the meantime, she had research to do.

. . . .

Maya sat down at a computer station, relieved the library was nearly empty and there wasn't the usual competition for spots. She searched online for images of DreamCoast. Most of the results were artist's renditions of the condo complex, not photographs. She couldn't find a single picture of the cabin.

She Googled Jonah Bishop—who appeared to be an upstanding citizen. He'd even received a civic award for "Best Business Owner of the Year." Curt—Dr. Curtis Klein—appeared to be equally upstanding. Out of curiosity, she typed in "Cadillac Escalade" and went to a dealer web site. She let out a whistle. More than $72,000 for an SUV? Curt must be one well-paid chemist. Or he was getting a nice bonus from Alan Kingston.

She thought for a moment. BEC had helped Kingston get the land use permits for his project . . . but what used to be at the site?

She asked a librarian for help, and the woman directed her to the county's web page. There were aerial photos going back several years and detailed maps and tax lot information. As far as Maya could tell, the DreamCoast site had been built on a patchwork of different properties, all of them forested. It looked like Alan Kingston had bought out at least five landowners. There were a few homes shown on the older aerial photos. Was one of them the cabin?

She jotted down the five landowner names on a scrap of paper. Her pencil hovered over one name. Recognition tugged, but she couldn't make the connection.

The clock on the computer reminded her it was time to meet Allison.

Maya slid the piece of paper into her pocket. She didn't have much to show for her research yet, but perhaps Allison had heard Harley say something about DreamCoast, something she hadn't realized at the time was important.

Maya logged off and headed outside. She needed a solid link between Sara and Harley—more than just a single phone call to Jonah. A reason for the contact. Did Sara have an environmental concern about DreamCoast, and she'd called Jonah to tell him? Maybe Harley had followed up after she disappeared.

. . . .

Maya waited on the street corner by the Coast Guard station. In one pocket was the list of landowners. In the other, an envelope stuffed with cash—the $1,600 for Allison, along with an IOU for the rest.

The wind gusted hard and the chilly breeze kept working its way under her jacket. Rain dripped. Goose bumps rose on her chilled skin.

7:15 p.m. Allison was late.

Maya gripped the fat envelope in her pocket, uncomfortable with having so much cash on her. Had Allison forgotten the gerbils and swung back home to get them?

She stamped her feet, trying to return circulation to her toes. Raindrops plopped onto her hair and ran down her cheeks, dripping from her chin and leaking under the jacket collar. Her stomach growled, reminding her she hadn't eaten since that slice of pizza at noon. She endured another ten minutes of misery before climbing into the Pink Beast. She called Allison's house on her cell but got no answer.

Where was she?

Allison wouldn't just blow her off, would she? Maya slumped in the car seat, staring out at the rain, at the Coast Guard flags that whipped hard with every gust. Staring at the empty street corner where she and Allison were supposed to meet.

She wiped her wet face and neck with her shirt sleeve. Harley's death had sliced a gash through their friendship. And there were moments—like that awful fight at Allison's house—when it felt like the relationship could never be repaired. But there were other times—like talking to Allison on the phone last night, making plans to meet—when Maya remembered everything good. She and Allison just needed time. They'd get back on track.

After fifteen more minutes of waiting, she gave up and drove home.

. . . .

Her phone was blinking again. Two more messages? She listened, expecting an apologetic Allison. But both calls were from Nick. The last one said, "Are you all right? I thought I would have heard from you by now."

Maya sighed. She did need to return his calls, but not right this minute. She set down the phone, willing it to ring. Willing it to be Allison.

After ten minutes, the phone remained eerily silent. Maya dialed the house in Toledo. It went to voice mail. She left a long message, telling Allison she'd been flushed out at BEC and she had news to share. "I thought . . . we were meeting for dinner tonight. I have your money to give back, too, minus a loan. I'll explain. Call me when you get home. And please don't handle the gerbils."

She set the phone down. Where could Allison be? She wasn't usually this flaky. Could something have happened to the baby?

Maya paced her apartment.

The phone didn't ring.

She dialed Allison's house again. Still voice mail.

When she hadn't heard back by 8:45 p.m., Maya knew something was wrong.

She called the Clam Strip and asked if anyone there had seen her. A girlish voice she didn't recognize—must be the new waitress—said Allison had worked earlier. "I think she's left by now. I'll check, but we're super busy. Can you call back in ten minutes?"

The phone went dead.

Maya grabbed her car keys and headed out.

Forty-Three

When she walked into the Clam Strip, Willy hustled over to the hostess stand. "What are you doing here?"

"Looking for Allison. Is she around?" She scanned the room behind him.

"She left early." He frowned. "I knew you were a bad influence on her. She's turning unreliable on me." Willy ran a hand through his slicked-back hair. "And she was always the one I could count on."

"What do you mean she left early? What time did she leave?" Her voice cracked.

"Around noon. She got a phone call and went flying out of here. I tried to reach her this afternoon, to make a change in her schedule. But she never called back. Unreliable," he muttered.

"She left at noon today?" Maya's stomach flip-flopped with anxiety. "Wasn't she supposed to work until 2:00?"

"She was." Willy motioned to a waitress across the dining room. "I had to call Britney in." It was the new girl with the straight hair, probably the one she'd talked to on the phone.

"Did Allison seem okay when she left?" Maya asked. "Was she sick? Upset?"

He shrugged. "She did look kinda pale. Crystal said she was throwing up in the bathroom earlier. That's all I need. Vomiting waitresses! Makes my food look bad." He lowered his voice. "Crystal might have said something about . . . 'female troubles.'"

Maya gulped for air, but couldn't get a full breath. The room spun. *The baby.*

"You're not going to faint on me, are you?" Willy's brow wrinkled in concern.

"No." She used her cell to call Allison's house again. Still no fricking answer. Maya fled out the door into the darkness.

. . . .

As she drove, her headlights beamed bright. She stared blindly at the road, trying to talk herself out of panic mode. *It hasn't been that long since Allison left the Clam Strip. A few hours.* A car whizzed past her and Maya flinched. *Allison might be home sleeping, just not answering her phone. The ringer's off.*

Another car whizzed past. *She would have called by now. Did she go to the doctor? The hospital?* Maya gripped the steering wheel harder. Even taking the faster route on Highway 20, the drive to Toledo felt like eternity.

Allison's Subaru was sitting in the bungalow's driveway. She must have come home after the Clam Strip. Relieved, Maya rang the doorbell. The cat gave a plaintive meow from inside, but no one answered the door.

She pressed the bell again. The chimes pealed.

Still no one came.

Maya's hand trembled as she reached under the planter box for the spare key and let herself in. The open doorway sent a blast of cool, damp air into the house. FuzzyBear meowed loudly.

"Allison?" Maya stepped over the threshold. "Are you here?"

She hurried through the house, checking each room. The living room was empty. In the bedroom, the comforter was pulled up, the bed neatly made. No one was in the kitchen or bathroom.

She raced down the basement steps and checked every gloomy corner. Allison wasn't here.

Where could she have gone without her car?

On the kitchen table was an empty plate dotted with toast crumbs and a bowl coated with dried milk, a few Cheerios sticking to its sides. Breakfast? Her gaze swiveled around the room.

The gerbils' aquarium sat on the kitchen counter, and FuzzyBear was watching it intently. On the floor, the cat's food and water bowls were bone dry. No wonder she'd been meowing. Had Allison been in a rush this morning?

Maya poured kibble and water into the bowls, then checked on the gerbils. A scant ounce of fluid remained in their water bottle, and their food was ransacked. When she reached in with a fresh handful, they scurried over, clambering across her hand to get to the food. What was going on? She'd asked Allison not to "handle" the gerbils, but she didn't have to starve them. And the neglected cat . . . This wasn't like her. Not at all.

Maya walked back outside. The doors on the Subaru were unlocked. Her unease grew. Allison had apparently left in a hurry. By herself—or with someone else?

She headed for the kitchen phone. She'd better call the police. When she picked up the receiver, it beeped.

Maya punched in the number for voice mail, which Allison had conveniently posted on the wall next to the phone. As she listened, she sucked in a breath. Willy's message and every one of her own messages from today—about the gerbils, about getting fired from BEC, about the money . . . They were all here.

As *new* messages. Allison hadn't heard any of them.

Oh my God. It was almost 10 p.m. Nobody had seen her since she'd left the Clam Strip at noon?

Maya looked wildly around the kitchen. When she'd arrived, the front door had been locked. Had Allison locked it herself?

Her eyes narrowed on the cat bowl. Next to it was a small smudge of grit. Slowly, she tracked the trail of brown smudges all the way to the front door. Had the cat made those? Or could it be mud off someone's shoes?

Her heart pounded as she dialed the Toledo police, spewing panicked phrases into the phone: *My friend's gone. She could be in trouble. Hurt.*

"She's an adult?" the man asked. "Over eighteen?"

"Yes."

"When was the last time you saw her?"

"Me, yesterday. But she was at work until noon today. And then she just *vanished*."

"Vanished?" he said. "It hasn't been that long. Are you sure she's not just—"

"Nobody's seen her . . . for almost ten hours." Maya gasped for breath. "She was supposed to meet me . . . meet in Newport tonight. She didn't show. And this isn't like her. Not disappearing . . . not without a word. She's gone missing, like Sara Blessing. She could've been kidnapped. Kidnapped! We need to go looking for her. Send the cops."

"Ma'am," he said. "Please calm down. I need to get some information from you, and I can't understand what you're saying. What's this about a kidnapping?"

Maya let her breath slow. She needed help from the police. She explained the situation again, much more slowly, and he said he'd send someone.

She expected sirens, a line of police cars, and a house crawling with cops. Instead, she got one patrol car. One guy. He looked like he'd already worked a 24-hour shift and couldn't wait to get home.

The weary cop introduced himself as Officer Raymond and asked her a bunch of questions. She showed him the unlocked Subaru outside and led him through the house, pointing out the dirt smudges on the kitchen floor. He didn't seem too perturbed, not until she told him Allison was pregnant. Then, it was like flipping a switch. He turned alert and interested. His wife was pregnant, he said. Three months along. They had two daughters already and he was praying for a boy.

"We'll look for your friend," he said earnestly. "We'll find her."

"Is there anything I can do?"

"You might as well head home, get some rest. Not much you can do tonight."

"Shouldn't I stay here?"

He shook his head. "You might destroy evidence without meaning to." He must have seen her confusion because he added, "We'll check the hospital first. If this really is a kidnapping, we'll come back and go over the house with a fine-toothed comb. But don't worry. Most of the time, it turns out to be nothing more than a misunderstanding. You get some rest. I'll be in touch first thing in the morning." He took down her home and cell numbers and handed her a business card.

Frowning, Maya accepted the card. He was probably right. There wasn't anything she could do here. At least if she went home, Allison would know where to reach her. "I'll take the gerbils with me," she said.

When Officer Raymond didn't object, she carried the aquarium to her car. She debated, then went back in and grabbed FuzzyBear and the bags of pet food. Might as well bring the whole menagerie. Allison wouldn't want her cat left here alone.

The drive back to Newport was a blur. Her hands shook on the steering wheel and it took everything she had to concentrate on the road. Where could Allison be? Maya prayed she was all right.

She parked the Pink Beast in front of her apartment and carried the cat up in her arms, setting it on the futon couch. She heaved the gerbil aquarium up the stairs and put it on the kitchen table. The little creatures were going crazy, running everywhere. "Sorry for the drama, guys," she said. "It'll be smooth sailing from here out. I promise." Her breath caught. She couldn't promise a damn thing.

Not until they found Allison.

Harley's photos were still strewn across her kitchen table. She scooped them up, carried them to her bedroom, and opened the dresser drawer. Her gaze stopped on the bone, its knobby ends sticking out from the t-shirt wrap.

She reached for the pictures again, shuffling through them until she got to the image of brown dirt. That blurry white blob in the corner. Could it possibly be . . . a bone?

Maya pulled Harley's and Sara's bones from the drawer and set them on the dresser top. What if these bones had come from DreamCoast?

Julie had said she occasionally found wildlife bones, especially when scavengers had dug them up. Harley and Sara could have gone to DreamCoast and found a few bones there. They might have visited Kingston, tried to pass off their bones as human. Maybe they'd even told him the site was an ancient burial ground. He'd panicked and halted construction.

No. Harley's bone was huge. Nobody could mistake that for part of a human skeleton. It was clear they were animal bones. Dan had said so.

Besides, Alan Kingston wouldn't have shut down the whole Dream-Coast development for two lousy bones. There had to be something more.

Something Kingston was hiding.

Forty-Four

Maya stirred, her muscles stiff and unyielding. Daylight beamed through the window shades. When had she fallen asleep last night? She was lying on her bed, on top of the covers, still dressed in yesterday's clothes. A cat was curled at her side. A cat?

Maya sat up quickly. Did the police have any news about Allison?

She dialed the number on Officer Raymond's business card. He answered right away, but sounded half-asleep. He said they'd confirmed Allison wasn't at any nearby hospital and her doctor hadn't heard from her. It didn't seem to be a medical emergency.

Good news, sort of.

"We're still looking. Do you have any idea where she could have gone?" His voice was weary.

"None at all." And that terrified her.

Maya showered and got dressed, putting on a peasant blouse, embroidered skirt and leggings in honor of Allison, who was always telling her she should wear something besides jeans. Her heart wrenched. Allison might never see her in this outfit.

It wasn't until she'd had her first cup of coffee that she remembered mentioning Harley's laptop. Could Allison have gone to the Coast Defenders' house to ask about it? What if she'd talked to Tomas? He might have gotten angry and . . . her breath seized.

She punched the buttons on her answering machine until she got to Nick's messages. He'd left his phone number in one of them. Somewhat reluctantly, she dialed.

"Maya?" he said, answering immediately. "Where are you? I've been trying to reach you."

"Sorry," she hedged. "Something awful happened yesterday. Allison's gone missing."

"*Missing?*" His voice rose. "What do you mean?"

"I mean no one's seen her since yesterday at noon, when she left work. I was wondering if she came to the Coast Defenders' house afterward. Did you see her there?"

"At the house?" A beat of silence. "I was there most of the day, but no, I didn't see her. I can ask around, though. See if anyone else did."

"Would you? Call me back if you hear anything, okay?" She started to hang up.

"Hold on, Maya. This sounds serious. Do you think we should go look for her? The group truck's here. I could swing by and pick you up."

"Thanks, but . . . I'm not even sure where to start looking." Maya bit her lip. "I'm supposed to wait here. Let the police do their job." As if she could just sit around while Allison was missing.

"You sound miserable," Nick said. "I'm coming over. We've got to do something." He hung up before she could respond.

Maya stared at the receiver in her hand. No. She couldn't deal with him right now. And she sure didn't want to go on a wild goose chase. Most likely, the answers to her questions wouldn't come from the Coast Defenders, but from DreamCoast. From Alan Kingston.

She called Officer Raymond again and left a message that she'd be out, and to try her cell phone if he needed to reach her.

She went into her bedroom and grabbed Harley's photos from the dresser.

The list of former landowners, the one she'd made at the library, was sitting on the dresser top. She picked it up and read through the names again. Her gaze stopped on the "Dearborn." She'd seen that name recently, but where?

Dearborn. Dearborn.

And then she remembered. It was in the article she'd read at the taxidermy shop. According to Dan, his Uncle Walter used to live "in the country" before he bought his oceanfront condo. Walter Dearborn must have inherited the property from his father. That's why she hadn't recognized the name Arthur Dearborn.

Two generations of taxidermists could produce a lot of animal bones.

. . . .

When Maya walked into Walter's Big Bucks Taxidermy, Dan smiled broadly, his gaze traveling with appreciation over her skirt and blouse. "Hey, you're looking nice today. Did you bring me another bone?"

"Not this time."

He saw her face and came around the counter. "Are you all right? What's up?"

"My friend Allison is missing. The friend I gave the gerbils to."

His face fell. "I'm so sorry. What happened?"

"I don't know. The police are looking for her. And I'm trying to figure out if she could've gotten involved in . . . something bad." She paused. This was awkward, but she had to ask. "Where was your uncle's taxidermy studio, the old one?"

Dan looked puzzled. "South of town. He had a few acres."

"Did he sell his land to Alan Kingston, the developer?"

"Kingston? That sounds right. I remember Uncle Walter thought he'd won the lottery, getting so much for the property. It was mostly forest, a couple of streams." Dan's eyes widened. "Why are you asking? What does this have to do with your friend being missing?"

"Maybe nothing." *Or maybe a lot.* "I'm just wondering . . . your grandpa and your uncle must have processed quite a few animals through their business. What did they do with the parts they couldn't use? The carcasses and bones?"

Dan's eyebrows rose. "I don't know. They probably took them to a rendering plant. Lots of folks did—before the plants all shut down. Knowing my grandpa, it's possible he held a bonfire or two."

"Could they have buried the carcasses?" This winter's heavy rain or the construction equipment would have exposed the bones.

"You're talking about quite a few animals over the years." He swept his hand around the shop, encompassing all the mounts. "Not just these, but all the work they've ever done for customers. And carcasses can carry diseases. If you buried them, it could—" He stared at her. "Wait a second. You're not suggesting my family did something wrong, are you? Because back then . . . "

She had to know. "Back then?"

"You're acting very strange." Dan's voice was heated. "What's going on?"

"Those bones I brought you to identify, it's possible they . . . " her voice trailed off.

"Came from my uncle's land?" His gaze darted to the mounts on the wall. "But that means . . . "

"I don't know for sure." Her heart twinged. Dan obviously loved his family.

"My uncle wouldn't do anything illegal," he said. "I know he wouldn't."

"I'm sorry. I have to go." Maya turned toward the door. The bones were the trigger, but there was more to it. Kingston wouldn't shut down his development over a few bones—or even a few hundred bones. She had to find the rest of the story.

Dan hurried to hold the door open. "I'll be working until seven or so. Come back later, okay? We can talk more about this. I don't want you to think—"

"Okay." She flew down the street.

"See you later?" he called. She waved to him, but kept moving.

. . . .

At the library, Maya checked her phone to make sure Officer Raymond hadn't called. There were no messages.

She headed for the computers and double-checked the tax records. Kingston Development *was* the new owner of Arthur and Walter Dearborn's land. Had Dan suspected where her moose bone and deer/dog bone had come from? How had he not guessed?

Perhaps he had. Maybe Harley's bone wasn't from a moose at all. Maybe it was elk, and Dan had told her that story about moose to put her off track, make her think the bones had nothing to do with Newport. He'd said he visited his grandpa and uncle as a kid. He could've watched them bury carcasses. He just didn't want to admit to anything that could get his uncle in trouble.

Maya stared at the computer screen, her hand frozen on the mouse. Dan had mentioned someone asking his Uncle Walter about a bone. Could it have been Sara? If she'd found her bone at DreamCoast, it made sense she would tell Harley about it. They were friends, partners in the group. Maybe he'd gone back with her to look for more bones. The night of February 27th?

No, she decided. Harley couldn't have been with Sara that night. Because if anyone had tried to hurt her, he would have protected her.

So he must have followed up after Sara had disappeared. He'd retraced her steps to DreamCoast and discovered the moose bone—and her locket. *That's* why he'd been so agitated about her disappearance. He'd figured out that someone connected to DreamCoast was responsible. At the brewery, Harley had hinted about a "huge" story, the reason he couldn't leave the group. But he'd told the wrong person—a person who'd betrayed him. Was it Tomas? Curt at BEC? Alan Kingston?

She leaned forward in the chair, pressing her feet to the floor. If Walter Dearborn and his father had buried every animal they'd ever mounted, there could be hundreds, even thousands, of bones underground. But a wildlife graveyard wouldn't shut down DreamCoast.

Kingston could just tell his work crew to dig up the bones and dispose of them properly. And wouldn't his crews have found bones themselves, as soon as they started digging?

Maya shuddered. Sara and Harley hadn't called Kingston. They'd called Jonah. BEC. They'd found something bigger than bones . . . something that involved Bishop Environmental Consulting.

An environmental crisis, maybe a cover-up of pollution.

She thought of the shelves in the back room at Walter's shop, all those bottles and jugs of chemicals. That mangy hawk on the shop counter. The arsenic dust.

Dan had mentioned his grandfather using DDT to protect his mounts. He might have used other pesticides, too. If he'd dumped them . . . the DreamCoast site could be heavily contaminated. Definitely the soil, but the groundwater or nearby creeks could be polluted as well, carrying the toxins off-site. Her pulse raced.

That had to be it.

And the current owner, Alan Kingston, would have to pay for the cleanup. Past owners, such as Dan's uncle, would be liable as well. They could face huge fines, a legal nightmare.

What kind of pollutants would there be at DreamCoast?

Dan had said his uncle was being treated for cancer. Could that cancer have been caused by the products he'd used? She browsed the web, checking out web sites that sold supplies for tanning hides and home taxidermy. They listed hundreds of chemical products, many of which *sounded* toxic.

But she needed to find the ones used historically. After more research, Maya wrote up a list of possible contaminants: arsenic trioxide, sodium arsenate, lead arsenate, mercuric chloride, DDT, strychnine, ethylene dichloride, and formaldehyde. It looked like many of them had been banned and were no longer in use.

She detoured to the archives of an old taxidermy chat room, where people were talking about chemical products—like good old DDT—as if they still had them on their shelves. And if Walter had begun his taxidermy practice in 1968, his dad—Dan's grandfather—might have worked on his mounts in the early 40s, or even late 30s, when all this stuff was regularly used.

Maya tried a few more searches for pollution or dumping related to taxidermy. She discovered a commercial leather tannery near Portland that had apparently dumped hides, animal parts, bones and chemical waste on nearby farmland. The contamination hadn't been discovered until years later, after several homes had been built on polluted soil. It became a multi-million dollar cleanup.

If that kind of contamination had been found at DreamCoast . . . Kingston couldn't afford to remove *all* the toxic soil. It would kill his project. There'd be no condos. No community garden. No playground. The clean-up, not to mention the legal wrangles, could take years.

Was it a strong enough reason to make Sara disappear? To silence Harley? And—even more frightening—did it explain why Allison was now missing?

Maya jumped up. If the DreamCoast site was tainted from decades of dumping hazardous materials, BEC's soil and water testing should have revealed it. Curt had to be involved. He'd covered it up. But how could she prove that?

Her thoughts jumped to the cash Harley had borrowed from Allison. What if her brother had taken his own soil and water samples at DreamCoast to show Jonah—and had borrowed that money to pay for lab testing? Maybe the results were sitting a lab somewhere, waiting for payment.

She needed someone knowledgeable about environmental contamination. She needed a Coast Defender. She needed Nick.

Forty-Five

Maya made a quick stop at home for the bones. She re-wrapped them in t-shirts so they were completely covered and slid the bundles into a cardboard box.

With the Coast Defenders' help, she would finish what Sara and Harley had started by making Alan Kingston admit what was wrong at DreamCoast. She'd force him to reveal if he had anything to do with Sara's disappearance or Harley's death.

And . . . her fists clenched. If he knew why Allison was missing.

Maya checked her phone. Still no news from Officer Raymond.

Should she call and let him know about the pollution? *Not yet.* DreamCoast wasn't his jurisdiction. And this had a very a tenuous connection to Allison—if any connection at all. Alan Kingston was a major public figure, friends with the mayor. She'd learned her lesson with Jonah. She would get Nick's help first, figure out exactly what the pollution issue was, and come up with a plan. Then, she'd let the police know.

If she rushed into Kingston's office to accuse him, he'd probably have her arrested. She couldn't be sitting in a jail cell. Not until she found Allison.

. . . .

On the front porch of the yellow bungalow, two bodies were inter-twined, pressed so close they could be one. Hands roved up and down, tousling clothes and massaging shoulders.

Maya climbed out of the Pink Beast, carrying the cardboard box with the bones. As she walked closer to the house, she saw the black spikes of Kelsey's hair. Her gaze swung to the guy pressed against her. A long, dark ponytail. It couldn't be.

Oh, yes it could.

Nick reached out and placed a hand on either side of Kelsey's face, drawing her in for a deep kiss. He'd used the same technique on her.

Mouth agape, Maya backed away. The box of bones fell to the sidewalk with a thud. She reached down to grab it and turned toward the car.

"Maya! Wait!" Nick called.

He ran after her. When she didn't stop, he grabbed her arm.

"Kelsey's dad died recently," he said, as if that was a reasonable explanation for making out with her on the porch. "She needed comforting. It's not what it looks like."

"Really." Maya pulled free of his grasp. "Because it *looks* like you're a two-timing sleazeball. But maybe I need to get my vision checked."

His eyes flashed anger. The charmer who'd talked her into bed was gone. "Let me explain."

Maya snorted. "Seriously? I may be gullible, but I'm not brain-dead." She moved to the driver's side of the Pink Beast, putting a rooftop between them. "I can't believe I slept with you. What a colossal mistake."

"I came by your apartment," he said. "You weren't there. Where'd you go?"

"Listen, this is over. Do you get that? "

Nick stared at her, slack-jawed. "You're dumping me? Talk about a colossal mistake."

"You know what? I don't give a damn. I've got other things to worry about."

"Like searching for Allison?" he asked. "You seem pretty worked up about that."

"Wouldn't you be?" The way he was looking at her, his eyes so dark and intent, made her uneasy. Maya opened the car door and tossed the box of bones onto the floor in the backseat. If he was trying to get under her skin, it was working. But she'd had enough. *Enough.*

"Wait," Nick said. "I'll come with you."

"No." She climbed inside.

Before she could lock the car, he yanked the passenger door open and slid onto the seat. "I have a few ideas of places we could look for her. But they might be a bit of a hike. You up for it?"

She stared at him. Had he gone insane? She wasn't going anywhere with him. "Get the hell out of my car. And if you're so gung ho to go hiking, take Kelsey along. With any luck, you'll both get lost."

He got out, slamming the door so violently the sound left her ears ringing. When he glared through the side window, Maya pressed on the horn. He jumped backwards.

She drove furiously down the street. Forget Nick. Forget the Coast Defenders.

She'd confront Alan Kingston on her own.

. . . .

The offices for Kingston Development were sandwiched between a defense attorney's office and an accountant's office. Maya drove past her destination twice before spotting the subtle brass sign. Alarm company stickers blanketed the windows.

She parked the Pink Beast and slid the bundle of bones under the car seat, taking the empty box with her.

The receptionist sat behind a marble-topped counter, complete with an elegant vase holding a white orchid. She had straight blonde hair, perfect makeup, and manicured nails. *Figured.*

"I'm Laura Miller," Maya announced. "With Bishop Environmental Consulting. Jonah Bishop asked me to deliver this important package to Alan Kingston. In person." She held up the now-dented box.

"Oh?" The receptionist eyed her nervously. "Let me check with Alan."

When Maya set the box on the marble counter, the woman flinched. Maya picked it up again. She didn't want her to think it was a bomb.

"One moment, please." The receptionist pressed a button on her phone and spoke into the receiver.

Maya held tightly to the box. *I hope I can pull this off.*

The receptionist hung up, looking surprised. "You can go back." She pointed toward a narrow hallway. "It's the last door on the left." Maya walked down the hall.

Alan Kingston was standing next to his desk, a cell phone pressed to his ear. He gave her a sharp glance and kept talking.

She studied him. In his plaid shirt, jeans and work boots, he looked more like a construction worker than a rich developer, but something about him seemed familiar. Maybe from his picture on the brochure. Kingston had several deer and elk mounts on his office walls. If he'd used Walter's Big Bucks Taxidermy, that explained how he'd found out about the property.

He hung up. Vivid blue eyes probed her face. "You're Laura Miller? You work for Jonah?"

She nodded. It wasn't as big a lie if she didn't say it aloud.

"Is there something I can help you with . . . Laura?" Another sharp glance.

Did he know she was faking? "You can start by telling me when you last saw Allison Rafferty," she said.

"Who?"

"My friend Allison. Did she come here and ask you about DreamCoast?"

"No." His face was guarded. "I don't know anyone named Allison."

Maya stared at him. She'd been sure he'd hold the answer. But maybe they were both lying to each other. This was her last shot—she had to use her leverage. She handed him the box. "Special delivery."

He opened the lid and looked inside. "Is this some kind of joke? It's empty."

"I took the bones out."

"Bones?" His voice quavered.

"You know, wildlife bones . . . like the ones people keep finding at DreamCoast."

"Are you with the Coast Defenders? I'm calling the cops." He picked up his desk phone.

"Go right ahead." She crossed her arms. "Because I've got quite a story. I'm sure they'd like to hear it, too."

Looking uncertain, Kingston set the phone back down. "Who do you think you are, barging in here . . . " His eyes narrowed. "I know. You're that waitress from the Clam Strip."

Maya gaped at him. She'd never seen this guy at the restaurant. And he couldn't possibly have recognized her in this disguise. Someone had told him.

Her breath caught. If Allison had found something that led her to Kingston, she might have come here to talk to him. "Are you sure you don't know Allison Rafferty? She's Harley Rivers' girlfriend."

His face went ashen.

The blonde receptionist strolled into the room, carrying some papers. "Alan," she said before she noticed the tension. "Oh. Excuse me." She started to back out.

"Darcy," he barked. "Get the police chief on the line. Tell him to get his ass over here. Now."

Maya scrammed. She hustled down the hall and ran out the front door, glancing back to see if Kingston had followed. He was standing in the building's doorway and his hands were balled into fists.

She hurried to her car and drove it partway down the block, letting the engine idle as she tried to figure out what to do next. If the police were on their way, she couldn't get taken in for questioning. Could Allison have gone to BEC instead—to Jonah?

No. Kingston had reacted strongly to Harley's name. He knew something. Maya slumped low in the car seat, using the side mirror to keep an eye on the Kingston Development office. Now that she'd stirred up the hornet's nest, things were bound to happen. Kingston might not know the name Allison Rafferty, but he'd definitely known who Harley's girlfriend was. This was the best lead she had.

She picked up her cell phone and dialed Officer Raymond's number, her hand shaking so hard she could barely hit the digits. She'd better bring him up to speed.

Maya caught movement in the side mirror. Kingston had rushed out of the building and climbed into a white truck. It roared down the street, right past her. She tossed the phone onto the passenger seat and took chase.

It was impossible to hide her super-sized pink car, so Maya trailed far behind him. The white truck turned down Olive Street, just blocks from the Coast Defenders house. She stopped her car, watching as Kingston parked in front of a trendy café and went inside.

Disappointed, Maya was about to drive away when a gold Escalade jerked to a stop at the restaurant's curb. Bonus: a two-for-one special.

She waited a minute for Kingston and Curt to get settled, then went up to the café counter and ordered a coffee to go. She snagged a few free peppermint candies from the basket by the register and slipped them into her skirt pocket. Who knew when she'd have time to eat next?

Across the room, the two men were deep in conversation. The café was quiet—post-lunch service—and they were the only customers. Maya headed toward their booth, sipping her coffee and holding the wrapped-up bundle of bones under one arm.

Curt blanched. "What are you doing here?"

"I could ask you the same thing." She propped a hand on their booth.

"I'm, uh, meeting with a client. So if you don't mind—"

"I do mind. I have some questions."

Alan Kingston remained silent. Neither of them had touched their Danishes, and ice was melting in their water glasses. They weren't here to eat.

When Kingston finally looked up, his blue eyes were chilly. "After that stunt you pulled in my office, you have some nerve following me here. I've got the mayor on speed dial, you know. I could make your life a living hell."

"Settle down. I just stopped in for a coffee." Maya held up her cup and took a slow sip. "I saw Curt and thought I'd say hi. We worked together at BEC."

Kingston turned a sick shade of green. She stared him down. If he'd covered up an eco-crime at DreamCoast, if he had anything to do with Sara's disappearance or Harley's death, he deserved to suffer. And if he'd done something to Allison . . .

Kingston stared hard at Curt, who looked down at the table.

Maya set the bones, the ends sticking out from the t-shirts, on the table in front of them. "Take a look at what Harley and Sara found at DreamCoast."

Curt eyed the bundle as if it were a coiled rattlesnake. Kingston's jaw clenched. Both men watched intently as she unrolled the fabric, revealing the two bones. "Do you have the police chief on speed dial, too? Because now would be a good time to use it."

Kingston threw his napkin on the table and stood up. "This is your goddamn fault," he growled at Curt. "Fix it."

He brushed past Maya and walked out the café door.

She slid into the booth across from Curt, the one person she hadn't talked to about all this. "Where is my friend Allison Rafferty? Did she come to BEC yesterday?"

His breath was labored and his eyes darted around, settling anywhere but on her. "I have no idea what you're talking about." He reached into his wallet, slapped some bills on the table, and stood up.

"Not so fast." Maya rose, too. "What did you cover up at Dream-Coast? Taxidermy chemicals. DDT. Arsenic. What else?"

His mouth opened, and he gasped for air. "You're crazy. I haven't done anything. There's no cover-up." With a lunge, he grabbed the two bones and fled for the door.

Maya jogged after him. "Liar! Thief!" As she crossed the threshold, she tripped and fell. By the time she got to her feet, Curt was already at his car.

She raced after him. Kingston's white truck was long gone, and the gold Escalade coasted away from the curb. The Escalade that Curt had probably purchased with blood money from DreamCoast. It disappeared down the street. The bones were gone—her evidence. Harley and Sara's evidence.

And she still didn't know where Allison was.

Forty-Six

Maya sat in the Pink Beast. What now?

A hand rapped on the passenger window and she jumped. Then she realized who it was and rolled down the window partway. "What do you want?"

"I saw you fall just now. Are you all right?" Tomas asked.

"No." She frowned. "Allison's gone missing."

"Missing?"

"Nobody's seen her since she left the Clam Strip yesterday at noon. The police are looking for her." Maya picked up her phone from the car seat. Still no word.

Tomas' face tightened. "She came by the house yesterday. I saw her."

"What time?"

He leaned in the window. "Around 12:30."

Maya stared at him. "Then you were the last person to see her."

"Oh, no," he said. "Don't try to pin this on me. Several of us were there. We all saw her leave. She drove off in her Subaru."

That didn't make sense. Where would she have gone? "Who else was there?"

He thought for a moment. "Kelsey. Ellery and Venus, the blondes. And Nick."

"Did any of them talk to her?"

"Nick did," Tomas said. "Maybe Kelsey, too."

Nick, who'd lied about his relationship with Kelsey. Maya's stomach churned. Why had he said he hadn't seen Allison yesterday? Or was Tomas lying? She didn't know whom to trust anymore. Sara and Harley had relied on the Coast Defenders—and look what'd happened to them. Maya had been blaming everything on Kingston and BEC, but what if the Coast Defenders were involved, too?

Tomas was no dummy. He knew something was up. He leaned closer, putting his head inside the car. She shrank away, pressed against the driver's door.

"Tell me what's going on. I can help you," he said.

She shivered. If Nick had lied about not seeing Allison yesterday, had he lied about Tomas, too? "Nick told me about the bumper repair on your truck. He found the receipt."

"What receipt? And the last repair I had done was a water pump. After that huge bill, I won't be fixing bumpers anytime soon."

She stared at him. "But if you didn't push my car off the road, who did?"

"I don't know." He got quiet. "I started following you because you seemed to have the inside track on Harley's death. Maybe somebody else realized that, too."

Maya flinched. Nick was the other Coast Defender who'd stuck close. But no—Tomas had seen Harley the night he died. He'd said things about Sara and the bottom of the ocean. "When did Harley tell you about the vandalized sailboat? When you met him on the Bayfront, at Newport Nature Tours?"

"You don't seriously think . . . " Tomas frowned. "What the hell? I didn't set the fire. I didn't even see him that night."

"Then how did he 'mention' the sailboat to you?"

Tomas rummaged in his pocket and pulled out a cell phone. He opened it up, punched some buttons, and showed her through the open window. "He sent me this." On the screen was a picture of a sailboat with jagged cuts in its side.

"You could have taken that yourself. Right after you did the damage."

Tomas showed her a text message from Harley: *Hey T, guess what I found tonight at Rocky's? Photo coming.*

Fat raindrops dotted the windshield. "Can I get in?" he asked. "It's about to start pouring."

Maya exhaled slowly. Her brother had apparently trusted Tomas. Could she? She nodded and he climbed inside. "I want to know why you've been following me."

He gave a slight smile. "Believe it or not, I was worried about you. After what happened to Harley and Sara . . ."

Maya let this sink in. Tomas was worried about her? That was a new wrinkle. "Yesterday, when you saw Allison at the house, did anyone leave around the same time she did?"

Tomas looked surprised. "Nick left about twenty minutes later. Or more. I wasn't really paying attention."

Nick again. Maya picked at the fuzz on her leggings. This black fabric collected everything: cat hair, grit, random fibers. Her fingers plucked off a piece of long, straight, dark hair. She stared at it. Had this come from her house? Or from Allison's? A chill ran through her. "Does Nick live at the Coast Defenders house?"

"He has his own apartment, but I'm not sure where. You didn't know?" She shook her head. "He's never invited any of us there—not even Kelsey," he added.

"Is he at the group's house right now?"

"He left. I thought he said he was looking for you."

The chill moved deeper. "When did Nick join the group?"

"Last November."

"Where did he move from?"

"Colorado."

Colorado? He told me California. The avocado farm. More lies. Harley had set that bulldozer on fire in October, and if Nick had showed up soon afterward, it wasn't coincidence. Ever since he'd arrived in town, the vandalism had escalated. And, according to Tomas, Kingston owned property in Colorado. He and Nick might know each other.

Maya felt sick. Tomas leaned over, peering at her. "What's wrong? You're white as a sheet."

She'd been wrong about Nick. *So* wrong. She couldn't say anything—not until she knew how deep the betrayal went. "It's nothing." Her voice shook. "I'm just worried about Allison."

"I need to get going." Tomas scribbled his cell number on a scrap of paper from his pocket. "In case you change your mind, call me. I'm on your side."

She took the paper, unable to speak.

Tomas got out, and Maya prayed she hadn't just sent away the one person who could help her.

She sat there for long minutes, thinking. Nick had been at the house yesterday. He'd seen Allison, talked to her. He'd left not long after she had.

Her stomach clenched. She'd told Allison about her dates with Nick, so Allison would have trusted him. He could have followed her home to Toledo. Maya suddenly remembered his strange offer to "search" for Allison. To go hiking together. He'd wanted to take Maya somewhere, too.

But where was he now? Who would know?

Forty-Seven

The Coast Defenders' house looked eerily deserted. The crack now careened all the way across the front window, and yellow paint had chipped from the siding.

Kelsey was curled up on the wicker loveseat, weeping. Her spiky hair lay flat and dark trails of mascara streaked down both cheeks.

"Where's Nick?" Maya demanded, taking the steps to the porch two at a time. Kelsey didn't answer. Maya tried the front door, but it was locked. She rang the doorbell and pounded on the wood. "Do you know where he is?"

Kelsey gave a sob. "Nobody's home. No one's here but me."

Terrific. "When did you last see him?"

"He left after you came by." Kelsey's eyes narrowed. She swiped her hand underneath them, smearing the mascara even more. "What were you two arguing about? He was furious. I've never seen him like that. I tried to talk to him and he pushed me away and took off."

Maya pulled out her cell. "Look, I need to reach him and I don't have his number with me." She stared Kelsey down until she got a mumbled answer. Her call went straight to his voice mail and she hung up without leaving a message. "Did you see him with Allison yesterday? Or today?"

"Allison?"

"Harley's girlfriend. She's tall." Maya held her hand high. "Long blonde hair."

Kelsey pursed her rosebud lips. "You and your friend need to stop chasing after my boyfriend."

"Chasing?" Maya blinked.

"After he broke into your apartment to get the files, he thought you'd back off. Instead—"

Her mouth dropped. "Nick broke into my apartment?" When she'd told him about the intruder, he'd been shocked. If Kelsey was telling the truth, he was a gifted actor. "Did he run my car off the road, too?"

When Kelsey's face paled, everything clicked. "That was you," Maya said.

Kelsey nodded. "Yeah. Sorry."

"Sorry? You could be arrested for hit-and-run. You almost killed me."

"I barely tapped your car. My dad's truck, the one I was driving that night, it doesn't have a mark on it." Kelsey looked away. "I didn't mean to hurt you. I just wanted to scare you a little, keep you away from Nick. I didn't know you were going to go all freaky and drive off the road."

Maya wanted to blast into her. But the accident wasn't important—not compared to Allison. "Where is Nick now?"

Kelsey shook her head.

"Where is his apartment?"

Another shake of the head.

Did the girl really not know? Maya would have to go looking for him. But she'd need a weapon. Because if he had Allison with him . . . She thought for a moment. "Do you guys have any pepper spray or a tire iron?"

"No." Kelsey stared at her. "What do you need those for?"

"How about a big shovel?"

"We have garden tools in the shed out back. But why—"

"Best if you don't know." Maya darted off the porch and headed into the overgrown backyard. The grass was so tall, it licked at the hem of her skirt.

Kelsey followed, blasting out questions. "Why do you need a shovel? *Pepper spray?* What are you up to? This doesn't have anything to do with Nick, does it?"

Maya ignored her. Nick knew where Allison was. He'd suggested a hike. Could that mean DreamCoast?

The shed was locked with a shiny, new padlock. But when Kelsey joined her, she had a set of keys in hand. "Open it," Maya said. "Or I'll report the hit-and-run to the cops. And to your dad." Meekly, Kelsey unlocked the door.

The shed's interior was cluttered with bags of mulch, an assortment of plant pots, and a pile of garden tools. Maya picked up a square-edged shovel. It wasn't ideal: too heavy, too unwieldy.

She glanced around. It was dim in here, the afternoon light starting to fade. She pointed to a large, locked cabinet. "What's in there? Give me your keys." Kelsey handed them over.

Maya opened the cabinet and searched the upper shelves for a possible weapon. Mostly junk. She dropped to her knees to poke around the bottom shelf, pushing aside a bottle of lighter fluid. *Lighter fluid?* Stuffed behind the bottle was a bundle of rags, an ax, and two cans of green spray paint. *But that meant . . .*

She glanced over her shoulder. If Kelsey realized Maya had found the group's vandalism supplies, she might attack. But Kelsey's mouth hung open in surprise.

"Who did the vandalism?" Maya asked.

Kelsey stared, wide-eyed. "I don't know."

"Nick."

"No, he wouldn't do that. We'd get in huge trouble." Her eyes showed her uncertainty. "The cops would toss us in jail and throw away the key. I wouldn't get out until I was really old . . . like thirty."

Maya picked up the square-edged shovel. "You should report this. If you didn't do the vandalism—if you didn't know about it—they'll probably let you make a deal."

"I'd never squeal on another group member," Kelsey said. "And Nick's my boyfriend. I don't want him to get in trouble."

"Trust me. He's using you."

"He's not." Kelsey crossed her hands over her chest. "He loves me. We just have a few issues to work out."

It was the same naïve way Maya used to feel about Frank. "Nick and I slept together," she said. "He was using both of us."

Kelsey turned white. "What? You *slept* with him? When?"

"The other night."

"That cheating bastard!" Kelsey seethed. "He said nothing was going on. I *knew* I couldn't believe him when he said you were just friends."

"That's what he told me, too."

"Oh! He's gonna be *so* sorry."

"He betrayed your whole group." Maya stepped outside. "And I need to find him. Now."

Kelsey's bottom lip quivered. "Let me show you something."

"I don't have time. Nick took my friend Allison somewhere. She's been missing since yesterday. I need to find them."

"Allison was asking about Harley's computer. I heard her. Come upstairs. I want to show you something." She trotted toward the kitchen door.

Maya hesitated.

"I found his laptop," Kelsey said over her shoulder. She slipped into the house.

Maya leaned the shovel against the kitchen wall and ran up the stairs after her, praying for a clue that would help her find Allison.

Upstairs, Kelsey was standing outside a closed door. "This is my room." She turned the knob and ushered Maya inside. The space was spotless—and extremely pink. The bed had a flowered comforter. Apparently even Goth Girls channeled their inner princess.

Kelsey reached between the mattress and box springs, and slid out a Mac laptop with a blue sticker on it.

"Where'd you find that?"

Kelsey's face pinched tight. "After Allison asked, I searched the whole house. I finally found it in a cupboard, hidden under some books." She opened the laptop. "Someone tried to wipe the hard drive, but they were no expert. They just deleted files. I restored them." Her fingers swished across the tracking pad.

Maya leaned over Kelsey's shoulder. Her gaze halted on a jpeg file on the desktop, labeled Class Reunion. She pointed. "Click on that." The grainy image, a screenshot off the web, showed a page from a high-school yearbook. Maya took the laptop and zoomed in. The center photo showed a smiling teenager with blue eyes and short blond hair. His high school was in Colorado. She gulped. The name under the photo was Craig Kingston. And his eyes were a familiar shade of blue. Vivid blue. Just like Alan Kingston's.

Her breath tightened. *Was it possible?* The image was years old, but she could see the resemblance. He'd darkened his hair, grown it long, and worn brown-tinted contacts. "Nick is Kingston's son," she murmured.

"What?" Kelsey looked hard at the picture. "Oh my God."

Maya couldn't stop staring at it. Nick had been playing her the whole time—fooling everyone. He'd done the vandalism himself, hoping to discredit the group. He'd probably killed Sara for threatening to expose the pollution. And then he'd murdered Harley. Her mouth went dry. What had he done to Allison?

"I can't believe this," Kelsey moaned.

He must have taken Allison to DreamCoast. Was he trying to stop her from asking more questions—or getting back at Maya? That coldness in his eyes, when he'd tried to convince her to go with him—he'd wanted them both in the same place. He wanted them gone. Like Sara.

"I need to use your phone." Maya flew down the steps to the main floor. If anything bad happened to Allison or the baby, she'd never forgive herself. Ever.

She stopped in the dining room to call Officer Raymond, but got his voice mail again. Weren't the police supposed to answer their damn phones? She left a message saying she had a good lead on Allison and was heading to the DreamCoast construction site. "Meet me there as soon as you can. Please." She hung up.

Kelsey hovered around the desk. "You're going there now? By yourself?"

"I have to." Maya picked up the phone again. Toledo was miles from DreamCoast—even if Officer Raymond listened to his voice mail in the next five minutes, it'd take him too long to get there.

She dialed 9-1-1. "This may sound crazy," she said into the receiver. "But I think this guy named Nick—or Craig—took my friend Allison Rafferty out to the DreamCoast property. He kidnapped her from her house in Toledo. I'm worried he'll hurt her." *Or he already has.*

Kelsey's eyes widened.

"Kidnapped? In Toledo?" The dispatcher said. "Where are you calling from?"

"Newport."

"Just wanted to make sure I had that straight. It looks like your current location is . . . the Coast Defenders house?"

"I'm not a group member," Maya said. "That's not why I'm calling. My friend Allison was kidnapped and taken to DreamCoast. The construction site owned by Alan Kingston."

There was a long pause.

"She's been missing since yesterday," Maya said. "If you don't believe me, call Officer Raymond in Toledo." She pulled his crumpled business card from her skirt pocket and rattled off the number. "Please. Can't you help me?"

"The property appears to be outside the city's response area," the dispatcher said. "But the Sheriff's office can send a deputy to check it out. I'll let them know."

"Thanks." Maya hung up. She ran into the kitchen and grabbed the shovel. "Can you call Tomas and let him know I went to DreamCoast?" Kelsey nodded.

When Maya drove off in the Pink Beast, she glanced in the rearview mirror. Kelsey was standing in the doorway of the Coast Defenders house. She pulled a cell phone from her pocket.

Maya sincerely hoped she wasn't calling Nick to warn him.

Forty-Eight

The swing gate across the road was closed and locked. Either Nick hadn't brought Allison here or he'd re-locked it after going through.

Maya backed up the Skylark a few feet, letting the tires slide off the pavement onto the muddy shoulder. She jumped out, grabbed the shovel, and peered down the road toward the highway. No lights or sirens. She couldn't wait for the cops.

She climbed over the gate's metal arm and started hiking up the steep, winding road, her lungs pumping hard.

She had to stop several times to catch her breath and transfer the heavy shovel from one hand to the other. Her flimsy ballet flats slapped against the pavement. The wintry chill penetrated the thin fabric of her peasant skirt and top. Not too smart. She'd rushed here without grabbing a jacket, hiking boots or a flashlight.

The clouds dripped raindrops, keeping the air moist and misty. Late afternoon light barely infiltrated the forest on either side of the road. How long until dark? An hour or two? Maya continued hiking up the hill.

At last, she reached the clearing. It was much bigger than she'd imagined—she could barely see the other end.

She scanned the site, searching for signs of Nick's presence. A curving line of asphalt snaked through the construction zone. On either side of it, wood stakes poked from bare dirt. A backhoe and forklift were parked next to a portable toilet, but aside from the new road, the site wasn't any more developed than in that aerial photo she'd seen at BEC. A photo taken weeks ago. Sara and Harley, or the discovery of environmental pollution, *had* slowed down Kingston.

Maya's brow furrowed. There were no cars or trucks. Maybe Allison wasn't at DreamCoast at all.

On the far end of the clearing, buttressed by dark woods, sat a small cabin. She squinted, trying to see it better from this distance. *Yes.* It had gingerbread trim on its eaves, like the cabin from Harley's photo. The place appeared abandoned, but she couldn't leave without checking it out.

Maya headed up the curving road through the construction site. When the pavement ended, she stepped into muck. Mud coated her shoes. Everything felt damp here—the air, the ground, the dripping trees. A creek roared nearby, swallowing the sounds of the forest. She kept hiking toward the cabin, using the shovel like a walking stick.

Something howled behind her and the hairs rose on the back of her neck. Coyote? Cougar? She blew out a panicked breath. Being here alone was freaky enough without wildlife. Suddenly that rundown cabin looked mighty appealing.

She hustled the last few hundred feet. The cabin's wood door was swollen with moisture and she had to push hard to open it. Heart racing, she stepped inside.

With the curtains drawn, the front room was dim. She waited for her eyes to adjust: a couch against one wall, a deer head, missing an eye, mounted above it. A file cabinet, coffeemaker, and card table with folding chairs. Not abandoned, then. Had this been Walter Dearborn's home?

A faint moan came from down the hall.

"Allison? Is that you?" she called softly.

Nobody answered. But she hadn't imagined that sound. Maya walked toward the back of the house, her wet ballet shoes leaving muddy tracks across the floor.

Two closed doors. She put a hand on the nearest knob. "Allison?" she whispered against the wood. Silence.

Maya swung the door open: a small bathroom with old-fashioned fixtures, the toilet bowl stained with rust. She stepped inside the room. Cobwebs coated the ceiling and walls, and when she pulled back the shower curtain, a huge spider scuttled toward her. She bit back a scream.

Maya crossed the hall and opened the other door. Even darker in here. She should have brought a flashlight. She peered around the space. In one corner was a bed with knobby metal posts and a bare mattress. The floor was thick with stirred-up dust. Holding her breath, Maya crouched down and looked under the bed. No one there.

She stood back up. On the opposite wall was a door. A closet? "Allison?"

Another moan, this one louder. Maya put her hand on the closet's doorknob. It twisted freely, but the door didn't open. She inspected the edge. Locked. "It's me, Maya." She tried to peer through the keyhole.

"Maya?" Allison gasped. "Get me out of here!"

Maya took the shovel and maneuvered the tip of the blade into the slit between the door and frame. With a grunt, she pulled back.

Nothing happened.

She tried again, pulling harder. This time, wood splintered and the frail lock broke.

Allison lay curled in a fetal position under the bottom shelf. Her face was swollen and streaked with tears. She had a black eye and a bruised cheek, her skin as pale as her white sailor blouse. She was shivering, the skimpy Clam Strip uniform no match for an unheated house. A handkerchief hung around her neck like a noose. A gag she'd pulled off?

"What happened?" Maya cried, dropping to her knees. "Are you okay?"

Slowly, Allison uncurled from the tight ball, extending her limbs like a hermit crab emerging from its shell. Straining with effort, she rolled onto her back, her knees propped up and hands protecting her belly. "It hurts."

"Where?"

Allison pointed to her head and legs. Her stomach. "Did Nick find you?"

Nick. Maya shook her head. "Is he here?" She glanced over her shoulder.

"I don't know," Allison whispered.

Maya angled her body so she could watch the bedroom doorway. Could she have missed seeing him? "How'd you get here?"

"I went to the Coast Defenders house to ask about Harley's laptop and Nick said you were waiting for me in Toledo. So I rushed home . . . He showed up a few minutes later, tricked me into coming here with him. At first he was nice, but then he started asking questions. And when I wouldn't tell him what you knew, he lost it. He was swearing and hitting me and . . . Oh, God, it hurts."

"And then he left you? How long's he been gone?"

"He comes and goes—" Allison gasped in pain. "Just get me out of here."

"I'll be right back. I need to check something." Maya hurried to the front door. She stared out into the clearing. Nick didn't appear to be here now . . . but he'd return. She couldn't carry Allison back to her car. Maya pulled the cell phone from her pocket. No sign of life. The hills here must be blocking the signal or it was too far from town. She bit her lip. She'd have to take the Pink Beast and get help. But that meant leaving Allison here alone.

She returned to the bedroom. Allison had crawled out of the closet and was sitting slumped against the wall, pale and spent. "I need to get help," Maya said. "I'll be back as soon as I can."

"Don't leave me!"

"Then you have to walk. We have to go *now*." Her voice rose in panic. "Can you even stand up?"

"Cut me some slack," Allison snapped. "I haven't had any food or water since I got here. It's not my fault I'm weak." She sat up straight, bristling.

Cranky was good. Maya could work with cranky—it was way better than helpless. She fished the mints from her skirt pocket and handed them over. "Here. Have a sugar jolt."

She scrounged through the main room and found a half-full bottle of artesian spring water. She handed it to Allison. "Drink up. We need to be gone before he comes back."

Allison sipped.

"C'mon. Let's go," Maya said. "Nick is a killer. He set that fire to murder Harley." Allison stared at her. "And I don't plan on losing any more family. We need to get out of here." Maya grabbed the shovel.

At last, Allison struggled to her feet, holding onto Maya's hand and the wall as she rose. She whimpered with pain as they walked through the cabin, resting her weight on Maya. They made it outside about twenty feet before Allison sank to the ground. "I'm sorry. I can't do this."

Maya pulled her back up and half-pushed, half-dragged her toward the woods near the cabin. She scouted for a place for Allison to rest. By that old spruce? Its roots were so big, they almost made a bench. She led Allison to it and leaned the shovel against the trunk. "I'm going for help."

Allison grabbed her hand. "Before you leave . . . if it sounded like I didn't want Harley's baby . . . " Maya held her breath as Allison continued, "I *really* do."

Maya smiled. As she stepped away, headlights flickered across the far end of the clearing. Someone was driving up the road to the development. Her heart leaped with hope. The cops?

And then she remembered the locked gate. Whoever was driving up had a key. *Nick.* He couldn't have missed seeing her Pink Beast. He knew she was here.

Maya turned back to Allison. "Go into the woods. Hide. I'll get help." She handed over the shovel. Allison needed a weapon more than she did. "If he finds you, hit him with this. Hit him hard."

She hugged Allison and left, hoping it was the right choice. Maya stopped behind a tree to watch. A white Kingston Development truck hurtled across the bumpy ground and came to a screeching stop outside the cabin. The driver got out and slammed the door.

It was Nick, no longer hiding his relationship to his dad.

As he walked toward the cabin, she shivered. If he'd arrived ten minutes sooner, they'd have been trapped inside. He stopped at the cabin door and turned, searching the site. Had he spotted her? She slid further behind the tree trunk. As soon as he discovered Allison was gone, he'd come looking for them.

The moment he headed inside, Maya ran over to his truck. She tugged on the doors, but they were locked. And he'd taken the keys with him.

She headed back to the woods, scooting along the edge of the clearing. Branches whacked at her arms and legs. Roots pierced her thin-soled shoes. Spiderwebs clung to her skin.

She glanced back. He was still inside the cabin, too far away to see clearly. Could she make it to the road downhill? It was only a few hundred yards away—and it soon took a sharp bend. If she could reach that spot, she'd be out of sight. But to get to the road, she'd have to enter the wide-open clearing. She felt a tremor of fear. What if he found Allison before she got back?

Glancing toward the cabin again, Maya stepped away from the trees and started jogging toward the road that would take her to the highway. Two hundred yards. A hundred yards. Fifty. She was going to make it.

Then her body went sprawling. One shoulder slammed against the dirt. Her ankle twisted. Sharp pains shot up her leg and she had to bite her hand to keep from screaming. What had just happened? She looked back and saw the wooden stake poking from the ground. She'd run right into it.

Once she could breathe again, she rotated her ankle slowly. Ouch, that hurt. Was it broken? She slipped off her leggings and wrapped them tightly around the area. The ankle was already swelling. Pain throbbed, but she could move it. Sprained, not broken.

She crouched low in the dirt, paralyzed with indecision. Was Nick still inside the cabin? If he spotted her, he could catch her easily. And her Pink Beast wasn't parked for a quick getaway. Maybe it'd be better to hide in the forest near the clearing. That way, she could draw him away from Allison if needed. She crawled toward the trees on the opposite side.

In the distance, the truck's horn blared. "Maya! Where are you?" Nick yelled. "I know you're here somewhere."

His harsh voice galvanized her. She pushed herself to standing and attempted a few wobbly steps, sucking in a breath of sheer pain. She glanced over her shoulder. Nick was standing next to the white truck, his back toward her. He was looking down at the ground. Had he seen their footprints in the mud, leading from the cabin into the trees?

He started walking toward the woods. Toward the spruce tree. She had to do something.

Maya cupped her hands over her mouth and yelled, "Hey, Nick! I'm over here!" As soon as he turned, she staggered toward the forest, hurrying for cover.

His head swiveled, but he didn't move from the spot.

"Over here!" she yelled again, waving a hand. This time he saw her—and started running.

With her lame ankle and so many trees, roots and shrubs to navigate around, her pace was slow, but she kept moving, going deeper into the woods. Those same trees and roots would slow him down, too.

"Ma-ya!" Nick called her name. "Wait up!"

Right.

"Ma-ya!" His voice got closer.

Much closer.

She came to a small creek with muddy banks. Should she cross? She might be able to lose him on the other side, then circle back to Allison.

The water was rushing fast, but the creek wasn't too wide. She stepped into it, gasping as the numbing cold water soaked her bare legs. She waded across and heaved herself up the other bank.

"Don't run away!" He sounded angry. "I know you're not far away. I can hear you splashing."

Why had she thought she could escape him? She had nothing left. Her body shivered uncontrollably, and her ankle delivered agonizing pain with every step. A few yards ahead was a fallen log, rotting in place. Decomposition had hollowed out the core, making a space just big enough to hide. She had no choice.

She slid backwards into the gap and tucked her head down.

Forty-Nine

Her hiding spot smelled of musty earth. Insects crawled across her skin, but she let them roam, willing herself not to squirm.

Nick thrashed through the underbrush. He was so near she could hear his every rough exhale, hear him mutter, "I'm coming for you, bitch."

Her heart thumped.

Another ragged, angry breath. More muttering. Louder muttering.

She kept her head low. If her dark hair blended with the log, maybe he'd pass without seeing her.

His footsteps drew closer.

"Gotcha!" he cried.

Maya raised her head. He was only yards away. She pushed herself out from the log, scrambled to her feet, and took a few limping steps. Pain shot through her ankle. As she crumpled toward the ground, Nick grabbed her.

She screamed bloody murder, but no one heard. No one came.

He gave a manic laugh and clamped an arm over her shoulder, yanking her upright. He smelled of sweat and fury. Moisture dripped off his forehead and ran down his cheeks. His eyes were crazed.

Maya swung at him, but he dodged her fist easily and tossed her to the ground. The back of her head slammed against dirt. She screamed again and his hand clamped over her mouth. "Shut the hell up."

His weight landed on her.

Sobbing, she twisted away. She fought for breath, writhing and kicking, but his fists pummeled her until she was still. She swallowed spit and tasted the rusty tinge of blood.

Nick climbed to his feet and yanked her arms over her head. Dragging her by the wrists, he pulled her toward the creek. The ground scoured her skin. She shouted and kicked, trying desperately to get free, but there was nobody in the woods to save her.

Water roared in her ears.

Abruptly, Nick let go of her hands and rolled her onto her stomach. Before she could move, he pushed her headfirst over the creek bank. She slid toward the water, grasping frantically for a rock or branch to slow her fall. All of a sudden, her body jerked to a stop. He'd grabbed her legs, pinning her in place. The top of her head dipped into the icy creek.

"No!" Current tugged at her hair. She pressed her hands into the rocky creek bottom, trying to keep her chin above water. Her arm muscles started to quiver and her fingers went numb. Nick was still holding her legs, his hands like vise grips around her ankles. Every squeeze of his palms sent pain shooting through her swollen foot.

Her head drooped lower. When she took her next breath, water filled her mouth. She choked, coughing it back out. Was this what had happened to Sara . . . he'd watched her drown?

"It's your fucking fault," Nick said. "If you hadn't stirred things up, everything would be fine."

Another mouthful of creek.

He cackled. "Thirsty?"

Her muscles shook, quivering so hard she could barely stay propped up. She angled her head to one side, her mouth just above the waterline. "I've told people about the bones, you know. You'll never get away with this. The police are on their way."

"What?" Nick's weight suddenly shifted. The hands around her ankles tightened and he dragged her up the bank. With a grunt, he flopped her onto the ground.

She rolled onto her back, peeled one eye open. Could she escape? She'd never outrun him. She needed a plan.

"Who have you told?" he demanded.

She tried to sit up, but Nick pushed her back down. Her teeth chattered. Maybe talking could buy her time. Oh, why hadn't she told anyone the full story? People knew pieces of it, but nobody except her could put it all together.

"You don't know anything." His hands circled her wrists, trapping her. He was so strong.

She squeezed her eyes shut, willing herself not to fight. Not yet. She had to catch him off guard. "I know you hurt Sara."

He frowned. "She made a bad choice. I couldn't let that go."

Maya gave a shaky breath. "Is she . . . dead?"

"Stone dead." The words lingered.

"I'm sure you had . . . a reason." Her voice trembled.

"I found her digging here at the construction site. I caught her stealing bones. She was going to *tell*." He sounded like a petulant child.

A shiver rolled through her. "Was your dad here with you?"

"No." He rustled. "You know about him?"

"I know everything. Except how the pollution was discovered."

Maya tried again to sit up, but he shoved her back roughly. Her muscles shook uncontrollably. She was soaking wet and chilled, bruised and battered. Her skirt was hiked up around her thighs and she'd lost her ballet shoes somewhere. How could she even fight? Her ankle wasn't strong enough to run on. She stirred, testing his grip.

"You have to understand. We had no choice." His fingernails dug into her wrists. "Curt found some strange readings in his soil samples." With his free hand, Nick wiped the sweat from his face. "We couldn't let that happen. My dad put millions into this project. If the bank called in the loan, we'd lose everything." His fingernails dug in again. "It was too risky. Toxic chemicals in the dirt? No one would buy condos here."

"So your dad bribed Curt." Her voice wobbled. "To make it look like nothing was wrong."

"Actually, that was Curt's idea. And it wasn't a big deal," he assured her. "We could have put a cement slab over the dirt . . . or something. There was no risk to people."

"Walter Dearborn has cancer, probably caused by those same chemicals."

"Oh, Christ. You know about him, too?"

"And what if the pollution got into this creek or the groundwater? What about the community garden? The playground? Kids."

"You sound just like Harley. He couldn't leave things alone."

"So you murdered him." Maya couldn't keep the rage from her voice.

"I didn't have a choice," Nick snarled.

"Because he found Sara's locket?"

"Oh, you fell for that? I put her locket in that box of files when I broke into your apartment. I thought it'd freak you out so much, you'd stop digging. But you didn't. So I found another way to keep you . . . occupied."

Heat surged through her. *Asshole.* "You're a good actor," she managed.

"Two years of theater training." His hand traveled over her wet blouse and down the skirt to her bare thigh. "Thankfully, it wasn't a strain. You're quite the tiger. In bed and out."

Maya swallowed hard. She looked around surreptitiously, straining to see in the dim forest light. A few feet away, a thick branch lay on the ground. If she could reach it . . .

He ran a hand up her thigh. "We're gonna have some fun. Before—"

Before? She shuddered. "Why not?" Closing her eyes, she whispered, "You were fantastic in bed. I can't wait to see what you do with a creek bank."

He ignored her sarcasm and reached for her blouse. She let him push it up, biding her time. When he let go of her wrists and leaned over to yank down her bra, Maya lunged.

Go for the eyes. That's what the instructor had said in her self-defense class. Go for the eyes. Maya held her breath as she shoved her fingers into Nick's eye sockets.

His eyes disappeared under a sea of blood. Nick screamed, clawing at his face. The sound seemed to go on forever.

Bile rose in her throat, but she choked it back.

It was him—or her.

She clambered to her feet and grabbed the thick branch. Yelling like a Samurai warrior, she slammed it over his head. *Take that, you bastard.*

He slumped to the dirt and stayed there.

Maya's fingers plucked at her blouse, the white fabric streaked with blood. What had she done? As she limped away from Nick's body, her legs wouldn't stop shaking. She looked back. He lay still. *Dead* still.

Her head swam with dizziness. She reached out, grabbing a tree trunk to stay upright. Nick couldn't hurt her family now. She'd seen to that.

But what did it make *her*?

Under the canopy of evergreens, the woods were already dark. Soon, the sky would darken, too. She needed to find Allison.

The creek roared. Maya stared at the water, praying for guidance. Which way was the construction site? If she followed the creek downstream, would she end up there? She took a few faltering steps toward the water, wincing as pain shot through her ankle. The rough ground scraped at her bare feet. When she reached the creek bank, she turned downstream, following its curving path.

After she'd been walking for two or three minutes, she heard a faint noise. A cry?

Maya stopped to listen. Only the rustling of the forest. The wind in the treetops. Flowing water. She remained still, tuning her ears to the slightest sound.

Nothing.

She stepped forward and heard the noise again. Her gaze swiveled, searching the underbrush. What was that pale thing by the tree? She strained to see. Not just pale—a bright, unnatural white. Her breath caught. Had Allison crossed the stream, too?

Maya hobbled toward the white *something*. Blood pulsed in her ears, thumping so loudly it masked the creek's roar. One step, and then another. She leaned forward. It *was* Allison!

She was curled up on the ground next to a fern. Maya fell to her knees and touched Allison's cheek. Her body was still. "Allison! Are you okay? Talk to me!"

No response.

She took Allison's wrist in her hand. Thank God—a faint pulse throbbed. And her chest was rising and falling. But her skin felt ice cold. Maya glanced down. Her own blouse and skirt were sopping wet. She had no way to keep Allison warm. She had to get medical help.

Maya looked back at the creek. If Allison had reached this spot in her weak condition, the construction site couldn't be far. She squinted. Beyond the creek was an opening in the trees. The clearing?

She let go of Allison's hand. There was a tiny object in the dirt beside Allison. Maya stared at it. A bone. This one looked fresh. Recently buried animals?

Her hand quaking, she picked it up and slid the small bone into her skirt pocket. Her evidence. "I'll be back. I promise." She gave Allison's hand a squeeze before she staggered to her feet and headed for the creek.

Two trucks were parked in the mud outside the cabin. One was Nick's. The other, a dark-colored pickup. Friend or foe? Maya stopped on the edge of the woods, her heart pounding.

She was about to step into the clearing when the cabin door opened. A man walked out. She watched, breathless, as he hurried over to the truck and opened the passenger door. In this dusky light, all she could see was his silhouette. Was it Alan Kingston, searching for his son?

Moments later, a second man emerged from the cabin. This time, she sagged with relief. He wore a uniform. The cavalry had arrived.

She let out a soft whoop and stepped into the clearing.

The man by the truck ran toward her, and she was shocked to see it was Tomas. He stared at her, equally open-mouthed. "Are you okay?"

She nodded, her teeth chattering. Tomas took off his jacket and draped it over her shoulders, and she hugged it close. "Kelsey told me what you found at the house," he whispered to her. "Sorry it took so long. We had to convince the cops that DreamCoast was really the right place. And then this guy"—he motioned to the officer coming up behind him—"didn't want to break the lock on the gate. I talked him into it."

The officer jogged up. He was carrying a large flashlight and had a big gun in his holster. He looked way too young to be bearing weapons—like a Cub Scout playing cops and robbers. "What's going on here?" he demanded, staring at her mud-coated skirt, wet blouse, and bare feet. Slowly, his gaze moved from her scratched-up face to her bare arms and then her hands. She clenched them into fists, hiding the blood on her stained fingers. "We received a report about a missing person," he said. "Is that you?"

"No. But I found her." Maya angled her head. "Allison's on the other side of that creek. I'll show you." She turned to leave.

"Hold on. What's *your* name? What happened to you? Is that blood on your shirt?" He peered through the dimness.

"I'm Maya Rivers . . . We need to go. It's getting dark and Allison needs medical attention."

"I'll radio for an ambulance, but whose truck is that?" He pointed. "Is someone else here?"

Her eyes darted to Tomas, who gave a helpless shrug. Maya debated. If she told this baby-faced cop about Nick now, that he was dead in the woods, they'd be more interested in hauling her off to jail than rescuing Allison. Maya slid her blood-stained hands into the pockets of her skirt, hiding them. Her arms shook. She still couldn't believe she'd killed a person. Killed him *dead*.

The deputy persisted with questions. "How did you get so banged up?"

Maya gulped. "I tripped over a log. Got a bloody nose," she said. "Please. Allison is pregnant. She needs our help."

"Pregnant?" The deputy lurched into action. "Let me radio for that ambulance."

"I'm not waiting." Maya hobbled back into the woods, with Tomas behind her. At the very least, they could cover Allison with his warm jacket.

With her lame ankle setting a slow pace, the deputy easily caught up with them at the creek. "Told you to wait," he said.

"She's right over there." Maya stepped down into the water. The freezing current numbed the pain in her foot. With a heave from Tomas, she made it up the other bank.

The deputy clambered up, too. "Which direction?"

She closed her eyes, pointed right. "I think she's that way." Her breath tightened. *And so is Nick.*

They headed into the woods.

. . . .

"I thought this was the right spot," Maya said, now fully disoriented. The deputy and Tomas forged ahead of her, calling Allison's name.

Then Maya spotted the flash of white. She headed over. "I found her!" she called, taking off the jacket and laying it over Allison. She clung to Allison's hand, willing her to regain consciousness.

Her eye caught on something in the dirt nearby. Another bone? This one had a chunk of flesh still attached. Animal? Or . . . dear God. Maya screamed.

Tomas arrived first, thrashing through the underbrush. The deputy was nowhere to be seen. "We've found her!" Tomas bellowed.

Maya pointed to the bone in the dirt and Tomas let out a gasp.

At last, the cop came rushing over. He was breathing hard. "What the hell is going on at this place? I just found a man behind those trees." He pointed. "He's coated in blood."

"Uh . . . it . . . was . . . self-defense," Maya stuttered. "I *had* to kill him."

"Oh, shit." Tomas started backing away.

"I didn't say the man was dead." The deputy pulled out his gun, aiming at her chest.

Shock washed through her. "He's not?"

APRIL

Fifty

"Harley would have hated this," Maya said.

Allison laughed. "So true." They stood side by side on the Bayfront, listening to Mayor Roan give a long speech about the history of Newport's fishing industry. Allison said, "I'm only here because Willy invited me to lunch at the Clam Strip afterwards. Now that my nausea's gone, all I can think about is eating."

Maya laughed. "You know my motto. Never turn down a free meal." She glanced at Allison's hand, where a diamond-sapphire ring should be sparkling. It wasn't. The cops hadn't yet found Harley's backpack. Not in Nick's apartment, the Kingston Development office, or at DreamCoast. Maya was pushing them to keep looking.

A search team had found Sara's body on the site, buried in a shallow grave. Animal scavengers had dug up and scattered a few body parts, including the small bone Maya had found, a finger bone. Allison had discovered a chewed arm, freaked out, and fled into the woods. After she'd crossed the creek, she'd gotten lost.

"Nick" was denying everything. Even now, three weeks after their encounter at DreamCoast, he claimed he had no idea how Sara or Harley had died, or how her bike had ended up in the bay. He'd never set a fire, never done any vandalism. Never broken into Maya's apartment. He suggested she was "unbalanced" and threatened to sue her for blinding him. For ruining his promising future.

The lies made her burn. Good thing he was stuck in the Lincoln County Jail and she couldn't get to him. And one day, he'd go to trial—she knew he'd break then. Maya had a lot of people ready to testify, including a raging mad Kelsey. Beware the woman scorned.

Mayor Roan was still talking. "We're gathered today to honor the Bayfront's rich history as a working waterfront." A group of fishermen's families applauded in the corner. The mayor added, "We also recognize the value of tourism and appreciate how our historic Bayfront draws thousands of visitors to our community each year."

Roan put his arms up in the air like a TV evangelist. "I hereby dedicate this site to a unique partnership that will merge two businesses in one scenic location."

Maya stared at the billboard behind him. The image showed a two-story building overlooking Yaquina Bay. Happy customers lounged on the upper-floor deck, cocktails in hand. The building's lower floor displayed an ocean-scene mural with a kayaker and a gray whale. The white banner hanging in front of the sign read "Future Site of Newport Nature Tours and Willy's Oyster Bar."

To her and Allison's surprise, Willy had joined forces with Doug Sammish. Apparently he'd always wanted to open an oyster bar and he'd grabbed the chance to do so on the popular Bayfront.

Maya leaned closer to Allison. Her belly was starting to round. After much testing, the doctor had announced the baby would be just fine. What a lucky little guy he was. She was planning to spoil him immensely—if Allison would let her.

A man walked up behind Maya, standing too close. She jerked away before she realized it was Tomas. His t-shirt read, *Compost: A rind is a terrible thing to waste.*

"The cops done grilling you?" he asked.

"Yeah. They knew it was self-defense."

"It would have been justifiable homicide, too. I wish you'd finished him off."

Sometimes I do, too. "I already have quite the reputation," Maya said. "The other day in the grocery store, a woman actually backed out of the aisle. I don't think she wanted to take her eyes off me."

Tomas grinned. "I'm sure she secretly admires your street-fighting skills."

"Or she's terrified of getting on your bad side," Allison suggested. "I know I am." She was practically glowing today, her hands wrapped around her baby bump.

"You'd have made a great Coast Defender," Tomas said. "I wish we'd known, before the group split up." His eyes dimmed. "At least we accomplished our mission, to shut down DreamCoast. Thanks to you. And once Alan Kingston cleans the site up, we're going to talk him into turning the property into a nature center. A place to bring school kids. He could name it after Harley and Sara. He owes us that."

Once the DreamCoast story had appeared in the national media, the condo development had fizzled quickly, the combination of murder, toxic soil, and animal graveyards proving too much for buyers. Ironically, when scientists had tested the soil and water, they'd discovered the contamination was limited to one area, and the site could be remediated without huge expense.

Alan Kingston was crying poverty over the clean-up, but he'd managed to pay his bail and hire a hotshot lawyer. His spin was his son had infiltrated the group to "keep an eye" on their actions, but he'd never imagined Nick would hurt anyone. Maya didn't buy it. Alan Kingston's silence had gotten Harley killed.

Fortunately, Curt was trying to broker a deal. He'd incriminated both Nick and Alan Kingston, even admitting he and Nick had been at DreamCoast the night Sara disappeared. According to him, he'd driven the truck away, leaving the younger Kingston behind.

Willy stepped up to the podium. He couldn't stop beaming as he plugged his new restaurant. "When we open, I hope y'all will stop by for some aphrodisiac oysters. Not to mention the hot waitresses." A wave of laughter rolled through the crowd.

"That leaves me out." Allison pointed to her stomach. "I won't be able to squeeze into a miniskirt much longer. It may be time to find a new job."

"Don't worry. I've got a plan."

"A plan?" Allison feigned dismay. "Good God. I hope it isn't like the last one."

"Very funny." Maya had gone to Jonah Bishop with a simple request. He'd apologized profusely for not believing her, even offered her a job with the firm. *No, thanks.* Instead, Maya had made him feel so guilty about what Curt had done, he'd offered to set up a scholarship at the community college for Allison. She was saving it as a surprise for Allison's birthday.

Maya turned to Tomas. "Now that the group's splitting up . . . what will you do?"

"I'm heading to Portland. I want to be around people who think like me for a while. I won't have to always fight for what I believe in."

She laughed. "Apparently Harley never told you his fable about spawning salmon. They inspired him with their 'never give up' attitude. I've adopted it."

Tomas studied her. "I underestimated you. You're stronger than I thought."

"I'm stronger than I thought, too." She felt a pulse of envy. Portland did sound inviting, but Newport was *home.* Harley's child would grow up here. Her family.

Tomas said goodbye and drifted into the crowd as silently as he'd approached. The talking heads on the stage prepared to cut into a broad purple ribbon.

Maya spotted Dan standing on the sidewalk nearby. He was still running his uncle's taxidermy business. The last time she'd seen him—literally bumped into him on the street—he'd mentioned his Uncle Walter had no plans to return from Mexico anytime soon.

She waved, but he didn't acknowledge her. Disappointed, she turned back to Allison.

Moments later, someone appeared beside her.

"Are you here to take the Wild Ocean Tour?" Dan motioned to the Newport Nature Tours sign. "There's no building, but they have a boat ready. And they're offering free trips this afternoon. Gray whales to see. You should come along."

Friends? Or was he asking her out? Maya grinned.

Dan smiled back. "So?"

She turned her head toward the bay. Behind the Newport Nature Tours boat, water sparkled in the sun. Thinking of Harley, she blinked back a tear. He'd wanted her to be happy. To find herself again.

And somehow . . . she had.

She turned back to Dan, linking her arm through his. "C'mon. Let's go see some whales."

Photo by Meghann Street

ABOUT THE AUTHOR

Christine Finlayson is a writer, editor and avid mystery reader. She loves to explore the trails and towns of the Pacific Northwest, on foot and by bike, and has dipped her triathlete toes into many ice-cold lakes. Nature inspired her early. In fact, Christine attended her first "save the plants" protest in a baby backpack (her mom's sign read, BLOOMS NOT FUMES). *Tip of a Bone,* her debut mystery, is set in one of Christine's favorite spots: the scenic Oregon coast. For more information about her writing, visit www.christinefinlayson.com.